Wretched

AN ECHOES OF HOME STORY

M. L. RAYNER

Wretched

AN ECHOES OF HOME STORY

Crane Publishing

First published in 2025 by Crane Publishing

Wretched M. L. Rayner.
ISBN: 978-1-7385585-3-7

Cover Design by: Crane publishing
Promo: Crane publishing
Audio Rights: W.F HOWES
Interior Design: Steven Pajak

"The true measure of a man is how he treats someone who can do him absolutely no good."

— Samuel Johnson

Prologue

9th March 1847

I am leaving, if only for a short time. Having a property located at Oban, it seems only fitting for me to visit now more than ever. These past few weeks have been utterly exhausting, but I'm sure the change will do me good. I dare say it will give me time to add some additional poetry to my works. I may even take the short ferry ride over to Lismore. The nature there is quite marvellous from what I recall as a child.

As I waited for the carriage this morning, the house seemed so quiet. It felt as though I was, in fact, viewing its rooms for the very first time.

The carriage arrived shortly after midday. A man dressed in rather ragged black attire saw to my baggage while I comforted myself on the seat. Peering through the carriage door, I took one final look over the house before calling out to the driver.

I have come to understand this is not a goodbye to Elphin. No, far from it. More than likely my return should see me back during the summer months. Yet as the carriage jolted over the cobbled entrance, I felt as though I should never look upon this land with the same light again.

The driver made the swift turn to join the road whilst I continued to gaze out of the window. Clais Cottage stood in the distance, darkened by its past. A past that I myself willingly helped to forge. As we moved farther from view, I poked my head out of the window, the cottage now becoming smaller by the second. Its form cast in shadow. But as the sound of the horses' hooves echoed from the ground and the driver's tuneless whistle pierced through the air, I continued to watch on with a frightful stare. I saw two girls playing around crumpled walls. And a motionless woman standing above a freshly dug grave. Her eyes never left me until the cart turned from sight.

LESLIE WILLS SHIFTED UNEASILY IN THE WORN CHAIR, HIS EYES hooked on the elderly man seated across from him. The old gentleman, known as Dr Roderick, hunched over his desk. His fingers, seemingly riddled with arthritis, struggled to grip the documents he held awkwardly to the light. His weathered face, etched with deep lines and magnified by the spectacles resting upon the bridge of his nose, betrayed no particular expression as he studied the papers before him.

In many ways, the office where Les sat mirrored the enigma of its occupant. Dust particles danced in the dimly lit room, illuminated by a single desk lamp casting a rusty-orange glow. The walls, once painted a vibrant shade, stood faded and worn, holding the weight of countless stories. Framed photographs hung with a slanted effect decorated the walls, capturing moments long forgotten, their subjects uncomfortably gazing back at Les with distant familiarity.

Stepping into the office just a short time ago, a musty odour filled the air, mingling with the scent of ageing paper and decaying wood, as if the room had been left locked and untouched for decades. It seemed like a relic from another era, a time capsule of the man's career. On the feature wall of old shelves and tarnished books, faded blue wallpaper weakly clung to the wall in tattered strips. The paint on the wooden panels that wrapped the perimeter of the space had long lost its lustre, leaving behind a patchwork of peeling layers.

In the centre of the room stood an impressive oak desk. At first glance, it struck Les as far too large for the already cramped office. Its surface was cluttered with countless scratches and stains. The wood, once polished to a shine, bore the scars of neglect and carelessness. Piles and piles of yellow-stained papers were scattered chaotically across its surface, with many strewn on what little floor space remained left to tread, paying homage to the man's unfinished business and forgotten dreams.

"Marvellous," Roderick murmured softly under his breath. His gaze remained fixed, his eyes unblinking, as he turned to the final page and proceeded to read in silence.

It was obviously clear that Roderick was a man in his mid 70s, most likely past the age of retirement. His clothes consisted of a slightly worn yet respectable suit that bore the signs of many years of use. The tweed fabric stretched around his figure, accentuating his large and sturdy build. And his salt-and-pepper hair was perfectly combed into a side parting, though it sat an inch or two out of place on his head, revealing wisps of distinguished grey at the temples. Despite his somewhat scruffy appearance and the way he kept his office, Roderick received exceptional respect as the most revered historian in the Highlands.

His reputation as an archivist and custodian of history preceded him, earning him admirers amongst scholars and historians all over the country. He had written many books during the peak of his career. And with his vast knowledge and keen dedication to his craft, he had spent decades committed to documenting the area's history of events and unspoken stories. However, despite being cherished by the community, the elderly man remained elusive, reclusive, and nigh on impossible to reach.

Les had spent considerable time and effort before finding himself seated in what he had anticipated to be the somewhat intimidating office of Dr James Roderick. It had been several months, in fact, several months of crafting letter after letter, as well as making regular visits to the office hoping to catch even a slight glimpse of the secretive fellow while he was off guard.

However, it was entirely by chance that on a bitter Friday evening in April 2006—just a few days before Easter—Les found himself wandering the quiet streets of Ullapool. He would make the trip into town at least once a week, if only to visit the dingy, old book shop that stood on the corner of Quay Street. After that, Leslie would often find himself strolling the banks of Loch Broom before taking rest on a bench at the end of the path that overlooked the town's harbour. The bench was typically unoccupied at that hour, which was precisely why he found the spot so pleasing. People went out of their way to avoid the chilling cold. The presence of towering hills on either side of the water, along with the vast loch that extended towards the ocean, created a wind tunnel leading straight to the dock.

It was on that very cold evening that Les instantly recognised Roderick from the rear covers of his books. The covers depicted a dashing man approaching the prime of his life and, without a doubt, the very same man sitting on his spot, breathing in the scenery of rocking boats and salt-filled air. Thirty years had passed, and Roderick had certainly undergone changes in appearance, which Les considered only natural.

Needless to say, Les's entire experience thus far had been an underwhelming one. However, he learned from life's teachings that appearances could often be deceiving. If that were the case with Roderick as he sat there, his tongue half gliding over his lips while reading the final entry, it would have to be the most deceptive of all.

"Marvellous," Roderick repeated as he collected the papers and neatly stacked them on his desk only to quickly fan them out again. "Tell me, Wills, was it?" He sounded somewhat disgruntled, pointing a crooked finger at the guest across from him.

"That's right," answered Les. "However, please, it is Les to my friends."

"Hmm," he acknowledged. "Where did you come across these papers, Wills?" he asked, his countenance alternating between a fleeting smile and a stubborn frown.

"Elphin," replied Les. His tone remained cool and collected. One might have even said professional. "Elphin Cottage. You may have heard of it?"

The old man's ears seemed to prick at his answer. "Elphin Cottage, you say?" His expression lightened as he marvelled at the pages on his desk. "I should have known. Where else would one find records of such a personal nature? I expect you found them in some secret hiding spot, did you? Below the floorboards or behind some panel, no doubt. A very fortunate discovery, I must say, considering the house's recent state."

"You'd think so," remarked Les as he leant forward, listening to the chair sigh under his weight. "But I actually stumbled across what you have there within an old shed, the loose papers found within a jumble of stacked boxes."

"A shed, was it?" he exclaimed with the raise of his brow. "In that case, we are extremely fortunate, indeed, that such records have even survived."

"Survived?"

"Oh, most papers of this age don't take kindly to the elements, you know? The cold and damp, well, it ruins everything. However, what you have here," he repeatedly tapped to the papers, "is an authentic account from March 1847, written by none other than the landowner, Mr Peter A Daily, himself. A true piece of history, my boy. One that if I were a betting man would wager has never been declared as found. Its value, dare I say, priceless to the right buyer."

Leslie cleared his throat awkwardly as he watched the man's excitement flourish at the glance of every page. "I'm afraid I have no interest in its worth, Dr Roderick."

"No interest?" The old man grew silent, his attention for the first time suddenly drifting from the papers, if only to study his guest. "Very well," he muttered. "Though you are aware, Mr Wills, that what I have set in front me does have historical significance."

"Not to me," replied Les. "To me it is nothing more than it appears—a stack of papers hosting the written word of a cruel and heartless man."

"Ah, that very well may be, but nevertheless, if you are not interested in their value, which I might add is the reason why most people sit in the chair you are, why bring such records to me at all?"

Leslie Wills slouched back in his chair, his eyes locked on the man. "An offering," he simply stated.

"Offering?" questioned Roderick, slightly taken aback by the comment.

"Yes," said Les, somewhat hesitantly. "Well, an exchange, then."

"Exchange?" echoed the elderly man again, both elbows planted on the desk, his fingers bridged below the groove of his chin. "I tell you now, I do not hold the funds to pay for such an item. It is a common misconception about a writer, you know? Especially one who has been acclaimed to be the best in their field. Many of us do not wish for wealth, but purely the recognition that our work is loved, cherished. Oh, and it will deem you well to pay little attention to the title Dr. It really is meaningless."

Roderick leant his neck forward and, with thumb and finger, slid his glasses along the bridge of his nose. "Allow me to share something with you, Mr Wills, something I have, in fact, shared with many," he spoke bluntly. "Never become a writer. The work is tedious and the pay is all the more miserable. It was, at least. And before you know it, you have four decades of writing behind you, five best sellers under your belt, and as you can see by my humble facilities," he waved his hand, "barely enough money to get you by. There are royalties, of course there are, but in the publishing business, there is only one who gets to take the pot. Never will it be the creator."

Les sat there frozen, somewhat surprised by the man's incessant babbling. It was clear he thought of his work very passionately, regardless of the fortunes it provided.

"I am sorry for your troubles," said Les in the most empathetic way he could manage. "But as I mentioned before, I have no interest in money."

"No?" blurted Roderick, still attempting to disguise the discomfort that throbbed throughout his fingers. "Then what is it you want?"

"Purely information," said Les, the word rolling off his tongue, just like he had seen in the movies.

"Information?" repeated Roderick in a deep grumbling voice as he rocked back on his chair. "What kind of information?"

Les took a deep, steady breath. "The papers that lay in front of you tell a story, Dr Roderick, as I'm sure you very well know. But despite everything these words reveal, I'm afraid it is only a partial story, at best. You have studied this man, Dr Roderick, and as you have plainly stated in your previous book, dedicated countless hours to his life, something no other researcher has yet to share."

"Neither have I, may I remind you," he remarked almost defensively.

"Which brings me to the reason I am here, sitting across from you now."

"Why?" grunted the old man.

"Because I lived in the house where those very words you see were written. I know of the horrors Daily committed and, furthermore, the cruelty he inflicted. I know, more than anyone, of the pain he left behind."

"Ah, save me your stories, Mr Wills," interjected Roderick as he waved his hand with impatience. "I have heard them all before. Every man has his troubles, whether he has led a hard life or a blessed one. I imagine you, of all people, carry your fair share. In fact, I am quite certain you do. Yes," he agreed with himself. "I can see it in your eyes. It is written there as clearly as the words spread out in front of me."

Les paused as he attempted to gather his thoughts. His mouth suddenly felt dry, his nerves heightened, as a hot flush waved over him. Little did he realise that his fingers dug deeply into the chair's armrests, his nails penetrating the worn-out leather.

"Come now, Mr Wills," continued Roderick, breaking the silence between them and lifting himself from the chair in such a way that indicated he meant business. "State your terms. And please, do get to the point. I do not have time for your riddles, and even if I had, I would not be obliged to entertain them. What is it you're after?"

A large lump formed in the young man's throat—so large it seemed near impossible to swallow it down as he watched the man lean over his desk and tower above him.

"I..." he gulped, "just wish to know what happened to this Daily character, that's all," answered Les in a rather cowardly tone, a tone he felt quite ashamed of voicing.

"Do you, now?" muttered Roderick with a clear hint of weariness, the harshness of his eyes unmoved. "And as curious as you are, Mr Wills, you must forgive that I find it only reasonable to ask you in return what you hope to unravel here?"

"The truth." He gulped again. "Nothing more."

A single brow raised halfway up Roderick's forehead, leaving the other to furrow.

"I have asked everyone," Les continued, "read every book, searched every record. Every single document available to the public. Months upon months of research. And yet ..."

"Yet?" the old man pressed as he leant in closer, shortening the gap between them in a rather intimidating manner.

"And yet, not a single document exists of this man after the 9th of March 1847, the very date which is clearly marked on the papers you see in front of you."

The old man pushed himself away from his desk, bringing himself to full height, which, in fact, wasn't very tall at all. But what he lacked in height he certainly made up for in stubbornness. "There is no death record, then?" added Roderick. "No papers of burial?"

Leslie returned a frustrated look. "Yes, there are such papers." He rolled his eyes. "Of course there are. And with the utmost respect, Dr Roderick, I think you, of all people, know that. Yes, I think you know that very well. Besides, the record provides little information—particularly regarding the cause of death. It merely notes that the man was found dead in his home, and I might add that this was some time later."

The old man smiled for what may have been the first time since their meeting, or so Les could recall. He slowly removed himself from the desk, burying his brittle fingers into the depth of his pockets as far as his jacket would allow. "That I do, Mr Wills," he replied most mysteriously. "That ... That I do." He made his way to a small rectangular window that overlooked the sleepy harbour street. There he stood for a moment, his frame blocking what little light tried to make its way through the glass. He breathed deeply, as though he was a man who carried nothing less than the weight of the entire world upon his shoulders.

A short silence followed.

"The papers you brought me," said Roderick, his silhouette unmoved as he watched a lonely passerby walk the street below.

Les's stare moved from the man and back towards the small stack of records, still placed neatly on the old man's desk. "Yes?" he asked.

"I will tell you everything I know, and the papers," Roderick cupped both hands behind his back, "the papers, they belong to me?"

"Deal," replied Les without any further thought. "You tell me what you know, and I'll happily have them gift wrapped for you."

The old man turned on the spot, his features partly blocked by the halo of light behind his head. "That won't be necessary, Mr Wills," he spoke in a low tone. "However, I thank you kindly for the sentiment."

Les wasn't sure how to respond to that. Nor did he really need to. Instead, he just smiled as the old man's attention swiftly shifted from the chair where he sat towards an old metal cabinet that stood draped by shadows in a lightless corner.

"Wait a moment," Roderick exclaimed, lifting his finger into the air. With a sudden burst of energy, he hurried towards the cabinet as fast as he could. The door groaned with rust but yielded to his force, swinging open to unveil what appeared to be the old man's treasured collection of personal papers, his most precious documents. They were stacked haphazardly, forming disorganised piles, causing the ageing shelves to sag under their weight. He scouted each one, his fingers gently sweeping across the toppling piles until his gaze descended to the lowest shelf. There, he halted. "Ah-ha," he whispered under his breath, bending down and causing the joints of his knees to crack. "There you are, my dear," he affectionately remarked as he straightened himself and returned to the desk, clutching something in his hands. With utmost caution, he placed it before him as he once again found himself slumped in his seat. It was a weathered brown folder, its corners frayed and tattered.

Leslie leant in, his gaze fixed on the gloomy-looking object before him as he attempted to make out the letters written across the folder in faded black ink.

"And this is?" he asked.

"That," replied Roderick, resting his veiny palm to the folder's sleeve, "is all there is, and all there ever will be, of the very man you've been searching for."

"You have records of Peter Daily?" asked Les, sensing an excited flutter within his chest. It had, after all, been months of searching without so much as a slight find.

"Oh, far better than that," replied Roderick with a noticeable gleam in his eye.

"Better?"

"What I have here, young man, are documents written by none other than Mr Peter Daily himself. That's right, you heard me. Three hundred pages to be exact, give or take. What you have provided me today, Mr Wills, is the final piece of a rather overdue puzzle, the beginning of a story that I've spent the best part of thirty years trying to obtain. I thank you for that. You wish to know what happened to the man after his departure from Elphin in the spring of 1847? Well, it is all here, my boy." He gently patted the folder. "Every bit of it. However," he added, picking up the tattered folder and holding it firmly to his chest, "I feel it only right to warn you that the writings within these pages are no pretty story. In fact, I have often referred to these entries as a glimpse into a dead man's soul. You will gain no comfort from what I'm about to share with you. Nor will you wish there to be any as we near its end. Mr Peter Daily," exhaled Roderick, "he was not a good man. In many cases, the worst. I can promise you only one thing, Mr Wills."

Les edged forward on his seat. His palms were sweating uncontrollably, and he wiped them on his jeans. "Yes?" he asked.

"The truth, nothing more," replied Roderick gravely. "A tale that has passed no man's lips since the day it was innocently placed on paper. I have kept it to myself, hidden from the world, shared it with no one. You may think it wrong of me, I have no doubt. But you will soon come to realise why I have done so for all these years. Yes," he mumbled to himself, barely audible enough for the young man across from him to hear. "You will soon understand. You wish to know the truth, Mr Wills?" he asked, opening the folder's sleeve and releasing the bundle of blotchy brown papers from their prison. He set them down as though they were his prized possession, objects as fragile as glass, and, with one hand, retrieved an old magnifying glass from the depth of his highest drawer. "Well?" He repeated the question. "What is it to be?"

Les sat in silence, unable to find the words to respond to the old writer's proposition. All the painstaking research, the countless hours he had spent sifting through files and books, the fruitless telephone calls and dead-end conversations with people he had hoped would hold the answers, all led to that very moment. An uncontrollable wave of excitement, mingled with a sense of anxious anticipation, washed over him as he locked eyes with the aged man and gave a subtle nod.

"Very well, then." The old man spoke plainly, moistening his finger and turning to the first page. Leaning forward, he rested his forearms on the desk, using their support as he directed the glow of the lamp. "I would inquire about your belief in ghost stories, Mr Wills. However, considering the purpose of your visit, such a question seems unnecessary."

"Oh, why is that?" asked Les.

"Because, Mr Wills," he said listlessly, "it is quite clear you are already in one."

Chapter 1

10TH March 1847

The sound of the horses cruelly roused me from yet another restless doze. Each laboured groan pierced into the crisp night air as the carriage forged ahead with its relentless twists and turns.

The day grew colder as the wind howled with force on that eerie night. It whistled through the trees and rocked the carriage with its unseen hands as we made our way towards the treacherous crevices of Ardmair, a steep, winding trail that carved between the rocks.

With an uneasy hand, I promptly drew aside the poorly hung curtain and gazed out upon a bleak and sombre village. It was little more than a pitiful improvement on the many deserted settlements that littered this forsaken land, its quiet dwellings masked by the dimness of the rocky hills and misty shores stretching far and wide across the open road.

In complete surprise did the carriage come to a halt, as though it had struck a dry, earthen drum. Following that, the coachman, Mr Campbell, a somewhat slovenly figure to be sure and by all accounts not the most learned individual, descended clumsily from his station. A loud and raspy cough escaped his lips as he clutched tightly to a flickering lamp that trembled in his grasp.

"Sir?" he ventured, his words barely more than a whisper as he delicately tapped upon the door. "May I have a moment, sir? I should be much obliged."

The latch of the door released, slivering open to reveal the young man's face, which seemed to glow with the radiance of a fat full moon.

Mr Campbell raised the oil lamp at arm's length, its light illuminating the shoddy dryness of his cracked skin and the frizzy coils of flaming red curls peeking from the rim of his hat.

The man hesitated, shivering violently in his thin frame as he hastily pulled his tattered collar tight around his neck.

"Forgive the intrusion, Mr Daily, but …"

"But what?" I snapped, gazing at the man whose face had been left red and bitten by the fierce winds.

"'Tis just the horses, sir," the man mumbled.

"The horses?" I echoed, curiously peeking past the door's gap in an attempt to catch a view. "What of them?"

The coachman attempted to regain his balance, one hand feebly shielding his face from the violent gusts of wind.

"If it pleases you, sir," the coachman went on, "it has been a little more than a day since we took rest. And with the road ahead long and the weather most grey, I fear—"

"You fear?" I interrupted the man as I slumped back into my seat. "Your fear is irrelevant, especially to me, Mr Campbell, an emotion suited only to the weak, never the strong."

The young driver's eyes, wide and glassy, drifted momentarily from my own, briefly settling upon the pair of waiting hackneys.

"Begging your pardon, Mr Daily, but they are, after all, only mere creatures. Simple creatures, if honestly speaking, sir."

"You needn't inform me of mere creatures, Mr Campbell. I have endured my fair share. A lifetime. Nevertheless, what is it you're implying?" I questioned with a tilt of the brow.

"Nothing, sir. Nothing other than simple creatures require the simplest of needs. A half pail of water and a few hours rest will see them well come morning."

I slouched forward on my seat. My eyes glowered into his. "You're suggesting we retire?"

Campbell stood his ground, an inkling of worry smeared wide across his face.

"Aye, sir," the man nodded. "If it is to your convenience," he replied hesitantly through the chatter of his teeth.

"Convenient?" My jawline clenched at the thought. The very notion of staying there! "It is most inconvenient."

"But, sir," the young man mustered up the courage to speak. "Without neither food nor water, I dare say the horses may not make it as far as Inverness. It would be most unfortunate if such events were to occur purely due to the neglect of a little food or water, wouldn't you agree?"

He paused anxiously, listening to the howling wind that cried through the hills in response.

"And not forgetting there's my employer, Mr Ramsey, to consider, sir. He'd be awful cross should anything happen to his personal property under my watch. Right livid, if truth be told, sir. Mark my words, so he will."

I took a deep breath, trying my best to rein in my rising temper. I could not stay there. I would not. I needed to leave, to reach Inverness as soon as possible.

"And you mark my words, Mr Campbell," I warned him, my tone growing stern. I ripped the blanket from my lap. The sole of my foot landed heavily upon the carriage floor with a mighty stomp. "It is no concern of mine what you contemplate to be a reasonable request. The arrangement has already been settled with your employer, yes? The deal, indeed, struck?"

The young man gulped hard, acknowledging the restless sound of squelching hooves as the horses' feet stomped deep into the mud.

"And … What of the animals, sir?"

I sighed wearisomely, my breath hissing through my teeth. "Should the worst occur and your precious mares fall ill, I will personally see to it that your employer is duly compensated for the full value of, what did you call it? His personal property? I highly doubt a man of business will object to such an offer. No such men ever do, not in my experience. It is quite within one's nature to feed his pockets over morals."

"I beg your pardon, sir? Morals?" he asked, bracing himself against yet another mighty gust.

The flame of the lantern flickered, almost dwindling to darkness.

"Indeed, Mr Campbell, indeed. It is within every man that they believe to stand by their morals. Most men swear blind to it. It is the way in which we desire to be admired. That is unless coin is involved, of course. There is no denying it. Money can turn the kindest man into the commonest of scoundrels and the commonest scoundrel into the vulgar and destitute. Still, we desire it all the same, yearn for it. No, Mr Campbell, I'm afraid morals count for nothing in this life. Wealth is, indeed, everything."

The driver remained rooted to his spot while his flittering garments danced gracefully in the gale. "But," he muttered, casting the dim light towards the front of the carriage, "maybe we could …"

"See here!" I exclaimed, suddenly lunging from my seat and grabbing the scruff of his collar. My grip tightened fiercely, causing the thread of each button to spring from his draping shirt. "You are testing my patience, sir."

The youthful man looked taken aback, his unsettled expression peering intently into my own.

My stare softened.

"Where are you from, Campbell? Lochinver, if I am not mistaken?"

The driver pondered for a few more moments before wetting his lips, then finally found his voice. "Strathan, sir," he corrected promptly. "Though to any wanderer, they would seem to be one and the same."

"Is that so?" I replied listlessly, my eyes involuntarily rolling with disinterest.

"Aye, sir. Truth be told, work has been difficult to come by in any of these parts most recently. That is, since the land fell cursed and all. Be that as it may, I was most fortunate for Mr Ramsey to take pity and hire me when he did. I count my blessings for that."

"Blessings?" I mocked most amusingly. "If there's one thing I do know, it is that the deprived become dependent upon charity, accustomed to it. It is quite within oneself to take. Heed my words. Your good fortune will not last."

The driver writhed in his position. "And why, Mr Daily," he questioned, "might I ask?"

"No charity ever does."

"That may be so, sir. However, without it, I dare say my family's situation would've befallen the path of many others," he replied in a soft surrendering voice.

"And of what path, Mr Campbell, do you speak?"

The driver's expression altered some, his fear visibly drained away in the moonlight. His eyes widened with astonishment. "Why, death, sir."

The man's shirt slipped from my grasp, causing him to stumble before he clumsily regained his stance. An odd stare painted his face as he spoke once more.

Though, as strange as it was, I did not hear the man, did not see him. Instead, my mind wandered. My thoughts flashed with the recollections of the winter past. Tormented by voices. Cries. The vision of souls leering at my gate, their nails scratching. Shrieks bellowing. Screaming for want. Pleading for mercy. Begging for me. It was all far too much to bear. There was no escape from them. Those thoughts. Those dreams. Not even in rest.

An icy coldness shuddered within me, crawling up my spine and stopping at the nape of my neck. My hair raised like pins.

"Sir?" The young man's voice once more found its way to my ears. "Is everything alright, sir? You appeared a little out of sorts just now."

"Fine," I grunted, grasping the lap robe and draping it over my legs.

"Perhaps I may persuade you to retire for the evening after all, sir? To alleviate your tiredness, so to speak. Heaven knows you'll—"

"Enough!" I spat the word frothing at my lips.

From out of nowhere, a fierce gust blew across the plain, crashing into the carriage and flinging me backwards. The ceiling lantern swung fiercely, flickering to a shade of distinctive blue before fading into blackness.

"Can you see them, sir?" asked Campbell, his distant voice but a haze as it called out through the stillness of a settling breeze.

I climbed up from my seat, wincing as I did so, still partly preoccupied by the pain that had quickly formed on my head—a large bump. I stroked it gently, my fingers combing through the clump of wiry hair.

"Campbell?" I sneered, squinting out into the stillness of the misty roadside. My vision blurred briefly, most likely the aftermath of withstanding such a nasty knock. I tried to focus, attempting to adjust to what seemed like a dark, boundless abyss before me, though it appeared to be hopeless. I could feel nothing, discern nothing, beyond the faint outline of an earthy hill and the sound of the ocean waves thrashing from beyond it.

"Can you see them, sir?" the driver's subdued voice whispered again. The tone with which he spoke was loaded with the deepest compassion and lament. Yet without a doubt, I felt it was not towards me.

"Campbell?" I enquired, my foot reaching blindly for the nearest step. "What in the Devil's name are you playing at?"

The carriage creaked and tilted in response to my shift, the door slamming closed behind me with a deafening crash as both feet landed upon the hard road. I surveyed the nearby land quickly, my head swivelling left to right.

To my astonishment, the horses remained calm. Not so much as an inch did they stir, nor a sound did they utter.

"Campbell!" I yelled, wafting aside the marsh-like mist that lingered about my thighs. "Where in God's name are—"

I halted dead in my tracks, spotting what could only be the silhouette of a person loitering in the far-off shadows. Its hazy outline was flattened against a pitch-black mound which inclined so boldly from the ground, its top perfectly defined against the backdrop of glittering stars.

I called out again, my voice raised to the breaking point, echoing back at me from afar.

Still, the shade remained still. Lifeless, one might say.

Somewhat bewildered by the lack of response, I lowered my arm to my side, causing the fog to swirl and billow in a ghostly manner.

Frankly, I initially considered what lingered in the gloom to be nothing more than a simple illusion, a mind trick, as it were. Darkness has a way of influencing the senses, there was no denying that. Especially when one has been devoid of rest. What stood before me could merely have been confused for nothing but a harmless object. A small birch tree? Or, perhaps, a pile of farmer's equipment left carelessly out to rust?

Despite my thoughts, all that remained for me to do was wait, to watch as this indistinguishable stranger, concealed by the dark, silently gazed back at me, studying me. Or, at least, that is my assumption now, for I felt it then.

"Let this be the last warning, Campbell!" I growled, striding towards the roadside with an unsteady gait that caused me to trip and tumble onto the marshy grass.

"Is that you, Mr Daily, sir?" Campbell's voice whispered. "Is that really you?" His speech was muddled yet, in a strange sense, preserved.

"You know perfectly well it is," I snapped, wiping down my sodden jacket. I hastened my steps, my gaze firm on the figure's frozen stance.

As I approached, the mound behind him grew in size, stretching skywards, reaching for the blanket of clouds that began to cover the sky.

Just then, an acrid odour struck me, a putrid scent that assailed my nostrils, causing me to gulp for air. I gasped, snatching my handkerchief from my inner pocket and holding it up to my nose. The faint fragrance of lavender did little to mask the stench.

"What …" I found myself retching. "What is that ghastly stench?" I enquired, my voice muffled from the cloth.

I edged closer, watching as the man's form gradually began to clear with each step.

"Stench?" Campbell stared at me, his head tilted inquisitively. I noticed how his eyes appeared strangely distant, as if viewing me from a far-off place.

I heaved once more. "That vulgar smell!" I exclaimed, holding my breath as best I could.

"It is merely the corpses, sir."

Another cold gust crossed the ground with a powerful passion, forcing the valley to wave in motion like the unforgiving waters of a stormy sea.

"Corpses?" I repeated. My eyes darted anxiously, searching for the source. "I see no corpses, Campbell!"

The coachman paused a moment longer. His blatant stare was vaguely altered as the corners of his lips ever so slightly creased, widening into an unsettling and sinister smile. His head tilted back, gazing up at the moon. A beam of silver light followed, dispelling the shadows of the earthy mound behind him and revealing the grisly truth beneath.

Stunned, I recoiled in horror, unable to tear my gaze away from the gruesome scene that towered before me. "Good lord!" I exclaimed, my eyes bulging with disbelief.

Bodies. So many bodies, piled one on top of another, men, women, and children alike, discarded and forgotten, left to rot in fields. Many appeared unclothed or dressed in little more than rags, with twisted, bony limbs that intertwined and embraced one another like a puzzle. Their gaunt faces bore looks of unending agony, revealing that death had provided no relief.

"Dear God," I gasped, horrified.

"God?" whispered Campbell, turning to behold the repugnant sight. One lifeless arm hung loosely from the jumbled pile, fingers stiff and still. "Do you see God's hand in this?" he spoke softly. Gracefully bending to a knee, he reached out for the motionless hand.

"Campbell, what are you doing?" I barked, swallowing back the nauseating stench of rotting flesh. "Who are these people?"

"These be villagers, dear sir," Campbell informed me, not once taking his gaze off the limp form he was tending to.

"Villagers?" I asked him.

"Farmers, families, fathers, mothers, and their kin, all condemned to the same cruel fate."

I fell silent, unsure of what to say.

"Well," I interrupted him, reverting my stare back towards the bleak, soulless streets of the nearby village. "A proper burial for them, then?" I gasped. "You know these people, I assume?"

The coachman grunted, his eyes still fixed on the lifeless hand. "There will be no burial here, Daily," Campbell replied heavily, returning to his feet.

"No burial?" I enquired. "There must be some soul out there willing to see them buried."

"There is not," Campbell growled, his voice low and troubled.

The distinct smell grew more offensive by the second.

"No one at all?" I pressed him. "They shall be paid, naturally."

"You are too late for that," Campbell muttered, his eyes suddenly brimming with tears. "They are all gone."

"Gone?"

"All of them. The entire village. Perished. Abandoned without food. Left to starve. Condemned to their slow, sufferable end. Each one dragged from their sombre homes, tossed aside like filth. Only then were they forsaken to rot in the winter mud, without so much as a mass grave to mark them."

I said nothing. No words of comfort nor of meaningful sentiment could find me. After all, there was little more to say.

"No, sir," the coachman continued. "There shall be no burial here. Not tonight or any other." He ceased for a moment, catching view of the moon's gleam that was soon to withdraw from the sky.

I gazed intently upon the man as the same uneasy expression smeared across his face.

"No burial, sir," he finally uttered. "Not tonight."

Within the blink of an eye, the darkness descended upon us, a deep, inky blackness that left me feeling cold and hollow. There was no noise, nothing but the sound of my own shallow breath.

I stood dormant for longer than I cared to. My breathing soon steadied. My nerves collected even as the cold night air harshly nipped at my lungs. I stepped back, eager to depart, only to suddenly observe the moon as it peeked out once more from its refuge.

Its gleam shone brightly, brighter than ever before, casting its presence upon the world and revealing the festered bodies in front of me.

I froze solid. A thin layer of sweat covered the nape of my neck. My heart stopped. At least, I believe it so. For in that moment, I felt only stillness within me. Stillness, yet an undeniable sense of fear. The bodies—they remained in their unsightly state, each one piled, draping on top of the last. There was, of course, one striking difference, something I had at first considered quite impossible, out of the question. Yet I saw it all the same—the image of each and every lifeless face leering back at me.

I stumbled back in complete horror, falling bluntly to my rear and knocking the wind clean out of me. Both hands reached out in desperate panic, grasping for the mossy earth as my feet kicked wildly in the air.

"It cannot be." I shambled backwards, heels digging deep, carving my escape from the deathly glares. I pushed myself up, still half slouched to my side, scrutinising the very faces that captured me. Each neck was bent in my direction, each set of eyes gazed deeply into my own, judging me. Their grey irises were painted in the most perfect likeness of the rising moon.

Was this to be my reckoning? My end? There was little time to consider, little time for anything. For as I stood to my feet with buckling knees, the humble light again began to fade. That time however, it would not return.

Then the voices began.

Chapter 2

11TH March 1847

It was the sound of a heavy-handed thud that startled me.

The clean light of a new day seeped into the carriage, releasing my mind from the lounge of dreams.

I yawned heavily, my thoughts still hazy, whilst the tardy sun kindly kissed my skin, lulling me into a comfortable stupor. I heaved a heavy sigh, my eyes shutting for a final time, as if willing the day to commence.

Beyond, the commotion of a bustling street penetrated through my window—the clacking of hooves on the cobblestone, the faint echoes of merchants announcing their daily trade, their cries stifled by the hubbub of residents marching through the thoroughfare.

Civilization, I thought wistfully. I had almost forgotten what it sounded like.

The sensations of city life had grown distant in my mind: the sweet aroma of the High Street bakeries, the din of busy streets, and, of course, the alluring distractions of women.

Still, there remained many alternatives to occupy the mind in the absence of a woman's touch. The intellectual topic of conversation, for one. Though I must admit, the opportunity is indeed a rarity when one finds himself confined to the country. It was the perfect place, after all, to resist all temptations, that was unless one was rather taken to the drink. Not that I ever found the need to preoccupy myself with such habits. It is true, one can say a lot about a man who drinks alone, not one bit of it worth noting.

It was as I sat there that the distinct knock struck the carriage door. I jumped, cock-eyed, eyes blinking in an effort to disguise my fatigue as I smoothed the hair from my forehead.

The knocking sounded again.

The latch snapped open with a concussive click, soon followed by a quiet, nasal voice that would trigger a panic within me.

In that moment, my mind shifted back to the previous night.

"Good afternoon, Mr Daily," greeted the coachman, his torso leaning through the gap of the door. "A magnificent day, is it not?"

I sprang up like a cat doused in boiling water, distancing myself from him like a frightened rodent pinned to a corner. I gazed at the man, bewildered.

"You?" I struggled to voice.

"Aye, sir," the man replied, carrying a baffled expression. "It is, indeed, I."

"Campbell?"

"None other, Mr Daily," he said, pushing the door wider. "I presume you will be pleased to know that we have arrived?"

"Arrived?" I replied.

"Aye." He paused, waiting to be given instruction. "Inverness, sir?"

"Inverness?" I mimicked him, smearing the cloudy glaze that stained the small carriage window. "When did we?"

"I would estimate around one o'clock, sir," he replied, looking backwards towards the direction of our travel. "It was a trying journey, especially once the storm hit. Honestly, I was nervous that dear Patsy wouldn't make it at all."

I recoiled, pale and dazed. "Patsy?"

"Forgive me. My eldest horse," he confirmed. "Though, not to worry," the man said gladly with the casual gesture of the head. "The old girl's currently lapping up the comforts of her stable as we speak."

Whilst he continued to natter, I attempted to gain my bearings. The dreadful memory of the previous night was replaying its effects: the ghastly sight, the putrid stench of rotting flesh. Yet the man before me appeared untroubled by it all, his demeanour perfectly ordinary, as though the affair had been wiped from his mind.

"You," I growled, cutting him off mid-sentence.

The coachman abruptly ceased his babbling, his finger pointing towards his centre chest with a shock. "Me, sir?" he stammered, his eyes wide with surprise. He glanced over his shoulder, unsure if I was even speaking to him at all.

"Lure me out into the fields, will you? Permit me, your superior, to take view of that foulest sight."

The young man looked somewhat discombobulated, scratching at the gingery stubble of his chin. "I'm afraid I do not quite understand."

"The bodies, man!" I hissed, my voice low and discreet.

"Bodies?"

"Hundreds of them, piled high and left to rot, victims of the land's curse."

"The land's curse," the coachman parroted, somewhat bemused. "Sir, begging your pardon, but are you feeling quite well?"

I sat, frustrated. The images of the night before, the bodies, flashed before my eyes.

"Some do say that the wind on those roads can be quite fierce," the driver continued, oblivious to my distress. "It can howl like a wolf across the open moors, they say, and many have oftentimes misheard its cry for something far more sinister. There is no harm in such a thing, sir."

"Utter nonsense," I muttered hoarsely.

"Nonsense or not, sir, I can honestly say we'd encountered no bodies on our travels, as you say. Not one. Not so much as a wounded doe, to that matter."

"But Ardmair? The villagers?" I gazed sharply at the man.

"Ardmair has been abandoned for months, that much is true. Those who perished from the hunger were interred in a mass grave, some time gone by. I was present. I saw it all."

"But we … I … I saw them," I muttered, almost to myself.

"Not possible, Mr Daily." The coachman's voice lowered, soothing, as if he were attempting to ease my distress.

From out of nowhere came the sound of children's footfalls as they trampled their way down the street, fleeing past the carriage in a blur.

"After your strict instruction not to retire for the evening, I confess I found myself to be flat on my back," the coachman admitted. "As mentioned, the wind can get terribly ruthless around those parts, particularly during a rainy season. A single gust can emerge out of nowhere and send a man packing."

"And what does this have to do with anything?" I enquired, intrigued yet impatiently so.

"Why, everything, sir," the man responded with a jovial grin. "Not a moment was wasted as I rapidly gathered my bearings and made haste back to the carriage. Upon my arrival, what to my wondering eyes should appear, but you, sir, in a state of unconsciousness. I initially felt you had taken a tumble and suffered a dreadful blow to the head. Alas, a nasty surprise, indeed," he added, revealing his dingy teeth in an anxious smile. "However, upon hearing your somnolent murmurs, I breathed a heavy sigh of relief. Nevertheless," he continued, "I did not miss a beat, as they say. Without further ado, I scurried up to my post and swung the reins with remarkable swiftness and refused to halt until we reached Ullapool. I did briefly consider seeking immediate medical attention for you, sir, yet the hour was so late I made the choice to proceed with haste. I am overjoyed that you have, by the grace of God, not sustained any significant injury."

I was left with little to say, caught between reality and a dream-like state. Could it truly have been nothing more than a strange nightmare concocted by my own mental weakness? Surely not, for the entire memory of what had taken place remained untainted and vividly clear. And yet, the coachman's story held a notable amount of logic.

"If you would be so gracious," the coachman interjected as he began to ferry my belongings across the stones, "it would be my sincere pleasure to escort you to your lodgings. It is not a strenuous trek—merely down the neighbouring alley. You shall find a quaint building by the name of The Antler & Hare. I daresay, I believe the quarters shall suit your needs, if only for tonight." He stepped aside, gesturing in the direction with a pointed finger.

With no further exchange, I stepped out of the carriage and made my way along the dim and crowded street. The narrow city lane teemed with people on that particular afternoon, a trifle too many for my liking.

A long row of market stalls, mostly those of fish merchants, lined the road parallel to its winding course, cramping the already suffocating path. So strong was the odour that I could hardly doubt that it would cling to me for hours.

A chaotic jumble of voices filled the air that afternoon: laughter, cries, and muddled conversation, all merging into one. And despite the chaos, I maintained a steady stride, wandering aimlessly through the market, my mind determined on one thing as I wove forth through the throng.

Tall buildings loomed above in a dismal display of poorly maintained doors and dank grey stone. Linked together as one, they blocked the sun, shading the day's light from ever reaching the ground.

Looking up, I observed a slate grey cloud slink between a break in the rooftops, partially obscured by the smoke that gushed from towering chimneys, infecting the sky with wicked soot.

Despite it all, I continued onwards, scanning for a signpost that indicated the very whereabouts of Crane Alley, my strides never faltering as I plodded on, deeper into the reeking heart of the city.

Chapter 3

The Antler & Hare was found in the forlorn corner of the alleyway, wedged between two condemned warehouses. Its old stone was worn and faded, plagued by years of neglect. Its visage was a woeful one, overlooking a meagre courtyard ensnared by an iron fence. A ponderous sign swayed idly from its wall, presenting a half-faded image of a hare impaled upon the antlers of a stately stag.

Inside the building left little to the imagination. A dreary hall, furnished with several shabby seats, occupied the recess of a towering, murky window. The floorboards were so conspicuously crooked that one might easily have found themselves stumbling upon them. A shattered mirror was affixed askew to a chimney breast wall, its flowery-patterned paper marred by damp. The hearth, blanketed by untold layers of dust, was devoid of any flickering flame.

In a dim corner, a solitary candle quivered on a counter space, its feeble glow dancing to the tune of the biting draft that had seized the room.

A single set of footsteps trampled from the floor above, reverberating along the shadowy landing and descending towards the public space below. A large, bearded man with a heavy limp came into view as he struggled to clamber down the staircase. Sprawled in misalignment, his straining shirt hung haplessly over his plump physique, a trifling match for the last notch of his overtaxed belt. His lips curved in an appearance of greeting, though barely visible through a dense thicket of grey whiskers that had taken control of his face.

"Ah, I shall be but a moment," he offered in a cordial tone, the thud of his ailing foot rumbling all throughout the lower levels of the house.

Within little time, he found himself slumped behind the counter, retrieving a guest book from beneath and, without care, letting it thump against the dusty surface of the counter. An opening of the spine and unfolding of its pages swiftly followed.

"Well, then," he sighed. "Every guest must give their mark, state where they're from, heading to, and the nature of their business. Town rules, you understand?"

"I sent word ahead."

"Very good." He dipped his quill into the ink—once, twice, and a third for good measure. "May I have your name?" he enquired, squinting down and perusing the dimly lit page.

"Daily."

Upon hearing my name, the man cocked his head off guard. Yet a smile slowly returned to his eyes as he set his quill to the desk.

"Ah, Mr Daily," he exclaimed as he spread his arms out wide and welcoming. "I hope your journey was nothing short of satisfactory?"

"It was uneventful," I grumbled.

"Excellent, sir. Simply excellent," he replied as he scurried away from the counter, his plump fingers interlacing together as he made his way towards the array of large keys hanging from the wall.

"Your note arrived only this morning, sir. I must admit, I was quite doubtful you would make it. After all, your request seemed most pressing," he said, sorting through the mix of unmarked keys. "But be that as it may, I am most happy to accommodate you. I have just one room remaining."

My eyes swept across the shabby lobby, which led up to mould patches that spread wide across the ceiling in blotches of green and black.

"How fortunate," I replied.

The proprietor bowed his head, presenting me with a sturdy bronze key he had retrieved from the highest hook. "I hope you will find it to your liking. How long will you be staying with us, sir?" Again, he collected his quill. "A few nights, perhaps?"

"Lord, no."

A brief look of embarrassment loosened the muscles of his face, half veiled by the room's inner shadows.

The man nodded, seemingly unable to hide his disappointment. "Very well, sir. Just tonight it is. The room is on the third floor, just up the staircase there." He nodded. "Room eighteen."

I sighed, scanning the warped flooring for my luggage.

"Ah, everything is ready in your room, Mr Daily. I made sure of it personally," he said, bowing his head once again. "Now, if there is anything else I can assist you—"

"Your fire?" I asked, not giving the man a chance to finish. "Is it broken?"

The owner's eyes widened in bewilderment. "Broken, sir?"

"Yes, broken," I confirmed. "Or is it that you are incapable of lighting it?"

The man grew silent, peering at me cautiously as I inspected the room.

"Your establishment is far from respectable," I said. "Yet I have heard from close acquaintances that it offers the finest accommodations in Inverness."

"Why, that is most generous of them, sir," the proprietor replied.

"I would expect nothing less than a fire upon my return," I asserted, my finger trailing along a thick layer of dust on the mantlepiece. "And please, do something about the dust. It's suffocating."

"I will have my staff take care of it presently," he assured me, hastily scurrying away and squeezing through a narrow door that led to his private quarters. His voice echoed throughout the corridor as he walked.

MY MEAGRE CHAMBERS CONSISTED OF A CRAMPED L-SHAPED ROOM replete with a four-poster bed and single dresser, oddly situated beneath a small, cracked window. The bedframe, unsurprisingly, lacked any sort of canopy, while the rough, burgundy sheets and discoloured decor of interlinked, once white daisies were hardly pleasing to the eye.

Gazing briefly outside, my eyes fell to the dreary courtyard and miserable alley beyond. Heavy clouds draped the city like thick, wet wool, gradually smothering the rooftops and diminishing them to mere outlines, soon to vanish altogether.

I took rest on the lumpy mattress, pillowing my head on a thin, feathered cushion. Again, my thoughts drifted back to the previous evening, my mind allowing what had happened, or what I believed to have happened, to circle around and around in my head.

To state that I felt out of touch lately would be a gross understatement, for something about the experience—whether real or imagined—left me feeling on edge.

Was it merely a dream?

Perhaps. I had been having them a lot.

Lying there still, I took in the dark wooden beams that spanned the length of the ceiling, and I allowed my mind to drift.

I thought of Elphin, the image of its landscape surrounded with such perfect beauty that, for the briefest moment, I could swear that I was there. I could see the mountains jutting from the earth, their snow-capped summits lost in the heavens, the wandering streams that wove through open valleys and scattered groves spilling over churning falls and joining the open lochs. I could hear the cry of circling buzzards soaring gracefully below an endless sky of sapphire blue. I could see squirrels scurrying up the trunks of ancient trees, wild rabbits darting across open fields, their bushy tails bobbing as they disappeared into the safety of their burrows.

I recalled the house signed in my name, nestled amongst rocky hill-sides, the secret path behind the stables, leading down to the banks of the river, and peaceful moments spent beside the water's edge, observing the shimmering carp swimming upstream. They were sights I feared I should never witness again.

It went without saying that gatherings at the house that year had become a regular occurrence, a true calling on my part and with little expense spared.

My guests were distinguished acquaintances whom I had favoured over the years. There were friends and colleagues from far and near, and even successful men of business like myself longed to attend my dinners, if only to bask in my presence. If I was not a well-established gentleman prior to my purchase of Elphin House, I most certainly was afterwards. Everyone who was anyone desired an invitation, so very eager to discover what magnificent secrets Elphin held to offer.

I became the embodiment of their community, a symbol they admired and revered. Their time spent with me was so vitalising that some, too, were inclined to purchase properties close by. The memory of their joyous faces still lingers in my mind, congregated around the dining table, raising glasses in gratitude towards me, their host, each expression displaying the utmost gratitude and honour. All except for one—the shadowy figure of a woman gazing through the window, her sunken eyes piercing through the dark glass, deep into my own.

"LEAVE ME!"

With a sudden gasp, I bolted upright in bed, my eyes flitting about the room, trying to push the nightmare back.

Was I alone?

I scanned the room again, but of course I was. Scolding myself for my foolish panic, I lowered my head back onto the pillow.

"There, you see?" I said to myself.

I remained perfectly still yet watchful, sensing only the rise and fall of my chest as the shadows on the ceiling gradually sulked in accordance with the setting sun.

Little time had passed. How long exactly, I was not entirely sure, nor could I recall if questioned. One thing, however, was certain. A dreamless sleep swept over me.

I FOUND MYSELF AWOKEN SOME HOURS LATER TO THE BLEAKNESS OF my dim quarters. A velvet shroud of darkness cloaked my chambers, lending the space an air of gloom. The meagre window at my bedside offered scant light, sullied by grime which heavily obscured the view beyond.

Faint voices drifted forth from the floor below, loud laughter combined with the merry clink of glasses and the clang of utensils recklessly scraping upon plates.

My stomach grumbled, a weak protest against the emptiness it held. The sounds of merriment from the floor below only amplified the gnawing hunger. It had been days, perhaps weeks, since I last enjoyed a proper meal. Mrs Donald, my once reliable housekeeper, had vanished without a trace. A skilled woman in the kitchen, she had kept the house running smoothly, but her abrupt departure left me in somewhat of a bind.

Another burst of laughter echoed from below, a reminder of the life I was missing. Still dressed, I fumbled for my coat and hat, pulling them on in a hurry. I had to get out of that room, away from the joyfulness below.

The hallway downstairs was bathed in a warm, flickering light. The hearth, dormant a few hours prior, roared with life, its flames dancing across the walls. A collection of oil paintings, hung haphazardly, depicted scenes of fox hunts, men on horseback galloping across vast fields, their hounds in hot pursuit of a wily fox that held a gleam of terror in its eyes.

Outside, in the gloomy street, I caught movement, the owner prowling to and fro near the entryway, his bulky frame scuffling helplessly with several crates as he attempted to mount the steps.

"Ah, good evening, Mr Daily." He greeted me warmly on the doorstep, the boxes he held obscuring half his face as he continued to climb the steps. "Out for an evening stroll, are we, sir?"

"In a manner of speaking," I replied.

The man half grunted. The muscles of his arms trembled beneath the heavy load. "Do take care, won't you, sir?"

"Are the streets dangerous?" I asked him.

"One can never tell, sir." The man shrugged as best he could. "The streets, they can be a risky place," he cautioned, "just like any other city you may encounter. The belly of the town, prostitutes, thieves, they all come alive come nightfall. Stick to the main road, sir, and avoid back alleys."

"Alleys such as this, then?" I enquired.

"Aye, sir," he replied, somewhat offended. "The town is rife with alleys, a labyrinth for those unfamiliar with their twists and turns. Better safe than sorry," he added, before finally entering the inn with a distinct note of breathlessness.

I made my way back through the oppressive shadows of Crane Alley, emerging onto the expansive High Street. A thick smog permeated the night, reducing the dimly lit lampposts to a ghostly flicker. The crowds and street vendors who flocked to the street by day had long since retired. Shops lay uninhabited, shrouded in shadows, their entrances tightly secured under lock and key, their window fronts masked in darkness.

The evening air was crisp and cool, the slight breeze carrying with it the aroma of shit strewn about the cobbled path. The entire town appeared deserted, the streets lying dormant in a slumber, patiently waiting for the twilight to pass and for the moon to fade away.

From out of nowhere, the faint sound of sobbing pierced the air. A man—or so I presumed—sat nestled up against the gutter in the shade of an unforsaken corner. His knees were curled tightly up to his chest, his head lolling lifelessly between them. At first glance, the man appeared clothed in little more than rags, hardly fitting for the season. His bare chest was bereft of a shirt, whilst his trousers were rent and torn, bunched up to his knees, revealing two scrawny legs that descended to grubby feet. The ground on which he sat shimmered, glazed in a thin layer of moisture illuminated by the lamp above.

Another mournful cry escaped from him as he raised his head wearily, his desperate eyes fixed upon me. His bulging orbs mirrored his gaunt, sunken cheeks, damaged and weather-beaten. His dishevelled hair appeared unruly, standing messily on end.

I expected the man to lunge forward, a desperate plea for charity in his eyes. But he did not. He remained rooted, a pitiful figure against the crumbling backdrop.

A sound of misery, a low groan, emanated from the darkness, drawing the man's gaze away. His head bowed, his eyes following the sound. In his arms, he held a child, a young girl, her golden blonde hair matted with dirt. Her frame was as thin and frail as his own. She let out a heart-wrenching cry, her face contorted with anguish as she twisted and struggled in his embrace, burying herself deeper into his chest.

Regardless of his meagre efforts, the expression upon the desperate man's face spoke volumes. Not even he could aid her.

Unable to tear my gaze away from the scene before me, I stepped aside. My mind was so far away that I barely registered the sound of approaching footsteps.

A figure emerged from the swirling fog, brushing my shoulder as they passed. It was a gentleman, thankfully, clad in a long, black coat with a turned-up collar. The rim of his hat shadowed his face. He stopped abruptly, pivoted, and tipped his hat. His gaze was oddly inquisitive as he turned to retrace his steps.

"Peter?" enquired the gentleman. His youthful voice was stifled beneath the thickness of his collar. "Peter Daily?" He approached, scrutinising me with the utmost interest.

"That, sir," I recoiled, the words numb on my lips, "entirely depends on who is asking?"

The man's arms reached out of the fog. "Uncle Peter, it is you!" he exclaimed joyfully, clapping me soundly on the shoulders and pulling me in for an embrace. "Why, did you not recognise me, Uncle?" He removed his hat, his thick, bouncy ringlets swaying freely in the breeze. "It is I, your nephew, Jacob." He smiled.

"Jacob?"

"Indeed, Uncle. Indeed," he replied, nodding before releasing his hold. "You mean to say you honestly did not recognise me? How could you not, Uncle?"

"In this fog, my dear boy? One can barely find their way through the streets."

He smiled handsomely at that and repositioned his hat upon his head.

"I must confess, Uncle, this is an unexpected turn of events, is it not? It is delightful to see you. It really has been far too long."

"It has, I presume. A decade, I believe, perhaps longer. I cannot bear to count the years. The thought of time depresses me." I looked the lad up and down. "You, however, were but a boy back then."

"Ah, I am a man now, Uncle," declared Jacob, his milk-white skin glowing with the ingenuous charm of his youth.

"Yes, I can see that."

The young gentleman returned a smile at the compliment. "Are you presently engaged, Uncle?" he enquired.

To which I promptly responded, "I am not."

"Ah, splendid," said the young man merrily, applauding as he spoke. He seemed decidedly pleased to hear it. "I would be greatly interested to hear more about your travels, or perhaps how you have been spending your time of late. Mother grows incessantly anxious, as usual. She claims she has heard hardly anything from you at all these days. Please." He placed a hand to my shoulder. "Will you join me for a drink? Or if you prefer, a swift bite to eat? I know a place that is not far. It is just a quick stroll down Bridge Street. My time here is limited, you see. I depart by coach come morning."

I must admit, the thought of a warm meal and a shared drink did sound good.

"Ah, so you have become a man of the world at last, then?" I asked him.

"In a manner of speaking," he modestly acknowledged, "yes, I have."

"Well then, my dear nephew, as long as time allows, I shall appreciate your company on this dismal evening." I moved aside, insisting we walk. "Please, lead the way."

Jacob's smile, a flicker of genuine joy in his eyes, was cut short by a pitiful wail that echoed from the hidden nook.

It was the child, clutched tightly in her father's arms. She groaned convulsively, her tiny body wracked with pain.

Jacob recoiled, his face contorting in a sudden grimace. "Vermin!"

he exclaimed, his voice trembling. He hastily pulled me away, waving a hand dismissively. "Come, Unclc, come. We mustn't dally. We mustn't stay here!"

"My dear chap, what in heaven's name is the matter with you?" I asked, turning back to the child. "These are but commoners. One encounters them at every turn. The world, as you have learned by now, is littered with them."

"Not like this," muttered Jacob, his voice barely a whisper.

"Like this?" I repeated, my brow furrowed. "Like what, precisely? Are you in some peril, Jacob? Is it money? I should have known from the way you bulldozed past me. You can tell an awful lot about a man purely by the way he walks."

The boy's forehead creased with worry, his fingers finding respite on the bridge of his nose. "No, no, no, Uncle, you do not understand."

"Understand, my dear boy?"

"The streets, they are not safe," he hushed.

"Not safe?" I said in disbelief. "Nonsense!"

"I swear it to be true, Uncle," insisted Jacob discreetly. "The poor, they …" He paused for a moment, his eyes scanning the darkened corners of the street. "We should not speak of such matters, not here. Come, let us find ourselves away from this place, and straightaway."

And so we proceeded, myself trailing behind, traversing through the squalor of sludge-filled lanes and towering, dim dwellings. The echoes of anguished cries soon faded into the distance. The child's pleas died, silenced and consumed by an ever-growing shroud of mist.

Chapter 4

The sound of rain began to patter against the small window located just behind the old man's desk as Les, without hesitation, interrupted the storyteller in mid-stride.

"But …" said Les, standing to his feet and pacing what little space the small, cluttered room had left to offer.

"Yes?" answered Roderick, unamused, his eyes glancing up from the last read entry and using his finger as a marker to not lose his place.

"You mean to tell me this Daily had family?"

"Yes," repeated Roderick. "Of course. What man does not?"

Les's steps came to a halt. "But …" He scratched the back of his neck, deep in thought. "But I thought I had searched everywhere. I'm certain I did. I found no mention of his heritage, nothing at all aside from his grandfather."

"Then I'm afraid you just weren't looking hard enough," replied Roderick, leaning back in his chair and, just like magic, unveiling a tall glass decanter. “A simple enough mistake to make. You wouldn’t be the first amateur to overlook it, nor will you be the last, I’m sure.”

“Overlook?” repeated Les. He was confused.

“The name, my boy.” The old man grunted with amusement, reaching for a foggy-looking tumbler that still held the remnants of his last guilty pleasure. “When one restricts their search to a single name, well, it’s safe to say you will never get very far at all.” He tilted the decanter to the glass, causing it to *clink* on impact. “Was your mother born a Wills?” he asked. “What about your nieces? Your aunts?” He took the glass to his lips, sighing as he swallowed. “I thought not. The reason why you have not come across such a name before is because this man written here in black and white is no Daily, but one Jacob Durose, Daily’s sister’s son.”

“The man had siblings?” questioned Les, swiftly finding himself back on his chair.

“Only one,” answered Roderick, staring into his glass. “Meredith. Pretty name, isn’t it? And from what I have researched, her looks upheld her name. She bore only one son,” he added, tapping his finger to the ink. “However, I believe we are running off course, here. Please, let us crack on.” He set down his glass, his position settling into place as he cleared his voice to continue.

“Wait a moment,” blurted Les, holding out his hand on the desk in an attempt to stop the old man.

“Eh, what is it now?” the old man huffed, clearly displeased by the interruption.

Les flinched back. It was clear the man did not take kindly to it. But if he didn’t ask at that moment, he knew he would never have the chance again. Les wanted to know everything, all there was to know, and if it meant stopping the man in his tracks to obtain that knowledge, well, then he was damn well going to do it.

“Can you tell me about this nephew of his?”

“Jacob?” grunted Roderick, gazing at the young man suspiciously. “Why?”

“I …” mumbled Les, unsure of how to answer. In truth, he didn’t really know why, nor did he have a reason. It was purely a matter of interest, nothing more. A taste of curiosity. He simply needed to know. “Please,” he asked.

The elderly gentleman’s stare remained as hard as stone as his untrimmed nails tapped heavily on the desk in a rhythmic pattern.

“Well,” pondered the old man, “if you wish to hear about such events, I suppose it only makes sense for you to know the full picture. Alright, yes, I shall tell you what I know. Nothing less."

He leant back, allowing his neck to flop to his chair as he raised his glass to the lamp, entranced by the swirl of his beverage as he dreamily spoke.

"In his youthful days, Jacob Durose was rarely regarded as an impressive addition to the family. As a boy of tender years, he was often described as an uncommonly quiet, reserved, and peculiar child to most who crossed his path. In truth, one might say that he was a rather odd lad.

"In his early years, Jacob found himself immersed in solitude, a commonality shared by those children raised in the bucolic countryside. He was the lone offspring within the family estate of Hulton House, an aged manor situated upon the moorlands that straddled the territory between Staffordshire and its surrounding borders.

"It would have been a delightful place back then, too, a place that had often played host to his uncle, for it was where he lodged during winter months.

"Sir Silas Durose, Jacob's father, was a man of the cloth from Tamworth, whose acquisition of the family estate sprouted in the summer season of 1823, a gift from Daily's late father, with the eye and curiosity of a hopeful father-in-law aimed at his daughter, Meredith. Indeed, the vicar's profession sat well with Daily's father's expectations; so well that upon his passing, Sir Silas inherited the substantial sum of £40,000 and a modest family property situated on the remote isle of Lismore, a summer residence once belonging to Daily's grandfather and his forebears, where one might confine themselves in contemplation and evade the grips of life. A retreat to forget the world, I think would be most accurate.

"Despite the good reputation that accompanied Silas and the newly obtained riches, he remained what many would deem a stern and disciplined man. Little warmth or interest did he reserve for those closest in his company, even his own wife, for that matter. But I must say, none could match the disappointment that was his son. Being a devout believer and a well-spoken lecturer to his ever-growing congregation, Silas took God's words to heart and lived his life by them, sparing no exception for his own flesh and blood.

"Jacob, on the other hand, cared little for the topic of religion. Young and curious about the ways of the world, he possessed a free-spirited mind similar to that of his mother. Often found gallivanting about the woods that enveloped the Hulton estate, he preferred the company of nature, climbing trees and skipping stones along the riverbank.

"In the colder months, Jacob engaged his interests in less adventurous ways, focusing on drawing—a passion instilled in him, again, by his mother. He would tread the long halls of the house with scraps of paper in hand, sketching animals such as horses, chickens, and the occasional stargazing hare. Although his drawings held little talent to unappreciative eyes, his mother encouraged his interest nonetheless, insisting the boy was nothing short of an artist, a common enough flaw by most mothers. Together, they spent hours in each other's company, painting and drawing, with Meredith kindly filling in much of the silences.

"By the time Jacob reached the age of ten and four years, his talent had noticeably flourished. No longer content with remaining within the usual borders of the family estate, his sketchpad accompanied him several miles away to a neighbouring village. There he would sit on a park bench outside of the church, sketching locals as they went about their business. So great had become his ability that many of the villagers had borne witness to Jacob's work and requested him to render his services. For a shiny penny, he would produce casual portraits to bring light into their gloomy homes.

"However, word of his skills soon spread rapidly, and as it was inevitable, his father discovered his whereabouts. Consequently, Jacob was confined and punished within the walls of the estate by his father. The boy's actions were deemed as shameful to the family name, with his street trading bringing embarrassment to them all.

"No longer able to wander, Jacob was forced to read and educate himself on the word of the Lord. His drawings were destroyed and his materials cruelly fed to the open fire. The one thing that brought him meaning, his only escape, was lost.

"Weeks passed, and word of the clergyman's actions towards his only progeny soon spread. Mindless gossip made its way from door to door as Silas conducted his affairs about town. Women whispered as he passed by their doorsteps, and men hissed his name with utmost derision, all for the sole purpose of causing him shame.

"In the wake of such occurrences, a marked shift was noticed in the devotees of Silas. His once loyal followers seemed to have turned their backs on him. The numbers of his flock had dwindled, and confidence in him had ebbed away. Following in the footsteps of his shameful son, the hapless Sir Silas Durose was now condemned to dwell within the confines of the manor, his respected name irrevocably tarnished.

"In the midst of his isolation, Silas found no comfort in the lavish decorations and elaborate furnishings of his grand estate. His once marvellous gardens, sun-kissed and rich with life, turned into desolate fields of barrenness, a true manifestation of his own self.

"As the months slowly passed by, Silas grew ever more distant and disheartened, vexed by the son that had brought about his downfall. His lips remained tight on the matter, and he was often absent from meals and church, barricading himself within the small room of his study. Unresponsive to any requests for his attendance, he distanced himself from the world, imploring all to leave his family in peace. Despite his efforts, his request was honoured by few.

"With little choice left to him, come autumn's arrival, Sir Silas made the decision to sell his wife's beloved estate, whisking his family to the remote shores of Lismore. It was to be a new beginning, far from the spiteful tongues and scrutinising eyes of their former neighbours. On Lismore, he yearned to find peace.

"His move occurred abruptly, affording Meredith and Jacob little time to prepare. A multitude of worldly treasures were left behind in the estate: family portraits, a wealth of dresses his wife cherished, an irreplaceable grandfather clock, and row upon row of books that covered the reading room walls.

"Silas deemed these 'treasures' a pointless extravagance, useless to the needs of his family. A fresh, more solemn existence lay ahead for them, free from the plague of society.

"There are few records of the family once they settled on the island. Jacob was scarcely seen by the staff, his presence confined to suppers, where he displayed new bruises that blotched his skin. In the mornings, he languidly trailed behind his father to Saint Moluag, a small parish chapel situated a mile hence from the house, where he would withdraw himself for private study. Never again during his childhood did he exhibit a ravenous appetite for adventure. Never again as a child did he venture beyond the household's gates. His curiosity had, for some reason, waned, taking with it the boy he once was."

Les's head tilted curiously to its side. "What happened to him?" he asked, completely sidetracked by the young boy's story.

The old man returned a hand to the long glass neck of his decanter, halting mid-pour at the question.

"Are you asking what supposedly happened to the lad, or what I believed to have happened?" he asked, his concentration stolen by a splash of scotch.

"Isn't the answer one and the same?" asked Les, slightly baffled by the writer.

"I suppose," answered Roderick, snatching his glass and swirling it with an air of dignity. "However, I believe we are getting ahead of ourselves. May I?" he asked, once again peering down to the papers.

Chapter 5

As we walked briskly down the cobblestone streets, I noticed an overhanging sign above a small wooden door that read The Castle Tavern.

Inside, the dank space was decorated with tired furniture, from the woodwork on the bar to the lamps suspended from the low ceiling beams. The crowd was made up of mostly locals, all dressed in shabby clothing, throwing back drinks and engaging in rowdy conversation so loud that one could barely hear themselves think.

"Come, Uncle. This way," ushered Jacob, struggling to make himself heard over the din of drunken voices.

We settled at a small table situated in the far reaches of the room, a murky, unoccupied nook concealed from prying gazes and curious ears. A small blaze snapped and crackled at our side, emitting a fragment of warmth.

"Now, then," I sighed, my limbs languishing before the flames as I slipped off both my gloves. "Tell me, what on earth has got you so worked up?"

The lad leant down discreetly, planting his knuckles to the freckles on his cheeks in despair. "Oh, many things," cautioned Jacob, sinking back into his seat and hoisting his glass to toss back a healthy swallow of whisky.

"Troubles?"

He exhaled, the first gulp bringing tears to his eyes as he let loose a fiery cough. "Oh," he struggled to speak, "I fear I have plenty of those,

Uncle," the young man grumbled. "But this, well, I'm afraid it is dreadful business," hushed Jacob.

"My dear boy," I tried to assure him, "all business is dreadful," I remarked, unable to ignore the roar of merry voices from behind me. "Frankly, I have grown tired of it. Such chatter. Such business. Life is far too short. Let us speak of more enlightening matters."

The worried lad shook his head. "Ah, I'm afraid this business implicates us all." He slumped farther forward, tossing back the dregs of his glass and setting it down on the table with a harsh *thunk*. "In truth, it is the very reason for my premature departure."

I looked at him, puzzled. There was something about the way he spoke—the worry in his tone, the look upon his face. It was the look of a beaten man.

"Oh," I leant forward, piqued. "And of what matter do you speak, Nephew?"

The young man glanced about in a stealthy manner, his darting eyes skimming over the roistering crowd of tipsy patrons, cautious of those nearby, before pressing his weight on the table. "The poor, dearest uncle."

"The poor?" I mimicked.

"The poor," he nodded, his face momentarily lit up by the smouldering cinders which dimly lit our corner. "Surely you have noticed?"

"Noticed what, Nephew?" I asked softly.

"Why, the state of the city. And not just Inverness." He raised his glass in the air, signalling to the barkeep for another drink. "It is all most unpleasant."

"You speak of the Hunger, I presume?" I asked, my voice flat and weary.

"So, you are aware of the situation, then?"

"My dear Jacob, such matters are beyond us."

"Uncle!" he snapped under his breath. He reached out, clutching at my wrist upon the table. "How can you disregard them?"

"My dear boy, how could I not? The woes of the penniless are of no importance to me," I replied with the harsh shrug of my shoulders. "Why should I waste my time on such prattle?"

Jacob's grip loosened.

"I'm afraid it is much more than that," he replied as the barkeep approached the table. "They are swarming out of the country like flies. Soon every city in Scotland will be seething with them."

"You exaggerate, my dear boy," I muttered, waving my hand dismissively as the barkeep saw to it to top up both glasses and sink back into the crowd. "What business is it of yours should a wave of vagrants inundate the city?"

"It is not a matter of *if*, Uncle."

"So you made clear." I pondered the notion further. "Well, if what you suggest should come to pass, the workhouses and factories shall thrive as well as ever. The underprivileged may and will, as they have for many years, procure their necessities there. It is, after all, their very purpose, dear boy. Now please, calm yourself."

"The workhouses ..." Jacob paused, reaching out to hand me my beverage. Retrieving his second, he knocked it back. "I hear that the workhouses are overflowing. So great is the desire for employment that the wretched line the streets every morning, hopeful of some opportunity to be fed. They come from far and wide, these hordes of impoverished souls. I have never seen such destitution. Many are scarcely clothed, covertly dragging their weakened children along as though they are nothing but lifeless puppets."

I removed the glass from my lips and stared deeply into the flickering flames. "If this is true, then more remedial measures must be taken."

"But that is just it, Uncle," remarked Jacob with a sense of urgency. "The very actions you speak of have already been executed. Aid has already been dispatched to various regions of the country, not to mention the numerous public works projects that have been undertaken to alleviate the congestion of our overflowing workhouses. It is said that many have perished from sheer inability to labour."

"I see," I declared, watching as the young man squirmed about the subject. "Yet I suppose it is better they perish than suffer a life of misery."

"Indeed, dear Uncle, indeed," said Jacob, his speech by that point beginning to noticeably slur. "Although many still take to the streets in mere hope of succour. They reside in the alleyways, beseeching from poverty, bringing with them a contagion of filth. I must add, you have encountered them on this very night. However, these beings are much worse."

Before I could ask him, a group of drunken men perched on stools by the bar suddenly burst into a tuneless song. The words they sang were nearly impossible to decipher as one forgetful chorus merged drunkenly into the next. Their voices were hoarse and off-key, their clapping ill timed to the point I could not help but feel a mixture of annoyance for as long as the chant went on. As the merriment came to an end, the group of men erupted into raucous laughter, patting each other on the back, tankards raised high. I sneered, my attention shifting back to the table.

"Come now, worse?" I asked him. "Who are they?"

"The Irish."

"Irish? But—"

"News travels fast, dear Uncle," replied Jacob with a stare full of knowledge in his eyes. "Many state that Ireland is the cause of all this unpleasantness. It is said that their land has fallen under a curse. That it is where all of this unpleasantness began. That their crops have rotted to blackened mire come the time of reaping. And that now they seek their want elsewhere. On our land, no less! They are arriving in hoards, mainly by small vessels or cattle boats. Why, I recently heard that farther south is overflowing with nothing but vagrant beggars. Can you believe it? I most certainly cannot. I'm afraid it is only a matter of time before our beloved country is overrun by filth." He withdrew a small holder and placed a cigarette between his lips, struck a match, and inhaled deeply. His eyes rolled in a dreamy fashion as he belched out a thick cloud of smoke. "And that is not all," he added most anxiously. "There are whisperings."

"Whisperings?" I pressed him. "Of what nature?"

He inclined his finger, ensuring I lean closer. "Riots," he hushed. "An uprising, Uncle." His tone trembled with fear. "Set to occur tomorrow at precisely noon. A protest by the poor. Without a doubt, I shall have departed Inverness by then. I do urge you, Uncle, to do the same."

I considered what Jacob said for a time, my gaze seemingly fixed upon his silhouette as it shimmered along the wall space behind him.

"I thank you for your concern, dear boy," I replied with no shred of alarm in my voice. "Though please, do not fret. My stay here is also brief. I, too, depart come morning."

"You are?" Jacob remarked, his eyebrows raised with interest. He crossed his legs, delicately removing his cigarette with two fingers as the smoke softly escaped his lips. "Short-lived, indeed," he went on, a livelier colour returning to his face. The worry, for the time being, at least, was gone. "And may I inquire as to where you are headed?"

"Oban," I answered.

"Oban?" Jacob repeated, flicking his cigarette, the ash filtering down to the edge of the table. "Then you plan to board the ferry to Lismore, no doubt?"

My brow arched some as he asked, knowing perfectly well what he implied. It was too clear by the way he said it.

"Pardon me, Uncle, if I am being too presumptuous," Jacob apologised, his manner clearly sincere. "But Mother speaks of you often, and in the highest esteem. I am certain she would relish your company, even if only for a short time. The island can be a desolate place, a prison for those unaccustomed to its ways."

"I remember," I reminisced, my memory thrown back to a time on the island as a boy, the fresh air, the quietness, the emptiness. Yes, it was not so much a place of privacy as it was a place to be forgotten. I tried to forget, closing the door on it as best I could.

Jacob smiled.

I waited.

He waited.

"Your mother," I asked him, keen to change the subject, "how is she?"

"She is content in her ways," Jacob replied thoughtfully, his voice mingled with a hint of admiration for his beloved mother. "A remarkable woman, truly. She spends much of her days tending to her flower garden, a pastime that she has taken to with most enthusiasm. And in the evenings, she indulges in her love of music, playing sombre pieces such as Haydn, Bach, or God in heaven knows what else on the piano."

The mere image of her playing sent a shiver down my spine. I could still feel the phantom pain of those endless childhood hours trapped beside her, my eardrums throbbing as she butchered every single note. "There is no doubting that your mother may be a remarkable woman, Jacob, but expressing herself through the keys of a piano is not one of her strong suits. Indeed, she has a tendency to make even the most beautiful music sound quite dreadful."

"Then I must correct you, Uncle," Jacob countered, a small smile turning the corner of his lips. "Her technique has vastly improved over recent years—one might say since the passing of my father. Although, I must confess, she would never concede that fact."

My voice took on a mournful tone. It felt strange sitting there across Jacob, prattling on about life's pettiness while the weight of his father's absence hung heavily in the air. I was, in many ways, surprised that I hadn't even thought to mention it. Still, it felt like a gaping hole in our conversation, a silence that screamed louder than any words.

"Ah, yes." I attempted to approach the matter. "I was disheartened to learn of Silas."

"Pshaw!" Jacob let out a chortle of amusement. "I most certainly was not," he replied plainly. "He was not a good man, not like you. He harboured no affection for me, at any rate. Whatever traces of sentiment he may have retained were fiercely withheld from view. He was a man of few words during his final years. And if you could believe it, more unpleasant than usual. Months would pass where we barely spoke to one another. Not a word. After the funeral, I hastily encouraged Mother to leave the island, the house. Needless to say, she would not hear a word of it. Nor could she be swayed. She can be rather stubborn, you know?"

"That I do know," I replied with an all-knowing smirk.

"So you will visit her, then?"

I looked kindly at the boy, his eyes wild and hopeful. His intentions were only to mean well. "You have my word," I nodded. "Yes, I suppose I will."

"Ah, splendid!" Jacob clapped, turning the heads of the nearby tables. "I often worry about her, alone in that empty old house. Oh, how I so wish I could join you. Though I'm afraid my duties call me elsewhere. I believe I should not step back on the island until the summer leaves have begun to turn. I'm afraid I journey to Ireland tomorrow."

"Ireland?" I asked him, my mouth half hung, a dozen questions clinging at the tongue.

"That, Uncle," he insisted, "is a conversation that can wait. Now, another round perhaps?"

From the depths of the hidden kitchen, the scent of potatoes and piping hot pastry filled the lower rooms, momentarily masking the lingering smog of tobacco smoke that smothered and climbed across the ceiling. As we savoured our meal, our conversation drifted towards Jacob's youthful days in Staffordshire. He listened intently, his focus never budging even as he dug into the pit of his bowl.

Meanwhile, unlike the young man's appetite, I struggled to muster up any enthusiasm for the dish placed before me. Instead, I kept myself occupied with half-hearted nibbles that did little to satisfy my want.

"Uncle, are you quite alright?" asked Jacob, his knife delicately slicing into the succulent pie. "You have hardly touched your meal. Does the food not please you? If so, I can only apologise. It is usually rather good."

I shook my head, my attention swayed from the plate beneath my nose. "My boy, do not concern yourself with such things," I responded, laying down my knife and fork. "The food is adequate enough," I spoke truthfully. "It is simply my lack of appetite that ails me."

"You are not well?" continued Jacob, sinking his teeth into a tender chunk of beef. "I must say, I am quite concerned by your wan complexion and the fragile state in which you find yourself. Why, you appear like a wisp of smoke that might be blown away by the slightest gust. Perhaps it is the reason why I hardly recognised you earlier this evening. Yes, I suppose that would be it." He stabbed his fork into a fluffy potato, waving it in mid-air as he spoke. "Really, Uncle, you should try to eat something. If only a morsel more, at least."

Again, I dismissed the thought entirely. The very sight and smell, the idea of forcing down what remained on my plate, triggered a sudden need to gag. "I have eaten my fill, dear nephew. Besides, my appetite has not been the same for some time. Not since …" I paused somewhat awkwardly, choking on the remnant of my words.

"Since, Uncle?" encouraged Jacob.

My hand flailed, and my lungs begged for breath as I casually cleared my throat. "Not since my time at Elphin."

"Elphin?" The man glanced up with a puzzled glare. "Oh, the quaint little village. Yes, that's right. I had heard rumours about it. I hear the scenery is quite remarkable to behold that far north, a place of much beauty, where the lochs shimmer to the night's sky as though it were crystalline glass itself."

"It is quite beautiful," I agreed, if only in hope of swiftly changing the subject.

Jacob bobbed his head with great interest as he dissected his pastry with precision. "And not to mention there is the land you purchased, yes?" he asked, his mouth half full. "Farming land, if what I was told is true. Not forgetting the house that seems to be on the tongue of every respectable man and woman in Scotland. They say it is a home like no other, a place of finery for all who seek it."

"People are prone to exaggeration, Jacob," I grumbled. "It would serve you well to remember that."

"Ah, Uncle, you are too modest. I must say, it all sounds rather charming."

"Yes," I mumbled, and quickly glanced about the room, expecting to find watchful eyes.

"Ah, that's right, you've not been well. Forgive me," begged Jacob, setting down his fork to the plate and yanking the napkin from his collar. With a delicate manner, he dabbed his lips. "My thoughts can get carried away with me sometimes. Most times, actually." He chuckled. "Tell me, Uncle. Did something happen at Elphin? Something to prompt your leave? Something ghastly? I must admit, I had decided on travelling farther north later in the year. I would have, by chance, called upon you to observe your estate in all its glory."

The ringing of a bell echoed through the dimly lit room, the sound drilling from a point behind the bar. The shrill voice of a woman pierced the air, announcing the final call.

"Dear nephew," I proclaimed loudly, the bell's toll still resounding in my ears. "If you persist on this path, I will be forced to confine our conversation to nothing more than the weather."

The young man sank back into the comfort of his seat and nodded defeatedly. "Of course, Uncle," he mumbled. "As you so wish."

A handful of unspoken words settled between us after that, broken only by the gentle crackle of the fire, which faded into a soft murmur.

The locals, their faces flushed and their voices boisterous, hastily drained their glasses, their laughter spilling out into the street as they made their way to the exit.

"It is late," I remarked.

"It is," stated Jacob, glancing over his shoulder towards an old chiming clock that stood tall and forgotten in the corner. Its cloudy face was covered in a mass of retired, draping cobwebs. "I should retire, then. It will do me no good to oversleep. Besides, I fear that I have consumed enough to sedate ten men."

I acknowledge that.

"Ah, yes, of course." I had, in fact, almost forgotten. "You leave for Ireland first thing."

"How do you know, Uncle?" responded Jacob, a look of sheer amazement smeared right across his face.

"You told me."

"I did?" the young man mused. "Oh, yes, of course! Of course, my apologies."

"However, as of yet you have purposefully avoided telling me why."

"Why, Uncle?"

"Your venture, of course!"

Jacob wearily raised his hand to his brow, endeavouring to gain clarity of his thoughts. "Forgetful me," he murmured, settling back into his armchair and lighting yet another match to his lips. "I set sail for Ireland to retrieve that which is rightfully mine."

"Rightfully yours?" I enquired, drawn in by my nephew's troubles as the aroma of cherry tobacco once again filled the room. "What is it that you wish to retrieve? They hold nothing of true value, the Irish. Their only wealth is the land upon which they dwell."

"Indeed, Uncle," piped up Jacob, snapping his finger in agreement. "And that is precisely what beckons me."

Curious, I leant forward in my chair, grasping at the buckles of my knees with both hands. "You mean to say you have acquired a spot of land, then?" I asked him, my voice hushed regardless of the empty room.

"To say that I have acquired a mere plot would be sorely understated, Uncle." Jacob laughed, relishing the smoke that curled around him. "I have obtained much more than a plot—acres upon acres of farmland."

"Ah, to own land is to be wealthy indeed," I stated.

"How very poetic of you, Uncle." Jacob smirked, rising to gather his hat from the rack. "Though I must confess it has done me a fat lot of good."

"You do not profit from your land?" I asked, watching as the young man fumbled with the buttons of his coat.

"Profit?" Jacob snorted with disdain. His smile turned sour as he struggled to maintain his balance. "I have scarcely seen a penny in many a month!" he remarked with annoyance. "My tenants, they brazenly refuse to pay me."

"Refuse?" I echoed in disbelief.

"Allegedly," confirmed Jacob, baring his palms to the table if only to keep himself from toppling. "It is all feeble excuses, you see. They claim since their land has turned sour, they are unable to farm. And without their harvest, they have not the coin to pay me." He sighed heavily, glancing back at me with wide, desperate eyes. "I dare say I am at my wit's end, and if this should continue, I will find myself financially ruined."

For the shortest time, I could do nothing but stare at the man as he drunkenly swayed on the spot. I observed the worry in his eyes, the tired look of desperation that painted his face, a portrait I had indeed come to know all too well. Very much so.

"Do they eat, Jacob?" I questioned him, only to find the boy taken aback.

"Eat?" replied Jacob in a state of clear bewilderment as his tongue darted from his mouth. "My dear uncle, what an odd question you ask. How should I know? It is simply not my business," he remarked, turning up the collar of his coat. "However, should they have the money to see their bellies full, why should they not fulfil their financial obligations?"

My brow deepened with concern. "So, what are your intentions?"

"I have an informant at Cork," he replied sluggishly whilst attempting to readjust his hat. "A local man of sorts. Highly recommended, I might add. He will assist me in evicting the filthy little beggars off my land. The time for being reasonable has well-since passed. They shall be given an option: redeem their debt or vacate their quarters."

"I see," I replied, returning my attention to the smouldering flames near my feet.

"Oh come, Uncle, don't look at me that way. It disheartens me. I'm afraid I am left with little alternative," he explained, circumnavigating the table with a drunken stagger. "Now, if you will pardon me, I must retire for the evening. If I am unable to succumb to slumber presently, I fear I may even forget my own name."

"So be it, then," I acknowledged, slowly standing to my feet and shaking him warmly by the hand. "Do take care of yourself, won't you?"

The young man returned my stare with an absent daze. "Naturally, Uncle. Naturally." He beamed fondly, embracing both my hands in his. "It has been awfully good …" He paused, determined to regain his speech. "Pleasure. It has been an awfully good pleasure to see you again. Perhaps I will see you soon? That is, if your visit with Mother permits it."

"I shall await your arrival at Lismore," I told him, seemingly reassuring him in an instant.

"Ah, splendid, Uncle. Splendid," remarked Jacob, most excited as the evening air struck his lungs. "Until Lismore, then," he chimed as he stumbled out of the door and vanished into the fog. The sound of his footsteps soon faded into the bleak, twisted streets.

Chapter 6

As I finally returned to the Antler & Hare, the clock had struck well past midnight. A veil of darkness enveloped the inner hallway, unleashing a chilling breeze that flowed and curled down the staircase. The entire house lay in complete stillness, though standard for such late hours, as I made my way up to the topmost floor.

Once I arrived in my room, I immediately lit the lamp on the nightstand, illuminating the chamber with a warm, comforting glow.

I sank into the depths of my bed. As I did so, a menacing tingling came over me, my imagination unleashing my darkened thoughts with memories screaming to be heard. The events of the past few weeks coiled and slithered through my mind, and I was unable to shake the worries that troubled me so, worries that poor Jacob may yet know. May experience for himself.

Again, I recalled my time alone at Elphin House and the strange noises that tormented me throughout my final nights, the smell of death that lurked about every room, and, of course, the unfortunate circumstances that had befallen my tenants. The farmland spoiled. Every family gone, wiped out by hunger.

My thoughts drifted to the Ferrell family: the two small girls lying in their graves, their mother's face, haunting my every move, every thought. Even so far away from Elphin there was no escape, no relief, no way to see her gone. She remained with me at all times, not in person but in spirit, a never-ending feeling of someone lurking over my shoulder, loitering in the shadows, waiting to drag me to the dark.

Despite my fatigue, I could not bring myself to fall asleep. I lay in bed for hours, my mind racing, heart pounding. Finally, as the lamp's light began to fade, I drifted off into a fitful sleep, my dreams once more troubled by unwelcome faces.

I AWOKE DURING THE EARLY HOURS OF THE MORNING WITH A frightful gasp, causing me to convulse upright with a wild start, vigorously throwing the damp linen from my skin.

As I sat upright, doused in confusion and unsure of what had caused such distress, I let my gaze wander across the room, searching for any sign of intrusion, any sign that someone was there. Was some ghastly spectre lurking in the shadows, waiting to pounce upon me when I least expected it? A host of harrowing thoughts raced through my head, and the sweat crisply clinging to my brow only added further to my nervousness.

An unsettling ache nestled in my gut, slicing at my core like a heated iron to flesh, as I clasped my middle in a desperate attempt to nurse it. It was a sensation I had not endured before, nor would I wish to again.

A sudden commotion from downstairs pierced the silence. Laughter, the same boisterous laughter that had echoed through the house earlier, once again filled the air, mocking my solitude. It bounced off the walls, a playful taunt. Cheerful voices mingled with the clinking of glasses and the clatter of cutlery, all accompanied by the tantalizing aroma of roasted meats and vegetables.

My weakened body struggled to rise. Feet, heavy and leaden, swung from the bed, thudding onto the floorboards. "Silence!" I commanded, my voice weak and strained. But the noise continued, a mocking echo of my own helplessness.

Sighing, I pushed myself up from the bed, the mattress groaning under my weight. I shuffled towards the door, my hand trembling as I twisted the handle. I approached the narrow staircase. The jabbing pains within my stomach intensified with every step, fuelled by the aroma of food that wafted upwards from the staircase.

I reached out a hand to steady myself on the wall, the cold surface sending shivers down my arm as I groped my way down what felt like an endless series of steps.

After reaching the second floor, I limped along a lengthy hallway and halted at a door from where the lively noises came. Beneath the crack, a bright light glimmered, amplifying the cheerful sounds. I clenched my fist and rapped upon the door.

"You in there!" I shouted, pounding my fist upon the wood. "Open up this instant!"

But my efforts were drowned out by the clamour of voices from within.

Through the keyhole, I glimpsed a table decked with a vibrant red tablecloth and a feast consisting of plates filled with sliced goose, roasted vegetables, bread, cheese, and onions. The aroma of garlic intensified, causing my stomach to growl.

People sat around the table, giggling, their faces obstructed from view. Red wine sloshed carelessly into the finest glasses, poured down each throat, and returned to the table empty.

"I demand you open the door immediately!" I yelled over the ruckus, kicking at the door with my feet.

Suddenly, the laughter ceased. As I continued to peer through the keyhole, I watched in horror as the merrymakers around the table abruptly froze in their places, each one still, lifeless, frozen like sculptures.

With my face pressed against the gap, a sharp pang gripped within me. My eyes clenched shut in agony. My hand scraped fiercely against the door as I felt myself falling, falling downwards. Then, just as it began, the pain within was gone. Vanished.

A hand grasped my shoulder from behind, causing me to startle in panic. A bulky figure was concealed in the shadows next to me, none other than the master of the inn himself.

"Mr Daily?" He spoke with an air of surprise; his eyes narrowed in fatigue. "Pray tell, sir, is everything quite alright?"

"No," I snarled, pushing myself back from the door, still nursing my body. However, it was true. The pain I experienced in all its entirety was no longer there, as if it had never existed at all.

"Are you injured, sir?" the proprietor persisted, as several guests poked their heads out of their rooms, each disturbed by the commotion.

"I … I heard a clamour all the way from my quarters," said the burly man, attempting to hide a yawn. He failed miserably. "Shouting too. I dare say, I thought we were being ransacked by a bunch of ruthless thieves. I am relieved to see we are not."

"No," I replied, endeavouring to gather my senses. "No thieves, not tonight."

"Then," the owner pressed, "what is the cause of your distress? The hour is late. It is barely past three."

My brow deepened. "My distress," I began, a finger wagging through the dark, "is none other than the clientele you keep here."

"My guests, Mr Daily?" the man grumbled, trying to lower his voice. "Why, there must be some mistake. My guests are all reputable enough. Besides, everyone pays their way. We do not house any charity cases here."

"I speak not of charity," I remarked, my voice controlled and steady, "but of the scant regard your guests hold for others."

"Sir?" murmured the owner.

"You have guests within this room, do you not?" I pointed towards the door, the question firm.

"Guests?" he repeated.

"Indeed," I replied. "A small gathering. By chance, I heard them earlier, too, laughing and shouting amongst themselves like gleeful children."

Yet another door opened farther down the hall, revealing a slender man in nothing more than a nightgown and slippers.

The proprietor took a long, hesitant pause. "Without a doubt, sir, the walls within this house are thin. So thin that one might hear a pin drop. However, I am afraid what you suggest cannot be so. There can be no gathering within this room."

"You presume me a liar, then?" I growled, frustrated by the man's lack of trust.

"No, sir, not a liar. Of course not," reassured the owner. "I believe you did hear something, or someone. But this room …" The owner paused again, resting one hand on the doorframe. "Why, it is quite impossible."

Anger began to stew within me, a feeling I could only describe as my blood coming to boil as I observed the curious faces peering out over the portly man's shoulder.

"Unlock it," I demanded, my voice raised for all to hear. "Yes, unlock the door and you shall see with your own eyes."

The large man scratched his balding head before reaching up on his toes and retrieving a small key that lay hidden on top of the door frame. "Very well, sir," he obliged, inserting the key and wriggling it about until the distinct click of the lock released. He turned the handle as the door creaked open, revealing the unlit space beyond.

"There you have it, sir," muttered the owner, his large frame partially obstructing whatever view lay within. He casually stepped aside, allowing me the space to peek inside.

There was no one within, no one at all. I found myself looking not upon the magnificent feast of a well-laid table or the assembly of guests surrounding it. Nor were there the enticing aromas that earlier forced my mouth to water. Instead, what lay before me was the dim, cramped interior of a small cupboard, an unused space with a single bucket occupying a corner of the floor.

I stumbled back in disbelief, crashing against the opposite wall. "What is this?" I demanded, my eyes unmoved from the lightless space.

The large man glanced inside the cupboard without so much as a concern. "'Tis a bucket, sir," he bluntly stated, indicating a large crack in the ceiling above. "The roof, it's leaked for years. I haven't the time to fix it. Nor am I the young man I once was. The bucket there collects the most of it."

"Not the bucket!" I snapped, glancing from one pair of gaping eyes to the next. "The guests!" I remarked. "Where are they?"

The large man cleared his throat. "As I said before, sir," he expressed with a short, humorous chunter, "guests? Within this room? Quite impossible."

"But," I whispered, recollecting what I had witnessed only moments ago, what I heard, "the laughter," I exclaimed. "The voices, I heard them!"

"Aye," he nodded. "Most likely nothin' but a bunch of drunks loitering about the alley, sir," replied the owner as he secured the door back under lock and key. "They'll shelter anywhere or any place they can. Mark my words, Mr Daily, you won't be the first of my guests to complain about the scroungers of this city. Nor, truth be told, will you be the last. Now," he insisted, retracing his steps along the hall, "if you are quite satisfied, sir, I shall return back to my quarters. That is, if you require nothing more, of course?"

One by one, the guests behind him slowly slipped back to their rooms, closing their doors and leaving me alone with no one but the owner for company. His brow raised through the bleakness as he gestured his hand for my reply.

"Sir?" he repeated with a slight ounce of impatience. "Will that be all?"

I acknowledged the man with little more than a nod. As I stood back, watching as his broad frame slowly disappeared down the staircase, I found myself alone, my attention unmoved from the door and the distinct sound of laughter continuing to play on in my mind.

Sleep did not return that night.

Chapter 7

12TH March 1847

That morning, I ventured downstairs as the first rays of the morning sun pierced through the curtains. I left without so much as a word during my departure, though I couldn't help but think it was for the better. Last night had certainly been a strange occurrence of events, a night that by all accounts left me feeling foolish for my actions, most likely the result of something I had drunk while partaking in my nephew's company—some poorly brewed ale that had dulled my senses. Still, the entire affair had left me on edge for the remainder of the night.

Unable to find comfort in my confinement, I could do nothing more than pace my darkened room. After several hours, I turned to my notebook, the quill trembling unsteadily in my hand as I recorded the very event. I wrote down everything, all I could remember.

As I emerged from the squalid entrance, the doors slamming shut behind me, I was confronted by the putrid staleness that lingered in the morning smog. I took a deep breath, hoping to rid myself of the noxious scent. The city would soon be far behind me.

Fatigued, I stepped onto the uneven cobblestone, my shoes scraping against the rough, wet surface. The old, tired buildings that lined the alley seemed to tower above me, their dismal fronts casting deep, gloomy shadows onto the narrow passage below.

As I made my way, one couldn't help but notice the stark contrast between the filth and grime of Crane Alley and the grandeur of the busy street ahead. It was as though I had entered a different world altogether. Gone was the bleakness, the squalor, replaced by a brand-new day.

The street hummed with frenetic energy, as I had anticipated. Despite the early hour, a steady stream of people flowed along the cobbled road like a river of misery. Men, their faces etched with weariness, strode purposefully towards their workplaces in worn, filthy clothes, while women, dutifully carrying bulging bundles of laundry, stood in a patient queue to draw water from a nearby pump, idly gossiping as their children lingered nearby.

In the span of little more than a heartbeat, my carriage came into view, its large horses of a bone grey appearance, impeccably reined and ready to depart. As I drew closer, Mr Campbell—the epitome of composure—stood casually leaning against the carriage door. His hair, a thick mass of wavy curls, danced in the gentle morning breeze, brushing lightly against the collar of his tarnished shirt. With a gracious nod, he offered me a courteous greeting, but I remained speechless, lost in my thoughts, my mind elsewhere.

In no time, however, I found myself nestled within the carriage, watching intently as my luggage was deftly secured to the sturdy rails above.

As the bumpy carriage wound its way through the frenzied streets of the city, the sound of hooves on the uneven road resounded in my ears. The atmosphere was thick with the acrid tang of coal smoke, and a murky smog rose from the riverside, shrouding the faces of passing townsfolk in a veil of filthy grey.

As we meandered down the busy streets, the carriage wheels ground on, the sound rumbling through the air like that of distant thunder.

Suddenly the horses let out piercing whinnies, their hooves pawing at the stony ground.

Dazed and disoriented, I cast a gaze onto the busy street, searching for the cause of the unexpected halt. That was when I spied a crowd of people gathered in the middle of the road, blocking our way ahead. There were hundreds of them, perhaps thousands. The driver, his voice thick with curses, struggled to rein in the agitated horses, attempting to assess the chaotic situation as the carriage jolted fiercely from one direction to the other.

"Campbell!" I shouted, my hand thumping against the carriage's ceiling as my face pressed hard against the glass.

The scene outside was charged with tension as a sea of peasants cluttered the streets, their bellies rumbling with want. Many of them had stood in line outside the soup kitchens since dawn, hoping for a mere morsel that would sate their very cravings. But alas, just as my nephew had informed me, the supply provided by the works was insufficient, the demand too overwhelming, for the many figures that flooded the winding street.

As the queue grew ever longer, tempers flared and patience wore thin. The mass of destitute individuals seemed to grow increasingly restless, and what had once been a peaceful demonstration for charity soon devolved into a tumultuous uproar. Men, women, and children alike joined in a cacophonous chorus of angry bellows, each one demanding their fair share of food. A newborn's scream pierced out from the swarming crowd.

It wasn't long before the stench of burning wood and debris filled the air as carts were set ablaze, flames leaping against the backdrop of the streets. Windows were shattered. Bottles and bricks were hurled at the heads of authorities. No force could stop them; the raging crowd was driven only by desperate hunger.

"Whip the horses!" I cried out, jolting back in my seat as the carriage lurched forward.

The once peaceful streets of the city were consumed by chaos, the sound of fighting and anguished pleas filling the air.

As we hurtled through the streets, Mr Campbell urged the horses to greater speeds, his knuckles white with tension on the reins as the crowd attempted to dodge the horses' path.

I clung to the sides of the carriage, my heart racing as the view of bulging eyes rushed by in a blur, each set pressing into the carriage.

It was then that I noticed a sight beyond my window. A man sat hunched away, separated from the maddened riot. His sunken features were knotted in the utmost sorrow, his words too far to reach me. In his arms, he cradled a small child, a girl I had seen before, her face so much clearer in the morning light, her hair so much more golden, her body much more limp. Despite all that, she remained unnaturally quiet.

Still, the father leant over her, tears streaming down his face. He laid her gently on the hard, damp road, weeping as he did so. No matter how much he pleaded into her ear, no matter how much he consoled her, cried for her, the young girl's peaceful expression remained unfazed.

Her familiar cries never once pierced the cold, morning air.

Chapter 8

By some stroke of luck, we escaped unharmed from the chaos. After taking a brief pause at the turnpike and paying the fee, we resumed our journey along the meandering lanes, basking in boundless views of the open countryside. The change in terrain was stark, for we had long since left the rugged terrain of our earlier travels behind and were met with a much smoother and effortless passage ahead. The fresh country air was filled with the fragrant scents of wildflowers and of blooming trees. What had been a taxing journey had soon transformed into an adequate one, where the only distractions were the calming views of endless fields that seemed to change with each passing mile and the scattered clouds that cast shadows over the distant hills. The gentle country breeze wafted through the land, rustling the leaves of a lone tree whose pink petals had begun to vibrantly blossom. Blades of grass waved across the far-off mounds like ocean waves.

Throughout the day, our carriage continued its journey along the dirt lanes, its wheels never ceasing their rhythmic rumble, as we passed one small settlement after another.

I must admit, the repetitiveness of the driver's whistle was lost on me that day, for my thoughts were consumed by none other than the small child I had witnessed only that morning. The memory of her spluttering despair as she lay within her father's arms the previous night still weighed heavily on my thoughts. It was a memory I fear will stay with me.

As the hours passed and my thoughts deepened, my conscience

grew more and more troubled. Yet as the sun began to dip below the distant hillcrest, a stillness was soon to creep over the countryside, bringing with it an end to the day. It was then I realised my worries of that morning were in vain. Even if I had managed to help, what difference would it have really made? The riots would have persisted, and the poor and destitute would have continued to suffer their prolonged fate all the same. Saving a single life certainly would not have altered the course of such affairs. And the more I told myself that, the more I refused to allow guilt to devour me. The notion that I alone was responsible for the suffering of those I had encountered was preposterous. Besides, my dreams continued to confound me, leaving me uncertain if they were even dreams at all.

My arrival at Lismore could not come soon enough.

As the evening stretched on and night approached, my thoughts turned to my sister, Meredith. The memories of our childhood flooded back to me, and I couldn't help but feel a twinge of shame that I had not considered our relationship in many years. We had grown up together within the walls of Hulton House, spending nearly every waking moment by each other's side.

Looking back on those days, I realise that Meredith looked up to me. As the elder sibling, I suppose I served as a sort of father figure for her, guiding her through the world with the limited wisdom that I had acquired at my young age. I could not blame her for that; after all, by the time Meredith was merely nine years old, I was already becoming a strapping young man of ten and three.

Our mother, God rest her, had passed away some years earlier. We had laid her to rest in the family plot on the outskirts of our village, just a short stroll from Hulton House. It was a peaceful resting place that lay tucked beneath the boughs of a lonesome tree whose delicate lilac blossoms would burst forth each spring, imbuing the spot with a fragrant sweetness—a sweetness that would remind me of her.

I can still recall the scent.

Meredith and I would often visit the gravesite together, finding comfort in our shared loss and reminiscing about the fond times we held with our mother.

It was a sacred spot, a place where we could be together without any judgement or expectations from those around us. Meredith and I would spend hours in each other's company, blanketed below the delicate petals of our favourite spot. As the months passed by, those once vibrant leaves would wilt, their colours fading from life and covering the gravesite like fallen snow.

How I missed our time together. How I missed her.

Our father was a good businessman. As most men of business often did, he travelled the world to escape the untimely loss to which he clung so dearly. I recall there were years where he barely returned home at all. And when he did, he was not the man we once admired when our mother was alive. Something had altered him. He had changed somehow. Heartache, one would say, although I never understood it back then.

To conceal his suffering, father would withdraw himself to the confines of his library, admiring a large oil portrait of our mother that hung pride of place above his desk. At night, his whimpering could often be heard echoing through the halls. Though his love for his wife was unwavering, it was also a constant reminder of his loss, one he found unbearable to live with.

As young children, we tried to comfort him as best we could, but like most men, Father kept any emotion close to his chest. We could do nothing but watch helplessly as he slipped further into his own world of grief, a world that only he could inhabit, a world of which there was no escape. The only comfort he found was in the memories of his one true love, memories that seemed to keep him alive day after day yet also seemed to be tearing him apart. Because of that, he never ventured to her resting place again. He couldn't. Our father preferred to behold his love as she once was, her beauty frozen, her eyes forever watching over him from the canvas of a portrait as if the passage of time had no hold on her.

As the years slowly melted away, my sister and I drifted apart. The bond we once shared, forged in the pain and loss of our mother's passing, gradually dwindled. Our lives became consumed with our own pursuits, and naturally, over time, our visits to the family plot also became less frequent. So infrequent, in fact, that I barely returned to our spot beneath the tree at all. After all, our mother was gone, vacated from this life, leaving only the boldness of her name etched in stone to remind us she was ever really there. It was as if the world had moved on without her, leaving her memory to slowly fade into the distant past. The once vibrant flowers that had surrounded her grave had gone, replaced by an overgrowth of weeds that seemed to care little for her legacy. The trees that had once provided shade for our quiet solitude stood tall and indifferent, their limbs rustling with a disinterested sigh.

As I matured, I tried to hold onto her memory, to keep her alive in my heart and mind as best I could, but as years passed by, it seemed she was slipping away from me. The memories of our times together were little more than a distant blur in my mind's eye.

By the time I reached my eighteenth year, I decided to depart from my childhood home. The constant reminder of my mother's absence and my father's grief had all become too much to bear. With a heart full of hope and determination, I embarked on a journey by coach to London, a bustling city that beckoned with the promise of boundless opportunities, determined to prove something of myself. And prove I did. After several years of dedication, I became a partner in a thriving mill. It was a hard-won victory. For the first time in my life, I felt a sense of accomplishment, a sense that I could achieve whatever my mind desired. I had discovered a world beyond the narrow confines of our family home, a world full of endless possibilities that was merely waiting to be seized.

Certainly there were occasions when I reverted to my previous way of life and retreated to the once familiar rooms of Hulton House.

Whenever I did, it was not surprising to often find Meredith alone in the music room. It was a peaceful place with a large bay window that allowed light to filter in as she engrossed herself in the pages of a book or lost herself in playing the piano, her preferred method of escape.

During my visits, she would often perform for me, relishing the opportunity to entertain an audience as she tenderly stroked the keys. However, her devotion, she remained quite dreadful. She struggled with most pieces, hitting the wrong notes and fumbling over the more complex sections, causing one to cringe, displeased.

While her playing may have been far from perfect, I respected her determination all the same.

Life had certainly not been easy for Meredith since I left for London. Our close relationship had been torn apart by tragedy, leaving her alone with no one but our broken father. With no one else to turn to, Meredith retreated into a world of loneliness, spending her days lost in saddened melodies, imprisoned within the family walls. Despite the comfort her music gave, Meredith yearned for human connection, for someone to understand and accept her for who she truly was, for someone to see through the walls she built around herself, to offer her a way back into the world she once remembered and the love she needed most.

I could not even begin to imagine how I would find her now.

Chapter 9

13TH March 1847

The strangest of dreams occurred last night. It was a warm summer's day with a sky painted in the deepest blue imaginable and not a single cloud in sight. As I sprinted down the steep dirt path, the sensation of the tall grass tickled my knees. I looked back to see the sun shining on the country house atop the hill.

My father stood leaning against the darkened doorway, dressed in his finest waistcoat. A pipe was clenched firmly between his teeth. He took a puff, emitting wisps of smoke that danced amongst the warm summer breezes. He nodded in my direction. His familiar smile curled at the corner of his mouth, conveying a sense of comfort—a smile that only a parent could give.

I waved carelessly as I ran, losing my footing on the uneven path and tumbling harshly to the dusty ground, scraping my knees. When I glanced back again, my father was gone and the door and windows were closed tight, reflecting only the shimmers of the morning sun.

"Peter!" A distant voice travelled from afar. It was a voice I knew, a voice I thought I would never hear again.

I climbed to my feet, spinning on my heels. Nestled at the base of the hill, beyond the quaint picket gate, my mother stood in the midst of an open field, twirling about in a playful dance. Her vibrant spirit was clear in the graceful movement of her arms, which extended towards me in a welcoming embrace.

The sun shone upon her like a heavenly spotlight, illuminating her smile which beamed with an infectious joy as she laughed and twirled. Her long flowing hair half masked her face.

As I approached her, the overpowering aroma of wildflowers and grass filled my senses. The sounds of chirping birds and rustling leaves surrounded us.

"Come to me." She smiled. Her voice was like a soft lullaby, beckoning me nearer.

Her playful twirls soon slowed as she found me by her side. Within that moment, she opened her arms, reaching out and pulling me closer. Her touch was soft and tender, her fragrance carrying the faint scent of lavender and peppermint, a smell I could never forget.

As she pulled away from me, her gaze held mine. Her love for me was as unyielding as the very grounds where we stood.

"Peter, my darling. Where are you?" she whispered. Her voice sang through the air.

"I am here, Mother," I said with a grin so wide I swore my jaw would break.

Her smile widened as the wind swept the hair from her face. "We've been waiting."

Puzzled, I gazed about the open field. "We?"

She nodded, and her delicate touch lightly brushed my cheek. "That's right, my love. We have waited so very long. Come," she beckoned, offering her hand. "We have something to show you, something I'd like you to see, Peter."

I took hold of my mother's hand, and we walked. Her fingers felt warm and smooth against my own, and as we walked, our hands swung in a joyous rhythm in the middle, like two dancers lost in a score of music.

Suddenly, we found ourselves walking through the woodland. The light that had once bathed the open greens was gone, and the vibrant colours of the trees overhead had dissolved into murky shadows. Twigs snapped underfoot, and the damp smell of the earth paraded up my nose, mingling with the faint scent of decaying leaves.

"Mother, where are we going?" I asked, trying to keep up with her as she led the way. Her touch felt steadying, as if she was guiding me through a storm that was brewing.

Looking down, I was startled to see that my mother's feet were bare. They were covered in small cuts and bruises, and a thin line of blood marked her path.

"Mother, you are hurt!" I said, concern lacing my voice.

Despite my worry, she did not stop but continued to pull me

onwards, her grip stern. She had something important to show me, something that was worth her pain.

"Peter, I'm tired," a small voice moaned from behind me.

My head jerked quickly, and I saw Meredith straggling at the rear, her fingers already knitted in mine.

"How did you get here?" I questioned, watching as her stumpy legs raced across the ground.

My head turned straight. "Mother, might we slow down a little? Meredith is struggling to keep up," I protested, my gaze shifting to my younger sister, who was straggling along behind us.

But Mother paid no heed to my plea. Instead, her steps quickened and her grip on my hand tightened, urging me to match her pace. We weaved ourselves between the maze of trees, our gasping breaths the only noise that echoed in the stillness.

"We are not far now, dear one," she replied, unflinching, never once turning back in her stead. Her pull became harsher, her steps heavier. Just as I began to protest her grasp, Mother started to sing. Her voice was hushed and sincere, as if she was confiding a secret in rhyme.

We continued to trudge, the dense forest deepening, and my sister's desperate moans became clearer from behind. Her voice was laced with exhaustion. She clung to my hand with white-knuckled fingers as if she feared being swept away by the sea of trees.

"Peter, I'm tired," she whimpered again, her voice hoarse as she stumbled and swayed with each step.

I turned to look at her, my heart heavy with worry, hoping that in some way I could ease her helpless tears. But to my dismay, Meredith was nowhere in sight. My hand was empty, absent her hand, yet I could still feel the ghost of her touch, her fingers still interlaced with mine, her presence still with me. And I could hear her voice, so saddened, still pleading for it all to stop.

I closed my eyes tightly. When I opened them again, it felt as though we had never been walking at all. The woodland around us was still familiar, but the sun shone brighter here, beaming down in patches to the forest floor. Coral bells grew and thrived in the dappled shade, their petals providing a touch of enchantment. Moss covered the base of every tree, and the tranquil call of singing birds once more serenaded the treetops.

I looked up to my mother, who seemed somewhat different than before. She appeared older. Her face, once a picture of youth, was tied and gaunt. Deep creases etched the once smooth skin of her forehead, and her eyes, which were bright and lively, carried a heavy burden of weariness, of struggle, as if they had suffered a lifetime of pain. The clothes she wore, once radiant and alive with colour, were dull and frayed, the pattern worn away to a dreary grey.

"Mother?" I gazed up at her, and she turned to me, her eyes never straying from the ground ahead.

"Hmm?" she mumbled distantly, squeezing my hand in return.

"Where is Meredith?" I asked, my voice filled with concern.

"Who?" she uttered.

A chill crawled down my spine.

"Meredith, Mother?" I asked again.

She said nothing. Instead, she lifted her one free arm, curling out her finger peculiarly and pointing to a gap in the thicket ahead. Something lurked there, something concealed, hidden by the overgrowth. A secret. We seemed to be moving towards it, yet my feet remained rooted to the ground. Then, just like before, my mother began to sing.

I AWOKE WITH A FRIGHTFUL GASP, MY HEART THUMPING AS MY body jerked upright on my seat. My brow was slick with sweat, and I could feel my breaths racing in quick and shallow gasps. My eyes darted around the carriage, searching for some unknown threat that loomed in the darkness. But there was nothing. It was just a dream. Merely a dream. A dreadful nightmare. Yet it all felt so real.

The beat in my chest slowly calmed as I tried my best to shake off the panic that clung to me. As I leant towards the window, my head resting on the cool glass, I gazed out on a world shrouded by darkness. I shut my eyes, attempting to conjure up a peaceful image, but all I could see was the unsettling scene from my nightmare. It was like a never-ending loop of memory, playing over and over again. I was trapped, unable to escape it. I sat there uneased, listening to the steady sound of horses' hooves upon the dusty ground, my only source of comfort from an otherwise terrifying dream.

Chapter 10

That morning, I sat with quill in hand, fully absorbed in the world of poetry. The written word had long held a place of deep affection within my soul, and as I journeyed along the endless roads, I discovered peace in the intricate beauty of the verses. It was precisely what I needed during those trying times, offering a much-needed diversion from the weighty thoughts that burdened me.

Outside, rain washed over the countryside, falling from a sky of slate clouds that seemed to stretch on forever. The droplets of water cascaded down with a gentle yet persistent patter, cloaking the world in a muted palette of endless greys and greens.

The rest of the morning passed by in little more than a flicker. With few tasks to occupy the mind, I found myself sinking deeper and deeper into the comfort of my seat, lost within my own head as I watched the world roll by. Each mountain outside my window blended into the next until it was impossible to distinguish one piece of scenery from the other. The forests that dominated the nearby hills sighed with quiet conversation. The leaves, too, rustled and whispered, as if sharing old, forgotten stories of the world that existed long before my own.

With no letting up, the rain continued to fall, each droplet a tiny messenger from the heavens. A downpour would soon undoubtedly turn the landscape into a sea of mud and muck.

Despite the rain, the coachman remained unfazed. He sat perched on his seat with an air of contentment, whistling a tune that had stayed with him since Elphin.

From out of my window, an old castle loomed nearby, casting its shadow over the way ahead. The intimidating stone towered towards the sky, with large blocks that had visibly begun to wither and crumble. Two mighty towers stood tall and proud, their tops obscured by a thick mist that swirled around them. A large, open archway stood at the centre of the castle's front, inviting any curious traveller to explore the abandoned chambers within.

"Stop!" I yelled, thwacking at the roof.

The carriage slowed to a steady roll before coming to a halt, its wheels partly submerged in the mud.

Without delay, the young coachman secured the reins and jumped down from his station. The tired leather of his boots sank deep into the muck.

"There be a problem, sir?" voiced Campbell, his voice becoming clearer as he trudged his way to the door.

"What is that?" I pointed.

Campbell turned, raising his head as his feet squelched deep within the puddles. "'Tis a castle, sir."

"I know it's a castle!" I voiced, flaring my nostrils. "Tell me, what is it called?"

The young man removed his hat, scratching at his head in thought. "Kilchurn, I believe, sir. Can't be sure I can tell you much more than that, sir." He placed his hat back on his head and squinted through the rain. "Other than a few stories, that is."

"Stories?" I asked.

"Aye, sir, a few," replied the coachman. "It was owned by the Campbell Clan." He grinned somewhat amused. "A handsome name, if I do say so myself."

"Ancestors of yours?"

"Aye," answered Campbell proudly. "My bloodline, to be sure. Some several hundred years ago, in fact. Though I canna be sure of when exactly. I know little of such things, sir."

"Well, then, tell me what you do know," I urged him.

"Well, I know that the Campbells ruled most of these parts back then. They were indeed a fierce bunch, victorious against any other clan who dared to step foot on their land, a clan not to be trifled with." He stepped aside. "See over there, sir?" He pointed with his arm stretched high. "Just over yonder there. Just past those wee branches. The rear tower, or what's left of it. You see, sir?"

I cast my glance upwards. "I do," I agreed, making out the faint outline of the tallest tower that weaved amongst the mists.

"Story goes that it was that tower that got struck by lightning, seeing the end to the castle."

"Oh?" I remarked, visualising the bolt of light that had struck down from the sky. "I imagine it would have been quite the spectacle."

"Aye, sir. I imagine it would have."

"And the people who resided there. They all perished?"

"Many did, sir, so the story goes," hushed Campbell. "However, as you can imagine, some did make it out alive. Though once the fire played its part and the smoke began to thin, the castle was very much lost. One might say that what stands before you now is the very reflection of the day Kilchurn saw its end." He looked about him. "Some locals even say that on quiet nights, they can still smell the smoke, hear the sound of roaring flames. Hear the screams."

"Is that true?" I asked him, leaning out farther as he spoke.

"Ach, 'tis all just natter, sir," Campbell said with a dismissive wave. "The locals, they don't have much to do around these parts. And places like Kilchurn," he looked back up to the tower, "well, such gossip tends to spread as quick as wildfire. It keeps the locals' tongues waggin', that's for sure."

"What sort of natter?"

"Oh, just wee tales handed down from one generation to the next. Stories of lives that have long since departed. Ghosts, I suppose."

"Ghosts?" The hairs on my neck prickled.

"Aye," he agreed light-heartedly as the rain began to pool on the rim of his hat. "Superstitious rumours. There are many different versions, but I wouldn't put much stock in them."

A mighty gust swept across the road, roaring ferociously as it seemed to race towards the castle. The trees lining the roadside bent and swayed like ships caught in a violent storm, their branches bending in the wind's wake.

"There once was an elderly market trader," Campbell began. "The story goes that he was travelling past Kilchurn one evening when suddenly the heavens began to open on him. I suppose very much on a day like this. Desperately trying to save his precious stock, the trader sought refuge within the inner dorms of the castle, the only shelter he could find from the downpour. He huddled there and waited for the storm to pass.

"It was as he was gathering his cart from the castle entrance that something grabbed his attention, something that would raise the hairs on any man."

"Well? What was it?" I leant even closer.

"A voice coming from inside the darkened chamber. The very same chamber he had recently departed. The soft, elegant tone of a woman."

"A woman?" I repeated, my skin prickling with unease. "What did she say?"

"Ach, it wasn't what she said, sir, but more the way she said it. You see, she whispered something to him. The words played hauntingly in his ear as he began to retrace his steps. 'Set me free,' she spoke, her voice frail with sadness."

"And what did he find?" My throat turned dry as I looked back towards the castle's arch.

"Well, I'll tell you, sir." Campbell leant in closer, his face stern as stone as though he was about to reveal the greatest of secrets. "Nothin'," he said, a faint smirk stretching across one side of his face.

"Nothing?" I repeated.

"Nay, sir. Nothing," he confirmed, shaking his head and regaining his stance on the roadside. "Of course, there are many who say that he did witness something extraordinary. But throughout the years, many retellings seem to differ. Some folks believe the woman to be a victim of the day the lightning struck, trapped in the castle by the blaze. Others believe her to be some sort of witch, imprisoned in the castle grounds, still captured for all eternity."

"And what do you believe?" I asked, my eyes fixed on the imposing tower of Kilchurn.

"Me?" Campbell hesitated, his gaze also locked on the castle walls. "Like I mentioned before, sir, they're but stories. Nothin' more. Kilchurn is a dismal-looking place, I'll give you that. But there's nothing to fear here. The only thing those empty rooms hold is history. History canna harm you."

"No," I replied. "Of course not."

The sky above us rumbled with far-off thunder, as if God himself were angry, unleashing a surge of rain that pounded the earth, forming rivulets that snaked their way through the muddy terrain.

The coachman studied the road ahead. His appearance was soaked to the bone. "Now, if you don't mind, sir, we'll continue to make tracks." He craned his neck to the sky. "If the rain continues, we'll be as good as sitting ducks."

With that, Campbell left my side and climbed back to his station. The carriage momentarily shook and jolted as the wheels sloshed over the swampy surface.

As I glanced out the window, I watched the entrance of Kilchurn slowly creep by. There was something unsettling about such a place. Its soulless entrance seemed to beckon me, to call to me to explore its depths and uncover the secrets that lay hidden deep within its walls.

As the carriage made its way through a cluster of gnarled trees, the tale recounted by Campbell continued to play on me, its words etched into my mind like a deep scar. But it was those three haunting words that lingered the most, stirring through my thoughts like a mournful dirge: “Set me free.” They were so vivid, so clear, that I could almost hear them whispered on the wind, calling to me as we passed, forever fading in my wake.

Chapter 11

14TH March 1847

A flurry of lights shone weakly through the haze. The distant specs provided a soft, comforting glow as they shimmered through the darkness.

Oban, I thought with relief.

The town, nestled on the edge of the sea, was a welcome sight after such a treacherous journey. As we drew closer, the lights grew brighter and more distinct, revealing a bustling and vibrant community that seemed to pulse with life.

The first thing that caught my eye was the harbour, where a fleet of fishing boats bobbed up and down to the sound of the sea, their masts and rigging silhouetted against the night sky.

The air was alive with the sound of screaming seagulls and the songs of jolly villagers as they sang from their local ale house. Children ran like a pack of wild animals from door to door, their clothes covered in soot.

The carriage came to a stop for the final time as the door swung open to the sight of Mr Campbell, looking rather glum and weary. The aggressive weather that had raged across the land the previous evening had finally petered. Still, the coachman's baggy clothes and long, frizzy hair clung to him like a second skin, rendering him the appearance of a waterlogged rat.

Smiling through his discomfort, he announced, "Here we are, sir. Oban, as promised."

With a sense of eagerness, I stepped out onto the seafront. The air was crisp and unspoiled, and the playful sea breeze brushed over crags dotted with sitting gulls. The soothing sound of the waves gently lapped against the shore, while a beam of light reached out to me from across the water.

It was none other than Lismore—the island's lighthouse itself—with its bright beacon shining from afar, in many ways welcoming me back to a place I thought I would never return.

"Sir?" Mr Campbell enquired from behind me, his hands weighed down by my bags. He looked in my direction across the sea. "If you please, sir. It is late. There won't be any ferry to take you across the water this evening, not at this hour. Shall we find you some lodgings for the night?"

"There is no need," I answered him, breaking my gaze from the lighthouse.

"No need, sir?"

"No," I insisted, venturing away from the shore and striding into the confined space of a long, narrow street.

Behind me, I could hear only the coachman's heavy breath in my wake, struggling to keep up with my stride.

As luck would have it, I had acquired a property in Oban some years ago. It was a spur-of-the-moment decision, one that could be described as a spontaneous purchase. The estate was nestled in a picturesque spot that overlooked the harbour and the sailing vessels navigating the open waters. The view of Lismore emerging from the distant ocean on a clear day was nothing short of a breath-taking sight, rendering it a perfect refuge from the city.

However, the rationale behind the purchase extended far beyond its natural grandeur. The estate in Oban was an ideal location to be near my sister, a short journey should she ever have required assistance in her time of need. In many ways, I simply yearned to support her in any way I could. However, it was a purchase that to this day had yet to prove its worth.

The house itself had been preserved immaculately throughout the years. It was a quaint and secluded cottage nestled on the periphery of the village, not too far from the shore. I had made suitable arrangements for the upkeep of the household during my absence, of course. The linens were to be turned regularly and the rooms heated as though anticipating my long-awaited homecoming.

That night, I settled into a comfortable chair in front of the fireplace, enveloped by the soothing warmth of flickering flames and glad of the journey's end. I ate nothing that night. I had not the desire for it. Instead, I poured myself a generous helping of brandy and listened to the world outside as it gently rattled at the windows.

As I gazed, unmoved from my seat, my eyes were drawn to a distant light that lay beyond the blackened pane: the lighthouse from afar, illuminating the darkness and beckoning to me across the waters like a guiding star. It served as the reminder of my purpose and obligation to the sibling I abandoned all those years before. And as I reclined deeper into the armchair, causally swirling my beverage, I sighed with great relief as the sensation of heat washed over me. With my eyes barely open, my mind began to wander, uttering soft words of comfort that only I could hear.

"Soon, my dear. Soon …"

Chapter 12

15th March 1847

The soft golden rays of dawn filled the room, casting a glow on the dark oak furnishings and the dust-coated bookshelves. I stirred from my deep slumber feeling disoriented and groggy. As I slowly became aware of my surroundings, I realised I was still slouched in the same plush armchair, an empty brandy glass precariously balanced on my chest.

The faint scent of the potent liquor wafted up my nostrils, mingling with the musty smell of old books and settled ash from the hearth.

With a deep sigh, I gradually rose from the armchair, feeling the weight of my errors and the throbbing in my head as I sluggishly made my way towards the door.

Outside, low copper-edged clouds smothered the horizon, merging with a low fog that concealed the roughness of the open sea. I yawned tiresomely, searching through the haze that cloaked the distant island. Regardless of my efforts, I could see nothing. To all who looked, the land across the way had vanished in its entirety, gone, swallowed up like some hidden secret patiently waiting to be found. However, I would set sail for its high cliffs and rocky shore. That day, we would reunite once more.

The stay had been much brisker than I had anticipated, and before I knew it, I found myself strolling along the seafront that led back towards the village. The air was sharp and clean, and the ground still bore the moisture of the previous night's rainfall.

In but a short space of time, I found myself standing at the harbour, surrounded by men of all ages who carried nets and baskets as they made their way along the short rickety dock. Not one of them was paying attention to the scream of gulls that was harsh in the morning lull.

A sturdy man attired in a long grey coat and ivory cap bellowed out orders as he marched along. His face was half-concealed by a bush of thick, white bristles, and his skin bore the marks of a lifetime spent exposed to the spray of the sea. He made his way up the dock, his feet thudding heavily upon the old wooden planks, his brow furrowing into a canyon of deeply defined creases that appeared like scars on his face.

"If it's the ferry you seek," he grumbled, his high-arched brows framing a less-than-welcome expression, "you've well-nigh missed it."

Without thinking, I looked out onto the ocean. "Missed it?" I asked him.

I squinted into the distance, shielding my eyes from the dazzling glare reflecting off the water as I observed a small boat sailing out of view, quickly vanishing as it ventured into rolling fog.

"If you wish to go to Mull," the man continued, "the next ferry won't be until tomorrow mornin'. Departs at nine. Sharp. We dunna wait for no latecomers."

He settled himself onto a stool by the harbour gate, relieving the strain on his feet and leaning his head back against the railings.

"Mull?" I repeated, confusion etched upon my face. "You mean to say the Isle of Mull?"

"The very same," he acknowledged, tipping his cap forward to block out the glare. He breathed deeply, folding his arms across his chest, his eyes dropping to a close.

"Then you are quite mistaken, seaman," I corrected him. "It is not Mull that I require."

"Seaman?" he echoed, his brow furrowing inquisitively. "Harbour Master, if you'd be so kind," he corrected me, before dropping his head back into place. "And besides," he muttered, "if it's not Mull you're after, then where is it ye intend to travel, exactly?"

"Lismore," I replied plainly. "Just across the way."

With a newfound air of interest, the Harbour Master's eyes opened. "Lismore, is it?" He reached into his inner pocket, producing a darkly varnished pipe that he tapped against his lips thoughtfully.

"A problem, boatman?"

"Harbour Master," he corrected again. "And no, no problem. Just a wee bit of curiosity, is all."

"Curiosity?" I asked. "About what?"

"About what sort of business a refined gentleman such as yourself would have on the likes of Lismore Island," he replied, rattling a small box of matches. He struck one with the flick of his wrist and held it to his pipe, shielding the flame from the wind. He took several short puffs. "The island hasn't much to offer—nothing but empty fields and rocky shores. A perfect place for solitude, if that is what you are after. Very few inhabit the place these days."

"If you must know," I spoke with an air of sternness, "I have a prior engagement with a family member, a member whom I have not seen in some time. It is of the utmost urgency that I arrive there."

"Family on Lismore, you say?" he asked, blowing out another thick wisp of smoke. "Why, you must be mistaken. There hasn't been an eligible family that resided on the island for near on thirty years. The dwellings consist of nothing but a few scattered cottages inhabited by local folks. That is, apart from the old Daily manor. However, it is barely a sight to behold of late. It is homed by a widow, one Meredith Durose. A nice lass, that one. But she tends to keep to her house nowadays. Many locals rarely catch a glimpse of that one."

"Precisely why I must make haste," I insisted, my urgency palpable.

"Oh?" grunted the boatman, raising the shade from his eyes for the first time. "You are acquainted with the woman, then?"

"Acquainted, indeed," I remarked, exhaling with a hint of impatience. "She is my sister."

On that note, the Harbour Master perked up, his tone laced with curiosity. "I used to often ferry the lady across the water at one time," he told me. "At first, with her husband, strange man, so he was. Never spoke a word, not to me, at least. Quite the recluse, so it happens, with a stare so stern it would make any man want to crawl up his own backside. Of course, when he died, she was seen much less crossing the water to town. Once a fortnight, if I recall right. Never alone, mind you, always in the company of one of her staff. A servant girl. Sweet lass. Always laughin'. They'd make their way about the town, their arms linked, gathering whatever provisions the mistress required, and then sail on back to the island. This was her routine for some years onwards. That is, until the wee servant lass departed her employment. Since then, Mrs Durose mainly confines herself to the house."

"You mean to say she resides alone?" I questioned, feeling somewhat ashamed at having to ask. Being her only brother, it seemed fitting I should know of such affairs.

"Nay," replied the boatman, cracking his neck to the side. "The house," he groaned, "still has staff under the mistress's employment—an elderly fellow. He makes the trip to Oban once in a blue moon, never accompanied by Mrs Durose, though. The man, he travels alone, doesn't speak much. Then there's the lady's son, of course."

For once I knew exactly of whom he spoke of. "Ah, you speak of Jacob?"

"Aye," he snapped his fingers. "A good lad, very good. Unusually quiet, from what I remember. That said, he is all grown up now. He visits the island once or twice a year in between his travels. That is, once he's had his fill of drink and women at the whore house."

"What?" I enquired, unsure if I had heard the man correctly.

"Aye, the finest establishment Oban has to offer, I assure you," he whispered with the slyest smirk.

"Preposterous!" I exclaimed. "Why, Jacob is a respectable lad, a successful lad. What need would he have for such a place?"

"Respectable lad or not, my fine sir, every man needs the whore house," he replied with the briefest shrug of his shoulders.

The roar of the waves pounded against the wooden dock, the force of their impact sending a frothy spray high into the air. The salty mist seemed to hang suspended, catching the light of the sky before falling back into the churning waters.

"Listen here!" I yelled, my patience wearing thin. "Are you able to oblige me with your services or not?"

He shook his head sternly, a short, disgruntled chortle escaping his lips. "Ain't no ferry going to Lismore. The route has been closed ever since the island's quarry works shut down, near on several years ago now."

I stood there, bewildered, my fists clenching into tight balls. "Then why didn't you say so in the first place?" I snarled, my eyes never leaving the water. "I simply must get there!"

"Then you'll need to hire yourself a wee rowboat, won't you." He laughed heartily. "Shouldn't take little more than a few hours. I'd be careful of the fog, mind you. There have been many cases of men rowing into the brume only to find themselves lost," he warned gravely as he stood to walk away.

I looked out into the distance with great concern, the fog appearing thicker and more menacing than it had earlier that morning. It loomed like a wall of grey cloud, feeding on any approaching ships that dared to venture near.

"Wait!" I called out after him, my voice echoing across the docks. "What about you?"

He stopped abruptly and turned, gesturing his pipe towards his chest. "Pardon me?" he asked, his voice rough with a thick confusion.

"You have a boat, I presume?"

"I do. The finest," he responded, somewhat insulted by my questioning. "I'd like to meet a Harbour Master who does not."

"Then perhaps I could persuade you to see me safely to the island. Today? I'll pay you, naturally," I proposed.

"Oh, aye?" he replied, cocking a single brow. "And what exactly would you be offering for such an inconvenience?"

"Fifteen shillings," I offered bluntly.

"Ah, I'd do no less than twenty," he countered.

"Twenty shillings!" I exclaimed incredulously. "Sir, you—"

"You won't find anyone else willing to take you there," he interrupted, his tone low to a groan. "Not in this weather. Besides," he pointed towards the harbour, "many boats won't return here until dusk. By then it'll be too late."

My mouth hung open in disbelief. I knew there was little point in haggling. The man would not be swayed.

"Twenty shillings, then," I begrudgingly agreed.

He nodded in return. "Ten now," he insisted. "I'll take the other ten when the job is done."

"Fine!" I frowned, counting out the shillings as they dropped into his palm with a *clink*. "There!"

He jingled the coins in his palm before tucking them away. "You have yourself a boat, sir." He grinned. "We'll set sail in an hour's time."

"An hour? But—" I began to protest.

"Aye, gives me time to get the old girl ready, make sure she's shipshape and all. Besides, have ye no belongings to take with ye?" he observed, his eyes scanning me up and down.

His observation was indeed correct. I had almost disregarded the thought and felt rather embarrassed in doing so.

"An hour then," I agreed, turning back and beginning to retrace my steps towards the village.

"Oh, and sir!" the boatman yelled out.

I spun on my heels, glancing back towards the bearded man, who was walking in the direction of the small wooden pier. His boots thudded along the slippery planks.

"Yes?" I asked him.

"I hope you have a good pair of sea legs."

Chapter 13

With haste, I gathered my belongings for the journey, enlisting the aid of Campbell, who had slumbered soundly since the preceding evening, content within a small stable. He had intended to embark on the homewards journey that very day. Yet after little persuasion, I advised him to remain in Oban during my visit to the island. After all, I was uncertain how brisk my stay at the old family residence would be. At first, Campbell seemed hesitant, withdrawn, but soon warmed to the idea with the promise of added compensation for his time and accommodation. I would put him up at a small inn named The Tartan Tavern, found along the main street of the village. Furthermore, I resolved to correspond with his employer, expounding upon the situation once I settled on Lismore.

With scarcely a moment to spare, we set off through the clamouring streets and towards the bustling docks. The briny sea air filled my lungs just as it had before, while the gusting winds tousled the hair at the nape of my neck as we walked the slippery planks along the crooked wooden pier.

Nearby, a band of fishermen unloaded their bountiful catch, their raucous voices carrying over the din of crashing waves and screeching seabirds.

I lingered for a spell, scouring the dock for the Harbour Master, though to much dismay, it was evident he was nowhere to be seen.

"Perhaps, sir, he has already departed?" suggested Campbell, his voice hoarse with fatigue as he dropped the bags on the planks.

"Taken himself to Lismore?" I retorted, waving my hand dismissively.

"Then perhaps we are merely late, sir. Perhaps the man considered that you had changed your mind?"

"Be quiet," I snapped, scrutinising the hands of my watch, its glass glinting in the light. "Why, it has scarcely chimed the hour. The man should be here."

And so we waited, watching as vessels sailed past one by one and the distant fog gradually thickened. Soon the tide ebbed away from the shore, revealing the jagged edges of rocky outcroppings that lay concealed beneath the surface.

Just then, what should I hear but a voice calling out from somewhere behind us, faint at first.

"This way!" it bellowed.

I surveyed the dock with complete puzzlement, scanning each boat until my gaze alighted on a head poking up from over the side—the Harbour Master.

"Hurry along, then," he bellowed, applying a hand to the side of his mouth as though his voice would become all the louder for it.

Without delay, I made my way to the end of the dock, cautiously peering over the side. There, buoying on the waves like a cork in water, was the bearded man himself, perched on a bench in a rotting rowboat. Its once-pristine white paint had become dry and flaky.

"Mind your step, now," directed the boatman, his oars already in hand.

A sudden pause lingered between us.

"You mean to tell me you shall be voyaging in that, sir?" queried Campbell, leaning over the side to obtain a more promising view, a splash of amusement playing at his lips.

"I most certainly will not!" I snapped. My face flushed red with annoyance. "Y-y-you …" I could not help but stutter. "You informed me you had a ship!"

"I informed you I had a boat," said the man below, battling to keep himself steady. "Besides, she's as dependable as any other in this harbour, and quieter too, for that matter. It will give you the chance to enjoy the scenery."

"And the risk of plunging into the abyss should she sink."

"Sink?" echoed the boatman, his annoyance clear. "Why, I'll have you know I've never lost a boat yet. Not in all my days. I don't intend to start now, sir."

"That is quite beside the point," I yelled loudly over the wave. "I shall not be seen gallivanting on these open waters on nothing more than a dinghy. And one of such poor condition, at that."

"Then you shan't be travelling at all, sir," said the boatman, gathering the rope and preparing to moor back to the dock. He tossed the rope, gesturing for Campbell to secure a knot.

"Wait," I instructed, gazing towards the island that was shrouded in mist, and asked how long it would take to reach there.

"The isle?" replied the boatman, pondering for a moment. "A few hours if the sea is favourable. Perhaps a tad longer."

As I stood there, the sea spray stinging my face, I found myself at a critical crossroads. The choice ahead was a tough one. On one hand, I could decline the boatman's offer and wait until tomorrow for a more reliable vessel. But there was no guarantee I'd find one, and time was running short. On the other hand, the idea of setting out in a fragile dinghy across those choppy waters made my stomach knot with worry. The boatman's experience did little to ease my fears, yet I knew I couldn't let my fear take control.

"Alright, then," I sighed, stepping towards the boat. I lifted my foot to the swaying bow and glanced up at Campbell, who stood at the edge, the wind ruffling his hair as he watched my every move.

"What are you waiting for?" I snapped. "Lower my bags!"

THE SMALL BOAT GROANED OMINOUSLY, CREAKING UNDER THE strain of the turbulent waters. In that moment, I feared it might sink. Yet the intrepid Harbour Master pressed on, undeterred, pulling mightily on the oars, his only sounds the occasional strained grunt.

It felt like an eternity before the tumultuous waves began to ease. By then I was thoroughly soaked, my clothes clinging to me as water streamed from my cuffs and elbows, my neatly combed hair plastered to my forehead.

We ventured into the fog, the dense air wrapping around us like a shroud. The Harbour Master steered the boat with steady hands, his years of experience guiding us through the thick mist.

As we sailed deeper, the fog thickened to the point where I could barely see my hand in front of my face. An eerie silence enveloped us, broken only by the creaking of the boat and the gentle lapping of water against the hull as the oars sliced through the gloom.

My eyes strained against the haze, desperately searching for any sign of land ahead, but it was like trying to see through a thick veil—utterly futile. The motion of the boat forced me to lean forward, dizziness overwhelming me as I cradled my head in my hands, fighting the queasiness rising within.

Suddenly, a loud horn blared nearby, jolting me into a panic. The Harbour Master swerved the boat to port, narrowly avoiding a larger vessel that had emerged from the fog like a ghost. I could hear the shouts of other sailors as they passed, their urgent warnings echoing above the roar of the waves. But just as quickly as they appeared, they were swallowed by the thick fog, leaving us once again in disorienting silence.

"Close call," uttered the boatman, smearing the sweat from his brow with none other than the cuff of his sleeve. He gritted his teeth, manoeuvring the boat with a single oar, his stamina never ceasing to fail him.

"Close, indeed," I agreed, releasing a held breath that had gone unnoticed. "Tell me," I felt myself begin to heave, though I managed to hold back the urge, "how on earth do you know where you're headed? Why, this fog is so thick here I can barely see you at all!"

He stopped for a moment, retrieving something from his pocket. At first, I could not perceive what it was but soon came to recognise the spark of a match that lifted to his lips. For the briefest moment, his face was illuminated with a dreary orange glow. I could see his eyes peering into me, shortly followed by the familiar scent of black-cherry tobacco.

"Does the ocean disturb you some?" he asked, his voice low and gravelly.

I avoided his stare before answering. "Not at all," I lied, glancing back into the distant emptiness of a ghostly world.

In truth, the ocean had always been my bane, my weakness. From a young age, I had never been able to develop a fondness for it, no matter how long I had spent at sea. The relentless motion of the water, the spray that parched my throat, and the vast emptiness of the horizon that seemed to stretch on forever, all conspired to make one feel small and powerless.

"Should I be? Disturbed, that is?" I asked him.

The boatman shrugged at that right before breaking out into an infectious cough. "'Tis just fog, is all," he said, attempting with great effort to clear his throat. "Occurs regularly enough this time of year. Tends to roll in from the north. You're quite lucky, mind you. It often stretches to the shoreline and smothers the village like a blanket of wet wool, fog so thick you could just about choke."

"I see," I answered, my focus still fixed past the wall of endless nothingness ahead.

"Aye," he grunted with a mighty heave of his brawny arms. "Call it superstition if you like, but when the mist settles over the water like this, a day's fishing is bound to be lost."

"Fishing?" I enquired with an air of confusion. "You speak of fishing?"

He nodded through the slow-passing murk that drifted before his face. "Aye, fishing," he repeated. "When the fog announces its presence, many boats return to the dock after a day at sea empty-handed, without so much as a bite." He puffed several times more on his pipe, exhaling a long, deep breath through his nose. "It's as though all the fish just vanish, like something spooked them. I canna explain it. No one can, yet it happens all the same."

"Spooked them?" I enquired subtly. I had had quite enough of that to last a lifetime. "But there is nothing that surrounds us but the air and sea. As you clearly stated yourself, it is merely fog."

"True enough," he nodded. "But when you are alone out here on the water for days on end, well, the fog … It does things to you."

My head tilted up like a question mark.

"Plays with your mind," the man continued. "Trickery, I suppose. People hear voices that aren't really there, see things that simply should not be."

From high above, the outburst of a gull pierced the silence, causing me to startle in panic. The sound of its wings flapped frantically somewhere overhead, it, too, likely blinded by the suffocating fog.

"And what of these so-called voices?" I swallowed back the lump that seemed to have lodged in my throat.

The man mumbled under his breath. "It varies from local to local." He sighed and, for the first time since our departure, allowed his arms the rest they well and truly needed.

The boat soon lost its course and, for a time, lazily drifted with the current.

"Some have sworn to have heard the voice of a wee lass crying out for help, whimpering and splashing as if she herself were stranded out at sea. Others have said to have heard the innocent sound of soft singing, something of a childlike hum. They would spend hours searching through the mist, only to return to the village eager to share their tale."

"And they found nothing?" I pressed. "No sight of a child? No wreckage?"

"Nay, nothing," he grunted, finding his grip back around the oars. He gave another powerful thrust, jerking the boat in a forward motion.

Just when I was about to give up all hope of us ever seeing beyond the fog, out of the corner of my eye a large black form appeared into view, slowly emerging through the haze. As we drew closer, the shape loomed taller and larger, while the sound of foaming waves crashed violently against its darkened, gloomy form, as if the island itself was complaining loudly.

The boatman turned to look in a rather casual manner. "Ah, grand. The north cliff," he said by way of conversation. "Shouldn't be too much longer now. The fog will start to thin around the bend there."

And right he was. Within a short space of time, a gentle breeze began to stir, causing the sea mist to lift, rising from the ocean's surface and revealing the rocky beach and rugged cliffs of the island.

The boat grinded along the ocean floor, soon to run aground. The boatman leapt into the shallow waters and, with little effort, dragged the boat to the shore. His neck veins bulged with the exertion.

"As promised." He breathed heavily, holding out his palm as he attempted to regain his breath. "That shall be another ten shillings, if I recall right." It was more a statement than it was a question, his rough features betraying a hint of eagerness. One might have suggested he was slightly unsettled, that he wished to depart as soon as the opportunity allowed it.

I paid him without question, of course. I was, after all, a man of my word.

The boatman collected my bags, throwing them carelessly to the ground before pushing the small boat back out to sea and quickly clambering inside.

"Wait!" I yelled. "You're not just going to leave me here!"

"Aye," he called back. "My services are complete, your grace." He tipped his cap, swinging his leg into the boat. Grabbing onto the oars, he began to row with a steady pace. "Besides, I figure you'll manage from here. 'Tis but a short walk up the bank there to the old Daily manor. With a quick stride, you'll be there in no time."

I turned around, spinning on the sand to locate nothing but a steep path that entwined through a tight section of sharp, pointy rocks, a challenging climb for any man, let alone gentleman. How I was to manage without someone to carry my bags was beyond me.

My sight quickly revisited the boatman, my eyes scouting the shoreline, beckoning him to return. But it was too late. The boat was no longer in sight. He was gone, and with him, the splashing of paddles faded.

Chapter 14

For a short time, the sound of the waves rushing against shingles and the scream of gulls was my only company. I stood there, my heart quickening, thudding in my chest. The realisation of being abandoned on this forsaken shore, with no one to assist, was a thought far from soothing. I inhaled a long, deep breath to calm my nerves and eagerly surveyed my surroundings for any sign of life. There was nothing. Of course there was nothing: no visible abodes protruding from the hillside, no sight of locals sauntering along the sandy shore, no voices of men toiling, women chattering about their affairs, or petulant children at play. Nothing. The world around me was a canvas of human silence. The only sound was the lonesome pulse of the waves embracing the shore.

With all my might, I heaved my bags, wedging them under my arms, and began my ascent, my feet slipping on the loose sand and concealed rocks underfoot. The bags grew heavier with each step. Regardless of my efforts, I struggled to maintain my balance as my shoulders collided with one perilous stone after the next.

By the time I found myself atop the hill, my knees had already begun to buckle. My strength was gone. I released my bags, allowing them to tumble to the ground. The feeling of blood flowing slowly back into my fingers was returning.

The fog was much finer up there, the air somewhat cleaner. As my eyes scanned the desolate terrain, a bleak and sombre sight greeted me. The fields were barren, with nothing but a sea of tough, unyielding grass stretching out as far as the eyes could see. The landscape was without any signs of life, a desolate and lifeless wasteland that seemed to mock the very notion of existence. The narrow and winding road sliced through the dense greenery like a knife, its serpentine path following the curves of the land with a cruel and twisted intent. *No doubt my best course*, I thought. And in good time, it should surely lead me to the house.

The Isle of Lismore was not a grand estate—far from it. It was a bleak and desolate place. Its hilly terrain, harsh and unforgiving, offered a scattered woodland that tangled and grew like a maze. The entire island was little more than a deserted rock, a place of despair. A forgotten place.

I had ventured much of it as a young boy with my grandfather, often with my sister dawdling along by my side. How exciting it all was back then. We would explore the land during the summer months, venturing through the lush green fields and cliffside paths that overlooked the calm blue ocean, marvelling at ships sailing by. On the clearest of days, one could even spot Duart Castle across the coast. Yes, I remembered the isle like the back of my hand back then—every hidden path, patch of woodland, and gleaming loch. Although, that was many years ago.

The memories I once held, along with my keen sense of direction, seemed to have dissolved over the years. Such a long period had passed since those summer days. And as I approached the winding road, battling my way through the tall grass, I couldn't help but feel somewhat disoriented. I recalled nothing of where I stood. Nothing. Everything seemed to have altered from what I remembered. None of it, I might add, for the better.

A bleak scene greeted me as I trudged down the dreary road. A small stone sign jutted out from the roadside, its surface slick with rainwater and obscured by a thick layer of green moss, leaving the words illegible and weathered. Despite that, I collected my bags and pressed on, my feet dragging over the sodden ground as I followed the road that seemed to stretch on forever, vanishing into the trees.

I THOUGHT THE PATH WOULD NEVER COME TO AN END. I proceeded, my weary limbs struggling to trudge forth. It felt as though I had been wandering for hours, with no rest in sight. I hoped to have stumbled upon the house by then, or even a marker that would stir memories of my youth. However, my mind remained a blank slate, absent of any recollection of the route I trod. Not a single glimpse of familiarity could be summoned. The road continued to meander along the contours of the hilly land, winding its way past one untamed forest after another. It was only after some time passed that a single stone cottage came into view, its grounds abandoned and reclaimed by the ruthless force of nature. I presumed it was one of the old worker's dwellings, left to ruin for quite some time, leaving only memories of what looked to be a dismal past.

Several yards ahead, another cottage emerged on the fringe of the woodland. Just as before, it bore a striking resemblance to the previous, its door decayed from the frame and the walls so askew that they threatened to crumble. The chimney, too, had long since collapsed to the ground, shattering into a myriad of stones.

It wasn't until I chanced upon several more ruins ahead that I began to ponder their sad state of abandonment. Afterall, since my arrival, I had not laid eyes upon a single soul, nor had I witnessed any signs of villagers. It was as though the working people of Lismore had suddenly failed to exist, that they had simply vanished from their place.

A sudden noise interrupted my concentration—the wild sound of a twig snapping, dissolving back into an eerie silence that shortly settled through the woodland. I turned quickly, bags in hand, darting my sight from tree to tree.

"Who's there?" I called out, focusing my sight through the brume. "Is there someone back there?"

The woodland off the road's edge remained still, quiet, the shade within its depths of hanging limbs and overgrowth dark yet soulless.

As I briefly gazed up to the cloudy sky that broke between the treetops, one couldn't help but notice the light was already fading.

Snap! Another twig, much closer that time. The sound shot into the air with a violent crack, causing me to spin awkwardly from one direction to another. I searched left and right, determined to find the culprit, before suddenly freezing where I stood. There, directly ahead, was movement beyond the branches.

My eyes widened, and my jaw hung agape with anticipation. Someone was watching me from the woods, their face obscured by the mist and hanging limbs.

"You there!" The words finally formed and jumped off my tongue with a stutter. "I-I see you!"

The figure said nothing.

"I say, could you guide me in the direction of the old Daily manor? I'm afraid I've found myself to be rather lost."

Still there was no response. The only movement was that of the swaying branches dancing lazily with the afternoon breeze.

I turned to look back at the path I travelled, then back to the way ahead. "This way, is it?" I asked hesitantly, gesturing with a nod.

The wind died in an instant, casting an unnerving quietness over the woodland.

"Shush," the faceless shadow whispered, as a single finger lifted from behind the undergrowth and slowly pressed upon its lips. "*Shush.*"

Mesmerised, my chest tightened and my breath became shallow as I edged away from the eerie presence that stood back amongst the tree line. I turned my back on the sight and promptly continued down the path, too afraid to look back.

The sound of snapping twigs grew louder with each passing moment, like the footsteps of some fiendish creature stalking me, inching closer and closer, biding its time to strike.

My legs quickened their pace, soon to break into a frenzied sprint. My feet pounded against the ground as I raced away from the sound drawing ever closer at my heels. My breathing grew louder as I fled, desperate to escape what lurked so closely in my wake.

It was as if the demon was gaining on me, its breath hot on my neck. I dared not slow down. I could not, for I knew that to do so could mean my certain fate. Instead, I pushed myself harder, faster, willing my legs to carry me farther than I ever thought possible.

As I burst out of the woodland and into the open air, my body collapsed with exhaustion, falling to the boggy earth with a hardened thump.

While gasping for breath, I listened intently. The sound from behind had ceased. The presence of my follower's footsteps no longer echoed in my ears. I scanned the area, hoping to see someone, anyone, perhaps some islander who would take charity and assist me in my time of need.

An outburst of gunfire rang in the air. The unsettling cry of birds dispersed from the nearby trees, saturating the overcast sky. Their dark outlines ominously floated overhead like a haunting masterpiece, casting a dreary, disheartening shadow over the ground below.

My head drooped back to the ground, noticing a trail of sombre smoke rising from the distance. *A house,* I thought as my hand reached out, stretching for help.

What happened next, I could not say. For a time, all I could sense was the impenetrable cloak of darkness—a darkness that wholly engulfed me.

Chapter 15

It was the scent of smouldering wood and the faint hint of peppermint that gently stirred me from my sleep.

"Peter?" The fairness of a woman's voice whispered my name. Her delicate tone was soft and pleasant, comforting, as I floated between the realms of dream and reality.

"Do fetch some water," the voice went on. "And please, do hurry! If I am not mistaken, I believe he is beginning to come to."

The sound of a door latch clicked from somewhere close by, as though it was ever so tenderly closed, followed by the resonance of footsteps on solid wood, gradually fading down a distant hall.

"Peter?" The gentle, soothing touch of elegant fingers lovingly caressed my hand. "Peter, do you hear me?"

The footsteps soon returned, growing clearer on approach. The latch again clicked. The door pushed closed with a stern and careless *thud.*

My eyelids slowly fluttered, revealing a hazy blurriness that, for a time, distinctly occupied my sight.

The room in which I lay was dimly lit. Flickering candles dripped soft pools of orange light that shimmered down the walls. And as my heavy eyes, weighed down with exhaustion, wandered drearily across the ceiling, tracing the intricate patterns of a dark oak bedpost and down to thick burgundy bed sheets and ruffled blankets that enveloped me beneath, the faintest squeeze was felt against my hand. It was a comforting sensation, like a butterfly landing to the skin. In a dazed state, I gazed downwards to the touch, tracing the arm that led up to the stranger perched at my side. As her face became clearer, the curve of her lips lifted. A kind smile beamed across her mouth as she casually leant forward to speak.

"Oh, my dear Peter. How long you have slept."

A bewildered expression masked my face, unsure if the figure standing before me was a figment of my own imagination, my own dreams, though I was certain it was not.

"Meredith?" I breathed out her name in a low, gravelly voice.

She inclined her head once with acknowledgement. With a gentle stroke, she withdrew her hand from mine, allowing her fingers to brush softly against the strands of hair that clung to my forehead with sweat.

"Is this …" I scanned the room in disbelief, my attention soon returning to my carer. The room around me seemed blurred and distorted, as if I were caught in a hazy limbo. It was a feeling I had experienced many times before in my dreams, but never to that degree of clarity. "Am I still dreaming?"

"I dare say you are not." She smiled, her eyes dark and thickly lashed.

"Then you are real?"

"Quite real." She laughed lightly.

I lay speechless, my sole attention resting upon a visage I had not beheld in many years.

Her countenance glowed with beauty, enhanced by the flickering flame of a candle that had seen half its life at my bedside. Her hair, a shade of strawberry blonde, more lustrous than any I had ever known, fell in elegant waves around her pale, freckled neck. Her small, perked nose wrinkled at either side as she smiled. Yet as I peered more closely, I couldn't help but discern the faintest lines etched beneath her eyes. A sudden flicker of affection sparkled within them. It was the most divine beauty I had ever known. I had almost forgotten it.

"My dear sister," I murmured, sitting upright and clasping both her hands in mine. "How long has it been since I last saw your face?"

"Too long," she replied, bowing her head and casting her face into the shadows.

I reached up and gently cupped her chin, directing her back into the light. "Forgive this old man?" I implored.

"Oh, Peter." She smirked dismissively. "There is nothing to forgive."

"My responsibility to you," I persisted.

"I am not yours to claim responsibility for, Peter," she chided gently.

"My neglect, then?" I pressed on.

"Hush now," she soothed, removing my hand from her face and guiding it back between the bed sheets. "You are comfortable?" She doted, rising from the seat in which she had spent many hours tending to my needs, only to adjust a pillow beneath me.

As I sank deeper into the softness of the bed, a comforting stillness settled over the room. For a time, my mind drifted, unable to escape the thoughts of how I had come to be lying there.

"Meredith?" I spoke up through the bleakness, my voice filled with excitement. "How did I come to be here, in this room?"

"Calm yourself," she insisted, raising her palm mid-sentence. She collected a large brown jug from the bedside table and poured its contents into a cup. "Here." She extended her hand. "Take a little water."

I received it graciously, my fingers trembling as I swallowed every last drop, allowing some to dribble down my chin.

"You appeared to have fainted," she continued, her voice never losing that soothing touch. "Nothing more, thankfully. Exhaustion, most likely. But not to worry. We shall have you feeling like your old self again in no time at all."

"Fainted?" I asked, still somewhat dazed.

"I'm afraid so. You were found just on the outskirts of the woodland." She pointed towards the blackened window. "A short stroll from the house, in fact. You were carried back, of course. At times, you could even be heard mumbling as you slept."

"What words?" I asked her.

"Oh, nothing of significance, I assure you. Utter ramblings, if that. I'm afraid I couldn't make head nor tail of it. Though, at the time, my only concern was to get you back to the house, and as soon as possible. It's still terribly cold on the island at this time of year. And in this fog, well, one can easily lose their bearings. Oh, look at you, my poor dear. You're shaking like a leaf. You have experienced quite the shock," Meredith exclaimed, her voice again laced with concern.

"Quite the fright, indeed, Sister," I added. "Quite the fright." I gulped back another measure of water, managing not to spill a single drop. "I saw something in those woods," I tried to explain, placing the cup clumsily on the nightstand. "Yes, something dark lurking at the borders of the house."

Meredith's face clouded with confusion, an expression one could only perceive as disbelief.

"What in the Devil's name are you talking about, Peter?" she interjected. "I dare say you must be mistaken. Things, they have quite changed since you last stepped foot on the island. No one inhabits the land these days, not really. Nothing except the odd wildlife here and there. There are, of course, a few villagers at Port Ramsey. However, they reside on the north side of the island. What need have they to loiter here?" She considered it for a second longer. "No, you have gone through quite an ordeal today. I suspect you must have fallen harder than I thought."

I lurched up in bed, the covers flying from my chest. "I am no child, Meredith! I know what I saw."

"I did not imply you to be as such. I simply—"

"Then do not speak to me as one. I am of sound mind, am I not?"

"Of course, but—"

"Then believe me when I say I know what I saw."

Meredith flinched with widened eyes as she bit the inner skin of her cheek. "And what is it, exactly, that you believe to have seen?"

"Evilness," I sneered gravely. "A foul creature spying on me through the dusk. At first, I thought it to be nothing more than a villager, one of the settlers you mentioned from Port Ramsey, perhaps. However, when I inquired about the direction to the house, the thing did not answer, not a word. It was as though the very creature had lost its tongue, severed from its mouth. It followed me, Meredith. Followed me through the woodland, perhaps even followed me here. In my state of panic, I must have wandered off the path. A rather poor decision, I know that now. Please, don't look at me that way. Spare me your judgement."

"And do you recall anything else?" she prompted calmly.

I fell back to the softness of my sheets, my eyes clenched shut in thought. "I … I recall falling to the ground. It was soft, wet. The sound of crying birds shrieked overhead, circling me like death itself."

My heart raced from the memory. It was as though I was experiencing the events all over again. The vision replayed in my head like a nightmare, forcing my nerves to heighten. Suddenly, my eyes sprang open with revelation. "Gunfire!" I recalled with a gasp. "There was gunfire coming from the woodland."

"Gunfire, you say," she replied sheepishly. "On the boundary of the house?"

"Indeed, gunfire," I answered, "its roar as loud as canons."

Meredith flattened her palm to the base of her neck, her breathing noticeably quickening as both shoulders jumped with tickled amusement. "That is no creature of which you speak." She laughed light-heartedly, which grew more infectious by the second. "Why, it is none other than Mr Gibbs."

"Who?"

"Why, Mr Gibbs, of course." She giggled uncontrollably. "The groundsman. I allow him to hunt the local game of the estate. An elderly man on many accounts, though I do believe his aim has only improved with the passing of each season. Regardless, it was the very man himself who found you lying in the muck. You gave him quite the scare, too, you know."

"I gave *him* a scare?"

"Indeed. When he called upon me in a flushed and panicked state, I insisted he carry you to the house immediately. I thought it to be some wandering peasant desperately in want of food. Heaven knows we've seen our fair share of them. Little did I expect it to be my own flesh and blood. I dare say, I, too, have suffered quite the shock tonight."

My eyes locked with hers.

"What?" she asked curiously. "Surely you didn't think that I, of all people, would have been able to carry you back here alone. My dear brother, these days I have barely the strength to putter about the grounds. No, if it weren't for Mr Gibbs, you may very well have still been lying out there. You should be thankful, Peter. It gets awfully bitter this time of year. It's the sea air, I think. Although I'd hate to consider what might have become of you should you not have been found out there, all alone in the dark. The very thought upsets me. No, it doesn't bear thinking about."

"But who is he?" I tapped bluntly to the lumpy bedsheets.

She stood up from her seat, patting down the creases of her dress. "He is of little importance," she plainly stated. "If you insist, we shall speak more of such things tomorrow. For now, I implore you to rest."

I grunted displeasingly at that, folding my arms like some stubborn child as I released a heavy sigh.

"Can I get you anything more before I retire? Something more to drink? A spot of food, perhaps?"

She made her way to the foot of the bed and leant over a small table laid with glistening silverware and a black iron pot. She lifted the lid, allowing steam to quickly escape from its prison.

"I saw to it that a serving of soup was prepared. You know, just in case. I suspected you'd be rather hungry after such a trying journey." She picked up a ladle, stirring it about the pot before scooping up its contents and allowing it to hover under her nose. She closed her eyes dreamily as she pleasurably took in the scent. "Ah, vegetable," she stated. "Might I tempt you?"

Again, another troubled sigh escaped me. "I have not the appetite for soup."

"Then please, allow me to prepare something that will satisfy you. Anything you want."

"I'm afraid I have not the appetite for anything."

She placed the lid back onto the pot, capturing the steam inside.

"Very well, then," she muttered, laying the spoon gently onto the table. "Then let us hope that your appetite returns as swiftly as your recovery."

"You speak as though I am a gravely ill man who lies upon his deathbed," I said.

"Gravely, no," she replied with a tone of seriousness. "However, there is something oddly different about you, Peter, something you may not wish to tell me, although I sense it all the same. It is as plain as the look on your face, the gleam of your eyes. You are not the man you once were, nor the man you believe yourself to be. I fear that something unpleasant may have befallen you, maybe even changed you. Tell me, when was the last time you ate?"

"What are you getting at?" I snapped impatiently.

"Why, nothing," she said. "Simply that you do not look well. You seem frightfully pale. Sickly, one might suggest—your eyes dull and your cheeks sunken. If I am not mistaken, it appears as though life itself is draining you." Her voice grew vulnerable as she spoke. "You would tell me if something troubles you?"

"My dear sister, I am fine," I replied with as blunt a tone as possible. And despite my attempts to convince Meredith, the look of uncertainty did not falter from her oh-so-caring expression. In truth, it had indeed been some time since I last gazed upon my own weary reflection. Days, in fact. But after such a long and trying journey, I was without a doubt to appear a little worse for wear than usual.

"Then I am glad to hear it," she replied lovingly as the warm glow of the fire softly caught her smile.

"Meredith, I—"

"The hour is late," she stated, and with a swish of her dress, she slowly turned to make her way towards the door. "Let us speak once you have gained your strength," she whispered calmly. "I do believe the rest will do you good. Should you need me," she insisted, "my quarters are but several rooms down the hall. You remember the one? The service bell still works, to the best of my knowledge. However, there will be no one to call upon you should you truly need it. I'm afraid the servants' quarters have been empty for some years now." With those words, she made her way towards the door.

For a moment, silence returned to the room. Meredith stepped into the hall, the floorboards creaking beneath her as the door was slowly pulled in her wake. She stopped hesitantly.

"It is awfully good to see you again, Peter," she spoke through the crack. "I must admit that there have been many months in this lonely old house where I thought you would never come back at all." She paused briefly; the strain of her breathing could still be heard from the far side of the room. "Peter?"

"Yes?" I mumbled drowsily, my eyes unwilling to stay open.

"I forgive you."

Chapter 16

On that fateful night, I was once again visited by a dream of my dear mother, beckoning me to follow her upon the fields. Though I knew full well what was to come, I could not resist the urge to heed her call. Without hesitation, I took her extended hand as she led me deep into the woods.

I jolted upright, a choked cry escaping my lips as a feeling of dread washed over me. The darkness engulfed me, with only a feeble trickle of silver moonlight offering little comfort. The ethereal howl of the wind outside seemed to slither through every nook and cranny of the house, each gust causing the very structure to groan and creak as if writhing in some endless torment.

Time soon passed, and with time, my nerves settled and my mind somehow lifted from the disquieting thoughts of unpleasant dreams.

Again, sleep was almost upon me, and as I listened to the world outside my window, one could not help but sense the eerie stillness of the night, a quietness that seemed to shiver. Yet just as I was about to succumb to slumber, the slightest sensation ever so gently roused me. What exactly, I still do not know. Nor do I wish to.

With heavy eyes, the room's objects blurred through the inky darkness, their fuzzy outlines slowly taking shape. My mind struggled to latch onto familiar comforts, but an unsettling weight pressed against my chest. The shadows seemed to stretch and twist, creeping closer as if drawn to me. A cold draft whispered through the room, sending shivers as sharp as splinters along my skin. It was then that I noticed the peculiar form at the foot of my bed, a shape that mingled with the dark—a woman sitting silently at my feet.

My heart froze solid, and my breath caught in my throat. I tried to speak, though no words would form no matter how I tried. As I continued to observe, thunderstruck by the very sight before me, the woman remained still in her place—rigid and unmoved, never once alarmed by my panic.

"I'm so cold," a voice whispered softly, her line of sight remaining fixed on an empty space ahead.

"Meredith?" I asked, feeling utmost relief surge through my body. Within an instant, I could breathe again. I could speak again. "What hour is this? Tell me, are you alright?" I strained my eyes as best I could, trying to discern her form.

She gave no reply, but instead slowly raised herself up from the bed. She stood unmoving for some time, gazing lifelessly beyond the darkness, not uttering a whisper or twitching a single muscle.

"Meredith? What is it?" I squinted hard, watching as her silhouette gradually moved, sulking over to the far side of the room where she stayed fixed in the corner.

I clambered up from where I lay, the sheets rustling with my movement.

I could do nothing but watch, mesmerised by my sister, who stood lurking in the shadows, her back still turned to me, her face pressed deeply into the gloom.

It took only a moment for me to snap from my daze as both hands frantically searched the bedside in a blind attempt to retrieve a candle, longing to strike a flame. In my clumsy haste, I knocked it to the ground, causing a rather loud commotion that clattered throughout the room as the candle rolled to a halt beneath the bed. My gaze shifted back to the corner, only to meet the widest pair of eyes gawking back at me.

"Meredith?" I swallowed hard. The dryness of my throat made it all the more impossible to speak.

One foot after the other, I swung my legs from the bed. I trod with caution, edging nearer, the floorboards bending beneath me. All the while, those blank, soulless eyes pierced out from the dark, watching me. As I found myself drawing closer, the strangest thing occurred; the resemblance of my sister seemed to slowly drift away.

I was almost upon her, little more than a few short steps, when a loud knock heavily struck the door, forcing me to jump from my skin. The handle moved, its rusty latch twisting. Before I could say more, the door creaked open, slowly revealing Meredith on the other side.

The glow of a candlestick seeped through the crack of the doorway, extended outwards by the daintiest hand. The faint sight of frilled cuffs and a white nightdress followed afterwards, soon to reveal the concerned expression of my sister's face, her features accentuated only by that single flame.

Hairs prickled along the nape of my neck.

"Is everything quite alright, Peter?" she asked. "I thought I heard you calling from down the hall." Meredith leant in closer. "You appear somewhat flushed."

"The door!" I stumbled backwards, my back colliding harshly with the corner of the bedpost.

"Door?" repeated Meredith. She directed the shimmer of light across the wooden panel, confusion all the while clouding her face. "I do not understand."

"Behind it!" I pointed sternly, my shaking finger lost instantly to the dark. "Someone stands there," I remarked with a cowardly tone. "They've been here all along, standing over me as I slept, watching me."

"Trespassers?" she whispered. "In the house?" Meredith stumbled. The light of the candle intermittently dimmed with the swiftness of her movement. She crept forward discreetly, wrapping her fingers around the panel with care, and snuck her head around the door.

"No, wait!" I yelled as her hand gripped firmly, swinging the door back into its frame. A loud slam followed, echoing its way like thunder throughout the house and forcing the walls to shudder.

Silence followed as she steadily raised the candle, studying the corner of the room. A tall coat rack stood in place. Hanging from it was a long black jacket—my jacket.

Meredith turned to question me, the most sceptical expression lighting only half her face. "It is but a jacket, Peter. Yours, if I'm not mistaken. It was awfully wet. I saw that it was hung to dry."

A sense of speechlessness overcame me. For a time, I could do little more than stare into the room's corner, waiting for what once stirred within the shadows. Waiting for the slightest glimpse of movement. Waiting for what should not be.

Meredith soon broke the awkwardness. "Is this some kind of trickery of yours?" she asked. "Similar to when we were children? If so, I must say I find it rather ill timed. I sleep rather little of late, disturbed by any strange noise that seems to occupy the house. I do not desire you to be unsettled further. We, after all, are no longer children, are we?"

"I speak of no trickery," I assured her. "None on my part, at least."

Meredith gazed and wandered back to the corner, her face again swallowed by the dark. "You are quite serious, then?"

I nodded, still trying to make sense of what I had seen.

"You saw someone?"

"I believe I did." With the aid of the bedpost, I lowered myself to the mattress. "As clear as I see you now."

"Believing you saw and knowing are, indeed, two very different things, Peter. You of all people should understand that." She walked to the bed, her feet concealed by the long flow of her draping nightgown. "Tell me, who do you believe to have seen?"

A large lump formed in my throat.

"It was a woman."

"A woman?" she repeated.

"Yes, sitting at the end of my bed. I must admit, at first I had mistaken her to be none other than yourself. I recalled you doing such things as a girl. There were many nights you would often sneak into my room. I would often find you come morning resting soundly beneath the sheets. You had this impenetrable fear of being alone."

"A fear I have learned well to overcome," she replied bluntly, lowering the candle as she spoke. "This woman, what did she look like?"

I thought hard, my stare tracing back into the same spot, as if the very figure would reappear. "I do not recall."

"Think, Peter," encouraged Meredith. "You remember her face?"

"I recall her voice."

"She spoke to you?"

"I believe she did. However, now I cannot begin to think of what words stirred me from my sleep, only the sound. Her whisper. It all felt so dreamlike, so otherworldly."

Meredith paused, clearing her throat as she considered what to say.

"Then perhaps, my dear brother, that is exactly what it was—simply a dream, nothing more. You are tired and unwell, exhausted, no doubt. And like me, you will soon come to terms that within these once familiar childhood rooms, shadows lurk in every corner. There is nothing to fear. The mind, at times, just sees what it wishes. Or what it does not."

"Perhaps," I mumbled as the touch of my sister's head came to rest on my shoulder. "We should at least check the house."

"The house?" She raised her head suspiciously. "Whatever for?"

"To simply ease the mind."

"Come now. If by chance you had seen someone, there was little time for escape. There is no trap door within this room, no secret passages nor hidden chambers. There is simply no place to hide. Besides, the house is secured tightly under lock and key. I make sure of it myself, every night, without fail. Though rest assured, no one travels this far south on the island. Not at the dead of night."

"You have no staff that reside within these walls?"

"Peter, I told you already." She exhaled loudly. "The servants' quarters, they have remained unused for years. There has been little in terms of staff since my coming to the island. During my time here, I had, in fact, only one servant, although I do not wish to think of her as such. We became rather good friends, you see. Since her departure, I suppose I have become content with my own company. That and the generous services of Mr Gibbs. However, he does not lodge within the house." She breathed in deeply, her mind tracing back to fond times of memories past. "Yes," she spoke distantly, "things will be quite different from what you remember. The house, I'm afraid, is but a shadow of its former standing. A capsule, as it were, of the years it stood its best."

A cold draft circled about the room, prompting my shoulders to spontaneously shudder and the flame of the candle to wave and softly crackle.

"It will not be long before dawn is upon us," continued Meredith, whilst shifting a glance to the window. "But a few short hours, I'm sure. Let us at least try and make the most of it. You will be alright, yes?"

I offered a nod.

"Then I shall see you at breakfast. For now, I insist you try to get some sleep. Tomorrow is a new day. We shall speak more then."

On that note, Meredith pushed herself up from the bed and, with the faintest glow to guide her, made her way back towards the hall. She spoke not a word as she left.

For the longest time, I could do nothing but lay awake in my bed, my mind still racing with paranoid thoughts and unsettled visions, my eyes fixed like glue to the farthest corner. Hours dragged by, and sleep never came. The sensation of fear never dimmed. All the while, I longed for the light of day to chase away the shadows.

Chapter 17

16TH March 1847

A sharp morning light spilled past the heavy curtains as I sluggishly rose from the bed. Gazing outside, a crisp morning frost covered the surrounding grounds. The nearest trees were barely visible, camouflaged by a thick layer of mist that seemed to swirl about them.

I dressed myself with due care, taking time to unpack the belongings that had been carried to my room the previous night. For the first time since I could remember, I viewed my reflection in the mirror. The mirror itself was a work of art, framed in ornate gold and elaborately decorated with the most intricate details. The reflection that stared back at me was a familiar one yet, in a surprising way, seemed somehow different. My features were softened by the bright glare of the morning light, draining away any tiredness I was sure would be evident. My hair, as thin as it was, appeared tidy and slick. The puffiness of my cheeks was filled with a healthy shade of rose red. And within my eyes was a glimmer of something else, but not exhaustion. No. A sense of boundless energy, perhaps. Needless to say, I had not looked that well in years. I appeared somewhat younger, fresher. And despite my ongoing fatigue, lack of appetite, and the numerous aches and pains that riddled my body, witnessing my reflection I couldn't help but somehow admire the face staring back at me. I smiled pleasingly, marvelling at myself like a young man drunk upon his own rugged handsomeness. One thing was undeniably certain. Returning to Lismore may have been exactly what I needed.

The faint aroma of freshly brewed coffee wafted through the air as I found myself wandering down the hall.

On the staircase, a vast collection of large family portraits hung in the most obscurely slanted fashion. Each bronze frame was more striking than the last and coated by decades of dust that settled upon each surface like a sheet of timeless frost.

A resemblance of my grandfather hung pride of place at the centre of the staircase. He was a rather disgruntled looking figure, dressed to impress (as always), a cane held tightly within his bent and crooked fingers. By his side, a portrait of my father hung, an impression of him from his younger days, perhaps a man in his early twenties. Below his was my aunt Bethany, a round and rather grotesque woman who found more love in the pleasures of her appetite than in any man she ever deemed fortunate to meet. Her life was a short one, collapsing over a bowl of steaming soup in the spring of 1798, her sixth serving if I correctly recollect. It took ten men to remove her from the table.

One after the next I observed the paintings with the keenest eye, each visible brushstroke reviving a face I had long since forgotten. As I descended, the figures of my family's past watched suspiciously from above. The emptiness in their eyes and their blank, sombre expressions followed me until I reached my final step.

The main hall, which once stood bright and welcoming, displayed a dull and somewhat saddened look. The white floor tiles that had complimented the fresh morning light lay worn and cracked, matching the omnibus of the room. The once charming paper that patterned the entrance clung desperately to the walls, its colour all but faded from existence as though time itself was feeding on the house. In the corner, a large wooden clock stood tall and forgotten. Its tired old cogs were absent a tick, the hands forever at rest, marking the time of ten o'clock.

The briskness of my footsteps echoed throughout the lower floor of the house. Each step bounced off the walls of empty rooms and echoed through the house.

The dining room door stood ajar upon my arrival. The sound of soft humming, too, became clearer on approach as I knocked to announce my presence.

"Ah, Peter," greeted Meredith, her song brought directly to a halt. "Good morning."

She sat at the far end of the room, perched at the corner of the dark wooden table which boasted eight neatly tucked chairs at either side.

"Please, do come in. Sit," she insisted with the fairest wave of her hand. "I would ask if you managed to get at least some sleep after my leaving you last night." She paused, briefly studying me up and down. "However, by the look of you, I trust you did not."

I gave no reply. Instead, I pulled out a chair from the table. The weight of its legs grinded and screeched across the floors.

"You look tired, Peter," she quietly remarked, perhaps to counter my feelings. "Utterly dreadful!"

"How very pleasant of you," I grunted while slumping back to the chair. "Come now, I do not appear all that bad. In fact, I believe I feel a little better."

"You have certainly looked better," she mumbled, casually returning her attention back to the morsel of food on her plate. She continued to eat with elegance, pausing only briefly as a napkin was gracefully dabbed to her lips.

"Breakfast?" she enquired, dropping her fork to the table. "I no longer have the staff to serve you, but what I lack in service I make up for in supplies. Do help yourself. Try to eat something. If you do not, I fear the wind might blow you flat."

On the table lay a selection of silver plates topped with various dishes, each offering presented in the most refined display. There were beef marrow fritters, eels in a thick, colourful puree, hare patties, fresh fish, and an offering of miniature pastries stuffed generously with a helping of meat. Steam rose from the table like a cloud of smoke, carrying with it the mouthwatering fragrance of the feast.

"I was not quite sure what you preferred," said Meredith, gesturing her hand to the table. "So I saw to it that a selection was prepared."

"You did all this?" I asked, overwhelmed by the vast amount of food sitting in front of me.

"That I did," she confirmed. "Let it not go to waste."

I scouted the table for a moment longer, coming to rest at a large bowl of fruit that was mounded high from the centre. I leant forward, picked up an apple, and sank my teeth through its skin.

"Tell me." She cleared her throat, watching as I ate. "Was the room to your liking?"

"Satisfactory." I swallowed before continuing. "Our grandfather's quarters, was it not?"

"Why, I am surprised you remember. It was, yes," she agreed. "However, as time passed, I found it all the more suitable for Jacob to claim its space. That said, you'll find it exactly how grandfather left it, with not so much as a book out of place. I often recall him sitting in his chair by the fire, you know? Accompanied by nothing more than his simple fondness of reading. Do you remember? I suppose you do. You were much older than I back then."

"I do," I replied, taking another bite from my apple. "I also recall the old goat's temper. That and the three lashings I received for misplacing one of his favourite books. I forget the title. Celestina, I think. A dreadful book. The old man didn't even like it, you know? He made a point of telling me so. He said it lacked its own identity, whatever the devil that means." I tossed the apple core to the table. "Still, for a man who held the finest taste in literature, he was surprisingly strict when he chose to be." My eyes gazed into Meredith's. "I don't suppose he ever …"

"Me? No." She acted somewhat shocked. "Not once. Not ever. I remember only his kindness, the times I sat upon his lap as he read stories aloud for my pleasure. Many times, we would read long into the night. He was forever indulged while reading, searching the far off reaches of his imagination. You could see it in his eyes. It was all rather charming."

"Charming, indeed." I huffed at the notion.

"He never read to you?"

"He did." The memory faintly returned to me. "Once or twice. Although I never really cared for it."

"Oh," she countered, "and why is that? I loved his stories."

"Let us just say one finds it awfully unpleasant to sit while the sting of a cane is still fresh, let alone being in the same company of the very person who inflicted it."

Meredith's eyes rolled full circle. "Oh, you exaggerate, Peter!" She stood up and walked to the window, observing the nearby grounds as a layer of cold seeped in from the frame. "He was a good man, really. Kind and generous."

"Kind and generous!" I mocked loudly at her expense. "Come now, nobody expects you to say such things. You have the house now, after all."

Her brow furrowed. "Inherited from our father, need I remind you," she sternly corrected.

"Yes, yes, not to mention the collection of unsightly portraits that still hang proudly on the staircase. A fine inheritance for Jacob, I'm sure!"

"I suppose so." She sighed, disinterested, slightly preoccupied by the dismal view past the dining room window. "Honestly, I was never very fond of them. Ghastly things. There is something about past loved ones still being able to watch you that I find quite unsettling, even if it is through the eyes of an innocent brushstroke. I care little for them, as you probably have noticed."

"Their poor condition had caught my eye, yes," I admitted. "It shall not be long before their features begin to wither."

"As will the rest of the house," she bluntly remarked, finally turning her attention from the window and back towards her guest. "The house has seen little in terms of maintenance these past few years. It requires it, though I have not the fortune to restore it to its former days. Nor would I wish to if I had. For me, it is just a house, a place for one to lay their head or shelter from the weather. It is not the home where we grew up, nor will it ever be so. And Jacob …" She sighed troublesomely, as though a great weight draped from her shoulders. "He has neither the interest nor desire to call Lismore his own. For a time, I believed he saw the island as his own personal prison. I must admit, at times it can feel just that. However, once the shackles of his father were removed, Jacob couldn't depart my company quick enough. He still visits from time to time, summer months mostly. Oh, how I look forward to his company. You mentioned you saw him, did you not? Inverness, was it? Tell me, how is he? I hear he is doing rather well."

"That he is," I replied. As Meridith returned to her seat, eager to hear of her only son's ventures, I could not help but tell her more. I talked of our chance meeting, our conversation and drinks at The Castle Tavern, and the whole affair that would find her son stuck amongst the squalor of the Irish.

Meredith seemed drawn back by the thought, though quickly dismissed whatever concern she harboured as she poured herself another steaming cup of tea.

"Ireland." She briefly chuckled to herself. "Wherever next."

She placed the spoon into the cup, allowing the steel to chime against the cup as she stirred. "I hear there have been great troubles across the coast. In fact, I hear many of the Irish have vacated their homeland, travelling here, all in search of food."

A sudden sensation constricted my throat as I recalled the heaving riots of the city: the struggle, the screaming.

"They have travelled to Lismore, then?"

"Some," she replied without showing a hint of concern. "Although, I do believe the high cliffs deterred many who wished to try. For those who had managed to find themselves on the island, I'm afraid their joy would have been rather short lived. There is little here in means of food. And with many of Lismore's farming community now gone, the

Irish would've had little choice but to seek their needs elsewhere. That said, you still find one or two wandering about the island from time to time. We aid them in whatever way we can."

"You have helped them?"

"My dear Peter, what decent person would not?" she questioned before continuing. "What we offer is merely nothing. Some basic needs if that. A bowl of something hot and clothing to see them from the cold. Once they have regained some strength, Mr Gibbs sees to it that they are escorted from the island."

"Oh, where?"

"That I do not know," remarked Meredith. "Regardless, you have nothing to fear from them. They want only what you or I take for granted. What is a little food from my table if it can help another. A small price to pay, wouldn't you agree?"

My brow deepened at the thought, and when I looked into her eyes, I found myself frowning all the more.

"A price, my dear, that would soon see you to ruin, nonetheless."

"Oh, fiddlesticks, Peter!"

"Mark my words. You do not know the poor as I have known them. Once you take pity and show them good nature, their only ambition is to take, take, take!" I spat, my fist striking hard upon the table with a mighty thud, forcing the plates to quake. "They are like vultures, Meredith, pests, swarming the streets like rats. A nuisance. I have seen it myself, experienced it myself. Provided them my hand in trust, only to have it bitten in return, a consequence of my generosity." I paused, watching as she clung to my every word. "It will do you no good to comfort them."

It took a second or two for my sister to gather her response—a response most fitting to her nature. "Perhaps, though it shall do my soul the greatest good," she responded. The words proudly rolled off her tongue as she lifted her cup, sipping what remained of her tea.

On that note, my fist unclenched. My feelings of frustration towards her mellowed within the blink of an eye.

"You really are far too kind for your own good."

"I know." She smiled in jest, combing back a strand of hair that fell loose against her neck and tucking it neatly behind her ear. "Now, let us speak no more of such subjects. There are, after all, plenty of things to talk about, are there not?" She shuffled around on a closer seat to face me with an expression that could melt butter. "Tell me, what plans do you have for today?"

"I have not considered it," I answered tiredly, leaning back on my seat with a weary yawn. "A breath of fresh air. A short walk, perhaps. And if the mood strikes me, I may even put ink to paper."

"You are writing again, then?" she asked, knowing all too well of my answer. "How wonderful," she voiced with excitement as a beaming smile stretched the length of her face. "You shall read me something. After dinner?"

"Perhaps," I reluctantly agreed.

"Splendid," she repeated. "It shall be wonderful to hear poetry within these walls again. I may even play something for you on the piano."

My face turned sour.

"I have been practicing." She leant in closer with excitement in her eyes. "When time allows it, of course. What is your favourite piece? I would very much like to know. Perhaps I should walk with you? We can discuss our love of music on the way."

I stood up promptly, the chair jerking back from behind my knees. I studied her cautiously, choosing carefully what to say.

"If it is quite alright, I would rather stroll alone. It has been some time since I have written anything of worth. I feel the topic of music would only distract me."

"Oh, oh I see," she mumbled disappointingly. "Oh, yes, of course." Her line of sight panned to the floor.

"You do not mind?" I asked.

"No. No, of course not." She fluttered her eyes, purposely avoiding my own.

"I have offended you?"

"Nonsense," Meredith remarked as she elegantly stood, her tone again lifted. "A poet's mind requires peace and quiet. I understand that. They must become free of mind, embrace their surroundings, and not have little sisters drabbling in their ear."

I smiled at her in return, placing both arms on her shoulders. I stooped down and planted a kiss on her cheek. When she looked up at me, there was no doubt that her face once again seemed to fill with fondness.

"What was that for?" she asked, rather embarrassed. Or was it gratitude in her hazel eyes? I really wasn't sure.

"That," I cleared my throat, "is simply me showing my appreciation for you."

"Oh." She looked surprised as she glanced up. "Then I shall not expect it again anytime soon," she muttered, trying her best to conceal a smirk.

"Ah, most generous, and a joker. I am blessed to have such a sibling."

We chuckled heartily at that, an infectious laugh that seemed to control us both. For the first time, it felt as though we were children again, two small youngsters with not so much as a care to be had in the world.

"It looks rather clear out," she said, her interest reverting back towards the grime that smeared the windows. Her laughter ceased. "Are you sure you won't have anything more to eat before you go?"

I declined the offer with the raise of my hand, convincing her my appetite would easily keep until dinner. Nonetheless, she insisted I pack something light for my walk—a few apples, a slice of bread and butter. I took them without quarrelling. It was much easier that way.

"I will see you at dinner, then." She delighted in reminding me. "I dine at six, not a moment later. Do try not to get lost again. Might I suggest the willow path?"

"What path?" I echoed her, watching as she prepared the food before me.

"The willow path. You used to love the trail as a boy. You would often walk it."

My mind turned blank. "Well, that was a very long time ago."

"Dear Peter, one thing you must understand about this island is nothing ever changes. Nothing. Not ever," she said, handing me a small bag which contained the food she packed. "Now, take the path on the right, next to the gate. You know, the one beside the dead oak tree. Follow the mound up to the top of the hillcrest. There it will lead you to the cliffs. Keep to the trail as best you can, and you will find yourself full circle and back at the house within but a few short hours. I'm sure the rest will come to you on the way."

Without further thought, I gave my thanks and left Meredith standing at the windowsill, shutting the door behind me as I made my way back towards the hall. The heavy front door protested with a weary groan once opened, assisted by the morning breeze. I stepped through the threshold. The bright morning light pierced through the brume, making it all the more troublesome to see. Before leaving, I turned to look back on myself, my hand still resting firmly on the large brass doorknob.

From up high, a pair of eyes stared down at me, their stare hard and bitter. For only a second did I study their gaze, as the door slammed shut behind me, leaving the watchful face of my grandfather alone in the shadows of his former palace.

Chapter 18

After only a short stroll, a piercing pant caught my breath as I stood atop the hill. Looking back at the house, it appeared so small from afar, like a patchwork of memories nestled amongst the fields. Ahead of me, a narrow dirt trail wove its way through the nearby willow trees, obscured by overgrowth that seemed to relish in its duty of keeping the route a secret.

The willow path, I assumed.

I pressed onwards with little concern of the way, reserving my pace, never straying from the path that cut through the wilds. Overhanging branches choked out any glimmers of sunlight that dared to breach the trail below. The air was thick with the scent of moisture, while overhead, the songs of unseen birds echoed from their hidden homes.

As I delved deeper into the woods, the path began to narrow and dip and the trees closed in around me, their branches reaching out like bony fingers of the forsaken. The forest floor was a tangle of roots and mushy fallen leaves, and I stepped carefully to avoid any sudden stumbles. From somewhere on the ground, the rustling of small animals scurried away from my footsteps, driving farther into the thicket and out of harm's way.

As I walked deeper, I realised the mellow calls of birds had faded behind me. Only my heavy breaths filled the air, accompanied by the rustling leaves that whispered softly around me.

Although I had apparently walked this path countless times as a child, I struggled to recall it. It felt dark and dismal, a lifeless stretch of jungle that held no warmth for me. It was not the island I remembered.

My cherished memories were bright and joyful with vibrant pathways and hidden trails brimming with secrets. Wildflowers painted the landscape in a riot of colours—bog myrtle, bluebells, bell heather, and mountain avens—all thriving under the open sky.

What remained? Only dense thickets, stubborn thistles, and patches of nettles sprawling across the path. Like the old house, the island had begun to decay, losing its charm with each passing year. The colours drained from whatever life remained. I could sense the loss, reflecting on what once was and the undeniable truth of what could never be again.

I sighed with relief when the trail began to lose its treacherous twists. The maze of roots that once reached out from the ground had sunk back into their hiding places, and the squelching patches of mud and leaves were gradually beginning to wane. Sunlight streamed through the overgrowth like a lantern lighting my path.

Soon a break in the trees revealed itself, leading me out of the woodland and filling my senses with the cool island breeze. Sweat trickled down my forehead, and my shirt, drenched with perspiration, clung to my back like a second skin.

Ahead lay a large open field, its condition marred and empty. The ground split into two sections, divided by a long stone wall that had seen better days. Its stones, once a proud boundary, lay scattered on the ground.

The unmistakable sound of the ocean drew my attention from afar; the familiar call of waves crashing against the cliffs urged me to move with haste. As I crossed the field, the sound grew louder and more distinct, and the ground beneath my feet transformed into hard, rocky terrain as I approached the island's edge. For a moment, I stood still, my eyes fixed on the ocean below, a gasp escaping my lips.

As the waves crashed against the rocks with tremendous force, salty mist shot high into the air like a plume of smoke. I was reminded of the familiar sense of freedom and adventure I had felt as a boy, gazing out at the vast expanse of open water, curious about the countless stories it held. Oh, how I once longed to be a part of it all.

At that moment, standing with the tips of my shoes at the island's edge and the sea breeze ruffling my hair, I couldn't shake the feeling that a certain bleakness had settled over those once captivating waters. A sense of helplessness and despair washed over me as the treacherous waves vanished into the rolling fog, obscuring the distant land from which I had come. One thing was undeniably clear to me: even the waters that surrounded the island had changed.

I stayed for only a short while, and instead of dwelling on my boyhood memories, I decided to continue my journey. I stuck to the trail; the thought of getting lost again felt hardly worth the risk, not to mention the embarrassment it would cause. Before long, I found myself carefully navigating a steep, slippery slope. There were moments I nearly lost my footing, but when I finally reached the flat, marshy ground, I was greeted by a small stream trickling down the hillside, flowing alongside the path.

Without a second thought, I followed its current, admiring the brisk water as it wiggled around rocks and pebbles. Just when I began to despair that no beauty remained on the forsaken isle, the brook surged in pace, tossing and churning before merging with a small, secluded loch—a place I was certain I had never visited before.

I settled onto a large, smooth stone by the water's edge, allowing time to drift by and my fatigue to fade away. As the morning progressed, the sun broke free from the canopy of clouds above, shining down on the loch and making it glisten like diamonds. In an instant, the place where I rested seemed to breathe new life. Fish sprang from the depths, their golden-brown scales shimmering in the sunlight. Insects darted across the surface of the loch in a frenzy, creating a melodic hum that filled the air with a humming harmony.

As the warmth of the sun gently caressed my face and the wonders of life danced around me, I felt compelled to reach for my bag. Retrieving my quill and ink, I was drawn to the scene before me. Without hesitation, I began to write, letting the inspiration flow freely onto the page.

IT WAS SWIFTLY APPROACHING LATE AFTERNOON BY THE TIME I reached the gates of the house. The sun had long surrendered its brilliance to the encroaching darkness. The sky had transformed into a dull canvas, painted in shades of charcoal and dusky greys.

As I quickened my pace along the path, a gentle rain began to fall, drizzling upon the land as if the heavens were shedding tears. The air grew cool and damp, and the droplets fell to my skin, mirroring the unease settling in my heart as I glanced towards the house. It loomed before me, its presence as unsightly as ever, nestled in the shadows of the hillside.

Darkness clung to the building like a shroud, its silhouette a stark contrast against the already fading light. Smoke billowed from the tallest chimney. The windows, resembling hollow eyes, stared out along the path with a strange aura of sadness, their panes tinted in muted shades. The large front door, once a portal of welcome, stood ajar, its rotting frame proof to the abandonment of this once remarkable place.

As I stepped inside, quickly removing my coat, the smell of meat drifted in the passageway. With little to occupy my time, I wandered aimlessly about the house. I settled into the comforts of my grandfather's reading room. Dusty old bookcases lined each wall, their shelves filled with the old man's pride and joy, as if he was still alive.

Books of all kinds stood proudly in their places, organised alphabetically, with not a gap to spare. A lifetime of knowledge was compacted within a single space.

Not in the mood to read, I simply bided my time, content in the old man's chair. Outside, the blustery weather filled the silence as the heavy rain pattered against the windows, the very sound like restless fingers tapping upon the glass.

Chapter 19

The dining room was lit by a soft orange glow, casting dancing shadows across the wallpaper and adding an air of cosiness. At the room's centre, a long mahogany table stood pride and place, decorated with a delicate lace tablecloth and an array of the family's finest china. Glistening silverware and crystal glasses sparkled under the gentle light, as if they were patiently waiting for the feast that was yet to come.

Outside, beyond the tall windows draped in heavy velvet curtains, the world embraced the darkness of the night. The soft pitter-patter of raindrops that drummed against the glass earlier that evening quickly began to brew, transforming the once harmless rain into an unwelcome storm that swept miserably across the land.

"Peter!" Meredith's voice found me. She loomed by my side, two large dishes held in either hand. "Do you even hear me?" She rolled her eyes and set down the steaming plates, only to repeat the question. "I said …" She spoke with an air of impatience. "I suppose you tire of all this gloominess. It can be quite trying here at times. Although, I do hear the weather can be just as unpredictable higher north. Constantly rains, does it not?"

"It can be rather dull at times, yes."

"Dull, indeed," she remarked, picking out the chair closest to me. She reached out for her napkin, folding it out on her lap. "When the rain begins here, I fear it will never stop. Afterall, what is one to do with oneself? How does one pass the time? There are plenty of books here, it is true. Although I must admit, I do tire of their pages. There is, of course, my music; however, even the most masterful pieces of our years cannot compensate for the divine pleasures of conversation. There comes a point when one yearns for it—good, meaningful conversation. Don't you agree?"

"Quite," I grunted with knife in hand, poking about the dish in front of me.

The wind howled and whipped against the windowpanes, rattling them as if begging for entry. The velvet curtains, too, ever so slightly swayed in response.

"I can assure you, the mutton is quite delightful," she encouraged whilst watching me toy with my plate. "As a matter of a fact, Mr Gibbs informs me it is the best Oban has to offer."

There was that name again, Gibbs.

"Does he, now?" I replied, my words directed to the portion of thinly sliced meat in front of me. I twiddled with my fork before bringing it to my lips. Under watchful eyes, I took a bite and forced myself to chew. The familiar juices savoured on my tongue, and the taste of chalky gravy slid down my throat, promoting the unexpected urge to gag.

A hot sweat came over me.

"Perhaps mutton was not the best idea," said Meredith, slightly taken aback by my appearance. She placed her fork down and stood, attempting to remove the meal from beneath my nose. "I have overfaced you," she confessed. "Perhaps soup will be more appropriate?"

"No." I groaned, blocking her from the plate.

"It is of no inconvenience, really. Allow me—"

"I am fine, Meredith!" I scowled at her.

Shocked by my outburst, she dropped heavily to her seat with a sudden slump. "Well," she replied, reverting to her meal as she spoke. "I see you are going to be full of words this evening."

She reached for a bottle at the centre of the table and poured herself a rather generous serving of port, the fruity scent wafting from the bottle as she turned to offer with a single stare.

I nodded in return.

"Let us change the subject to something else, then," she insisted as the port flowed freely into my glass. "Tell me, how did you find your walk around the island?"

"It was," I threw back a swig from my glass, "uneventful."

"I see," she responded, somehow disappointed. "Well, I am pleased to hear that you at least managed to see some of the island again, even if it was unsatisfactory to your liking. Did it prompt any joyous occasions at all? Any memories?"

"No."

"None whatsoever?" she said with disbelief.

"Should it have?" I asked, reaching once more for the bottle.

"No," she mumbled. "No, I suppose not. A silly question, really. Forgive my asking."

"There is nothing to forgive," I grunted, taking hold of the bottle and filling my glass to the brim. "Besides, you are quite right. I thought I was sure to remember something of the land, some lost memory, perhaps. However, the land is not as I once recall it. It feels a darker place, somehow. Dare I say it, grimmer."

Again, I downed the contents of the glass with one fell gulp, wafting my finger midair.

"There was, however, one place which sparked my attention, a breathtaking place, most likely the last of its kind. Lismore's well-kept secret."

"Oh," paused Meredith, assuring to swallow her food before speaking. "And where is this secret you speak of?"

I leant slanted in my chair. "One could not possibly say, exactly. A small loch, little more than an hour's walk from the house."

"A loch?" She pondered. "Ah, you speak of Kilchernan," she replied. "Dreadful name, I know. There is something unusual about the Scottish tongue that I will never understand. Why they insist on such obscure names is utterly beyond me, especially for a place of beauty. That said, they have always seemed to lack the civilised tongue. No less, I, too, have found myself at the water's edge often enough: reading, painting, sometimes just to be alone with my thoughts. However, as you can imagine, loneliness is not difficult to come by, not here."

"No," I agreed. "I suppose it is not."

As the wind intensified, its gusts grew stronger, unleashing its force on the house. With each powerful blow, the structure seemed to tremble, causing the house to creak and moan in the most unsettling manner as the flickering candle flames swayed upon their wicks. In an instant flash, light torched the sky, sweeping through the crack of the curtains.

"It has turned rather foul out," I remarked, growing ever conscious of the storm beyond the walls.

"Nothing to be concerned of, I'm sure," replied Meredith. Her tone remained calm and collected. "I find it best not to think about it. Consider it as nothing more than nature's play, a dramatic scene, a reflection of poetry in motion. Which reminds me." She, too, leant forward on her seat. "Did you manage to write anything during your walk today? Something wonderful, no doubt. You always did have a way with words. Might I see?"

Without a moment's thought, my hand slipped into the inner sleeve of my jacket pocket, retrieving a folded piece of paper that, at first glance, appeared torn and wrinkled. I dropped it onto the table and, with two fingers, slid it across the old wooden surface.

"May I?" expressed Meredith, unable to disguise the hint of eagerness in her voice.

I briefly smiled at that. "A work in progress," I explained. "I'm afraid I am a little out of practice."

"And I'm afraid that you have always been too modest, Peter."

She unfolded the single sheet of paper and guided it under the glow of the nearest flame. With the strain of her face, her eyes weaved between the lines, squinting through the bleakness, studying the words in silence.

MEREDITH LOWERED THE PAPER FROM HER SIGHT. HER FACE, blank, was cast in shadow, her widened eyes distant as though she was in the deepest of thoughts.

"I did mention it was a work in progress, did I not?" I said with an open palm, gesturing for the paper to be returned.

Rather than hand it back, Meredith continued to clutch it tightly. Before answering, she found herself drifting to the ink once more.

"It is …" She stopped dead, leaving her word to hang.

"It is poor?" I asked.

"Wonderful," she whispered, her bulging eyes at last drifting up from the letters she held.

"You humour me, Meredith," I said, studying her.

"I assure you I do nothing of the sort!" she stated without a spec of amusement. "It is without a shadow's doubt the best thing you have written. The best thing anyone has ever written, or I have ever read, for that matter."

"Come now," I insisted, placing the poem back within the comforts of my pocket. "They are merely notes. Scribbles, really. And like all works of poetry, it shall take time and patience to perfect them."

"But there is nothing to perfect!" replied Meredith, her voice growing louder by the second, her face scrunched to a scowl. "Within little time at all, you have managed to create something so charming that I myself am utterly lost for words."

"You don't sound lost for words."

"Oh, Peter!" she barked. "You cannot alter this. You mustn't. Promise me that you will do no such thing. Why, if you did, I don't believe I would ever forgive you for it."

There was little sense in pursuing an argument, for I knew it would lead to nothing but frustration. Even from a young age, Meredith had a remarkable tendency to be opinionated, holding fiercely to her beliefs. She would engage in debates that seemed to stretch on endlessly, her face turning a notable shade of blue in her determination to have the last word.

"Very well, then," I spoke softly to her. "If it means that much to you, I won't. Not a word." I chuckled slightly. "How emotional you are this evening. Just like when you were young."

"I am not emotional, Peter," she declared bluntly. "I just know good art when I read it, and what I have read is purely that." She removed the napkin from her lap and tossed it outright onto the table. "Now, if you are quite finished, I wonder if you would join me in the music room. I would very much like to play for you," she added, already making her way to the door.

"Must you?" My heart sank.

"Yes," she answered proudly. "That is, if you do not oppose?"

Twiddling my thumbs, I could not help but ask. "Will there be something more to drink?"

"Drink?" She turned, unable to hide the confusion smeared across her face. "Why, yes, of course."

"Then please, do lead on."

I rose from my chair, and with measured steps, I closely trailed behind her, leaving in my wake only the stillness of an empty room, an icy breeze that whispered through the space, and the flicker of dying candles as they twirled their final waltz.

Chapter 20

A grand piano, its polished surface gleaming under the bleak light, took centre stage. A tall silver candelabra stood on its top, its freshly struck flames casting fine shades upon the instrument's keys, which were patiently waiting to be touched.

The dim room was decorated with old family tapestries depicting pastoral scenes of tales forgotten, their rich colours muted in the amber light as though the very substance of the night had been woven deeply into the fabric of the room.

As I settled myself upon the comforts of an armchair, I reached for a glass and indulged myself in a further helping of port.

With music sheets in hand, Meredith gracefully settled onto the piano bench, her posture aligned with perfect poise. Her hands, as if guided by an invisible force, tenderly caressed the keys, each touch a gentle expression of her deep connection with the instrument.

"Are you sure you do not mind my playing for you?" Her gaze shifted. She instantly recoiled her hands and cupped them nervously to her knees, as if the keys themselves were scalding hot.

It was a typical reaction of hers, one I had grown used to. It was so typical, in fact, I should have seen it coming. It came as little surprise that Meredith lacked a certain level of confidence as she matured into womanhood. Raised by a somewhat absent father and motherless from a young age, she had little choice but to navigate the complexities of life on her own. The void left by our parents lingered like a dark shadow, shaping her insecurities and influencing her reactions.

Meredith possessed an undeniable charm, yet she often doubted herself for it. Her self-esteem had been shaken like a fragile flame in the wind, susceptible to the slightest hint of criticism. She sought praise from those closest to her, yearning for their recognition, yet somehow managed to sabotage her own progress as if subconsciously believing she didn't deserve even one true chance at happiness.

Nevertheless, as I gazed across the room, I couldn't help but picture the small, vulnerable girl she once was, sitting at the piano, her feet swinging from the stool.

In my heart, I had always held a firm belief in my sister's potential. I saw glimpses of her true strength and resilience behind closed doors that no one else ever did. She had the strength to rise above her doubts and blossom into the confident woman she aspired to be. All she ever lacked was the courage; she just needed a gentle nudge in the right direction.

"Of course not," I reassured her. "Furthermore, Jacob informs me your playing has drastically improved of late. Quite the pianist, so I recall him saying."

I could see a trace of surprise and hope in her eyes, as if my words had touched a dormant ember within her. "Oh, I'm not so certain about that, Peter."

"Then play for me and we shall see," I insisted, drinking back the glass's fragrance, which wafted below my nose. "Play for me, and may each note reach the heavens."

In due course, she nodded, gracefully readjusting herself on the bench. Her fingers, trembling, swiftly rediscovered the keys. A heavy exhale escaped her nose, a demonstration to her focus. Without any need for additional encouragement, she seamlessly transitioned into playing, immersing herself in the music that flowed from her fingertips.

Her body swayed subtly to the rhythm. Her eyes closed. The room around her faded into the background as she entered a place of pure expression. With each delicate touch and fluent stroke, she poured her soul into the performance, allowing the music to speak for her in ways words never could. Despite all that, there was merely one problem. She wasn't very good.

She was bloody awful.

Her fingers, once shaking, revealed their limitations as they struggled to execute one intricate passage to the next. The melodies, though filled with much emotion, lacked the polished touch that distinguished any kind of masterful talent. As much as it pained me to listen, to stop myself from drowning out her music, I found myself with little choice but to sit and endure it, to accept it for what it truly was—nothing short of bad art.

The room eventually returned to its quiet and natural state. Meredith, as to be expected, turned to face me, watching me as the strings rang out their final notes.

She withdrew her hands.

"Well," she uttered softly as the blood returned to her fingers. "What did you think?"

Dreadful.

"It was delightful," I replied, trying my best to hide my dishonesty. "A true reflection of many hours dedicated to practice. I congratulate you for it."

The slightest smile touched her lips—a smile so well hidden that it lingered behind her stern expression, as if she was trying to conceal a private joy known only to her.

"Oh, Peter, that is awfully kind of you." She blushed. "Do you really think so?"

She removed herself from the perch, closing the piano's lid upon standing, and found herself across from me on a floral-patterned chair, directly opposite a cold, flameless hearth.

"I …" She bit her lip as I witnessed a single tear roll down the flushness of her cheek. "I'm sorry," she sniffled. "What must you think of me."

"It is quite natural for a musician to get strangely attached to their passion. I myself through the years have—"

"No," she interrupted, her glassy eyes unmoved from the room's corner. "I'm afraid you do not understand, Peter. Not this."

"Then you must tell me," I urged her, sitting forward on the edge of my chair and taking her hands in mine. "What is it?"

Just then, her deadly stare drifted away from the corner and down towards the cold touch that gently cupped her palms.

"It is just …" she mumbled as another tear broke free, falling to the lace around her neck. "What I have performed for you tonight, that piece, I have not played in some time." She paused, her shoulders taut with unspoken tension. "Not since *she* left the island."

"She?" I answered her, my brow furrowed, suddenly recalling our talk that morning. "Oh, the servant girl you spoke of earlier?"

"Oh, I'm afraid she was much more than that," she piped up. "To me, in any case. Not that I would expect you to understand, Peter." She whipped out a handkerchief from the depth of her sleeve and softly dabbed the redness from her cheeks, causing their glow to flourish.

"Although, you are quite right in some respects. There was indeed a time when she was nothing more than that. My Patty. A quiet girl from the island's village, hired by Silas for nothing more than simple services about the house. My husband always had a way with children, mostly never nice. He thought it rather proper to have another child about the house, someone around the same age as Jacob. Someone he could interact with, occupy his time. A plaything, I suppose. However, it didn't go according to plan."

Willing to listen and a touch curious, I urged her to continue with nothing more than a lingering glance alone.

"Well, as you know, Jacob was a rather reserved child at the best of times. He never took much liking to his father's enforced playdates. In fact, he showed little fondness for the girl at all. From day to day, he hardly acknowledged her existence. But who could really blame him? He was, after all, a boy of higher class, an educated child who carried a respectable name on his shoulders. Who was she? No one. Nothing but a scrawny peasant girl who resided with her younger brother and aunt. A rather obscure surname, not of our own tongue by any means. Ó Súilleabháin." She spoke the name with some trouble. "Quite a penniless family, I assure you, and barely able to speak a word of English. Her father had perished on some ship during a returning voyage from England, and her mother, well, her mother was taken ill by fever long before the girl had any real means to remember her.

"We paid for the girl's time at the house, naturally, never hearing a peep of objection from her aunt. They desperately needed the money, you see. What broken family does not? And having her niece provide a service was by far the most practical way of obtaining it—much more preferable than seeing the child working long hours down at the quarry, or worse, carted off to some mainland workhouse. They are, after all, no place for the likes of children.

"It will probably come as no surprise to you that her aunt never enquired about her girl's services here at the house. It mattered little, not to her, at least. But I suppose there was never much to tell. For several years, she attended the house like clockwork, always punctual. Never a day did she miss. And with child companionship failing miserably, it felt only appropriate to make some use of the girl. Nothing too strenuous, you understand. Mopping, cleaning, and such. Chores that gave her some sort of purpose.

"And so, that was the way it was. The girl frequently attended the house, and at the end of each week, her aunt received what was owed—a small price, really. I forget how much. However, it mattered not. Soon after, we found ourselves under the circumstance of having to pay nothing at all."

"The aunt abandoned the child in your care, then?" I assumed.

"I suppose in some way, yes, she did," said Meredith as her gaze turned towards the flameless hearth. "She died," she said plainly. "In her sleep, I believe. She felt no pain, or so I was told. Nasty business, however. That said, I do believe there is something quite soothing about the way she passed, to leave this world in the comforts of one's bed. Like slipping from one dream to the next."

"Or a nightmare," I added, and took a sip from my glass.

Meredith's head whipped in my direction, away from the breast of the hearth. A look of pure irritation brewed across her face. "Why must you do that?"

"Do what?" I countered.

"Why must you take everything you hear and turn it into something so sinister, so ugly."

"I do that?"

"Yes," she huffed. "It is a weakness of yours. You have always failed to see the beauty in people, even if it is in death."

We said not a word to each other for a moment, allowing the sound of the stormy night outside to once again make itself known within the house.

"And what of the boy?" I asked, if only to block out the howl of night. "The younger brother you mentioned. What had become of him?"

"Oh, my dear Peter, how should I know? I never met the boy. Nor was it my place. I should imagine he was likely taken from the island, placed into care, perhaps."

"So, the workhouse, then."

"Yes," she muttered, the name of such a place causing her tone to soften. "I suspect there is that. The child had no other family to care for him. And because of this, there was little choice to be made. Besides, it was not my doing. Young boys, they are quite feisty. I'm sure no harm would have come to him if that's what you are implying."

"And …" I cleared my throat casually. "The girl?"

"Well, by then she had already been coming to the house for quite some time. We looked upon her as if she was a part of the household. The family, of sorts. At least, I did. It would have been a terrible shame to see her depart from our company, especially after no wrongdoing of her own. I'd go as far as to say the place wouldn't have felt the same without her. No," Meredith agreed with herself, "no, it would not. So, I arranged for the girl to remain here on the island, in my charge, of course. I knew Silas would not object. He cared little for such things. And who else would oppose such a charitable offer? A young girl born into poverty, only to be raised up from the squalor she had been accustomed to? Quite the opportunity, would you not agree? I homeschooled her myself, of course, taught her to read, to write. And with no expectation, I saw that she began to speak correctly. Pronunciation holds much significance in conveying one's thoughts effectively. If one cannot do this, then perhaps one should be confined to never speaking at all."

With an unsettling flourish, a white flicker of light seared across the darkened sky, casting a blinding glow that momentarily bathed the room, sulking along the floor.

"You adopted this peasant girl, then?" I enquired, my voice tinged with interest as I leant slightly forward, eager to catch her response. My fingers tapped lightly on the table.

"Not as such," she quickly answered.

"Then I'm afraid I do not understand. You took the girl in under your keeping, raised her?"

"Yes, yes," replied Meredith, her brows knitting together. "All of that. Although, it was never legally bound. Yes, I know what you are thinking. You forget, I can read you like a book. A very predictable book, at that. It is true, we may have dismissed the necessary paperwork, but what we didn't lack was stability. The child would have a roof over her head, food, warmth. Much more than anyone else could offer her. Come now, you look at me as if I had committed some sort of unspeakable crime."

"And you were not concerned by this?"

"Concerned?"

"That someone might come looking for the girl."

"Oh, my dear Peter." She chuckled, amused. "Have you not seen where we are? This place, this island? You really must look around you. It is but a forgotten rock lost to the harshness of the ocean. Why, you could shout at the top of your lungs and no one would hear your plea. Not here. Hardly worth the trouble for anyone to go snooping about in hope of finding some missing girl. Besides, there was no record of the family having ever resided at Lismore. The children's births are rarely documented these days, and following the sudden death of her penniless aunt, the woman found herself with nothing more than a common grave. No gathering. No service. Just her body laid to rest without so much as a cross to mark her."

As Meredith's tale unfolded, I found myself compelled to refill my glass, once more topping it to the brim. That time, however, I extended the same gracious courtesy to her. I invited her to join me. She did. And as she continued to speak, her voice took on a gentle hush, as if delicately tiptoeing around the wrath of heartbreak yet to come.

"Now, where was I? Ah, yes," she said, her glass never once touching her lips. "It is rather funny, really," she pondered. "I always considered the passing of a loved one to break a child, leaving them devastated. But here this girl was, still standing, still breathing, even after the departure of her brother. Still, she raised little fuss.

"She moved into the house immediately after, residing in a room on the third floor—I believe the room directly above your own. I felt the old servants' quarters quite improper for such a young girl, especially under the circumstances.

"To my surprise, she settled in well. She spent her days about the house, hardly ever breaking her routine. The chores kept her busy, I think, a way for her to forget about her *situation.* I did not object to such things. After all, when a mind is troubled, one does what one can to keep it occupied." She took the first sip from the glass, sighing aloud after drinking. "And that was just the way it was.

"As the years passed us by, I watched the girl grow like the daughter I never had, thriving in this beauty that far exceeded my own. Time seemed to drift away so quickly back then. So fast, in fact, that before long, Jacob had already matured into a fine young man. He had his own dreams, however, his own ambitions to accomplish—ones that stretched far beyond the rugged shores of Lismore. I begged him to reconsider, to stay here with me. Selfish, I know, but I suppose the heart wants what the heart truly wants. He promised he'd return to the island as often as he could, a promise to this day he has kept close to his heart. I understand now that a man like Jacob isn't meant for this life. He desired freedom, respect, a chance to prove his worth in this world. He reminds me very much of someone I know." She smiled, throwing me a sideways stare.

"It is a man's purpose to forge his own path in life," I stated between gulps, my voice steady.

"And that he has," she said proudly as another flash of light shone brightly across her face.

"And so, from then on, it was just you and the girl?" I asked.

"Not at first." She sighed. "Not quite. You forget, it was several years before my husband's passing. For a time, life continued very much as it always had. When Silas's time did come, the house seemed so …"

Her voice trailed off, and a sense of melancholy filled the room. I leant forward, encouraging her to continue, to tell me.

She blew out a long breath, her eyes distant with memories, memories I believed she wished she no longer had.

"After Silas's passing," she went on, "the house felt like a hollow shell. The rooms that were once filled with my family's footsteps now echoed with silence. I found myself longing for companionship, longing for someone to share my days and fill the void."

"The girl?"

"Yes." She smiled. The warmth with which she spoke became stronger. "She brought life back into the house. Her laughter filled these silent rooms, and her presence breathed new energy into my days. We became great friends. No, not just friends. We became family, maybe not bound by blood but by the fondness we held for one another. Or what I held for her."

She paused, a smile playing on her lips as she thought of such wonderful times. "It wasn't always easy," she told me. "We faced our challenges, and along the way, together we found the strength to overcome them. The girl grew up to be a remarkable young woman, full of kindness and spirit. And I, in turn, found pride and purpose in nurturing who she had become. We would do everything together, just the two of us. During the long winters, we would spend our days reading in front of the fire. She always loved to read. And I, too, loved to listen. We would talk long into the night of stories—stories that our grandfather once shared with us, Peter. She possessed an undeniable fondness for the written word, a secret curiosity that stirred within her like a guilty pleasure. Romance literature, mostly. Many nights I simply observed as she immersed herself into the pages of a book, watching as an unmistakable transformation never failed to grace her face. It was as if she surrendered her own existence, becoming one with the characters she attached herself to, experiencing their joys, their sorrows, all the many emotions that Lismore had failed to offer her.

"As the harshness of each winter came to pass, spring would return in all its glory, painting the grounds with an array of lively colour. It was always a better time, and the summer months were no exception. When the days were warm, our time was well spent tending to the garden, and if the mood struck us, we'd set off on foot, wandering the island's many secret paths. Oh, how she loved to explore, to venture to new places she had never trod upon before. But there are only so many places one can discover on an island. And regardless of her frustrations, I do believe the fresh air did us both a world of good. During the evenings, we would often take a blanket and sit near the north cliffs. We'd watch the sunset, marvel as it vanished beyond the horizon as if sinking into the depth of the ocean. It was quite lovely."

Meredith stood with glass in hand and began to pace the old wooden floor. Coming to a stop at the window, she drew back a single curtain, gazing hard beyond the blackened pane.

Lightning again scorched the sky, silhouetting the far-off trees in the distance.

"She had become rather restless," said Meredith, her concentration unaltered from the strong reflection staring back at her. "She grew tired of the island. Bored. Once one has spent year after year confined to the same old paths, well, I suppose it is only natural to seek change."

"And so you let the girl travel to the mainland." I chuckled, knowing her all too well.

"You don't understand, Peter," snapped Meredith. "The girl begged me, practically pleaded. She said that if I was not willing to take her, then she would find a way herself, swim if she must. There was little I could say or do in the matter. And so I decided to—"

"Escort the young lady to town."

"Yes," she answered, allowing the curtain to sway back into place. "It was the least I could do to please her. And I do believe it did just that. So, once every fortnight, we would catch the ferry into town. She had never travelled across the water before and found the whole experience quite remarkable. She once told me she felt like a bird hovering above water. And I remember stating that it was quite a ridiculous notion.

"When we reached Oban, she seemed almost stunned. Gone was the loneliness she had grown used to, given way to a labyrinth of bustling streets. And people—so many people going about their business. I don't believe I had ever seen her so excited. Merchants lined the sidewalks, their stalls overflowing with an array of goods, enticing passersby with their displays. The air was filled with a blunder of sounds: the clatter of hooves on roads, snippets of conversations, and the occasional street musician adding their rowdy contribution to the din. She linked my arm tight, committing to never letting go as her eyes darted from one new scene to another."

As the hour grew late, Meredith continued to share her cherished stories, her expression infused with overwhelming bliss yet at times tinged with unmistakable sadness. As she continued to speak, her voice carried a soft rhythm, lulling me into a tiresome daze as I nestled myself farther in the armchair. The room around us faded into the background. All I wished to do was listen.

"It carried on this way for some months," continued Meredith as she restlessly paced the room, her footsteps never stopping. Not once. "Eventually, it was expected that we visit the town as often as we did. Not just by her, you understand, but by some of the townsfolk who resided there. We had made several acquaintances during our little trips, you see. Good people. Respectable people. People whom I could trust, or so I thought.

"When the days arrived, we would spend the majority of the morning replenishing our supplies. Nothing much, merely some simple provisions. The local storekeepers had come to know us both quite well by then. Too well, I suppose, not that it was any fault of my own. Young ladies, they love to gossip, as I'm sure you are aware."

"I am afraid I am not," I jested as I allowed my eyelids to close.

"Yes, well, it came as little surprise for the town to learn about our situation. Word spreads quickly, you know, especially within the busy streets."

"Oh, and what situation was that?" I asked.

Meredith's feet ground to a halt.

"Why, that the girl was not my own, of course. Not that I was ashamed. Far from it. I am very much a private woman, Peter. I may not have always been, but the years on Lismore, well, they have changed me some. The last thing I wish is to go about the town and hear people whispering, muttering my name beneath their breath, having to tolerate those gawking eyes. It is not what any respectable woman would want, to have their name dragged through the mud like that. After all, my business is my business, nobody else's. I would very much like to have kept it that way. So, on returning to the island, I felt I had little choice. I decided to do the only thing that felt right."

"You locked yourself away again," I said. "You and the girl."

"I did," said Meredith with much sympathy. "The poor girl, she wasn't at all pleased about the whole situation, but I suppose one must do what they can to protect the people they love. The world outside these walls can be a cruel place. I realise that now, and in time, so would she. All it would take was a little perseverance. She would come to understand my actions eventually, to see the reason that sometimes the most unfair decisions in life are often made for the greater good."

"Except she didn't, did she?"

Meredith stood speechless, the words failing to form past her lips.

Hesitant, she simply clasped her hands together, her gaze drifting to the floor.

"The Harbour Master," I continued with a tiresome groan, lifting myself upright, "he happened to mention that once you ceased travelling, this girl of yours was often seen wandering into town alone. Hardly the actions of an obedient servant."

"I told you already." She appeared cross. "She was much more than that! I stood my ground for as long as I could." She made herself clear. "Every command I issued, she dutifully obeyed. And for a span of several months, life continued as it always had. I found relief in that, and I believed she did too. Or perhaps I merely convinced myself of such. Yet as the relentless weeks wore on, a transformation gradually took hold of her. The once genuine smile that graced her face now wore a veneer of falseness. The gleam in her eyes, too, had vanished without a trace. I knew I had to take action, do something, but what path, I did not know, could not think.

"It was on a cool autumn's eve that I finally plucked the courage to ask, to discover the key that would once again reignite her happiness. Can you imagine her response?"

Fatigue weighed heavily upon me by that point, and I released a wearied sigh.

"She beseeched me," continued Meredith. "Pleaded for permission to return to the town." Her voice was stained with a hint of melancholy.

"And how did you reply?" I asked her sluggishly, my hand finding respite upon my forehead.

"What choice did I have?" She huffed, a pang of heartache evident in her words. "It broke my heart to witness her in such a way. So sorrowful. So shattered. It was as if I had stripped away the very source of who she was. At first, I couldn't grasp it, couldn't comprehend the reasons why. However, like all things in life, time reveals its secrets."

The echoes of the rusty clock resounded from within the depths of the house, marking the arrival of midnight. Each dull chime weaved a haunting melody through the stillness of the hour.

As I lifted my head, the delicate dance of moonlight filtered through the gap of the curtains, casting a shadow on my sister's face.

She stopped.

"I believe I have shared enough for tonight," she said, her voice trailing off as the last chime dissolved. "And I sense that you have had quite enough to drink. Come," she beckoned, "let us retire. I'm sure by morning's light the storm will be gone, and the island shall emerge all the better for it."

"No," I stated, my head rousing from the chair. "I wish to hear more," I replied, unable to control the slur of each word. "I wish to hear what happened!"

For a fleeting moment, my mind swirled with dizziness as my eyes danced hazily around the room, searching for the face of my sibling.

"Peter?" Her hand stirred my shoulder. "You are drunk. I suggest you go to bed," she advised, her voice motherly.

"I am not tired," I grumbled.

"No, but you are being stubborn."

"I would like to hear of your outcome."

"Why?" she enquired.

"I suppose I wish to know why the young girl held such significance to you."

Meredith's hand tightened its grip on my shoulder, each fingertip imprinting itself upon my flesh.

"Very well," she murmured, her grasp loosening as she uttered the words.

"From that day onwards, once a week I granted her the privilege of boarding the ferry and venturing into town alone, if only for a few fleeting hours. No more, no less. However, during those first few visits, something remarkable occurred, Peter. She changed. Instantly. Each evening, she would arrive back at the house full of excitement, a grin stretched from ear to ear. Her eyes sparkled with joy, eager to share the happenings of her day, the people she had crossed paths with, the things she had seen. I must confess, it was all very wonderful to see her act in such a way. It was as if she had transformed, returned into her delightful, old self. Oh, how I had missed that. The smile upon her face. The soft hum as she walked about the halls. And her laugh … Well, I feared I would never hear such a sound seep past her lips again.

"It carried on this way for quite some time, and as the weeks swiftly passed, her visits across the water became more frequent. It mattered little to me at the time; if she was happy, I was happy. But what began as a daily visit to the mainland soon turned into much more. Her time away from the island, away from me, grew longer and more noticeable. There were even occasions when she would arrive home much later than we had discussed, well after dark. As you can imagine, I worried terribly at the mere thought of anything happening to her. After all, she was but a young woman. But I suppose radiant youth often brings with it a certain amount of ignorance. On some nights, restlessness overcame me to such an extent that I would gather my coat and find myself sitting at the docks in the dead of night, anxious and hopeful for her return. Yet on many of those long nights, she never made it back at all. And when she finally did, I was met with the feeblest excuses imaginable. 'Oh, Ma'am, you worry too much,' she would say to me, laughing. And perhaps I did worry, but it was all for the greater good. All I ever wanted, all I wished for, was to do right by the girl, to keep her safe, you understand? The world can be a cruel, heartless place, and I know. I have seen it myself. And if anything were to ever befall her, well, I don't believe I could ever have forgiven myself. I simply couldn't. And just when I believed that nothing else could come between us, nothing further could drift us apart, fate delivered another arrival to my doorstep."

Chapter 21

Meredith lingered for what seemed to be the longest time, her voice trembling as she fought back the undeniable tears in her eyes. She tried to speak, to muster what she had kept bottled up for so very long. The thought alone was all too much to bear. The room fell silent as she took a long, deep breath, carrying with it the weight of countless pent-up emotions. The silence between breaths seemingly stretched time itself.

"She, she left me, Peter," she said finally, her voice broken and shattered.

"The girl died, then?"

"No, she did not die!" snapped Meredith, her manner instantly becoming a force to be reckoned with. "What would entice you to say such a thing?"

"I just thought—"

"Well, you thought wrong, Peter," she interrupted, nostrils flaring at the notion. "Very wrong." She let out a grunt of disapproval, followed by another heavy sigh. So heavy, in fact, it was as if she was releasing a thousand words in a single breath. She cleared her throat, fighting back the heartache, and, with one finger, slackened the lace around her neck. Only then did she continue to speak.

"It occurred on the most miserable of nights, a night strikingly similar to what we have witnessed this evening—cold and wet. It was late. I was alone. The rain pounded nonstop, spreading wide across the island. The wind howled most fiercely over the house. And as I recall, taking view from the library window, the clouds hung low in the sky, casting a dark and worrisome shadow over everything below. Lightning torched the heavens in the distance, briefly revealing the world outside before plunging it back into darkness. I remember it was on the third flash that I noticed something—something on the path. Or should I say someone, a figure from what I could perceive, approaching fast. I ran to the door, wrenching it open as quickly as I could and inviting the ghastly weather to seep into the very core of the house.

"There on the step, soaked to the bone, was none other than my darling girl, her hair weighed down flat upon her forehead, her white dress draping wet from her petite frame, merged with the paleness of her skin. For a moment she simply just stood there, utterly speechless, her wide eyes staring up at me. She appeared somewhat frightened, dare I say it, hesitant of me. Why? I simply couldn't imagine. I had never caused harm to the girl. Never had I struck her. I adored her. I still did.

"A trembling shudder took hold of her body as the wind effortlessly knocked her this way and that. I advised she come inside at once, beckoning her in, offering out my hand. Any longer outside and she would certainly have caught her death. I suggested that she get dry, remove her soaking wet clothes. Perhaps a nice warm bath to dull the chill. Still, her stance remained stern, rooted to the spot. She would not move, not an inch. I didn't understand it, couldn't contemplate why. So I asked her. I said, 'What is wrong with you?' Of course, she answered not. She merely looked away, staring at the ground as the rain continued to bounce about her feet. I asked her if she was in some sort of trouble, if there was anything *I* could do to help. She was, after all, still under my care, my watch. Regardless, she would not utter a single word to me. I bowed my neck low in an attempt to meet her eyes, yet she avoided my gaze completely. 'Has someone hurt you?' I persisted, stepping out into the rain and tugging her firmly by the arms. I shook her. 'If so, you must tell me,' I demanded as the deep rumble of thunder clattered overhead."

"And did the girl eventually succumb to your questioning?" I asked.

Meredith relaxed the tension in her jaw.

"She broke her silence eventually, yes," she answered. "She told me she was leaving. At first, I must admit I didn't know what to think of it. It all seemed so sudden, so surreal. I tried to escort her into the house, tried to convince her, but she wouldn't listen to a word I said. Not one. She resisted me, Peter. I was shocked, angry. After all, she had never resisted before. She had always been a good girl, a sensible girl. And when she told me of her reasoning, well, I very much lashed out. I shook her violently. I'm not proud of it, but I was desperate. I just wanted to talk some sense into her, make her see reason. Understand, I had no wish to harm her. She screamed. I screamed. And before I knew it, a flash lit up the sky and we were both falling back towards the ground, scuffling about the mud."

Without realising, I shot her a piercing look.

"A moment of pure instinct, I assure you," she remarked. "A rash decision, nonetheless. Looking back now, I feel quite ashamed of it all. I was frustrated. Upset. What I did was wrong; I know that now. I suppose I was just blindsided by the notion that she would rather be anywhere else but here, with me."

Again, I nodded in response, a weak effort to try to express the limited understanding I could muster, hoping to at least offer some form of comfort.

"But you still haven't told me why," I asked.

"Why?" she repeated nasally.

"Why the girl wished to leave."

At her sides, Meredith's fingers curled into a vise, her fists tense and trembling.

"Because she fell in love, Peter."

"Ah."

"Yes, love. Some young man who'd passed through the town, I was later informed. A simple farmer, of all things. Can you imagine that?" she huffed. "I forget his name now. What was it?" She thought for a moment and pinched the bridge of her nose. "Oh, I'm sure it will come to me. Besides, it matters not."

The wind outside became stronger, swiftly changing between gentle whispers and fierce roars as if the gale beyond the walls was telling a story of its own.

I watched Meredith closely, studying her as she paced the floor, and in that moment, she turned to me. Despite the sadness painted on her face, and the nervous way she acted, it was clear that the weather outside had begun to bother her greatly. For what reason, I was not sure; I could not comprehend. Perhaps it increased her already deep sense of loneliness, her commitment to a life alone. Or perhaps it simply served as nothing more than a reminder of the events that occurred on that unforgettable night.

"As you can imagine, I was quite in shock. She told me he had proposed and asked for her hand," continued Meredith as she exhaled, somewhat amused at the thought. "Fancy that! A man without so much as a penny to his name and not even a ring to offer her, not that wealth played any part in her decision. Truth be told, I don't know what did. His situation seemed to matter very little to her. She accepted him for who he truly was—lower class, a simple man. She told me he was kind-hearted, loving, her prince, or so she referred to him, disguised in commoners clothing. Regardless, his profession was the least of her concerns."

"But it concerned you?" I interrupted, with no desire to stir the pot.

Meredith frowned irritably. "What a ludicrous question you ask, Peter. Of course it concerned me. It concerned me greatly. After all, this man had nothing—no money, no property of his own. How was he to provide for her? To care for her in the way which I had?"

I did not answer as she stopped to look at me, but instead, I inclined that she go on.

"I enquired where she was going, where I might find her. A reasonable enough request, I thought. However, she simply wouldn't say, only that they planned to travel north. He would acquire a patch of land, find her a home, a place where they could be together always, maybe even raise a family. I must admit, it all sounded far too sudden to my liking. She was still frightfully young, after all. Far too young for marriage. I couldn't bear to see her throw away her youth like that, not to a man of such standards. She deserved so much more, so much care. Far beyond the capabilities of mere class. And as we both stood out in the cold on that dreadful night, soaked to the bone and covered in mud, I pleaded with her one final time to reconsider, to throw away this absurd obsession she had planted in her head. She, of course, said nothing. I expected no less. But when I yelled that she would never be welcomed back here, screamed that she would not step foot inside this house ever again, well, she responded in a way that words never could."

"How so?" I asked her.

"She embraced me," replied Meredith, enveloping her own arms around herself as if trying to relive the memory. "She held me tightly, resting her head on my shoulder, and in that moment, I could feel the strong thump of her heart racing against my chest. Tears streamed down her face as her breath fell heavily on my ear. With a trembling voice, she whispered to me—a simple sentiment, yet one that meant the world. 'Thank you,' she said. It may come as a surprise for you to hear that I said nothing in return. I couldn't. There was nothing more to say. No words of comfort. No blessings. I merely stood by, my emotions hidden, locked away.

"I was heartless, Peter. Cruel. I know that now. I have accepted it. And every day, my regret torments me for my actions of that night, the way I treated her. I didn't mean any of it. My words were meaningless, hollow. And despite my stubbornness, it wasn't until her arms finally released me and her fading figure slowly disappeared back into the bleakness of the night that I finally found the will to speak."

Meredith paused with quivering lips.

"I simply cried her name."

AS THE NIGHT DWINDLED ON, THE RAGING STORM OUTSIDE gradually calmed. Meredith let out a tired yawn as she wearily hoisted herself up from the chair, her hair all tousled and drooping.

"I think it is time we went to bed," she insisted, her tired steps faltering slightly as she slowly made her way across the room. She turned to glance at me, still slouched on the furniture. "I assume you'll be retiring as well?"

"I think I might stay for a while," I answered, nestling myself farther into the cushions and cocking one leg over the arm's rest.

Meredith lingered from the far side of the room. "Very well." She yawned infectiously. "Then I bid you goodnight."

"Yes," I replied. Then a sudden thought occurred to me. "Oh, one more thing."

Meredith halted, her figure caught in the doorway. "Yes, Peter. What is it?"

I sat up, my body twisted to find her. "Did that girl you mentioned ever come to realise the error of her ways?"

Meredith lifted her chin, contemplating my question with great thought.

"Are you asking if she ever returned?" she asked.

"I suppose I am, yes."

My sister contemplated deeply, pausing before responding. When she finally spoke, her voice carried the same undertone of sadness.

"No," she replied softly. "No, she did not. I'm afraid I never saw her again after that. However, I often find myself dreaming about her. When I do, the dreams, well, they are never pleasant. Her face still remains so vivid in my mind. There are moments when I awaken only to momentarily forget that she is no longer here at all. Silly of me, I know. I'm not quite sure how to explain. I believe I would fail miserably if I tried. She was a good companion to me, Peter, a true friend.

My only friend. One of a kind. The one person who I could rely on when truly I needed it. What I wouldn't give to see her here with me again, hear her voice. Oh, but it is all far too late for that," said Meredith, holding back her sorrow with the politest smile.

"Too late?" I asked. I didn't understand. "But why?"

"Because she is happy now, Peter. If she was not, I believe her shadow would have filled my door long ago," explained Meredith as her head gently rested on the doorframe, both eyes closed. "No, the girl I cared for so much has moved on. It is about time I did the same."

With that, Meredith remained in the doorway, allowing the precious seconds to slip by. A heavy hum escaped her lips, bearing witness to the grief she carried within. Despite her longing desire to let go, an undeniable truth still resided deep within her—she understood, with unwavering certainty, that forgetting would never come.

"Goodnight, Peter," said Meredith once more as she turned and walked away. Her footsteps resounded down the hall. With each step, the sound became fainter, echoing against the walls as she ascended the stairs, the rhythm of her footsteps mirroring the weight of her own aching heart.

Chapter 22

Several hours must have passed before I finally stirred from my sleep. At first, I thought the music I heard, and the slightest scent of perfume, was merely a figment of my imagination—the piano's song echoing in my mind.

Lying still, I kept my eyes closed, savouring the soothing melody that flowed from my sister's fingertips. Unlike earlier that evening, the soft music filling the room was flawless, nothing short of a masterpiece. No matter how late it was, I couldn't help but admire her talent. She was simply magnificent, a musician any pianist would aspire to be.

I turned slightly on the spot.

"You could not sleep?" I murmured, my voice heavy with fatigue.

To my surprise, Meredith didn't respond. Instead, she continued to play, seamlessly transitioning from one beautiful segment to the next.

With some effort, I pried my eyes open and gazed at the cracks on the ceiling, sprawling like tangled roots. As I did, the tempo of her playing noticeably faltered. It became sluggish and awkward, the notes blending into a jarring disarray.

"I believe that is enough music for one night, my dear," I said, my displeasure only partially hidden.

Meredith continued to play as if she hadn't heard me at all.

My head lifted from the chair's arm, the cracking of my bones audible in my ears as I swiftly turned to face her.

"I said, I think that is quite enough for one—"

My words cut off abruptly as the music that had filled the room came to a sudden, eerie halt. A chill ran up my spine, raising the hairs on the back of my neck. My gaze fixed rigidly ahead, I peered through the dim haze, my focus settling on the shape of the piano behind me and the empty stool, lacking a player.

With a jolt, I sprang to my feet, unable to look away from the unsettling sight before me. The cover that concealed the piano's keys was closed, and the stool was cold to the touch.

Without delay, a sudden urgency to leave surged through me. I hurried out of the room, my fingers gripping the doorknob as I firmly pulled the door closed behind me.

I rushed towards the hall, my heart racing in my chest. As I neared the stairwell, I grasped the railing, ready to climb. Yet just as I prepared to take my first step, something compelled me to look back.

The front door stood slightly ajar, its hinges creaking under the weight.

"Meredith?" I called softly, my voice barely above a whisper as I withdrew my foot from the step. "Is that you?"

A shallow breeze wafted through the gap, causing the door to sway gently. From beyond it, faint laughter drifted into the air. It wasn't the laughter of a single voice but rather the laughter of many, a chorus of amusement in the dead of night.

"Whoever you are!" I warned, my voice trembling and choked. "This is private property. You must leave immediately!"

The laughter continued regardless, undeterred by my warning. The voices intertwined, creating a haunting symphony that spilt in with the cold.

Filled with fear, I lunged towards the door, slamming it shut with a resounding thud. I turned the key, my hands trembling as the latch locked firmly in its place.

Beads of sweat dripped from my forehead as I leant against the door, gasping for breath. I pressed my ear against the solid wood, yearning for the haunting chorale to cease. It did no such thing. However, as I began to edge away, a slow and unwelcomed knock thundered through the house, each strike absent of any pattern, any emotion.

I stumbled backwards in sheer panic, my footing giving way beneath me, and I found myself sprawled across the tiles. My eyes remained stern, unblinking, as the thump of three more knocks solidly struck upon the door.

Knock... Knock... Knock...

"Who ... Who is that?" I demanded, each word barely escaping past my lips. "Who's there?"

An unwanted pause hung in the air. The knocking ceased, leaving only the lingering echoes of its presence. Yet my anticipation thickened as the faint sound of distant laughter continued to seep its way through the cracks and crannies of the house. Then it happened. My body stiffened as I bore witness to a motion—a dreaded motion. The doorknob turned, slowly, almost secretively, gripping me in its icy grasp. As the latch freed, the door unlocked, inching open, revealing the strangest sight from beyond.

As I struggled to find my footing, my knees began to buckle, each step a feeble hobble as I wandered forward in shock, drawing closer to the view outside and emerging beneath the open sky.

A thick snow appeared to engulf the landscape, stretching out before me like an endless white abyss. The sky was pitch black and cloudless, absent a single star, and as my first step crunched deeply into the soft blanket of snow, the wind, too, became calm. Silent. It was as though time itself had stopped.

I could not understand it. I couldn't explain how. It had not snowed at all that evening. I was sure of it. Nor was it the time of year for such weather. Yet there I stood, sinking knee-deep into the snow, the frosty air gnawing at my skin, invading my lungs with its icy touch.

"Hello?" I shouted, my voice belting out into the distance and returning to me from far away

For a few unsettling moments, there was silence except for the eerie sound of my footsteps mingled with the familiar crunch of snow underfoot. I rubbed my arms, desperate to shake off the cold that had quickly seeped into my bones. I turned around, intending to retrace my steps, to find my way back inside and escape from the chill. However, to my dismay, the door stood closed.

I reached out, twisting the handle back and forth in a frenzy. I pounded on the door, panic rising within me, peering through the keyhole and crying out through the lock. But it was hopeless. No matter how hard I tried or how loudly I called her name, Meredith remained oblivious to my pleas.

I slumped against the door, my body trembling uncontrollably. Just when I felt I had lost all hope, the sound of laughter drifted through the air again.

"Who's there?" I snarled through clenched teeth, my eyes darting from one snowy mound to the next. Something caught my attention—a faint glimmer of light peeking through a cluster of distant trees. I couldn't quite make out what it was. A house, perhaps? I had never noticed one so close before. Yet the allure of warmth and the chance to escape the biting cold compelled me to follow.

Without a second thought, I veered off the doorstep and ventured towards it, staggering as I navigated the uneven ground.

The snow grew shallower as I moved deeper into the thicket. Their branches intertwined above me, forming a canopy that obscured the empty sky. The laughter grew louder, interrupted only by the rustling of snow falling from the branches and my own laboured breath clouding the way ahead.

Summoning what little energy I had, I emerged from the dense woodland only to find myself standing before a large stone house nestled amidst the snow. Black smoke curled lazily from the chimney, while frost-kissed windows glimmered with a flickering glow of light, painting a warm, cozy picture from within. As I drew nearer, I listened to the symphony of laughter joined by the faint melodies of music, the clinking of glasses, and the dancing shadows that played upon the inner walls.

"Hello?" I called out, relief washing over me as my voice carried through the chilled air. I approached a window and pressed my hands against the frost-covered glass, peering into the room. In the centre stood a magnificent table, decorated with fine linens, that commanded my attention to its lavish feast. It was a banquet for kings. The table overflowed with steaming meats, vegetables, and an abundance of beverages that would warm any weary soul. Yet the chairs surrounding the table sat vacant, just like the rest of the room.

"Hello?" I repeated, my voice pleading, stinging from the cold as I tapped upon the glass, hoping that someone, anyone, would hear me. "I … I need help. Will someone please let me in?"

I fumbled towards the door, wrapping my trembling hands around the frozen handle and twisting, but it wouldn't budge—not an inch. A surge of voices erupted from within the house as I stumbled to the next window. I peered inside only to find another empty room aglow with flickering candles. I moved on to the next window, and then the next, but my search found nothing. Not a single soul was in sight.

I had nearly given up all hope of discovering anyone, but as I approached the final window, stumbling over hidden objects buried beneath the snow, a surge of relief flooded through me. Inside that room, a roaring fireplace threw out a warm amber glow at its centre. In front of it, a large chair was pulled close to the flames. A figure occupied the seat, a cup and saucer resting soundly on their lap; their presence was shrouded in shadow.

"You there!" I cried, pressing my face against the pane. "Could you possibly let me in?" The words stumbled out of my mouth, interrupted by the biting cold. "I … I seem to have found myself in a bit of trouble."

To my astonishment, the seated figure remained unresponsive, calmly relishing the comforting heat before them as the steaming beverage was lifted from the saucer.

"I say, can you hear me?" I yelled, rapping on the glass with tingling knuckles. "I urgently require your help."

The shadowed face slowly turned towards me, yet the person remained firmly seated, showing no intention of rising.

"Yes, yes you!" I confirmed, nodding hastily in their direction. "Could you please open the door?" I shivered, unable to stop the cold. "Please, do hurry."

At first, there was no movement from within at all. Not even a slight twitch could be detected. However, as I made my final plea, the stranger gradually rose from the seat, setting down their drink upon the hearth. It was revealed to be a man—a man dressed in what seemed to be the most exquisite evening attire. His face remained veiled, obscured by the silhouette of his dense, unruly hair. With a dignified stance, he stood upright, adjusting the cuffs of his jacket, before eventually turning to face me. He lingered on the spot as he watched.

"Hello," a voice replied, muffled through the glass.

"Yes, hello!" I responded, feeling a sense of relief.

Though the man remained motionless, his head tilted inquisitively, seemingly amused by my distress.

"May I come in?" I struggled to speak, grappling with a violent cough that pierced my chest like knives.

"Inside?" the voice answered, his tone laced with the strangest uncertainty.

"Please!" I shouted.

The figure within stirred, his movements drawing him nearer, too, until he stood directly in front of me, his visage revealed by the moon's pale light.

Dread coursed through my veins, paralysing me in its grip as I stared at the face looking back at me—a disturbing blend of my own true reflection and his. One face was consumed by terror, the other marked by twisted cruelty. They were one and the same, a face that was none other than my own.

I crashed to the ground, the blanket of white snow cushioning my fall. Frantically, I crawled, clutching at the icy surface. I stole a glance over my shoulder, unable to tear my eyes away from the haunting presence from within. Its eyes were so empty, so heartless.

Struggling to my feet, I summoned every ounce of strength to break free from the clutches that bound me. With my heart pounding, I ran, my legs carrying me as fast as they could back to the shelter of the tree line. There I stopped, slumping against a tree, shielding myself from view, my breath caught in my throat.

The resemblance of myself remained at the window, those hollow eyes still fixed on me. A malicious smile crept across its lips as the moonlight cast a ghastly pallor upon its face. Suddenly, the glow from each room of the house intensified, creating a stark silhouette of the watchful figure. Smoke billowed from the chimney like a ferocious beast, its dark cloud clawing at the air. As I cowered, the potent smell of burning filled my nostrils.

Flames engulfed the roof of the house, spreading through every room like wildfire, rising higher and higher. Windows shattered one after another, glass shooting to the ground like frozen shards, while the door heaved heavily with smoke. Heat washed over me, yet my likeness at the window remained unfazed. Even as the fire consumed him and the dancing flames licked at his flesh, his gaze remained locked with mine. It held firm until I felt myself falling, the world around me dimming into a hellish scene. Only then did the sound of laughter fade with the light.

Chapter 23

Leslie Wills leant back in his seat, his self-control slipping away as he shouted over the writer who was clearly in his element, just as he had done so before.

"What the fuck was all that about?" he blurted out, immediately regretting his outburst as he witnessed the old man's piercing gaze from across the desk.

"Pardon?" The old writer's head tilted. "What is what all about?"

"Well," Les fumbled, his unease evident in the way he nervously tapped his foot. "The blizzard, the voices coming from that house, the man who this Peter Daily claimed to have been none other than himself, and let's not skip the piano playing on its tod." He made sure not to miss that. "What's it all about, Roderick?"

"Ever heard of a player piano, lad?"

Les scrunched his face doubtfully. "Of course I have," he answered, unable to stop his eyes from rolling. "But you know as well as I that such a thing was not invented back then, not until the turn of the century, at least."

"No," mumbled Roderick, removing his glasses. He polished them with his jacket. "You are quite right. These entries were certainly before its time. However, you were slightly off the mark. It was the late 19th century, to be precise."

Les bit his lip, thinking of things he could have said but didn't. He had no interest in the man's common knowledge of history, nor would he indulge him further if he had. He simply wished to know one thing and one thing only.

"You avoided my question," stated Les, his patience slowly beginning to wane.

"I did not,"" answered Roderick, his reply just as stern. "I did nothing of the sort. I simply happened to answer your question with another. The truth is …" He thought for a moment. "The truth is, I cannot explain what is written here regarding the piano. Nor would I feel like an educated man if I attempted to fill your head with such mumbo jumbo. It is scientifically documented that many accounts like this have a logical and, might I add, a reasonable explanation."

"Accounts like what?" replied Les, folding his arms in the process.

"Well …" The old writer stalled and quickly pointed to the page with one finger. "See here!" he exclaimed. "It plainly states the man had been drinking. He admits it was so. And more than his fair share. I suspect the music he heard was nothing short of a dream-like state, his mind cheated by the drink. After all, many people over the years have claimed to witness oddities once stirred from their sleep. I dare say you have as well, at least once in your life. Tell me, why should we assume this to be any different?"

There was no denying it. The old man's words resonated with undeniable truth, casting a weighty shadow upon Les's thoughts. As a person who had encountered similar situations before, Les found it increasingly difficult to simply brush aside such a narrow mindset. However, a sense of restraint washed over him, compelling him to refrain from further challenging the old man's beliefs. Instead, Les simply let the old man's words drift away.

"Ok," answered Les. "And what of the other things?"

"Hmm?" uttered Roderick. His attention had already drifted from the topic and back towards the unread pile on his desk.

"You know," encouraged Les insistently. "What Daily found. The house. The fire he stood by and witnessed. What's he yammering on about?"

The old writer pricked up his ears. His expression quickly turned to a serious one, though despite his sternness, he was unable to conceal a mysterious smugness that spilt out beyond his stare.

"Ah," the writer extracted while returning his spectacles to the same small red markings that indented the sides of his nose. "It would not be prudent of me to provide you with the answer you seek. Not at this time. Not yet. And not when we have come so far in the retelling of this story. I'm afraid I do not deem it appropriate, Mr Wills. At least, not for this moment."

Les felt a slight sense of surprise at the old man's refusal. "Then what is appropriate for now?" he asked, his curiosity merged with a visible touch of frustration.

"My boy," replied Roderick, adding a rather humorous chuckle. "My boy, my boy, my boy. It is simply appropriate for you to listen. Nothing more. For you to gain what no other living ears have heard before. Do this, and I, in turn, shall ask no more of you."

Uncertain of what to say, Les leant back in his chair, determined to listen to the old man until the final page was turned and his lingering questions were finally answered.

Having broken the writer's concentration, Les offered an apology, well aware of Roderick's irritation. "I'm sorry," he said, slightly embarrassed. "I simply wish to find out the truth."

"In due time, Mr Wills," replied the old man in a gruff, low voice. "But one cannot simply unveil them all at once. We must first finish what we have already begun here."

Outside, a lonely lamppost blinked to life, casting a feeble glow that struggled to penetrate the small, suffocating window.

Roderick settled into a more comfortable position, adjusting himself before clearing his throat loudly. He refilled his glass and turned his gaze to Les.

"Rest assured, Mr Wills, you will receive your answers. I have no doubt. Now, if you please." He gestured towards the page waiting beneath his nose. "Let us continue."

Chapter 24

17TH March 1847

My eyes flickered open with a disoriented flutter.

As I lay there, my gaze turned towards the sky. Towering trees stood lurching above me, their lofty forms reaching upwards as if in an attempt to touch the clouds that calmly drifted by. The fresh morning breeze swayed their branches, creating a calming dance of shadows and light. I recalled thinking to myself as I lay unmoved on the cold, wet earth that I had never seen trees move in such a way before. There was something so lifelike about them, their movements imbued with a sense of consciousness—an observation I had chosen to ignore throughout my fleeting years.

"Come on, now," a voice bellowed, each word becoming louder and clearer than the last. "Take your leave!"

With great effort, my head lifted from the ground, feeling as heavy as lead and causing my back to spasm.

I must admit, it took a moment for my eyes to adjust, gradually bringing the scene before me into focus as a man looked down at me.

"Mr Daily?" the man enquired, his voice mixed with a peculiar blend of perplexity. "What is it you're doing out here, sir? And lying on the ground, no less."

I pushed myself up.

"I …" I commenced, my voice faltering as I pressed both palms into the sodden grass, seeking urgent leverage to stand. A bewildered look must have swept across my face, the recollection of the preceding night flooding back to me in an instant.

"The snow!" I said with disbelief.

The man wrinkled his nose, pausing before he finally decided to answer. "Snow?" he repeated rather stubbornly.

"Yes!" I confirmed, my words laden with astonishment as I clumsily climbed to my feet. "It has gone, vanished, every trace of it! Why, it is like it was never here at all!"

The man cocked his brow peculiarly. "Here at all, sir?"

"The snow!" I barked again, my gaze sweeping across the woodland floor. "Are you listening to a word I speak?"

The man returned a delayed nod.

"That I am," he replied, his face adorned with curiosity. Or was it worry? "Yet I regret to inform that we have not witnessed even a flurry of snow on the island in some months. Perhaps a little less. It is the salt in the air, you see?"

"Impossible," I muttered, my restless footsteps tracing a circuit upon the ground. My thoughts were still entangled by the memory, the events so clear in my mind.

I turned to look at him. "Who are you?" I asked, my attention drifting back towards the stranger.

The man did nothing but observe me from where he stood, a faint smile betraying his lips. Clad in a well-worn jacket and boots that had indeed seen better days, he displayed an air of quiet authority. His large frame, though not towering in height, possessed a commanding presence that hinted at a life spent toiling upon the land. His weathered skin and squinting eyes bore the marks of countless hours under the sky, etched with deep lines that told tales of tireless dedication to the island.

"Oh," said the man, clasping both hands behind his back. "We have already had the pleasure of meeting, Mr Daily." He chuckled humorously to himself. "But I must say, I am glad to find you awake this time."

I studied the large man with great interest, a mysterious smile displayed upon his face as he casually edged nearer to greet me.

"Mr Gibbs," he stated, tipping his hat in gesture and presenting the yellow tint of his teeth. "Perhaps my name has already been mentioned?" he asked, knowing the answer all too well.

"That it has, Mr Gibbs," I confirmed. I offered my hand. "A great deal, if I may speak so truthfully."

The man obliged my offer, reaching out and grasping my hand, which in turn he proceeded to shake harshly. His palm was dry and rough, no doubt the result of many years of labour. Nothing short of a worker's hand.

"Nothing too displeasing, I hope?" he enquired in jest, though in truth, one could tell he relished the thought of compliments. He released his grip and supported himself against the nearest tree.

"On the contrary," I remarked, making sure to assure him. "My sister, in fact, she speaks very highly of you. So much so that I believe she would be at an utter loss without you."

Mr Gibbs grinned in a most pleasing manner, his cheeks flourishing to that of the reddest rose as his eyes grew wider from hearing it.

"That is awfully kind of her, sir," he said. "It is always pleasing to hear that your services are well appreciated, regardless of what said services might be."

"Yes," I agreed, dusting off the muck that clung unsightly to my clothes. "My apologies, Mr Gibbs. I'm afraid I must appear in an awful state."

With a cautious glance, the man carefully viewed me from head to toe, as if he were a tailor thoroughly gauging my proportions for a set of fresh garments.

"Ah, what is a little mud, sir," he reassured me, his smile never shifting. "Although, I must admit when I saw you slumped on the ground as you were, I first mistook you for a wanderer." He chuckled heartily.

I met his eyes with a blank expression, his stare never letting go of mine until I was inclined to look away.

"Oh, do forgive me," he promptly apologised. "It is no secret that we get scroungers from across the sea from time to time. Beggars. Scum, mostly, desperately in search of food. When I noticed you amongst the leaves just now, I expected you to be …" He paused awkwardly, considering his words and position.

"You expected me to be one of them," I interjected.

Mr Gibbs hesitated, his shy manner urging him to change the subject as quickly as humanly possible.

"You say you spent the entire night here, sir?" he asked.

In truth, I couldn't remember if I had informed the man of that or not, nor could I recall exactly where I was. Everything appeared so different in the daylight, seemingly harmless. I made the decision to confide in the man. I told him of the voices I had heard, the vast expanse of snow, and the nearby house I had stumbled upon. I told him about the residents inside and the engulfing flames that consumed the inner rooms, claiming the souls from within.

All the while, Gibbs never said a word. He simply stood by, his expression absent, lingering on every word said, before finally asking for a simple clarification.

"A house, you say, sir?" He removed his weight from the tree, his hand caressing his beard. "Where?"

I cast a look over my shoulder. "Well, I believe it was in that direction," I responded, loosely pointing the way.

Seemingly confused, Mr Gibbs steered his sight beyond the army of trees, squinting his eyes until they were nothing more than narrow slits, as he hurriedly advanced ahead.

"Show me," he requested.

I took the lead, guiding the way. However, as we progressed, I was ashamed to say my sense of direction quickly became confused. I was lost, disoriented. Each passing tree blurred my recollection of the path, leaving me uncertain of the way.

Eventually, the denseness began to clear, revealing a small patch of green marred by overgrown, pestilent brambles and alder bushes. In the midst of the tangled mess, a small building stood at its centre. I approached cautiously as countless questions swirled inside my head. At first glance, it bore no resemblance to the house I had witnessed at all, not in the slightest. It appeared to be abandoned and neglected, a worker's cottage from years past, no less. Its door arch stood bare, its walls crumbling to the point it could barely stand. Indeed, it seemed that the faintest gust could see it flat, toppled to the ground.

"Is this the place you mentioned, sir?" Gibbs asked me, stepping to one side and observing me closely on approach.

Stuck in some kind of trance, I studied the stones for a moment longer, confusion clouding my memory as I swiftly turned to face him.

"No," I answered with certainty. "It is not." I retraced my steps to where Gibbs waited. "There must be another house nearby," I continued. "We must have overlooked it. Somewhere in that direction, perhaps." I pointed aimlessly.

Mr Gibbs subtly shook his head. "Not possible."

"Not possible?" I pressed him. "Why?"

"Because," he explained, "this hovel you see is all there ever has been around these parts. There's none other. I should know. If you did happen to stumble across a house last night, it would most certainly have been this one."

My attention was drawn back to the sorrowful shape as I scanned from one small window to another. Long vines and branches had taken over the house. The wall's stone was partially covered in a thick, damp moss, showing no signs of the previous night's events. There was no evidence of fire, no signs of damage, no sign of struggle. I drew in a long, profound breath, hoping to catch a hint of lingering smoke. Yet there was none. Instead, the earthy aroma of the soil filled my lungs. The piney scent of trees permeated the air, carried by a gentle breeze, while the cheerful chirping of crossbills sang faintly from their nests above.

I placed my head in my palms, running my fingers through my hair as I visualised the scene that had only hours ago unfolded before my very eyes: the grand house lit up, filled with laughter and music; the man who bore a striking resemblance to my own, staring vacantly through the blaze, his hair singed away, his flesh melted, consumed by flames; the smell. It all appeared so vivid, so lifelike. How could it possibly be untrue? No, Gibbs must have been mistaken. Of course he was; of course he was. There must have been another dwelling out there somewhere, some place deep within the wood. Somewhere unknown. Somewhere secret, even to him. I had to find it.

A firm hand landed on my shoulder, its touch commanding yet strangely kind. I flinched and raised my head, only to find Mr Gibbs standing beside me. His imposing figure cast a shadow as he spoke.

"Whatever you believe you witnessed here, I shall not pry any further, nor do you need to tell me," he said, his deep voice both soothing and blunt, like a father advising his child.

A tender whisper of the wind twirled and swept across the ground, causing the vines to sway and the underbrush to rustle in an eerie hymn.

"Allow me to accompany you back to the manor, sir," Gibbs generously offered. "I am sure the mistress must be concerned about your whereabouts by now. Let us not trouble her further, hmm? Besides, she would not appreciate our presence here."

I glanced up to him oddly. "Oh," I spoke as his grip loosened on my shoulder, swinging back down to his side. "And why would that be?" I asked.

Gibbs cleared his throat, delaying for a moment, wondering whether to voice his thoughts at all.

"Ah, forgive me, Mr Daily. It is not my place."

"No, I suppose it is not," I replied curtly. "However, any concern for my sister is surely a concern of my own, would you not agree?"

"I …" He pondered the question. "I suppose I do, sir," he replied.

"Then I implore you to tell me," I urged him. "In fact, Mr Gibbs, I insist upon it."

The gruff-looking man wrestled with his thoughts as he grumbled, scratching at the chalky stubble that powdered the base of his neck.

"I forget," he spoke openly. "How long has it been since you arrived back on the island?" he asked, knowing all too well the answer. "Three days, is it?"

"I dare say it has," I replied.

"Then I suppose you might have heard about the young girl who used to live up in that house?"

I subtly nodded, recounting my sister's tale.

"Hmm," he grunted to himself. "She was a nice girl, mostly quiet. She grew very close to Mrs Durose. And your sister, well, she cherished that girl as if she were her own daughter, her own flesh and blood. They were inseparable for a while; a true pair, they were. That was until the girl left, of course. I won't bore you with the details, Mr Daily. I only know what I know."

"And what is it that you know, Mr Gibbs?" I asked him. "And please, be frank."

"Well, I know that your sister hasn't been herself for some time now, ever since the young girl left," he answered, tousling his hair as he began to walk.

"What else?" I encouraged.

"Very little, sir," Gibbs said honestly. He turned his gaze back to the crumbling cottage. "I just know that she wouldn't approve of you being here, and neither would I, for that matter."

"Come now, there must be a reason?" I insisted, my eyes following his.

"So, you don't know, then?" Gibbs asked as though he were savouring the moment.

"For heaven's sake, man, know what?" I snapped.

"That the young girl who once held your sister's heart, the very girl who left this island and abandoned the one person whose sole purpose was only to do good by her, was born within those walls."

Chapter 25

As we returned on our walk to the house, Mr Gibbs told all he knew. The burden of his words was heavy as he spoke. Every now and then he would relax his pace and look back, purely to ensure I was close by. He told me my sister couldn't bear the reminders anymore, that the memories of happier times became unbearable for her over the years. And to rid herself of grief, she instructed that the cottage, the very place where the girl was born, be destroyed. She was adamant it would help her heal, to rid herself of the painful reminders that refused to give her peace.

"She believed that by tearing down the house she could finally forget," Mr. Gibbs explained, his voice marked with empathy.

"And did it?" I asked breathlessly, trying with all my efforts to match his stride.

Mr Gibbs displayed a sideways ogle. "I think, sir, we both know the answer to that."

We followed the sloping path round towards the rear of the house. The morning was grey and dull, casting a solemn hue over the rooftop. The air was heavy with fog as a drizzle started to fall, sprinkling droplets on the frosted leaves while our footsteps were muffled along the ground.

Through the grime that smeared the library windows, the silhouette of my sister could be seen sitting on her chair.

"Mr Gibbs," I questioned, my steps slowing to the point of stopping. "These wanderers you spoke of—who are they?"

Mr Gibbs abruptly halted his stride, the deep lines of his forehead furrowing as his gaze became vacant and distracted. He looked over his shoulder at me. "I believe that this is also something you know already."

"Perhaps," I murmured, fidgeting with the button on my coat. "But since I arrived on the island, I dare say that I haven't seen a soul. Not one, that is, except for yourself, of course."

"And you won't," he said plainly, his expression turned serious. "Not as long as I'm here. Filthy beggars, the lot of them."

"You ensure they are escorted off the island, I've heard?"

Mr Gibbs opened the garden gate, a small picket fence, aged and weathered, and patiently waited for me to pass through.

"I suppose," he breathed out slowly. "I make sure they leave the island, yes. What becomes of them afterwards is not my concern."

I paused for a moment, the sound of rain shattering the silence between us. "They do not head to the nearest town?" I asked him.

"Hah!" Gibbs exclaimed, both shoulders bouncing at the thought. "Oban wouldn't have them, sir. Any poor spotted wandering in those streets is swiftly chased away, and for good reason too. Once you catch one lurking in the alleys, you can be sure that more will follow. No," he agreed with himself and, with his one free hand, gestured for me to pass. "Best to have them gone."

I entered the garden, allowing the small picket gate to softly creak shut behind me. I turned back, observing Mr Gibbs, who in turn offered me the kindest smile, his eyes crinkling at the corners.

"Don't let it trouble you, Mr Daily," he tried to reassure me, bearing his weight to the gate. "These days, the most I encounter is the occasional body here and there. Any living souls that wash up on our shores are swiftly turned away. However, do find comfort, most of them never make it to land—a detail that I have managed to keep from your sister."

In that very moment, my mind drifted back to Elphin, picturing the lifeless bodies scattered far across the farmlands, each one starved, their limbs as brittle as dried-up branches. The realisation that the same fate awaited them on Lismore left me with a sinking feeling, a sensation I could not shake.

A sudden sense of light-headedness washed over me.

"Is everything okay, sir?" Gibbs asked, pushing himself off the gate with a look of slight confusion on his face.

"Yes," I replied groggily, struggling to hold my balance. "I'm afraid I too faced similar circumstances before arriving here. The memories of what occurred are … How should I say this—still quite vivid."

"Ah," he acknowledged and, without further concern, leant back against the gate. He blew on his hands before rubbing them together for warmth. "Yes, I had heard about what happened."

I regarded the man with a firm gaze, unsure by what he meant.

Gibbs's lips curled at one corner. "News travels fast, Mr Daily, even in these parts. Gossip eventually finds its way to us, nonetheless. Yes, I had heard about the matters in Elphin. Most unfortunate turn of events, I must say."

I glanced up at the library window, noticing Meredith was still deeply absorbed in her book.

"Does my sister know of such matters?" I asked him.

"Bah." Gibbs waved his hand dismissively. "The mistress won't so much as leave the island, let alone pay attention to any gossip that finally reaches her door. She has no interest in such matters."

A fleeting sense of relief coursed over me.

"No," Gibbs continued. "Whatever you may be concealing from her, I assure you it's quite safe. For now, at least. She will hear nothing from me. I give you my word on that."

"Then I am very much obliged to you," I replied, acknowledging the man with a slight nod of my head, a gesture Gibbs too promptly returned, his expression strangely reflecting a sense of mutual respect. Maybe it was even trust I saw in his eyes.

Mr Gibbs raised the collar of his coat and glanced towards the clouds. "Looks like another day of it," he grumbled, catching a few spots of rain in his hand. "Get yourself indoors and out of the cold, sir. Perhaps some rest. You don't appear all that well."

Without another word said, I left Mr Gibbs on the path and swiftly made my way to the main hall of the house. Ascending the stairs as quickly as my legs would allow, I locked myself inside the shelter of my room. Perched at the edge of the bed, unmoving, I remained alone with only my thoughts for the remainder of the day.

Later that night, the distant sound of Meredith's piano playing travelled from the floors below, touring the house with its saddened tone and reigniting my memories of the previous night. I could not find myself to leave the room again until morning.

Chapter 26

18TH March 1847

A piercing scream jolted me awake at the break of dawn. The agonising sound, brimming with despair, resounded from below, filling the house with an air of grief.

Without a delay did I find myself sprung up from the bed, my attire unchanged since the day before, and dashing out of the room in a panic, racing down the hall. I sprinted with all my might, my shoulders colliding with the walls at each turn, stumbling over the crumpled rug that snagged about my feet. Rushing towards the staircase, I clutched the railing tightly as my body swayed, climbing down the first few steps, my heart all the while thumping in my ears.

At the bottom of the staircase, my attention was quickly drawn to the open door. The bright morning light streamed into the large hallway, revealing a figure that bore a striking resemblance to Mr Gibbs, standing quietly at the threshold, a document of some form held firmly in his hand.

At his feet, Meredith sat huddled on the untidy tiles, her body wracked with convulsive sobs. Her head was bowed, her fists clenched tightly against her face, partly obscured by the cascade of her long flowing hair. Another piercing scream tore from her lips, her voice breaking under the burden. Without pause, I swiftly knelt beside her, tenderly attempting to ease her hands away from her face.

"Meredith, what is wrong?" I asked, gripping at her wrists, her skin becoming as white as snow.

Meredith released another harrowing cry. “No!” she howled, pushing back against my touch with a frightening force. Her voice pierced my ears. “No, no, no, no, no!” she wailed. The sounds were so filled with pain that I was sure her heart was breaking.

Still holding on to Meredith as she wrestled, I glanced up at the familiar face in the doorway. Mr Gibbs stood there plainly, his imposing figure creating a backlit silhouette against the morning light as he awkwardly cleared his throat.

“What have you done to her?” I demanded, losing my grip on Meredith as she continued to thrash for freedom, pounding her fists against her knees.

Mr Gibbs placed a calming hand over his chest. “Me?” His eyes widened defensively. “I assure you, I am not the cause of your sister’s distress. She has received some distressing news, sir.”

“Nooo!” Meredith’s scream echoed to the rooftop.

“News?” I barely managed to speak, my voice muffled by her endless sobbing, as I caught sight of the letter in Gibbs’s hand. “What news is this?”

Gibbs glanced down at the small, crumpled envelope gripped between his fingers. Despite its slightly wrinkled appearance, it was evident the seal had not been broken.

“I tried to convince her to open it, sir, but she wouldn’t listen to me. When I insisted that she take it, well, she blank right refused. I had no choice but to tell. I thought it was the right thing to do. I had heard about the events earlier this morning.”

Meredith pushed me away with force, curling into a heap on her side. Her legs furiously kicked the empty space around her.

“This morning?” I climbed to my feet. “Events? What are you saying, Gibbs?”

The large man finally crossed the threshold, bowing cautiously to avoid hitting his head, and ushered in the blinding light that had been held at bay, flooding it into the hallway. He extended his hand, the envelope wedged between his thumb and finger. “I believe,” he kept calm, “it is only appropriate that you read this yourself, sir.”

I glanced at the envelope then up to Gibbs. He nodded, urging me to take it.

Grabbing the letter, the seal snapped cleanly as I opened it, revealing the papers inside. For a moment, even the cries of my sibling and the impatient breathing of Mr Gibbs faded into the background.

“Well?” Gibbs asked, the tension clear in his neck.

I uttered not a word, nor did I need to. The expression on my face must have said it all. The colour drained from my complexion.

"So, it is true then," Gibbs remarked, stepping back until he found himself hard up against the wall.

On the floor, Meredith started to crawl towards the nearest bench beside the stairwell. Her cries had begun to fade, but the pain she endured could not be stopped in every breath she took.

Helping her to her feet, I guided Meredith to the bench, where I knelt before her. Our eyes met briefly, exchanging a flicker of glances. After several silent exchanges, I decided it was time to speak.

"My dear." I held her hands firmly. She clung to me, her fingers intertwined with mine as if her very existence depended on it.

"Oh, Peter," she sobbed. "It can't be true, can it?" Her tear-filled eyes beseeched me. "Please tell me that the words in that letter hold no truth, that what you're about to say shall spare my heart from shattering."

For a moment, I could only lose myself in those deep, unblinking eyes of hers. They were so wide and heartfelt I felt as if I could get lost in them, eyes so pure they revealed her soul. I squeezed her hand again, attempting to steady myself.

"My dear Meredith," I began, the words catching in my throat. "I am … sorry."

"No," she whispered with a violent shake of her head. "I cannot believe it. I won't."

"Then allow me to say the words, nevertheless," I pleaded, drawing closer to her as the clock in the corner began to strike the hour.

Meredith took a deep, shuddering breath, struggling to hold back her emotion, her pain.

She nodded.

"The message has come from Ireland," I informed her gravely. "I fear the news it bears is not of a joyful nature."

Meredith's hand grew limp in mine, her eyes turning even more distant with each passing word.

"It can't be," she murmured to herself.

"I'm afraid it is, my dear," I answered, guiding her hand to my cheek. "Your son, Jacob, is dead."

Chapter 27

Les's voice boomed within the small office, his body jumping to attention. "Dead?" he barked, nearly launching himself out of his seat. "What happened to him?" he asked anxiously.

Roderick's eyes rose from the documents, his expression stained with a blatant glare of irritation as he peered over the rim of his glasses, which hung low on his nose. "Well," he grumbled, "if you keep your trap shut for a moment and listen, you'll find out, won't you?"

Chapter 28

In an instant, Meredith sprang to her feet, wrenching herself free from my grasp. A pained cry escaped her lips, somewhat muffled as she covered her mouth with both hands.

"Lies!" she screamed, shooting me an angry glance. She paced back and forth, her complexion unnaturally pale. "All of it. Nothing but dreadful, unforgivable lies, Peter. Why, how could you, of all people? How dare you utter such things."

"Meredith," I began, observing her closely.

"No! I will not hear it," she yelled, cutting me off abruptly. Her face flushed with anger. The usual kindness she held was replaced, torn by tears that streaked her rosy cheeks. "I refuse to listen. I won't. They are nothing but cruel words. Heartless, cruel words. Nothing more."

"I'm afraid it is true," I insisted, extending my arm and offering her the letter to read for herself. "It is all here," I explained gently. "Plainly written, as clear as day. Death by gunshot."

Meredith recoiled from the letter, refusing to touch it or even entertain the idea of reading it. Her expression twisted into a bitter scowl you could hang meat from. She remained silent for a while, allowing her irritation to simmer at the grim possibilities regarding her only son.

In a swift motion, she stormed towards the door, pushing me aside as she ventured out into the garden, leaving behind a discarded shoe that had slipped from her foot.

"Ah, most unfortunate," piped up Gibbs, making his presence known from the corner. "He was quite an odd lad, I'll give you that.

Reserved, you might say. Always lost daydreamin' in his own thoughts. But there was an undeniable spark of brilliance in him."

Gibbs leant against the worn stair rail, his gaze drifting. "Still, he didn't deserve the end he got," he said, a touch of melancholy in his voice. "And the poor mistress," he continued. "Losing a loved one is never easy, especially when it's your own kin." He snapped from his daze, his attention suddenly drawn to me. "Might the letter provide some assurance about his final moments, sir? I'm certain it would bring comfort to your sister to know that the young master did not suffer greatly before his end."

From beyond the open door, the morning darkened, casting a gloom across the garden that crept into the threshold of the house.

"The boy was shot at close range," I remarked, pointing at the letter. "That's what it says here."

Mr Gibbs briefly planted a hand to his head and rubbed his temple. "Dear god," he muttered with a look of eager enquiry. "So the shot was intentional?"

"What gunshot is not?" I remarked. "I know of no one who raises a pistol without the intent to end another's life. Nonetheless, I agree. The entire affair is truly dreadful."

"Dreadful indeed it is, sir," agreed Gibbs. "Does the letter reveal more?" he asked, just as pressing as before.

"It does," I replied wearily as I began to read aloud. "It states here that he spent his final days in Cork, where he owned some land. During a visit to his property, he was struck down by one of his former tenants. Likely some farmer, no doubt."

"And with no apparent motive, sir?" Gibbs asked.

I recalled my last encounter with Jacob at The Castle Tavern. "I do remember him mentioning during our brief meeting that he hadn't received any payment from his tenants for several months. He was growing tired of waiting, weary of their excuses. So he decided to take matters into his own hands and evict the little squatters himself. The farmers must have resisted, and one thing led to another. Poor Jacob," I mused. "He was never a very physically strong lad. Strong-willed, yes, but not imposing. I suspect he never stood a chance. He was quite unlike his father in that regard."

"But, sir," Gibbs interjected with concern, "this doesn't make sense. Correct me if I'm wrong, but how could a man of the land, a simple farmer, obtain such a weapon? Many can't even afford to put clothes on their backs or food on their tables, let alone own a pistol—especially since the blight struck. I've seen their dire condition firsthand. There must be some mistake."

"There is no mistake, Gibbs," I assured him, straightening the letter with a firm hand. "According to this, the culprit stole the weapon several nights prior from a local officer—a young soldier, to be precise. It seems the young man had indulged a little too much ale and woke up the next morning unaware that his pistol was missing. By the time he realised, he chose not to report it, likely to spare himself the embarrassment. Losing a weapon so carelessly carries severe consequences. Perhaps he thought he'd take his chances. Regardless, the brute has been punished for his carelessness, and the shooter has been apprehended in Cork. He awaits transfer to Limerick for trial, where he will face the consequences of his crime."

"Then it will surely be the noose for him, sir," replied Gibbs, mimicking the act of tightening a noose around his neck, his expression reflecting a sense of choking.

"Let us hope so, Mr Gibbs," I replied. "Let us hope."

Gibbs took a step closer, his expression intense. "And does the letter mention anything about the young master's body, sir? Or what has become of it, for that matter?" Gibbs asked.

I quickly scanned the papers, my eyes darting across the words. "It states here that Jacob's body and all his earthly belongings will … Will …"

"Yes, sir?" Gibbs pressed, leaning in. "Will what?"

"Will be," I hesitated, my eyes lifting from the page, "transported here, to Lismore, it seems. He is set to depart on his final journey from Cork no later than Monday."

Mr Gibbs straightened his posture, squaring his broad shoulders. With one hand, he counted down on his fingers, repeating the motion several times before finally voicing his thoughts.

"Are you absolutely certain of that, sir?" he asked, his troubled gaze fixed on me. "I must say, the writer of such a letter must have been gravely misinformed."

"Misinformed?" I echoed, still partially distracted. "And what makes you think so?"

"Well, considering that Monday was two days ago, sir," he replied, his expression deepening.

"Was it truly?" I asked, worry creeping in as I realised I had lost track of the days.

"Indeed it was, sir," said Gibbs confidently. "In fact, I believe it was the very day of your arrival."

Overwhelmed by disbelief, I collapsed into the nearest seat only to spring back up again, grabbing Gibbs by his upper arms and shaking him urgently.

"How much time?" I asked, my eyes wide with desperation.

"Uh, time, sir?"

"How long will it take them to reach the island from Cork?" I pressed, my mind racing.

Mr Gibbs took a moment to consider. Having travelled to Ireland only once in his lifetime, he hazarded a guess, compelled by my urgent questioning.

"One might estimate several days, sir, perhaps a day longer assuming that the journey to the harbour went as planned and that the storm hasn't slowed them down."

For a brief second, I couldn't help but feel a surge of relief wash over me. "Then we still have time," I murmured, the situation still looming over me. "We must prepare for the arrival and ensure everything is handled properly."

My grip on Gibbs relaxed, and I began to pace the room.

"Time is running out," I muttered, my gaze fixed on the floor. Suddenly, I turned to him, a plan written on my face. "Gibbs, we cannot afford to waste any more time. We must find her," I insisted. The thought of her seeing her son's casket arrive on the shore so soon after learning of his fate would be unbearable. Only God knew how she would react to such a devastating sight.

The tall man agreed with a stern nod. "Very good, sir. This way!" Gibbs walked ahead, already stepping out of the house. "However, may I suggest we divide our search?"

"Divide?" I asked, trailing closely behind him.

"Aye, we would cover more ground, sir, and thus locate your sister's whereabouts more quickly," he explained.

"Yes!" I exclaimed. "Yes. Splendid idea!"

"Very well, sir," Gibbs acknowledged, somewhat pleased with his quick thinking. "I will check the old settlement and the loch. The terrain can be quite boggy in those parts. Might I suggest that you search the nearby woodland and the cliffs to the south? The mistress often walks those paths, so it's highly likely you'll find her along the way."

As I was about to agree, a chilling presence crept over me, a force that stopped me in my tracks and threatened to hold me still. It was a sensation I dreaded, yet one I had felt before—one that could bring me to my knees, as if a wicked beast had taken residence within the depths of my gut.

An agonising hunger gnawed at my insides, consuming me with its relentless torment. I felt myself wilting, drained of strength, my legs faltering beneath me in an unexpected weakness. Desperate, I clung to the man I had been shadowing in sheer hope of seeking his aid, as if he held the key to saving me.

Gibbs turned sharply, his piercing eyes cutting through the shadows on his face. It was clear that an air of suspicion dripped from his gaze, as if he too sensed the forces that riddled within me, his concern only magnified by the height from which he peered.

"Mr Daily, I must advise you to stay indoors," he said, his hand swiftly slipping under my elbow to offer support. "Your sister did mention your health of late. And although our encounters have been brief, I sensed from our initial meeting that you were not well. Please," Gibbs insisted, gesturing back to the door, "allow me to see you back indoors, sir. Regain your strength. Some rest and something hot to drink might do you a world of good."

Maybe the man had a point. Perhaps rest was exactly what I needed. But that wasn't the moment for it. Not then. Not when Meredith was still out there, wandering the island in her vulnerable state. Who knew what could have befallen her? After all, faced with such dreadful news, one might feel compelled to take matters into their own hands, regardless of the unwise consequences.

I wasn't about to sit idly and wait during such a critical time. There was no choice. I had to find her—before it was too late.

"Just give me a moment," I asked him, shutting my eyes tightly, longing for the sensation to pass. "You should go," I advised. "Search for her. I'll be right behind you, just a few steps away."

The burly man hesitated, unsure about leaving me alone at the doorstep. "I don't think that would be wise, sir. You must—"

"I will manage," I grumbled, leaning heavily against the doorframe and forcing a smile on my face. "I just need a moment, a chance to catch my breath."

Mr Gibbs stepped onto the path but glanced back at me. "Are you certain?"

I nodded through the pain.

"Find her, Gibbs."

"Very well, sir." He complied, distancing himself farther as he spoke. "And if I find her in distress?"

I gritted my teeth, trying to conceal the discomfort in my voice. “Say nothing, Gibbs. Nothing to further upset her. Just bring her back to the house. Ensure she doesn’t leave. If I don’t find her along the cliffs, I’ll find my way back here, hoping you’ve safely returned with her.”

“And what if we both fail to locate her whereabouts?” Gibbs dared to ask.

“Then it is likely she will behave in a manner unlike herself and will perish from a broken heart.”

Chapter 29

As I watched Mr Gibbs traipse along the garden path, passing through the gate and disappearing into the rolling green, his figure soon vanished amidst the shrubs that lined the hillside.

For a while, I remained rooted to my spot, bound by discomfort. Despite my eagerness to hurry, to dart across the garden with my arms outstretched like spears, I dreaded the consequences of any sudden movement. I feared collapsing onto the ground, wailing in agony at the force coursing through my core, my stomach in knots, and in despair of having no one to heed my call. I would be alone—alone with every breath becoming a struggle, every heartbeat pounding in my ears as a reminder that no help was to come.

As I raised my head, pulling my chin away from my chest, I glanced out into the garden, questioning whether what followed was a figment of my imagination. Straining my ears, I tilted my head upwards.

A faint voice reached me, carried by the morning breeze. It uttered no discernible words but produced a mournful wail that, at first, seemed to drift from a distance. Without a doubt, it was the sound of grief.

Lost in my thoughts, I soon found myself wandering along the garden path without realising it. The searing pain that had once threatened to bring me to my knees had faded, replaced by a growing need to walk. With measured steps, I approached the gate and lifted the latch.

I listened hard.

"Meredith!" I yelled as loudly as I could, though my exhausted voice seemed to falter.

Still the cries went on.

As I soon approached the woodland, a sense of unease settled over me like a heavy fog. The screeching gate from behind somehow indicated a point of no return as if the world I knew had faded into the background.

With little option, I pressed on, my footsteps muffled by the thick undergrowth. The branches were gnarled and twisted, determined to block my way. Each step was a battle, as if the very forest itself conspired to keep whatever it hid at bay.

As I walked deeper, the surroundings grew heavier. The covering of trees cast a deep shade, suffocating the sunlight. Shadows seemed to dance and swirl around me, whispering secrets I couldn't decipher, could not understand.

I called out for Meredith, my voice echoing through the stillness. Instead of reaching her, my words seemed to dissipate, stolen by the breathlessness that gripped me.

Exhausted, I sought rest upon a decaying tree stump covered in moss. I sank down, my limbs trembling. The air grew colder, and a chill crawled down my spine, sending shivers through my body. I felt as though unseen eyes watched me from the darkest places, their gaze filled with curiosity.

I struggled to regain my stance, and as I did, the unmistakable sound of hurried footsteps stomped from somewhere beyond a dense thicket. They raced along the forest floor, each step blending seamlessly with the next, accompanied by the rustle of leaves and the recognisable squelch of mud.

"Meredith?" I called out once more as the footsteps swiftly passed me by. "It is only I, your brother. Please, don't run away."

With no time to waste, I ran, relying solely on the footsteps to guide me. The sobbing grew louder, each cry echoing in all directions. With every step, nature seemed to resist me; overgrown branches reached out, snagging my clothes and scratching my skin. Roots emerged from the ground, threatening to trip me and send me sprawling onto the forest floor. Yet I did not fall. Instead, I pushed onwards, feeling my legs grow numb and my chest tighten as each laboured breath clouded my vision ahead.

With a frustrated grunt, I forced my way through a barrier of drooping foliage, using both arms to clear a path. At last, I emerged in a spacious clearing of lush, short grass, leaving the denseness of the woodland behind me.

The sight that met my eyes was bleak: a blanket of dark clouds merging seamlessly with the grey expanse of an endless sea. Violent waves crashed and churned against the rugged rocks below. With cautious steps, I inched closer to the ledge, my heart heavy with worry for my sister's safety, silently hoping she had not ventured too close to the edge. However, my worry was soon distracted. In the midst of it all, my gaze locked onto a lone figure in the distance that could only belong to her. Standing at the elevated edge of the land, she appeared both fragile and lost, swallowed by the vast gloom that surrounded her.

It was at that moment I became aware that the cries I once heard had seemed to drift away, replaced only by the sound of the wind rustling through the grass and the distant tune of white foaming waves that effortlessly climbed the cliffside.

I set forth, careful not to startle her. Step by step, I advanced along the cliffs, navigating the wet and boggy terrain. I trod carefully, my gaze fixed solely on her.

Meredith stood frozen at the ledge, her back turned to me as she gazed out at the endless ocean. The wind swept over the stony terrain, playfully teasing her dress into a wild flutter and sending her fiery red hair into a lively dance.

She took a step closer to the edge, her toes delicately hovering over the sudden drop.

"Stop!" I shouted, my hand instinctively reaching out as if to physically halt her.

Meredith abruptly froze, her body as still as a statue. Her stillness was so striking that I wondered if my voice had even reached her at all. Unmoved by my presence, she appeared untouched, as if I was merely a distant whisper of conscience brushing against her ear.

"My dear," I spoke, unable to stop the tremor in my voice. "Please step away from the edge."

With each step, I moved more slowly than the last, my movements becoming increasingly delicate as I approached the incline.

"What you have heard today is nothing short of a tragedy," I assured her. "Truly dreadful. No one can deny you that. But whatever thoughts are crossing your mind, I implore you to reconsider. We must think of Jacob now, Meredith. We must think of your boy. His destiny lies in returning to the island. I never wished to tell this now, not like this, yet you have given me no choice. Tell me, what purpose does it serve for your only child to return home if his mother has gone from this life?"

Meredith did not respond but instead appeared to sway in sequence with the passing gust.

"Please, I beg you," I beseeched her, extending my arm with outstretched fingers. "Come. Take my hand," I requested bluntly. "I shall escort you back to the house. We shall talk more then."

The sound of another triumphant wave crashed against the cliffside. Its roar was so loud the earth seemed to shudder beneath us.

Meredith tilted her head to the sky, taking view of the endless pallet of grey.

I asked her, "Will you not speak, then?"

For a brief time, it seemed as though she might have yielded to my plea. Her body continued to sway, caught between the force of the wind and the grief raging within her. But just as quickly as the spark of reasoning appeared, it faded, leaving behind a veil of doubt.

"I ... I feel so ... Cold," she whispered, her voice barely heard amidst the surging waves. "There is nothing left."

Her words lingered, intertwining with the salty mist that clung to our skin.

Drawing closer, I noticed that her dress clung to her frame. The fabric was torn and tattered, drenched as if she had just emerged from the very depths of the ocean. Droplets of water fell from the cuffs of her wrists, joining the dampened hem of her gown. Yet it hadn't rained since she left the house earlier that morning, not so much as a drizzle. Not even once.

The skin on her neck and shoulders appeared alarmingly pale, even paler than before, sickly, resembling the colour of candle wax. She seemed frozen, thoroughly soaked to the core.

Meredith's line of sight seemed to shift from the clouds down to the perilous rocks below, her right heel slightly lifted as if she was preparing for the final step.

"Wait!" I yelled again, my voice accompanied by an unfamiliar sound I had never heard before. I dared not move, not so much as a muscle. "Do not do this," I begged her. "A fall from this height would see the end of you. If the rocks do not claim you, the sea's current shall. There would be no return for you, Meredith. No mercy. Do you not understand?"

Meredith halted as if the words I spoke finally managed to reach her, persuading her to consider the foolishness she was about to endure. As she listened, the sole of her foot stepped back onto the dry earth. It was then I noticed both her feet were bare, a detail that had somehow eluded me until that very moment. Her other shoe must have been lost along her hurried path from the house, lost to the mud or perhaps flown from her foot as she ran. Yet in that moment, it felt to matter little as she gradually turned to face me.

Meredith pivoted on the spot, her body twisting as her long neck followed, revealing the horror on her face.

My heart stopped; its beat ceased. Dead. Lifeless. The rhythm was only slightly more than the loved one I beheld.

My sister, as still as ever, stared down at me from the ridge. Her expression was so gaunt that the thought occurred to me it may not have been her at all. Her face was vile and plump, swollen. Her skin was a ghostly white marred by unsightly purple blotches rooted beneath her flesh. The deepest shade of blue nestled on her lips. A prominent gash trailed from her neck, following the groove of her jawline and tapering off at the dimple of her chin. The wound seemed raw and gaping, widening with the rise and fall of her chest. Yet it was her eyes above all else that seized my gaze, her eyes that would haunt me in my dreams. Her eyes would remain with me for all time. Gone was their beauty, their gleam. They were like twin orbs that once cast a spell upon all who dared to gaze upon them. Gone too was their kindness, their warmth that once came from within, leaving behind a void filled only with the deepest shade of red—eyes brimming with blood.

I gasped, unable to control the fright in my voice. "What … What have you done?" My words faltered as I witnessed a peculiar smile spread wide across her face, a sinister curve of her lips. It was unlike any smile I had ever seen from her before. It was a smile devoid of sanity, an inhuman expression that spoke only of darkness.

I stood frozen, my mind grappling to make sense of the unsettling sight that loomed before my eyes. Meredith's head snapped back, her eyes fixated on the heavens.

A deafening rumble drummed through the air as if the sky itself had held its breath for far too long. What unfolded next I couldn't begin to explain, as a deathly stillness seized the land. The once strong wind ceased its fury, and the swaying grass froze in mid-motion with it. High above, a congregation of clouds hung motionless, trapped in a state of suspension.

Meredith's stare slowly wandered back to me. It was as if her soul had retreated from those eyes of hers, leaving behind an empty vessel. She no longer smiled but studied me plainly. And without any further reasoning, without any warning, Meredith dropped backwards, her body descending to the rocks.

A horrifying gasp wrestled past my lips, choked by my own disbelief. Time seemed to stretch as her figure disappeared from view, growing smaller and smaller, swallowed by what lay at the surface.

I rushed to the edge, fell to my front, and peered down at the jagged rocks and clashing waves, hoping to catch a glimpse of her. But there was nothing to be seen. Nothing. There was only the haunting memory of her departure, the final glimpse of her face as she fell, and the heartache that dwelled within me.

A roar again drummed overhead. As I remained hunched over the ledge, time seemed to slip away from me, engulfed in a haze of sorrow. Tears streamed down my face as I cried out for her, my sobs carried away by the wind's howl. Despite my grief, I could not tear my gaze away from the ocean below, its violent form cruelly concealing her lifeless body lost amidst the whirling depths.

She was truly gone.

"Peter?" a voice called out from behind.

I turned my head, scrambling to rise from the ground.

There, appearing on the grass where the incline smoothed to level, Meredith stood watching.

As you can imagine, I was in disbelief, shock, unable to trust my own eyes. Doubt lingered as I questioned the figure who awaited my response. However, there she stood all the same, emanating an aura I thought I would never see again. Her cheeks, slightly mottled and flushed, bore the traces of tears shed. Her appearance reflected weariness, burdened by her sadness. Yet despite it all, she presented herself as remarkably composed, radiating good health, in fact.

A profound breath escaped me, as if releasing a torrent of words, thoughts, and feelings all at once.

The same could not be said for her.

Meredith regarded me with nothing more than the oddest glance, her enquiry direct. "What were you doing just then?" she asked, her expression demanding a prompt answer. No nonsense. "Why were you playing in the dirt?"

My voice caught in my throat, leaving me utterly speechless. I struggled to find the words to explain. How could I?

"I heard you calling from the lake," Meredith continued, her tone laced with concern. "I found myself having to dash all the way here. What on earth is the matter with you?"

With little hesitation, I attempted to explain it all, everything, leaving no detail unmentioned. I recounted my journey from the house, the voice that led me through the woodland and towards the spot where

I stood. But as I spoke of discovering her on the ledge and the actions she had taken, Meredith showed little restraint in voicing her objection.

She remarked with a blunt tone. "Do you truly believe I am so reckless?" She clucked disapprovingly. "It is a perilous plunge, one that would spell the end for anyone foolish enough to take it."

I attempted to elaborate further, to make her comprehend, but she refused to listen. She refused to hear me.

"Enough of this, Peter," she demanded. "I am not in the mood for you. Not today."

With much effort, I held back my frustration, biting my tongue. There was no reasoning with her, not at that moment. Not then. Not after all she had been through, regardless of my woes.

"We should return to the house," she proposed, breaking the silence between us. "However, I would prefer to walk alone."

I nodded. "Very well, of course."

Her brow deepened some. "I was not seeking your permission, Peter," she replied.

The heavens growled once more, their rumble trembling across the horizon of raw bone cloud, as if in agreement with her tone.

"I will see you at the house, then," Meredith said, her voice absent of warmth as she retraced her steps in the direction of the woodland. "I would not take too long," she called out, her voice trailing behind her. "The clouds, they seem awfully grey."

Only then did the first drop of rain fall.

Chapter 30

21ST March 1847

Several days passed before Meredith found the strength to emerge from her chambers—three days and four nights, to be precise. Throughout that time, she chose to seclude herself, ensuring that even I, her own brother, respected her need for privacy. She spoke not a word during that time. And like most grieving women, Meredith sought comfort in the embrace of an armchair which stood at the foot of her bed, cocooned in her son's thick woolen blanket lazily draped over her shoulders, her face entranced by the flames of the fire at her feet, her son's image perfectly preserved in her mind's eye. For a time, the world outside her door became a distant one and, by no means, equally unimportant, as if it belonged to an entirely different reality.

Time seemed to stand still within those four walls as time, may I remind you, often does when one is consumed by grief. During those long days, memories of her son haunted her every waking moment. His joyful laughter and smile filled the corners of her mind. One might go as far as to suggest she clung desperately to the memories she had left, afraid that if she let go, she would lose the last traces of him forever, gone with the distance of time. She would not sleep, nor would she eat, not so much as a morsel, regardless of what dish was placed outside her door.

It was a habit I found myself subjected to. Perhaps it was out of guilt for the sibling who had already lost so much, a way for me to sense what she sensed, feel what she felt. Or perhaps it was simply nothing more than a way for me to deal with my own sense of loss, a way for me to overcome the absence of a nephew.

As each morning gradually settled into the late afternoon, it came as no surprise that Mr Gibbs would, without any instruction from me, find himself calling at the house unannounced as he had done for so many years past. However, his unexpected visits posed little inconvenience; instead, they provided me with an opportunity for brief conversation, regardless of what that conversation might have been.

Mr Gibbs was indeed a man of many words, kind and courteous as he was, though not in any sense a refined fellow. Nor was he a man of the world. He spent much of his time at the house talking mainly of his life on the island. His interests were limited to such things as fishing and hunting the local game, to which he never failed to personally deliver his finest kill, wild hares mostly. Their scruffy fur and long bushy ears were matted with blood as he carelessly dropped them on the counter. "An island delicacy," or so he proudly stated.

Like clockwork, he would perch himself on the same old stool which stood beside an old, rusty stove, located in the far corner of the kitchen. There he would remain for several hours, content with a hot tea in one hand and a toasting fork in the other as he hovered a thick slice of bread over the stove and waited for the chill to escape him. It was only after he had slurped the very last dregs of his drink that Gibbs diverted whatever conversation was at play to the well-being of his mourning employer before donning his hat and casually making his leave, his boots ringing out down the corridor.

As the hours grew late on those lonely nights, and with little to do, I found myself wandering the house, often finding myself alone in the library, writing at my grandfather's desk. Why, I am not sure. I suppose the scratching of the quill on parchment and the scent of aged books surrounding me provided a faint sense of comfort, a fleeting distraction from the events that had unfolded over the previous days. One might say that the library had become my refuge, a sanctuary where I could retreat from the misery that engulfed the upper level of the household. A place to escape it all.

In the quiet stillness of the night, I poured my emotions onto the paper before me, penning words that attempted to capture all that troubled me. As the ink flowed and the words took shape, for a brief time, I found myself almost forgetting, my worries dwindling away like the dimming wick of a candle, petering out, lost in the depths of the written word.

By the time I retired to the confines of my chamber, ensuring that the doors of the house were securely bolted and the windows shut firmly in their place, the moon would already have reached its highest. The bed curtains were tightly drawn, leaving no gap for even the slightest glimpse of light. Exhausted from worry, my head would sink heavily onto the pillow. For those few nights, I lay there, restless, staring wide-eyed at the ceiling.

The house remained in its silent state, elevating every creak of the floorboards and every whisper of the wind outside. For the longest duration, I felt that time stood still, frozen, as I waited for the hours to pass, for the faintest chime of the standing clock below to strike each quarter, for the darkness to reach its end, and for the spill of dawn to lurk beyond my curtains. Though, I am obliged to tell you that nothing more happened on those long nights. I was not alarmed, not chased from my bed, nor did I bear witness to any scraping or sinister sounds. The room, once consumed by an unsettling stillness, remained just as I remembered—quiet and undisturbed. The only haunting sound that reached my ears was my sister's distant cries, echoing painfully through the night.

Chapter 31

25th March 1847

The funeral took place at a small chapel known to the islanders as St. Moluag's. It was a dreary spectacle of a building for those who beheld it, its white stone walls shrouded by a fine mist and long-forgotten headstones strewn about the confinements of the churchyard. Their tired inscriptions were mostly gone, washed away over time.

It was on that very soil that Jacob's story came to an end. A small gathering of just my sister, Mr Gibbs, and myself made our way across the marshy grass towards the back of the chapel grounds. The family burial plot rested in the farthest corner of the churchyard, a secluded space where many generations of the Daily family had been laid to rest, including Jacob's father, Silas, who had passed some years earlier.

The ground had been prepared in advance, the freshly turned soil ready to welcome its newest occupant. As the coffin was carried from the church to its sacred resting place, the weathered wood creaked under the weight of the deceased, mirroring the burden of grief shared by those who stood by to witness.

As the coffin slowly descended into the earth, I noticed Meredith's glassy gaze fixed on the scene before her. A heavy silence fell over the yard. It was she who was struggling, the memories of her son threatening to overwhelm her. With each scrape of soil on the coffin, the thud against the lid reminded her of farewells that would linger forever.

After the last clump of dirt had been gently scattered on the grave,

Meredith lingered for what seemed like only a fleeting moment, staring at the flowers she had placed upon the mound. She remained silent, in many ways reserved, refraining from uttering any prayers or sharing cherished memories. Whatever thoughts or feelings filled her remained tightly concealed, locked within the depths of her being. Perhaps there was little to express, for no words could ever resurrect her cherished son, no matter how much she wished it so.

Despite my many attempts to console her, reaching out and placing a hand upon her shoulder, Meredith strongly rejected any form of comfort. Instead, she would simply coldly and bitterly shrug off the gesture. The priest, a man with wiry silver hair and a chalky beard of no more than four days' growth, discreetly left his post to return to the inner chambers of the chapel. Meredith shortly followed after him, though her leave was not destined for the church but back towards the woodland: a long and lonely trail for any grieving woman, leading her back towards the empty house.

I turned quickly, eager to escort her back to the house. It would have been unwise to let her walk that path alone, especially under such dreadful circumstances.

As my foot sank into the yielding earth, the moss beneath it felt spongy. I was ready to march after her, ready to call out her name in hopes of stopping her, but a firm grip on my elbow held me back, urging me to reconsider.

"If I may be so bold, sir, I would advise against it," Gibbs said, his voice a low, gravelly whisper. He spoke so quietly that I initially thought he wanted to keep his words private, or perhaps it was a sign of his respect for the sacred ground we stood upon.

His grip on my elbow loosened as I stepped back, returning to his side at the grave. "She needs time, sir," Gibbs continued. "That is all. It would be wise for you to ensure she gets it."

Observing her hurried pace, I watched her soon disappear along the path.

I sighed heavily, turning back towards the headstone that was yet to display our Jacob's name.

"It is all such nasty business, isn't it?" I asked.

"Nasty business indeed, sir," agreed Gibbs. "The nastiest. To lose one's kin is to lose a part of all we live for." His head bowed deeply into his chest as he spoke, as though he was about to recite a prayer. "No," he mumbled. "It is not right for any guardian to outlive their child, to witness the life that they have brought onto the earth only for it to be cruelly taken, snatched away without mercy. It was not God's will to see him from this life, sir. Nasty business, as you so rightly said yourself."

"Yes," I replied, watching the mist drift over the narrow mound of dirt in the churchyard. "I suppose we can be thankful that the boy did not suffer, at least not too much. I was reassured that his death was quite instant and that he felt little pain in his final moments."

"Then we shall be thankful for that, at least, sir," replied Gibbs whilst clasping his hands behind his back. "The boy is now at peace."

I nodded fondly at that remark. "At peace," I repeated. "At peace and reunited with those he cared for most."

Gibbs lifted his chin from his chest and cocked his brow in the most peculiar fashion. "How do you mean?" he bluntly questioned, throwing me the oddest glance.

"The boy's father, Silas," I answered whilst studying the groundsman's expression. "I am correct in saying that the man was also buried here? It is, after all, what is written upon the stone." I pointed ahead.

"He was," answered Gibbs, his hardened stare promptly drifting from my own and settling on the letters boldly chiselled into stone. "What of it?"

"Well, I ..." I pondered for a moment, slightly bewildered by the groundsman's stern yet baffled reaction. "Well, I am simply expressing that if Silas Durose lies beneath the very ground where we stand, surely there can be no other plot more fitting for the resting place of his only son."

"A reunion of sorts, then?" Gibbs said as he knelt and took a handful of soil, which he respectfully scattered over Jacob's resting place.

"Precisely," I assured him.

The old groundsman, still kneeling, did his best to hold his tongue. He merely grunted in response, avoiding any true opinion, until a short burst of laughter escaped him.

"This matter is amusing to you, Gibbs?" I asked.

Gibbs groaned heavily as he pulled himself up to his feet. "No," he answered. "Not at all. In fact, quite the opposite. It is more the sentiment you speak of."

"Sentiment?" I asked rather begrudgingly. "What sentiment? What I was trying to say was—"

"Jacob despised his father, Mr Daily, despised him as much as any man could possibly despise another. He hated Silas to that extent, loathed the very ground he walked on, the very words he preached. You truly mean to tell me that you did not know this?"

"Know?" I snapped, unable to prise my eyes away from the smooth, vacant spot on the headstone. "Of course not."

Mr Gibbs tilted his head in my direction. His stare was hard. His eyes were so narrow that one could easily have mistaken his expression as squinting through the bitter cold.

"Well, there might have been the odd remark," I went on, my mind trying to recall our last meeting. "He suggested that he never felt emotionally involved by his father's passing. That Silas, despite his position, was not a good man. I must admit, I paid little thought to what he had to say at the time. He had been drinking rather heavily—far beyond his means. When a man depends on drink to find his voice, you can rest assured that most of his rambles can be taken with nothing more than a pinch of salt. However, with Jacob, it didn't seem to be the case. There was a difference in him for certain, his words far beyond that of a drunken rambler. There was something deep within, behind his eyes, as he spoke. Unhappiness, one might guess, shrouded by a mask of hatred. Or bravery. One can never really tell. Gibbs, if there is something more, you must tell me."

With a humble gaze, Mr Gibbs stepped back from the graveside, gently brushing against my arm as he made his way towards the winding path of the churchyard. The path was nearly hidden beneath a curtain of overgrown grass and entwined vines cascading from the chapel's walls, almost easy to overlook. Undeterred, he continued on, his raspy breath forming dense, foggy clouds that mingled with the crisp morning air.

In that moment, he slowed, his stride coming to a reluctant halt as he glanced back over his shoulder. "Walk with me," he invited.

SILENCE SURROUNDED US AS WE WALKED, NOT A WORD exchanged between us. The only sound accompanying our brief journey was the gentle scuff of our footsteps faintly disturbing the morning stillness.

As time passed, it became clear that the man beside me had no intention of breaking his silence. This struck me as unusual, for Gibbs was not one to hold back his words for long. Though my acquaintance with him had been brief, it was evident that something troubled him deeply. His usual light-heartedness had given way to a visible unease, casting a shadow over his wrinkled face and revealing a burden he found difficult to share.

The tip of the manor's rooftop appeared beyond the trees.

"The father … He used to beat the boy," Gibbs revealed, stopping to catch his breath against a slanted fence where frost-blackened vines sprawled wildly over the pickets. "Beat him senseless, so he did."

I stood next to him. "My dear Mr Gibbs," I responded wearily, "it is not uncommon for a boy to experience the hard hand of his own father. It after all instils discipline, a form of respect. Why, without a few firm beatings, I doubt I would have become the very man I am today."

Taken aback by my reply, Gibbs shifted his gaze from the frost-bitten field beyond the gate. His fists visibly clenched. "So, I suppose your father was also fond of lashings, was he?"

I grimaced at the word.

"Aye, I thought not," confirmed Gibbs with a stern nod. "Whether it was a sturdy cane, a harsh belt, or any object that could inflict marks upon the flesh. Day after day, I heard the ruckus coming from the house for myself, hearing the screams beyond the young lad's window, the cries from his mother as she could do nothing to stop it. Nothing but beg. She was overpowered, helpless, her only choice to watch that poor young boy be turned black and blue."

A deep weight settled in my chest, leaving me momentarily breathless. "But why?" I finally managed to ask.

"Why does any man inflict cruelty on the weak?" asked Gibbs, his voice filled with uncertainty. "It's a question I wish I had the answer to, sir." He pushed himself off the fence and resumed walking along the path at a more leisurely pace. "Only heaven knows what goes on inside another man's head. In the case of Jacob's father, I suspect he was a rather troubled man. During his final days, your sister confided in me that the island never agreed with her husband. He changed somehow after they arrived, becoming aggressive and resentful. He was no longer the Silas she once knew. But I, for one, can't share that sentiment. To me, he will always be the man he was on the island—a sick character who inflicted his own struggles and pain on his child."

I couldn't believe what I was hearing. "Well, this certainly sheds some light on everything," I said as we walked beneath the sprawling branches.

"Everything?" Gibbs enquired.

"Why, Jacob's lack of loyalty towards his father, or should I say his disloyalty."

"Disloyalty would be an accurate enough description, sir," Gibbs muttered, taking the lead on the narrow, winding trail. "And who could blame the lad? No reasonable person could. Not even his kind-hearted mother. When his father died, I believe it brought much relief to them both, a burden lifted from the hidden scars that covered his body. Jacob wanted to escape the shadow of his father—a shadow that seemed to persist long after his untimely death. The boy worried that it may have eventually become a part of him, you see.

"There were whispers, you know?" Gibbs continued, occasionally glancing over his shoulder. "Whispers that young Jacob was responsible for the clergyman's death. Just rumours, of course—nothing more." He waved his hand dismissively as he walked. "Some say he was poisoned on his deathbed. If that were true, I suppose it would be nothing less than what the old man deserved. I hope you don't mind me speaking so frankly, sir."

I told him I did not. As we walked beneath the final branches, dappled sunlight filtered through the leaves, casting a gentle play of shadows on the path before us.

"To escape the memory of his father, Jacob did what most in his unfortunate position would do."

"And what is that?" I asked, my voice strained as my foot stumbled over a protruding root.

Mr Gibbs twisted his neck as far as it would go, casting a sideways glance, his one visible eye unable to meet mine. "He ran away, of course, packed up whatever he could carry and fled. The young man wanted to make something of himself, I suppose—to prove he was more than the worthless son his father had claimed he was. So, without hesitation, he set his sights on the mainland, leaving his mother behind, along with the humble peasant girl she had taken in as her own.

"Oh, he made sure she was well provided for, that goes without saying, returning to the island once or twice during the warmest months. But he made it a point never to stay long—a few short days here and there, a week at most, before setting off on his travels again."

"And now he shall remain here for all time," I spoke with a heavy heart, "never to step foot off this rock."

"Indeed, sir," said Gibbs, his tone mirroring my own as he ventured onto the expanse ahead, pausing beneath the presence of the house that stretched across the hillcrest—a bold landmark and yet not a glimpse of happiness to spare. "Pardon me for saying, but one might suggest that the whole ordeal is quite ironic."

"Ironic?" I asked, watching as the clouds moved above the house in sequence with the grass below.

"Well," replied Gibbs, chewing on his words. "One cannot help but sympathise with the young man's shortcomings. There is certainly no doubt about that. But if you were to consider the events that led your poor nephew to his end, the troubled childhood, his abusive father he endured, not to mention his longing to leave it all behind, the end of the lad's story is indeed a saddened one."

"I'm afraid I don't understand, Mr Gibbs. Please, do speak bluntly," I replied, mulling over the groundsman's riddle whilst hunching my shoulders from the cold.

"Is it not evidently clear, sir?" answered Gibbs surprisingly, his nose beginning to shine with the darkest shade of purple from the cold. "After all he faced as a child, after all his determination to leave Lismore, here he will remain forever, his only destiny to become one with the earth that surrounds him. Imprisoned by it. Laid to rest for all eternity beside the very man he wished to escape in life."

THE GROUNDSMAN SPOKE TRUTHFULLY—AS TRULY AS ANY MAN could. The very thought of young Jacob rotting there, lying alongside his late father beneath the cold, damp earth, was a chilling thought to bear. Mr Gibbs, despite his unreserved manner, was always honest. He wielded what many would call a gilded tongue, possessing a remarkable skill to shape one's perception of a mournful situation, often making it feel even more grievous.

Yet as we became better acquainted, I could not help but appreciate his peculiar views on life. The gentleman spoke nothing but the truth, living his life with his heart laid bare on his sleeve. A kind enough man, without question.

The groundsman let out a sigh as he reached into his waistcoat and pulled out a worn, silver pocket watch. Its tired clock face bore faded numbers, and the hands were slightly askew as he struggled to read the time.

"Ten o'clock, sir," he muttered simply, snapping the lid shut and sliding the watch back into the depths of his pocket. "I must be off. I have an engagement—one I'm afraid I cannot miss. My responsibilities won't attend to themselves, after all. Please extend my sincerest condolences to your sister, will you? Regrettably, I won't be visiting the house this evening. We're expecting a shipment at the docks this afternoon. Nonetheless, I'll ensure the pantry is replenished by morning."

With that, the groundsman doffed his hat and turned towards a break in the tree line. He set off briskly, tracing the curve of the fields until he dwindled into nothing more than a mere speck, soon vanishing from sight.

Chapter 32

It didn't take long before I found myself outside the old house. Thrusting my hands into my pockets, I swiftly paced up the large stone steps that stood weathered and cracked. As I briskly made my way along the garden, I observed the flowerbeds, filled with weeds and patches of lifeless, grey grass that climbed and spread wildly across flagstones.

The house itself flung a long shadow that loomed over me like a blackened cloud, casting over the many weeds and bushes that quivered in the late March chill. Its two upper windows resembled that of saddened eyes as I drew nearer, inspecting me as I weaved my way across the garden, a garden that resembled the same love and joy of the very house itself.

As I neared the entrance, it would have been dishonest to say that Meredith didn't occupy my every thought. After all, she had already endured so much—so much heartache, so much pain. With Jacob's unexpected death looming over her like a constant torment, I could only foresee the worst to come. Would she remain there forever, left to wither away like the very house that chained her, like the garden that gave no life? Alone, without anyone to care for her, to cherish her in her remaining years? I could not let that happen. No, I would not. As long as I drew breath, I would see to it that my sister found happiness once again.

I would whisk her away from the island, far from the prison that had robbed her of life. Together we would embark on a new venture, beyond the sights of that dismal rock. Our hearts would finally be content, and we would both rediscover happiness once again. It would be a new chapter for us both, a new life, a fresh chance to reclaim what we had held so dear all those years ago but had lost as time slipped by.

Of course, there was a chance she would outright reject my offer, and given what had come to light in recent days, I wouldn't expect anything less. However, I refused to give up on her so easily. In time, her heart would surely heal; that was the nature of healing. When that moment came, we would finally bid farewell to our childhood home, leaving its rooms to wither and decay like the broken hearts they once held. We would sail away together, side by side, my hand tightly entwined with hers, resentful of the lives that meagre house, that scrap of land, had taken. Together, we would put an end to our time on Lismore. We would never return again.

A wave of excitement washed over me, urging me to quicken my pace. I felt a pressing need to find my sister in the library at once and explain everything, share all the plans, the possibilities I could offer.

With purposeful strides, I hurried along the side of the house, a smile on my face as my feet barely touched the ground. I was just a few steps from the door, mere seconds away from calling out her name, when the slightest movement through the window caught my eye through the window—someone inside the house.

At first, I mistook it for none other than Meredith herself, watching me as I pranced by, the oddest expression on her face.

Overcome with excitement, I couldn't contain myself and shouted, my voice filled with joy as I retraced my steps with a shuffle.

"Meredith, we must speak!" I cried. "I have the most wonderful …"

The smile sponged away from my face. My voice faltered, as if an invisible hand had clamped around my throat, the words trapped within a tightening knot. For a moment, I dared not blink, dared not move. As I stood by, feet rooted to the ground, my eyes became locked, grew wider, unable to stray from the strangest of sights before me.

There was a man. That man too stood frozen, staring out the window of the house, his features somewhat hazed by the daylight which reflected strongly upon the murky glass. His eyes pierced into my own, eyes so wild that I could not tear free from their hold. As I studied his face, a sudden wave of recognition washed over me, though I could not quite place where I had seen the man before. His skin was sickly and pale, almost white, and his unkempt hair clung to his scalp in matted strands. Deep lines chiselled his sunken face, accentuating the weariness and suffering of his deep, hollow sockets.

"Who ..." I stammered, my lips quivering with unease. "Who is that?" My finger trembled in tandem with my voice, rising purposefully to a point, only to witness the figure on the other side of the pane replicate the very same movement.

The man did not reply. Not so much a sound did he voice, but simply continued to gaze through me. His brow deepened with disgust, his stare somehow vacantly lost.

In the blink of an eye, my mind was transported back to the words of Mr Gibbs, his stories of ragged beggars roaming the island, their ravaged souls driving them to desperate lengths. They would stop at nothing, their urge relentless, as they scoured the land in search of food, showing no mercy in their quest. Like spectres from a lawless world, they would trespass into homes, pillaging whatever personal possessions they could lay their hands on.

I thought of my dear nephew, cut down in his prime, fallen victim to those despicable beings who stood half alive, half dead in front of me.

Wanderers.

Fuelled by a rush of anxiety, I ran to the door, swinging it open with a mighty thrust as I stepped inside the house. All was eerily still. My heart raced, pounding in my chest like a hammer striking at the stubborn nail of a coffin, as I made my way to the room where the mysterious man had stood.

Yet as I barged inside, he was nowhere to be found. The room lay bare, as if no man had ever been there at all. Driven by hope, I hurried along the hall to the library, praying to find my sister unharmed, still seated in her favourite chair.

The anticipation choked my breath as I pushed open the library doors. As I rushed into the room, my hopes were dashed. The chair where she once sat was empty, its cushion untouched and cold. Panic seized my chest, tightening with each passing second as I called out her name, my scream echoing off the walls.

The silence that returned was deafening.

I bolted for the stairwell, tripping and fumbling, my footsteps matching the beat of my own trembling heart. Sweat clouded my vision as I hurriedly burst from one soulless chamber to the next, exploring every shadow within, every hidden corner.

"Meredith?" I called again, my voice strained. Each room began to swirl into a whirlwind of hazy objects.

Despair engulfed me, leaving me unable to breathe or think. Time seemed to freeze all around me as I helplessly leant against the wall.

And just as I was on the verge of surrendering, ready to collapse in a heap upon the floor, a gentle touch brushed over the back of my head, delicate, like a whisper, its touch so hauntingly vivid—the last tether to reality before the light failed and the abyss engulfed me whole.

Chapter 33

My mother is by my side, just as she always has been. The birds have ceased their song now, their shrills that fall down from the sky like glistening ribbons have come to sing their last. The forest is darker now, lifeless despite a faint orange glow peeking through the branches, signalling the approaching dusk.

A familiar chill envelops my small, childlike hand with a gentle squeeze. It's a touch I recognise all too well. I raise my eyes to meet my mother's, observing as the strands of orange light crown her head like a burning halo. She looks different somehow, compared to other dreams. Her hair, once thick and brown, now hangs wispy and grey, lacking any liveliness it once had. No longer does her face display the same glow, but rather the shiver of dread, as if a ghost returning from a life they long wished to forget.

She does not speak, not a word, but simply looks ahead. Her glare is fixed on a gap within the tree line, just as she has always done before.

"What lies beyond, Mother?" I ask her, though deep down, I do not truly wish to know. But before I can fully make sense of it, the distance between us begins to shrink. I try to pull away, to escape her grasp, but when I glance down, our feet remain rooted to the ground. We're not walking yet we move closer through the shadowy passage ahead all the same.

Low-hanging branches conceal our path like an old, torn curtain draping from above. I reach out to push them aside. The air is thick with the scent of wet earth, and even though my feet remain still, I can feel the sticks and mud squelching between my toes.

I close my eyes, knowing all too well that this is where the dream should end and I would awaken from whatever lies ahead. But this time, I don't. Instead, the ground grows bleaker, and soon all I see is blackness.

The tunnel of wilderness thickens as we move forward. I quickly glance up at my mother's face, seeking comfort, but she too has been swallowed by the dark. All that remains is the hand I cling to and the rapid sound of her breath falling against my ear, a breath so heavy that it feels as if her face is right beside mine, resting at my shoulder, her wide eyes staring at me through the dark.

There is a faint light ahead, its shade of the fairest glow, a light so inviting it ignites the darkness, dulling the unknown horrors that linger at my side. It moves closer, its orb becoming brighter, signalling our end to this dreadful place. We are soon engulfed by it, cleansed by it, and before my eyes have time to adjust and this dream has reached its final scene, the sensation of something tender flitters down against my skin.

We stand before an old tree in full bloom, its limbs twisting and bending upwards, reaching ever higher. The blossoms burst with colour, camouflaging the setting sun. Its roots stretch wide across the forest floor, protruding from the earth like filthy claws, choking any other life they touch. Yet despite the ground it claims, the tree itself is dying. Its branches begin to droop and wither, their tone fading to a dull brown. Petals drift down in a calming flurry, their lively blooms now brittle and lifeless, settling like lilac snow upon an icy ground.

At the base of the tree, a small headstone stands crooked, leaning with the uneven ground riddled with roots. Thick moss covers its top, and the words are hidden beneath a layer of fallen petals.

I know this headstone. I have seen it many times before—sometimes as a child, sometimes in my darkest thoughts. And despite its weathered state, with rough stone marred by deep cracks and letters hidden, I know what lies beneath its cloak. I know who rests beyond the surface.

I turn to look up at my mother, whose shadow still lingers at my side, wanting to ask her why she has brought me here, why now, after all this time? But as I turn to look up, she is gone, nowhere to be seen. I search behind me, glancing around, but there is nothing—no one. When my focus returns ahead, hypnotised by the delicate petals twirling from above, I see her again. She stands just behind the headstone, her hand gently resting on its top.

I ask again why we are here, but when she opens her mouth, no words form. She cannot speak. Or I cannot hear. I try to respond, to tell her we must leave, but when I begin, no sound escapes me, no matter how hard I try. And the more I try, the more I realise that the woodland is steeped in silence. It's so quiet that I cannot hear a thing—nothing at all. The world has become deafening.

I plead with my eyes, beckoning her to follow as I attempt to edge away. I feel the pain of my feet as they trudge across the thicket, the earth pressing sharply under heel. Yet, the more I step back, the closer I come to the gravesite. I am so close now that I am almost upon it.

Mother, she's pointing at something, her brittle finger urging me towards the writing hidden under leaves. I shake my head unwillingly. Not because I am afraid, no, but because I already know what I will find etched upon the stone. I see it always, every time I close my eyes, every memory drifting back to my childhood. I see it letter by letter, word by word. And if I see it now, if I dare to wipe away the petals on the stone, then that means the woman staring down at me is not really here. That she has never truly been here at all.

With a slow motion, my mother reaches out and clasps my wrist, her bony fingers wrapping around it tightly like the roots that snake the ground. Her hand is cold and slippery, moist like wet earth on a drizzly day. At first, I try to resist her, yanking and thrashing with all my strength.

But as her grip tightens, my eyes shut, clenched so tightly that I can somehow hear the waves of the ocean in my ears.

When I finally open them again, her grasp has vanished, the sensation evaporating like the burn of a lantern snuffed out by the rain. She stands there, gazing downwards, a blank expression cast across her face. It is only then that I am startled by the cold stone against my palm, the petals clumped between my fingers like paste, and the familiar letters in clear view.

It is my mother's name, a name of such beauty that it seems utterly lost in such a dark and dismal place.

I trace my fingers along the grooves, memories all the while flooding back like a surge of lost whispers. I remember her for who she used to be. Yet here she lies, forgotten, confined to her miserable resting place. There is no one to keep her company anymore, no one to care. Like a filthy secret, she is hidden, the trees concealing her from all she knew, all who knew her, trapped until the very end of time.

I'm kneeling on the ground, my head bowed low, observing my knees, which sink into the dirt. I know I am crying although I cannot feel the tears. My body is numb, senseless. The only thing I feel is grief.

I glance up, expecting my mother to be gone, for the remaining shadow to have dwindled away, replicating the words half washed away in stone. However, there she still stands. Her long, wet hair clings to her face and covers the glare of her eyes.

I try to get up, to find my feet and wrap my arms around her, to tell her all the things I wish I had done before but never had. But I cannot. Something is holding me back. I try again, straining, but still I remain slumped upon my knees. I am unable to move, bound to the spot.

A faint stir upon the ground grabs my attention. It slithers, concealed beneath the earth's surface, disturbing the soil in its wake. There are hundreds of them, perhaps even more. What it is, I do not know. Nor do I think I wish to find out. But just as I begin to scurry, to reach out to my mother, something sinister pulls me from behind.

Roots ensnare me, coiling and entwining like serpents, endless in their grip. I wrestle against their tightening hold piercing into my flesh. I strive to break free, yet more roots emerge like grasping hands from the earth, seizing my limbs and pulling me downwards. A scream wells up within, but only the chilling slither of roots pervades my ears, binding me in a haunting embrace, their whispers echoing as one.

Something is happening. The ground beneath me begins to shift and churn, the soil parting as if an ancient force has awakened, pulling me down as its prey. I don't know what to do or think. But there is little time for either. Without warning, I sense myself slowly beginning to sink.

My head lurches up, and with one free hand, I fight my way through the tangled lines in hope of reaching my mother. I pray for her to find me, to latch onto me once more. For her to take my hand and rescue me from this awful place, to carry me back where I belong, back to the comforts of fields, the fragrance of grass and dandelions that billow beneath the scorching sun. But as I strain my neck, my chin grazing through the dirt with clenched teeth, my eyes are met only by that of the solitary headstone, devoid of a loved one's touch.

She really is gone.

The ground trembles and convulses beneath my feet; its rumblings call to me. I hear it, a voice carried on the wind and through the earth, beckoning me to release my grip on life's fragile thread. It begs me to surrender, to yield to the unknown. I fight with all my might, thrashing and contorting, digging my nails into the earth, desperate to resist the pull. In spite of all my efforts, all my will, I find myself sinking even deeper, unable to halt the descent.

Thin vines begin to encircle my throat, at times blinding my sight like nature's cruel mask, obscuring my view of the world around me.

The ability to breathe is becoming harder as I sink deeper into the abyss. The air itself grows thin, each breath a laborious task. Time slips away, fleeting and elusive, leaving little time for me to think.

With a final gasp, I draw in a desperate breath, the largest and most terrifying gulp my lungs have ever known. But before I can finish, darkness envelops me, swallowing the remnants of daylight and obscuring my view. The last gleam of sunlight filters away, leaving me to descend farther into a gulf of blackness. I slip deeper, my head vanishing beneath the soil from which there is no return.

The end draws near, and an undeniable truth resonates deep within my bones. Its arrival is imminent, a relentless force poised to claim what it deems rightfully its own. The earth presses in around me, exerting its weight to plunge me deeper into its deathly snare. An eternity of frigid darkness awaits, a bleak existence devoid of everything but my own paralysing fear.

In this moment, a realisation strikes me, searing through my mind—a thought that I will be forever alone. Forgotten, unspoken of, left to decay without so much as a loved one to mourn my mark, to grieve the loss of my existence. I shall become a mere mutter of a wagging tongue, a thing of what all men fear the most, an echo that fades into obscurity, a name lost, devoid of all its meaning.

The moments that linger slip away with alarming swiftness. With trembling fingers, I strive to reach the surface, to bridge the divide between my fading existence and the living world beyond. Suddenly, something brushes against my palm, a touch so soft I swear it can't be real. It can't be, but it is. It grasps around my hand, linking at my wrist, and, without further delay, sternly begins to pull. I no longer feel myself drifting farther but instead swimming to the surface, returning to the light, back to where I know I belong. The earth wades over me as I climb to break free, the strong grasp never losing its fight as my head emerges from the ground.

Mud and dirt fill my eyes. I cannot see. But for now, it seems to matter little. I inhale a long, desperate gasp, allowing the cold, crisp air to funnel into my lungs, still clutching onto the loving hand that saved me.

It feels so much colder here now, as though the winds have changed within a heartbeat, and the sting of winter bites my skin. The ground remains the purest white, just like before, layered from the debris of fallen petals. I can just about make out the figure holding my hand. It is her. My mother is crouched down beside me, her hair concealing her face as her grip remains faithful to mine. I watch her closely, squinting through the blurriness with the greatest love I think I have ever known. But before I have the chance to speak, to ask if we can go home, Mother's head cranes to her side, her neck cracking as it comes to a peculiar stop. Like this, she appears to stay, frozen, her stare fixed to the headstone.

A shallow gasp overcomes me as I turn. The words are so familiar to me yet haunting all the same. Gone was the name of my mother, gone as though it were never truly there at all. In its place, a new name rests, a shuddering sight, each letter just as harrowing as the last.

Meredith Durose
Forever tormented, never made whole

I lurch backwards, pushing against the ground, locked beneath the shadow of the towering stone.

Meredith is not dead. She cannot be!

I will for the dream to end, long for the forest around me to dissolve and for the twisting branches overhead to transform back into the cracks of my ceiling. I close my eyes tightly, hoping that by some unexplainable miracle I will find myself gone from this place—somewhere far away. Far, far away. A place where I can hide and feel safe, where dreams can no longer reach me.

With a sudden burst of energy, I struggle to climb free, scurrying from the hole, my mother's hand firmly interlocked with mine for leverage. The ground gives way beneath my feet, shifting with every step. I reach out, grasping at whatever ground surrounds us. But as I do, I come to a jarring halt. The ground is cold. My palm is wet, freezing. At first, I don't understand; my thoughts are lost, dazed. There is ice on my hand, tingling my fingers to numbness. And at that moment, I realise that the once-white petals spread wide across the ground have turned into the thickest layer of snow.

The hand gripping mine begins to tense. Its wrist leads up to a watchful face. The expression is gaunt and distant—a face that belongs not to my mother but to the soulless stare of Martha Ferrell.

Chapter 34

26TH March 1847

The room I found myself in was dark—empty and cold save for a single lamp that hissed in the far corner, casting a faint light. Outside, the night felt calm and content, a stark difference to the harshness that had plagued the house in recent days. The weather, much like me, appeared drained of its strength, its fierce gusts weak and weary, as if waiting for something—though I knew not what.

Beyond my window, the shadowy shapes of trees stood still at the edge of the grounds like guards holding back their urge to stir.

Exhausted, I let out a groan as I pulled myself up, slipping away from the nightmare. My shirt, damp with sweat, clung to my skin like a cold blanket, peeling away as I rose.

"So, you have finally decided to awaken, then?" said a voice.

I craned my neck over my shoulder. In the far corner, just beyond the lamp's reach, Meredith sat in a small chair, wedged beside the narrow window and a sturdy wardrobe that extended several feet from the chimney breast wall.

"You have been sleeping for some time. Several hours, I dare say," she continued in little more than a whisper, never once shifting from her shadowed spot. "I have been watching over you."

Instantly, my nerves relaxed and my breath returned to a more casual pace. "My dear," I groaned drearily. "You've been watching over me all this time?"

I could make out but a faint nod captured through the darkness.

"I have," she replied bluntly.

"Why, I am quite alright," I replied. "A little tired, no doubt. That said, I assure you, there is absolutely nothing wrong with me. It is I who should be caring for you."

Through the haze, the form of my sister hunched forward, the sound of her fingernails scraping against the chair's arms, stabbing through the stillness.

"Oh, but I do believe there is something wrong, Peter," she replied. Her voice was hushed as if she had pledged to disclose the deepest of secrets. "Something terribly wrong."

Uneasy about her tone and the implications it carried, I strained my eyes through the haze.

"You speak in your sleep. Did you know?" she asked, shifting slightly so that a strip of moonlight fell coldly across her cheek. Her eyes flickered momentarily away from the lamp as she leant farther forward, eyes shadowed by sleepless nights.

"I did not, no," I replied, somewhat taken aback.

"Indeed, you do," she confirmed, a slight curve of her lip hinting at something deeper. "Just as you have since your arrival back on the island. At first, I thought it was merely the effects of a tiresome journey. But now I see it's something quite different—something more. You have changed." She looked at me with a curious gaze. "Don't ask me why, but you have. I can see it in your eyes, the way you speak in your dreams at night, the way you carry yourself, the way you look. It's etched on your very face, Peter, from the lines of your brow to the groove of your chin. You are hiding something. Don't dismiss it. Remember, I know you better than anyone else. I can read you like a book. You've brought whatever it is all this way with you, hoarding it deep inside, allowing it to consume you bit by bit. Soon, I fear there will be nothing left of you at all."

"Oh, balderdash!" I replied, shaking my head dismissively. "They are merely dreams—nothing more. Unpleasant dreams, yes, but still just dreams."

She paused for a brief moment, letting the stillness of the night respond to her as her face slipped out of the light and back into the gloom from which it came. She rested back in her chair, the old wooden legs creaking beneath.

"Dreams," she continued, speaking as if to herself. "They have a way of releasing whatever we keep locked inside—the pain we suffer, the heartache. Without such an escape, I'm sure we would burst. I should know." She hesitated slightly. "I have indulged in such dreams myself."

From the shadows, a chilling draft slithered into the room, slowly easing the door open with an unsettling creak as it nipped at the nape of my neck.

"And these dreams," I asked her. "You believe they reveal things to you?"

"Reveal?" she snapped, her head jerking forward. "No," she mumbled, almost reflexively. "Nothing I do not already know, at least. But they provide an undeniable clarity. No matter how desperately you try to flee from your troubles, the outcome remains the same: anger, grief, guilt. It all surfaces eventually; you only need to allow it. Speak the words you've feared to voice, and only then will your mind accept your burdens. I have suffered guilt—plenty of it. Now with Jacob's death hovering over me, I fear I'll have to confront it all over again." Her neck bowed low, meeting the form of her hands as if she was on the brink of tears.

"You speak of such things like the boy's death was your doing."

"I never said it was," she sighed. "It is not his death that causes my guilt, but more the many other things I could have done for him when he was alive but simply didn't."

I scratched at my scalp, pondering her words as the voice of Mr Gibbs echoed in my mind. I recalled his story from earlier that day—a tale of a young boy tormented by his father, abused and punished for simply being himself, and a mother who could do nothing but watch from the sidelines, witnessing every vicious act, every cruel punishment. She listened to his cries, to his misery, helpless to protect her child.

"Guilt," she continued, her voice delicately cracking, "it is such a wicked burden for the mind to bear. In many ways, it is cruel. Yet we are all victims of our own wrongdoings, a sentence we must endure. Do you not agree?"

"I'm not at all sure what you're implying," I replied.

"Guilt," Meredith repeated, her gaze locking onto mine. "Come now. Let us not linger on this subject longer than necessary. We are of the same blood, are we not? Cut from the same cloth. Whatever troubles you, whatever guilt you've locked away behind those eyes of yours, will not simply vanish come morning. No matter how much you wish it, it will remain with you, Peter—inside you. Don't you understand? It will become part of you forever, festering in your soul until you have no one to blame but yourself. I know this because I have lived that very life for far too long, imprisoned by it, trapped within my thoughts. I see you, and I dare say I recognise the very same. A good man. A kind, generous man who is far too proud to seek comfort in sharing. A man too stubborn to reveal his feelings. Why do you deny it? Something is tormenting you."

With a surge of energy, I found myself upright, pacing the floor in a swirl of unease. There was no doubt that what she said had struck a chord of truth. I had indeed been hiding something—not just from her, but from myself, a heavy burden borne of guilt, yet it felt like so much more. It felt as though every secret I had tried to forget and bury deep within had suddenly resurfaced, clamouring for release. The memories of Elphin, the harrowing nightmares, the visions that plagued my every waking moment—what did it all mean?

I collapsed back into my seat, my legs giving way beneath me, the memories of my lifeless tenants flashing before my eyes, accompanied by the haunting echoes of their desperate pleas.

Gradually, my breathing calmed. The frenzied panic, too, subsided, along with the harrowing voices that clamoured within my ears.

Emerging from the shadows, Meredith rose from her chair and quickly nestled herself by my side. She extended her hand, intertwining her fingers with mine, gripping tightly—ever so tightly. "Speak to me, Peter," she implored, the tension in her forehead easing as she spoke. "I am here to listen."

With a heavy sigh, my gaze drifted towards the window, which offered little but blackness in return. "Then I shall tell you," I whispered softly. "I will tell you everything."

"If you may recall, I was once the owner of a flour mill on the eastern side of London. In many ways, the mill was like any other—perfectly situated beside the river, distributing the finest flour that all of London had to offer. And oh, what a place it was! The five-storey building teemed with workers, a fortress of a good, respectable business—a place I had built from the ground up. It feels like an eternity since those days.

"Be that as it may, it was not to last. Fate dealt me an unexpected blow when my only business partner, Arthur Fritton, a man renowned for his charity work and respect for his employees, tragically fell ill.

Some sort of peasant fever, they said. Quite the coincidence, one might say, that despite all his efforts to provide relief to the poor, it was, in fact, the poor who brought about his end. A cruel twist of fate, without a doubt. And as a result, I was left as the sole shareholder of the estate.

"For the first few months, I did all I could to carry on the operations of the mill. But the burden eventually became far too overwhelming for a lone man to bear. After all, time had taken its toll on me, and I was no longer the sprightly young man that many once admired. I had become old and tired of it all, devoid of passion. And as time slowly slipped through my fingers, the weight and pressure of my departed partner's absence soon began to gnaw my conscience. Afterall, how much longer did I truly have before I, too, would follow in his shadowy footsteps? Was I destined to simply wait, anticipating the inevitable? To find myself one day bedridden in a hospital, tended to in my old age, stripped of all dignity? I would then surely regret having dedicated every waking moment to those old mill walls, a life shackled to nothing more than obligation. And for what, I ask you? Success? Wealth? Well, in truth, they all hold very little importance. I had not known such things when I began my venture. I was blinded in many ways, ignorant. I was driven solely by the pursuit of a good name and a handsome profit. Nothing else mattered, not to me, not to my acquaintances or workers, and as much as it pains me to admit it, not even to my own family." I paused, my gaze lifted. "Not even to you."

Meredith recoiled slightly, her bosom rising and falling with each breath, desperately trying to find the man she knew long ago but couldn't.

"I never married, Meredith," I went on, fighting off her lingering gaze. "You know this all too well. Nor in all my years did I ever fall in love. Not in the deepest sense, I don't think. There were romances, of course there were, seasonal flings that began abruptly and by my own choosing ended just the same, none of which were ever meant to be. I suppose, to me, love was just too much of a complicated circumstance to find myself in. A four-letter word. A sensation for which I never did find the time nor strength. Nor did I entertain the notion of seeking it. Time held too much value for me, far too precious to be squandered on a fleeting emotion like love. And although it may surprise you, the affection I cherished resided not in the eyes or touch of another, but rather in the satisfaction of holding a quill in one hand and a prosperous purse in the other. I was wedded to my work, you see? Driven by my own success. Little did I know that it would consume me if I allowed it so.

"So, one day, I made a firm decision. Enough was enough—I would not allow myself the same fate. I would move away, far removed from the grim and watchful streets of London. I would travel north as far as possible, find myself a charming little spot in the Highlands. A new place to call home. Somewhere quiet and secluded. A fresh chapter. A place to call my own.

"And so, without hesitation, I swiftly sold the mill to the first buyer, severing all ties to my life's work. My workers, the fruits of my labour, and everything I had built—gone with the stroke of ink. To my surprise, it was some days later that I read the mill had been demolished in its entirety, pulled down to its foundations, leaving all the workers to venture out into the cold. Needless to say, I gave the matter little thought. It was no longer my concern, my cross to bear. And as you can imagine, my mind was somewhat elsewhere. My ambitions changed.

"And so… you wandered off to Scotland?" questioned Meredith, her focus unmoved. She sat slightly hunched, her head tilted as if trying to unravel every word before the story reached its end.

"I did," I confirmed, massaging the stiffness in my neck. "However, the journey was far from pleasant—quite the opposite. The days seemed to stretch on endlessly, and the nights brought even more restlessness. We wasted little time during our travels, somewhat anxious whether we would ever reach our destination at all. Fortunately, the weather remained dry for the most part. But when we finally arrived on the outskirts of Ullapool, it had been little more than a fortnight since we left the bustling crowds of London. As you can imagine, I was utterly exhausted, longing for the simple comforts: a warm bed and a good night's sleep.

"I remained in Ullapool for some time after that, regaining what energy I could muster and taking in the surroundings the small town had to offer. Tell me, have you ever found yourself there?"

"Ullapool?" Meredith asked, the place rolling off her tongue. "I have not."

"Ah, then one day I shall take you there," I offered, before swiftly returning to the point. "It is quite a beautiful spot. Quiet and quaint. A simple place in many respects, inhabited by nothing but simple people leading the simplest of lives."

"I would like that very much, Peter," she replied, her faint smile barely visible through the dim light.

"I did not stay there long, of course," I added. "A week, perhaps. Maybe a day or two longer. After all, I had further business to attend to, a life to build. And if my memory serves me correctly, it was on the evening of a cold Saturday when I received word about a most promising purchase—a house located just a few miles from the town, a rather isolated spot known as Elphin. The gentleman who disclosed such an opportunity went by the name of Angus, a slender man with a nose as prominent as a peacock's. As it turned out, he was a local book-keeper and a long-serving member of the town's committee. When he offered to accompany me there himself, I agreed almost instantly. I mean, who would not?

"We set forth the following morning, venturing through the winding roads that trenched along the mountainsides. I must admit, the land-scape was nothing short of glorious, and by the time we arrived a few hours later, well, what greeted me was nothing short of breathtaking.

"There before me, curved in the shape of the rocks, sat the most alluring house I have ever known. Not vast in size by any accounts, but what it lacked in stature, Meredith, it made up for in undisputable charm. The grey stone walls stood proud, blending perfectly with the landscape. A thatched roof crowned its top, its golden shade comple-menting the cool tone of the stonework."

"It certainly sounds wonderful," said Meredith. Her smile tightened, almost as if she found it a struggle to hold it.

"Yes," I said. "Needless to say, I didn't give the purchase much consideration. I was hasty. Foolish. Yet I couldn't control the sudden surge of excitement that had completely overwhelmed me. The desire to own a property like this, a property that, let me remind you, was far beyond anything I had ever dared to imagine, was simply irresistible to me. I had to have it.

"Of course, I returned to town that day with a newfound sense of life. A whistle danced upon my lips as I happily strolled along the village streets. So elated was I that I decided to indulge in a few glasses of ale to celebrate, extending the invitation to Mr Angus, who unsur-prisingly was more than willing to oblige. We drank long into the night, joyously discussing my plans to further develop the house. Nothing too drastic, mind you. No, it was far too special for that, far too significant. I simply wished to make a few improvements, to make some minor changes here and there. Mr Angus agreed, without opposi-tion to any of the suggestions. And as the night grew late and our tankards remained full to the brim, it was quite clear that the man sitting across from me had no doubt drank his fill. He began to ramble in a drunken manner. His sentences slurred. At first, I thought nothing of it. I simply humoured the man. It wasn't until I returned to my lodgings in the early hours of the morning that his words began to play on me."

"And what do you believe this man to have said?" pressed Meredith, leaning in even closer.

"Believe?" I repeated, spitting out the word. "My dear, it is not a matter of what I believed I heard, but rather the greatest concern of what was said by the man who said it."

"And what was that?" Meredith persisted patiently.

A heavy sigh escaped me. "He said that he was certain my new tenants would welcome me with open arms."

Chapter 35

Meredith arose from her seat, the sound of her long skirt swishing softly as she moved. Crossing the room with an air of purpose, she found herself rummaging through a set of shadowed drawers and, by chance, discovered a single candle.

With graceful poise, she struck a match, its flame dancing to life, casting flickering shadows on the room's walls.

"Tenants, you say?" she enquired, her voice laced with inquisitiveness. With a mere flick of her wrist, she extinguished the match, causing a faint scent of smoke to waft about the room. "What do you suppose he meant?"

"That, my dear," I answered, trying to dispel the humour in my voice, "is precisely what I found myself asking."

"Surely you don't mean to say the man was disloyal to your agreement?" She placed the candle carefully on a small, round table which stood at the centre of the room.

"Disloyal. Deceitful. They are both very much one and the same," I replied, reigniting the resentment within me. "But I have come to think of it as nothing more than an unfortunate event."

"Unfortunate event, indeed," agreed Meredith as she resumed her place by my side. "Please, do go on."

I cleared my throat and proceeded to speak.

"Despite my sudden weariness regarding the nature of Mr Angus, it transpired, much to my astonishment, that the man was indeed everything he claimed himself to be, and even more so."

"More so?" asked Meredith.

"Untrustworthy, dishonest, and by all accounts plagued by a number of troubles. It seemed that the man had managed to drum up a considerable amount of debt—debt he had accumulated in high-stakes card games. And so, driven by desperation and consumed by the fear of facing the consequences, Mr Angus grasped at any opportunity that presented itself, even if that meant selling his estate to the one person willing to take it. I made every attempt to locate him, as one would naturally do. But to my dismay, it became apparent that the papers documenting the transfer of ownership had already been marked, the purchase complete, and Mr Angus, much to my surprise, had long departed from the outskirts of Ullapool, leaving me with no means of reaching him."

Meredith sucked in a breath and adjusted herself upright, her back straight, her chin nuzzling into her neck as she asked, "So, what did you do?"

"My dear Meredith," I shrugged defeatedly, "what could I do? The man himself had already fled, dodging the cause for justice, as it were. There was little more to be done, little option. My only choice was to retrace my steps further north with my head held high, preparing myself for any expectancies to come."

REMAINING RESTED IN THE CHAIR, I LET MY HEAD SAG WEARILY. My eyelids drooped, longing for the pounding in my temples to subside.

Shortly after, Meredith returned from the lower floor, bearing a teapot decorated with intricate floral patterns and two cups that emitted a delicate *clinking* as she walked. With a graceful precision, she set the tray down before me, the polished surface glimmering under the light. Without delay, she tipped the teapot, releasing a plume of steam as piping hot tea swirled into the cups.

"Is there anything stronger, perhaps?" I asked, hopefully.

"No," she responded curtly, her focus unmoved from the task before her. "Only something warm to alleviate the cold." With a gentle smile, she placed the cup onto a saucer that presented a few minor blemishes along its rim and extended it towards me.

"Very well, then," I sighed. "But I must confess that a strong drink, given the circumstances, possesses certain qualities for such a night that a hot cup of tea simply cannot replicate."

"But a hot cup of tea possesses the power to soothe both body and soul, does it not?"

I gave no reply to that, but instead raised the cup to my lips, blowing delicately before daring to take a sip.

"Now then," continued Meredith, once again settling down to her seat and holding her cup with such a refined elegance that suggested she was hosting a lavish dinner party. "If you are quite through yearning for the bottle, might I suggest you continue?"

My hand trembled slightly, causing the cup which sat upon the saucer to briefly tremble with it.

"Yes, of course," I murmured. I bent forward, clumsily placing the beverage on the table.

"I suppose it was some weeks later that I found myself returning to Elphin. It afforded me time, you see? Time to ensure the house was in proper order before my arrival, as well as to guarantee that the staff were adequately prepared.

"The day itself was undeniably dreary, in fact quite miserable as the coach came to a steady halt outside the house. But despite my unfortunate encounter with Mr Angus, stepping out of the carriage that morning and looking upon what was now my new home seemed to make all feel right again. I spent the following mornings puttering about the house, afternoons writing letters to my associates back in London, if only to assure them that all was well. In the evenings, I would find myself comfortably nestled in front of the fire with a brandy in one hand and a blend of my favourite pipe tobacco in the other. I was content, Meredith, perfectly happy with my spot amidst the hills."

Meredith's eyes rolled with a touch of exasperation. "So, if I understand correctly, you encountered very little trouble, if any at all?" she asked, pausing to take a sip of her tea.

I looked at her bluntly, withholding the urge to spit out my drink. "On the contrary. But yes, at first, I must admit that all appeared to be going rather well. I would even confess that whatever worries I once had swiftly dwindled away."

"Then what changed, Peter?" pressed Meredith, her expression brimming with all the more curiosity. "There must have been something?"

"Everything changed," I confided, a sudden tension constricting my throat, compelling me to slacken the collar of my shirt. "Things were never to be the same again. You see, I grew tired of the property grounds. One morning, I took it upon myself to venture farther—nothing too strenuous, merely a short wander of the estate. It was, after all, a glorious morning, clear and bright. The kind of morning that kindles a yearning desire to explore.

"And so, I walked, following the trail down to the river and crossing the bridge, which led me to a small incline some distance away from the property gate. With little desire of retracing my steps back to the house, and a feeling that one can only describe as a further want for adventure, I decided to push onwards, trudging my way to the hill's crest. By the time I neared the top, I had grown awfully tired. The air, though crisp, felt somehow foreign to my lungs, unfamiliar as they were to the unspoiled freshness of the Highlands, having long been acquainted with the foul stench of the city. And so, there I stood, my breath panting, only to be greeted by a sight which caused my fists to knot."

"What?" asked Meredith.

"Tenants."

Meredith dropped back into her seat with the expression of complete surprise. "So, this Mr Angus spoke the truth, then?"

I nodded sharply, my response distant, unable to shake away the scene that still played true in my head. "Yes, what he had disclosed to me on that drunken evening appeared to be, in fact, the truth," I told her. "Without a doubt quite possibly the most genuine words to have slipped the man's tongue all evening."

A gentle touch brushed against my knee as Meredith's face leered over my shoulder.

"In the distance," I continued, both eyes tightly shut, "countless roofs of small dwellings were scattered about the landscape, not few in their numbers, I must be clear, but many. Hundreds. All farming off the land. My land," I remarked, prodding a finger to my chest. "Spoiling the very earth with their presence, the very soil which was now legally my own. I could not allow it. Would not! And so, as I looked out across the endless settlements, observing the thick, dark clouds which swiftly rolled in from the sea, I swore to myself that a price would be paid for my humiliation, that this situation, as it were, would not be my cross to bear. And so I left, retracing my steps to the house, never again to return to that spot upon the hill, never again to witness the disgust of what I beheld that day. Or so I thought."

Suddenly, and without realising, the hand that grasped my knee turned firm.

"And so," interrupted Meredith, encouraging me further with a stern yet pressing nudge. "Then what happened?"

"Then …" I replied, studying the lace which travelled the course of her arm.

She looked at me anxiously, her brow bent.

"Then the rains began."

Chapter 36

Beyond the window, the moon briefly sank behind a shroud of nothingness, casting the space with little light and causing the room where we sat to feel all the colder for it. I asked if we might light the fire, which she did not oppose but instead relapsed into silence, refraining from any further questions until a small hearth was lit.

"For several months, it felt as though it had done nothing but rain," I went on, extending my arms towards a single flame in an attempt to fight the chill. "Depressing," I grunted. "The kind of weather that fills one with an undeniable sense of gloom. Not that you are unfamiliar with such."

Meredith responded not with words but rather a soft hum of agreement.

"With the rain never ceasing, most days I found myself confined to the house. After all, there was little else to do. And with time on my side, I devoted much of it to writing letters to London, particularly to a lawyer by the name of Scrimshaw, whose reputation exceeded his wealth. Our professional lives had intertwined in one way one or another. In fact, it was I who had offered much support to him during his darkest hours. However, that is a story better suited for another time. Nevertheless, regardless of our acquaintance, I held a glimmer of faith that, in return, Mr Scrimshaw could shed light on my minor predicament and, in doing so, help rid the settlers from my land.

"This exchange of letters went back and forth for many weeks. And much to my disheartenment, it appeared that my efforts were leading me nowhere. I had almost given up all hope. My patience waned. But on a dark and dreary morning of late November, a letter from none other than Scrimshaw himself found its way to my door, a letter that by all accounts would change my outlook on everything. He suggested, and much to his persistence, that considering the dwellers were well within their rights to be there irrespective of my oversight, that I should consider commanding rent for their use of my land."

"Rent?" asked Meredith quietly.

"Not by any means a substantial amount, my dear, but more a reasonable sum for plots they had obtained. At first, I must confess, I was uncertain of what to think. The very idea of charging these people had never truly occurred to me. Never. And so, with the utmost urgency, I found myself seated at my desk, quill in hand, replying to London.

"Now, you must understand, Meredith, that I had no intention of proceeding with such an act. None whatsoever. I place my heart on that. Do believe me. May I remind you that my coming to the Highlands was never an incentive for my own gain, as I believe I have mentioned before, but purely to enjoy what few years I had left, away from the grinds of business."

Meredith acknowledged, her head nodding in the direction of the fireplace.

"In any case," I continued, "how, I ask you, would charging these farmers for the use of my land assist me in my most pressing endeavours? It certainly would not have seen them gone from their dwellings, that was for certain, but simply compensate me for the inconvenience. To that, I held no interest."

"And did the lawyer, this Scrimshaw, oblige you with a response on the matter?" asked Meredith as she returned her stare from the blaze.

"He did."

"And?"

"He advised me that although he admitted it would not resolve my burden instantly, the decision to introduce such a scheme for these meagre plots could possibly work to my advantage. You see, the people that lodged within these small huts were nothing more than simple farmers, not familiar by any means in the way of the law. Neither were they educated, to that matter. Most could neither read nor write. From the very day they were born, their lives were simple, their sole purpose to reap from the earth in order to stay alive. So, when Scrimshaw expressed that many would, in fact, decline the idea of having to pay and, in doing so, have little choice but to move on, the very notion struck me as a promising one. After all, those who chose not to settle their debts would simply leave. And those who remained, accepting such irrational charges, would, all in good time, follow in their neighbours' footsteps.

"At first, the very concept worked out rather splendidly. Within but a few short months, the population of settlers had drastically decreased by little more than a quarter, with no clear signs of stopping. Initially there was some resistance, as one would expect. However, that soon turned to uproar. After all, what man, regardless of their background, would willingly surrender what they believed is rightfully theirs?"

"No such man exists," Meredith remarked softly, her voice barely heard as though it travelled on the breeze.

"Precisely," I replied

Suddenly, a loud commotion clattered through the room. The noise bounced from wall to wall, directing my attention towards the window, instantly recalling the memory of a bone-like hand smeared across the glass, of a face with eyes so sunken, watching me from the cold.

A wave of fright washed over me; an unsettling dread triggered my palms to sweat and my legs to weaken at the knees. Yet no matter how long I bore witness to the abyss beyond the pane, no matter how hard I stared, waiting for that very hand to rise from the ledge, fingers outstretched, or for that sickening face to emerge, no such display occurred. For those few seconds, everything remained exactly as it had been before, if only for the briefest of moments.

A gentle tap struck the glass, jolting me backwards in my seat, my trembling finger all the while pointing in the direction of my darkest fear.

Meredith's head swiftly followed. "Why, what on earth is the matter?" she enquired, taken aback by my peculiar behaviour. She stood quickly and, with no concern, made her way over to the window, peering out as best she could. She turned to look back. "It is simply a bird, Peter, a small jackdaw, nothing more."

As to whether or not I should have chosen to believe her at that moment, I truly could not say. Yet despite her attempt to dispel my unease, a gnawing doubt persisted.

"A jackdaw?" I cowered, my stare moving away from her and back towards the window.

There, on the ledge, a small bird perched, its feathers as black as night itself, its sheen appearing to weakly glisten in the soft moonlight.

"Yes," Meredith replied, her voice steady, though her uneasy expression remained true upon her face. "While the island may not teem with creatures, the common jackdaw seems to thrive. They nest in the woodland beyond the garden gate, just there." She gestured beyond the pane. "They have a peculiar habit of taking flight during the late hours. Perhaps the lack of light and the fog obscure the house. One can often discover their broken bodies lying stiff across the garden path come morning.

The stunned bird quickly turned its head, locking its gaze to me, its eyes as black as the depths of a coffin.

"Come now, truly," said Meredith, her voice attempting to allay any concerns. "There is no need for such alarm."

There was not a shred of doubt that the presence of such a small creature stirred something within me just then, something far deeper than mere fright. Not that I ever considered myself to be a suspicious man, of course. But as I sat there observing its beady stare and its beak tapping against the glass, it felt as though the arrival of this creature was no mere coincidence. That, that it carried with it a message meant solely for me, a message that I could not begin to decipher.

"Peter?" Meredith's voice gently intruded my gaze, pulling me back from the jackdaw's soulless eyes.

I mustered a forced smile. "Did you say something just now?"

"I asked where we left off," she repeated, her brow slightly furrowed. "Your story …"

"Ah, yes, of course," I replied, my mind settling back into focus. The tightness in my shoulders began to loosen as I nestled deeper into the crook of the chair. "Let me see," I mused, running my fingers across the bristles of my chin. "For many weeks, a sense of quietness seemed to have fallen over the land. I had intentionally distanced myself, perhaps excessively so, demanding that I received visits from my tenants only when their monthly fees were due. It continued like this for quite some time. Eventually, I took it upon myself to employ additional staff—a representative of sorts—to collect the funds on my behalf, thus sparing me from the predictable visits that, like clockwork, arrived at my doorstep. I entrusted this matter to a local individual highly recommended by my trusted housekeeper. He was a reticent man who went by the name of Coull."

Chapter 37

Roderick flinched, the wheels of his chair jolting slightly backwards, as his guest's voice boomed across the desk.

"Wait a second!" Les's voice raised, his tone harsher than he initially intended, scaring the old-timer out of his wits.

"What is it?" Roderick grunted, his eyes wide with shock as he placed a hand firmly on his chest. His breathing appeared rapid. "Are you trying to give this old man a heart attack? Really, there's no need to shout like that." He gestured with his thumb and forefinger, signalling to lower the volume. "Bring it down, will you?"

"I'm sorry," Les replied, sinking back in his chair. Truth be told, he didn't feel too guilty for startling the old man a little. Within the short time that he had spent in the writer's company, it was abundantly clear that the man had a slight flair for dramatics. "I just, I have a question," Les asked, his voice hushed.

The writer's focus shifted back to the cluttered papers on his desk, his gaze fixed on the lines he had just recounted.

"*Reticent*?" he repeated in a condescending manner. His eyes peered over the rim of his spectacles, pupils widening. "It means reserved. Quiet."

"I know what reticent means," snapped Les, his annoyance made perfectly clear. Les may not have been the most educated person, far from it. After all, he had barely made it through his high school years. And for the qualifications he did somehow manage to achieve, Les was never really sure what to do with them or what future they could shape for him.

That said, Les was never one for big dreams like many of his former friends, nor did he ever long for them. In many ways, Les considered himself to be a realist, his future already scoped out by supporting his remaining family, which up until his sudden move to the Highlands had consisted only of his dear mother. His working life had consisted of factories, working long hours with minimal pay. No, he wasn't overly bright, but what he lacked in academics, he made up for in reading.

Reading was Les's one true passion. From a young age, he found himself immersed in books, and in many ways, he found he had more in common with the characters he read on paper than with anyone he had ever met. They were his escape from the real world, his open door to relieve the pressures of life. However, new books were always difficult to come by for a boy tied to a class far beyond his means. His mother had always considered it a useless hobby, a dedication that could be better spent elsewhere—doing what, exactly, Les was never quite sure. Neither was he overly inclined to explore it.

Every Sunday, he would accompany his mother to church, a practice she insisted upon with great merit. Nonetheless, it held no interest for Les. For him, the sermons preached every week were false promises, a way to entice the weak and vulnerable into thinking the church was all they needed, a clever trick to enlist the elderly. Les knew better than to fall for that load of bollocks. Far better. But despite the cold, old hall and the hard wooden pews that caused his arse to grow numb, Les never missed a service and all for good reason too. Once a month, a donation of books was gifted to the church, some of which were assigned to the small chapel library, the rest to be sold at fundraisers or used as raffle prizes to help raise money for the parish.

Needless to say, seeing all those books come in month after month did something for Les. It caused his heart to flutter a little, seeing the haul piled up as they were. After a few discussions with his mother over the dinner table and a rather feeble proposition from the vicar, Les struck a deal to organise the monthly donations by category and, if time allowed it, alphabetical order. His cut? To take any two books he desired from each drop-off. "Just two. Nothing more," he recalled the vicar telling him, his wrinkled finger inches away from prodding Les's face. He was always a tight-arsed git. Despite the small reward, Les was more than happy with the arrangement suggested, regardless of the old goat's temperament. And so, for at least an hour after service, he would find himself huddled away in the dusty back room of the church, sorting through countless piles of books.

As an adult, he had often thought this was where his fondness of reading, or more suitably put, his addiction, began, widening his thirst for stories and his eager desire to consume all he could. Somewhere along the line, he gained a great fondness for the work of Dickens, a 19th century novelist whose books were easy enough to come by. There was never a monthly drop-off that went by at the church where he didn't come across one title or another. After only several months, Les owned the writer's entire collection, which had taken pride and place on his bookshelf. Perhaps it was the slum-like characters that Les had grown to admire, in many ways the heroes of such stories. Or maybe it was simply the striking resemblance between Les's own hardships and how they related to the lives he had come to admire solely through the pages.

As the years went on, Les would broaden his search for classics. He became engrossed in works by Wilde and Hugo, the haunting telling of Irving—one story featuring a schoolteacher pursued by a headless horseman. He always did like that one. Then there was Shelley, of course. He had attempted to read Austen once or twice, the books recommended to him by none other than the ladies of the church, but very much like them, he found the stories to be exceedingly dull and tiresome, with characters that mainly revolved around the likes of women gossiping at home, yapping on and on about men and forcing their fannies to tickle.

"I don't have all day. What is your question?" asked Roderick. He removed his glasses and polished them briskly on his shirt. "By gosh, man. It will be late soon, and I'm afraid I have a pressing engagement. I simply cannot miss it."

Pulled back from his memories, Les looked over the old man's shoulder and out through the small window, noticing the distant light of a boat coming into port.

"The name you mentioned," Les began to explain.

"Name?" remarked Roderick, both hands rummaging about his papers. "What name?"

"You mentioned a man named Coull."

"Coull?" the old man grunted, holding up the papers to the lamp and repeating where he left off. "Ah, yes, Coull. What of it?"

"Nothing," replied Les, feeling rather foolish for asking. "It's just, I knew a man of the same name, back in Elphin."

"Is that so," answered the old man, allowing the paper to freely drop. "A family name, no doubt, most likely of the same bloodline. It is nothing unusual. I have seen it before, many times. The name Coull has been documented in such parts as early as the 16th century, none of them high in status, mind you. Farmhands, really. I know. I have researched the line intently."

With a noticeable cramp in his leg, the old writer stood, turned, and found himself limping to the window.

Outside, the darkness had fully set in, bringing with it a group of rowdy fishermen that loitered outside a pub across the street. Their voices became so loud that the old man could barely hear himself think.

"Then you must know of the man I'm talking about?" asked Les.

"Uh?" grumbled Roderick, his attention still fixed on the drunken crowd below.

"Coull?"

Roderick twisted his neck over the length of his shoulder, his expression clouded in thought. "There was one," he finally answered. "A Coull. I met him, why, it must have been some ten years ago now, perhaps a bit longer."

He removed himself from the window, latching his weight onto a tall filing cabinet that stood surrounded by clutter in the corner. One by one, he slid open the drawers, pulling out files and folders which he tossed carelessly to the floor, muttering beneath his breath. "Where is it? Where is it?" He groaned, slapping each drawer shut after his search. "Ah ha!" rejoiced the man. He picked up an old brown folder from the final drawer, its contents clearly lacking in paperwork as he wafted it about in delight. "I knew it was around here somewhere," he said, making his way back towards the table, his limp suddenly gone. "Now, let's see." He flipped open the folder, pulling out the few crumpled pages from within. "Ah, that's the one." His memory instantly returned. "Mr Michael Coull." He looked at Les. "A charming gentleman, very beneficial to my work, so he was. More than you might think. I have often wondered from time to time how the man was doing."

Les couldn't help but hesitate a little before answering. "I'm afraid he is not doing too well at all."

"You know of him, then?"

"I did, for a time. Very much. We had become good friends, Coull and I. The closest of friends, you might say."

"He is unwell, then?" pressed Roderick, filing away the folder to the floor. "If so, I ask that you pass on my regards, should by chance you see him soon."

"I will," replied Les, clearing his throat. "But I wouldn't expect the same courtesy in return. After all, you never do get much out of a headstone."

"Ah," voiced Roderick, a brief sense of sympathy masking his tired, old face. "Pity," he remarked. "He was a good man, a fine fellow. A knowledgeable one at that. I had the pleasure of meeting him in person from one time to another. After speaking on the phone once, the man insisted I travel to his home—an old cottage, huddled amongst the rocks. Yes, I recall it well."

Les stared blankly, but in a strange way, he felt a sense of happiness at hearing his friend's name spoken by someone other than him.

"I met him, as I said I would. It turned out what he had to say was extremely useful for my research. Critical, actually. Coull seemed to know more about the area's history than I anticipated, more than any other historian I've had the displeasure to meet. The man shared practically everything with me, especially the events leading up to what we have discussed today. I suppose you have had the pleasure of such teachings yourself?"

Les's eyes drifted to the ceiling, watching as the batten bulb above his head displayed a constant flicker. He thought about his time with his old friend, his memory sweeping back like it was only yesterday, following the old farmer's footsteps through the snow as they reached the famine village, a place that by that time was nothing more than scattered rocks. He thought about his time at the Dram Inn, sitting opposite Coull while the storm played havoc on the world outside, and the experience (unknown to him) Les beheld while he was there, an experience that was nothing short of impossible, yet he had witnessed it all the same. The guests at the inn—he had seen them as clearly as he saw the old writer perched across from him at that moment. Certainly, he had his doubts about what he had observed that night. Needless to say, many evenings went by when he even doubted his own memory, a trick of his own mind, he tried to convince himself, brought on by nothing but the drink he had partaken in and the chilling story that went hand in hand as he sat beside the fireplace, listening to Coull's tale.

Yes, there were times after the passing of his dear friend that Les contemplated endlessly on the thought, open to the idea of dismissing it all entirely, every single part of it. After all, how could it have been so? Those poor people, dead and buried in the churchyard, the same grounds that his dear Coull came to lay in, no less—how could he have seen them when he did? How could they all have been there at the inn on that harrowing night?

He lay awake on those nights, tossing and turning on the notion, the very recollection, the question rattling about in his brain. But no matter how much he mulled it over, no matter how much he tried to reason with himself that the whole experience was nothing more than the strangest of circumstances, Les eventually found himself with no other choice but to gradually move on, to let what he had seen slowly ease into the back of his mind. To accept it. After all, if he could accept what he had experienced during his time at Elphin cottage, accept the story of Martha Farrell, who was he to doubt the events of that unforgettable night at the old Dram Inn? Ghosts were real.

"Well?" Roderick's voice found its way to Les. "Did the man speak of his heritage?"

Les sat upright, blinking himself from the daze. "His heritage?" he asked. "No. But he did speak of the past, and with much passion. He was very proud of it, was Coull."

"That he was," agreed Roderick. "That he was. But you must never mistake word of mouth to be the God's honest truth, my boy. Stories," he gestured with his hand, "they can get muddled over the years. Many what I call important facts can get lost along the way. I suppose what I'm trying to say is Mr Coull knew his past from the stories he was raised up with. But let us not forget it is the hard evidence," he pointed out, "documentation, if you will, that always solves the puzzle. Without such papers, we resort to simple hearsay, you understand?"

Les glanced down to the scribblings on the writer's desk and, rather than indulge the man in his art of fact-finding, simply asked, "Did you share your findings with him? Coull, I mean?"

"I did," the old writer mumbled. "Never have I met a man so intrigued to hear such knowledge." He let out a short, humorous chuckle. "Other than yourself, that is. It is funny that we should all have crossed paths the way we have. Nevertheless, when the time came for me to disclose the involvement of his ancestors, Coull wished to hear no more. He simply closed the subject, asked me to leave and for me to take my papers with me. That was the last I heard of the man. However, I am sorry to learn of his passing. That said, a man such as Coull could not smoke the way he did and not be subject to some repercussions. We are only human, Mr Wills."

Again, Les's memories of this old friend consumed his mind: the endless cigarettes, the way he looked during his final days, the illness, the retching, the blood-spattered marks upon his wrist as he coughed. Les would have given anything to change things, to see his friend not go the way he did.

"Why would he oppose hearing about his own bloodline?" asked Les. It didn't make sense. "I mean, it was his family."

"Who can say," replied Roderick with a somewhat dismissive shrug. Drawing his attention away from his guest, Roderick once again settled back to his papers. "Maybe it was the fear of knowing what might come, that the name he claimed so proudly could, in some way, have been mixed up in this whole despicable mess. Maybe he had already chosen not to believe what I was about to tell him. Or maybe he was simply content with his own teachings, proud of the story that he knew, the story told to him by his father and most likely his father before him. That is, at least, the way I prefer to think of it. Nothing more, nothing less. Now, Mr Wills, if I may?" asked Roderick, a magnifying glass ready in his hand.

Les enquired no further but casually tipped his head. The image of his friend lying on his deathbed during his final days remained strong with him. No matter how much he tried, Coull's face never left him, even as the old writer continued to read.

Chapter 38

"Coull, by many accounts, was a reserved and strangely quiet sort of chap. I was told that he had previously worked on the property, a groundskeeper, so to speak. He took care of various tasks around the grounds, tended to the horses, and was responsible for maintaining the house in case of any little damage. Considering his background, it seemed like a natural choice to employ the man when I did. And for good reason too. He was just the man I needed, not just for his loyalty but for his pure brute strength. He was a large man, in many regards a somewhat imposing figure—the kind of man who could plough a field without the need of a horse. He was tall in height and compensated for his lack of hair with a beard that fell about his chest. His tattered sleeves moved in the breeze as he farmed the field, revealing forearms the size of tree trunks.

"Apart from his daily responsibilities of the grounds and the stables, I also instructed Coull to visit the farming plots once a month to collect the rent. I insisted that he should take matters into his own hands if necessary, not to settle for anything less than the full amount owed—no negotiations. That was the rule. The man challenged little in regards to such demands, but instead often returned my gaze with gentle eyes, acknowledging only with a bow of his head.

"And so, every month's end, Coull would come to the house, bringing with him the coins he had gathered that day. He would often stand by quietly in the doorway, his hat clutched tightly in his hands, refusing to budge until every coin was accounted for and books carefully balanced. Rarely did he find the voice to speak, his quiet words barely heard over the scratching of my quill. When he did, he often would share the difficulties faced by the farmers, describing how selling their harvest to pay me left meagre means for them to survive. Perhaps Coull believed that, considering the nature of my requests, I would display some form of sympathy towards their plight. But in truth, I barely spared a moment. To me, they were merely feeble excuses, that was all, a natural case to express such matters. After all, it was their way of life. I had encountered such people for countless years—those who wouldn't lift so much as a finger yet sought the most generous charity in return. No, if they could manage to provide for their families, then surely they could afford the roof over their heads.

"Coull remained silent thereafter, offering no voice for the months that followed. Yet I couldn't help but notice the broken look that was etched upon his face when he next returned to the house, his gaze filled with shame and his eyes cast downward. It was as though the man knew what was to come."

The strands of Meredith's hair appeared to shimmer, reflecting the flames of the fire. She had long since finished her tea, yet the cup remained firm in her grasp as I spoke.

"What was to come?" she asked, and placed the cup upon the table.

Clearing my throat, I gathered what little voice I could muster. "I'm afraid what I'm about to tell you will not come easy to your ears, nor will it be easy for me to speak of, I assure you. Believe me, I have tried."

Rising from my seat, I paced the room calmly, the weight of my footsteps creaking the floorboards. "You must trust me when I tell you this. If there were any other way of explaining the events that were to follow, I would choose to do so. But I can do no such thing. The truth stands as it is. There is no dividing it."

Remaining seated, Meredith did nothing but observe me from across the room, her unbroken attention never straying from my restless feet as I ceased circling the floor. With her hands placed delicately on her lap, leaving no room for distraction, she urged me to go on with her look alone.

"It was the following spring when everything fell apart, catching me completely unaware. I never expected it to happen, and really, who would?

"Payments had been few and far between during the winter. There were even some months when I didn't receive a single penny at all. I was furious, as you can well imagine, overwhelmed with frustration. The very thought that these people, these common peasants, were making a mockery of our agreement consumed me greatly. In fact, I was so angry that on a blessed Sunday evening, I lay in my chambers long into the night and thought of nothing else. Things could not continue as they were. I would not allow it. Could not. So, I decided to take matters into my own hands.

"The very next morning, I summoned Coull to join me in my office. In his same old punctual manner, he arrived, stepping into the room with a furrowed brow and laboured breath, leaving the impression that he had hastened his way there with some urgency. I motioned for him to take a seat, and after some consideration, he reluctantly stepped forward and obliged. He had the same worried look upon his face, like that of a child waiting anxiously, knowing that a beating would come. And rightly so too. At the end of the day, what good is a money collector who lacks the ability to collect the funds?

"With a stern manner, I looked the man up and down before shooting a glare so intense, so furious, that it sent him shrinking back into his seat. A sense of fear widened his eyes. I warned him that should he return from the settlement again that day without a single coin in hand, he would find himself without employment, and furthermore, he would never find work within several miles again.

"At first, the man was silent, his face filled with the same self-pitying look I had grown accustomed to. Finally, when I demanded that he speak, he found himself momentarily speechless. After a few seconds, in a tone tinged with sadness, Coull informed me, with much dithering, that there was no more money left to be had. The farmers were penniless.

"Now, it goes without saying that I was slightly taken aback by such news, and with a thump of my fist to the desk, I insisted that he explain himself immediately.

"Coull's stare never wandered but instead stayed fixed upon me at all times. He appeared somewhat surprised by my questioning, casting a fleeting shadow of doubt on whether I was aware of what he was referring to at all. And with a touch of hesitance, a mannerism he often displayed in front of others, Coull soon found himself in the uncomfortable position of having to divulge it all—every little detail. He told me that my tenants were starving, their want for food so agonising that the spectre of death loomed over them all. He told me that the land they had farmed for generations had suddenly turned sour, leaving them without the means to feed their loved ones, to pay me. As you can imagine, this all came as quite a shock. Until that day, I had heard nothing of the sort—no rumours, no gossip, regarding the blight. So, when I found myself cutting him off in mid-sentence and questioning why the tenants would simply not leave and find means elsewhere, he simply enquired, "Without a coin to their name and starving to death, where would you expect they go?'"

With her fingers knitted tightly together, Meredith's eyes rolled in the weakened light. "Surely you don't mean to say that you hadn't heard a word of the ordeal?" Her nose creased slightly. "Truly?"

I waved off her question with a passive shrug. "Granted, I had spent much time confined to the house. Perhaps a little too much, venturing outside only when the fresh air appealed to me, a short walk around the boundaries of the house. Nothing more. I suppose when one grows used to living in such seclusion, isolation itself can become quite the addiction. But if I had heard such news prior to then, if I had travelled to the nearest town, I'm sure I—"

"If you had listened to the man in the first place," interrupted Meredith with great purpose, "you would have heard that the majority of the Highlands were or already had been facing the same dreadful dilemma." Meredith tutted. "I mean, really, Peter," she breathed through her nose, "how could you not have known? You, a man of such education. Why else do you think the peasants of Ireland are so desperate, so determined to abandon their homeland, crossing over in their masses? There hasn't been a piece of news this past year that hasn't revolved around potatoes—this and that. Even here, shortly after the rumours began, our crops began to fail. They turned black, Peter. As black as coal. Why else do you believe the old village that sits on the outskirts of this house is abandoned, the cottages left to ruin?"

Stepping over to the fire, I leant against the hearth and allowed the warmth to take me. "I assumed the work in the quarry had ceased operations," I stated bluntly. "I assumed they had simply left."

"They died, Peter," said Meredith, her expression as solid as stone. "Perished. Not all of them, but enough. I took it upon myself to help where I could, providing a hot bowl of soup or whatever fabric I could obtain to shield them from the cold. But the demands were far too great. If starvation hadn't taken them, then sickness surely would have. Towards the end, there were hardly any people left, and those who remained would have lasted little more than a month. With little else to do, I took it upon myself to ensure everyone's safe passage from the island. At least on the mainland they might have had a fighting chance. At least, I would like to think so."

Still at the hearth, absorbed by every word she spoke, I couldn't help but ask, "You sought relief for those people? Strangers?" I paused. "Paid for it yourself?"

"Every penny," she stated proudly. "All from my own inheritance, I can assure you of that. I had little choice. Who else was there to help them?"

The fire spat and crackled, throwing embers across my feet and causing me to flinch.

"I had no idea," I said, accompanied by a softened stare.

"And why would you?" she asked. "I would not have expected as much, especially when you claimed to have no idea of the misfortunes that had befallen your own land."

Another strand of hair fell from the bun on her head, settling loosely upon her cheek. "Regardless," she continued, "after hearing of such hardships, I assume you did whatever was within your power to help those poor people?"

In an instant, an unyielding burden seized hold of me, rendering me speechless as my eyes traversed the room, my trembling hand finding comfort upon my brow as if to shroud my face from her.

"Oh, Peter, you didn't?" Meredith remarked in nearly a whisper, her eyes shutting tightly, awaiting my response. "Please, please tell me you didn't allow those souls to suffer. Not after you discovered what you did. Not when you had the means to help them. You must at least assure me of that."

"My dear Meredith, how could I have known?" I retorted, swiftly turning on my heels and locking my gaze with hers. "Initially, I dismissed it as mere exaggeration, a ploy by the tenants to appeal to my charitable nature. You must believe me when I say this. I had no idea of the horrors these people endured. Truly, I did not."

Meredith's brow furrowed even deeper, accentuating the lines on her forehead—a look that conveyed pure disappointment, as if she were wrestling with thoughts too heavy to voice. "But surely, after hearing the groundsman's account, you must have had some suspicion? If not a trace of curiosity?"

Regrettably, I found myself with not a word to say.

"And you never even considered visiting this patch of land you fought so hard for, if only to reassure yourself of the matter?"

The memories flashed before my eyes in the blink of a moment—the dark, haunting images I had tried so hard to forget.

"I did. Although you must understand that by this time, the news of failed crops was everywhere. There was not a place in all of Scotland where talk of the poor had not fallen on the tip of every man's tongue or the wagging of every woman's. Furthermore, what could be done to stop it?"

"But," huffed Meredith, her frustration reaching such heights that her heel began to tap, "you must know that the only path to achieve such an outcome is through relief."

It went without saying that her statement was undeniably true, and in many respects, I could never have anticipated anything less to fall from her lips as she said it. She was a rare creature in many ways, with a heart that cared not only for herself but also for the well-being of others, even those she had not met.

"Yes, but," I protested calmly, "you speak of relief as if it were some meagre cause, as though a few meals would cease their torment. Of course measures were introduced to aid them. I suppose it is why I found myself doing nothing. I relied solely on the words of others. After some time, it was said that supplies of food had arrived to the few areas that required it most, shipped from abroad. Heaven knows what they received. But those who went without were simply left to fend for themselves, scavenge. And with little to be sourced from the ground, many were left with only one choice—to leave their home and walk by foot to the nearest towns."

Meredith looked almost too worried to ask. "And what awaited them at the nearest towns?"

"The workhouse," I stated plainly. "That is, if luck was on their side. For those who were not so fortunate, I heard they would walk barefoot through the bitter cold only to be turned away at the door. Even now, as we speak, they line up at the gates, barely clothed, leaning and pushing against one another like scoundrels, desperate for the slightest morsel. A dreadful sight."

"Oh, how awful," muttered Meredith with an air of grief.

I observed her closely, watching her eyes as she fought to hold back tears. It was clear that what I mentioned had affected her in some peculiar way. Perhaps the notion stirred memories of her own misfortunes, her son, fuelling whatever grief she carried. Or perhaps her thoughts wandered elsewhere, to the island's inhabitants, forced to leave for the mainland, longing to know if they still remained a part of this world at all.

"Yes, the workhouses are indeed an unsightly place," I added.

"Truly."

"Nevertheless, its purpose is a necessary one."

"And what of the families?" asked Meredith. "I hear that many cannot reside together, that they are torn apart: wives from husbands, children from their mothers, some never to lay eyes upon each other again. A terrible thing."

"And no concern of ours," I stated as I patted my pockets in hope of finding my pipe. "Besides, it is not within the house's interest to keep families together. Nor is it to ensure that every man, woman, and child is cared for. It is a workhouse, nothing more. Those who are fortunate enough to find a place within their walls should realise just how fortunate they truly are and, further to that, be all the more grateful for it."

Meredith bowed her head low, sniffling pathetically as her chin came to rest on the collar around her neck. "That is an awfully cruel way to think, Peter," she said quietly, unable to shy away.

"Why, I don't believe so," I remarked. "You forget, you have not seen the world as I have, Meredith, cooped up here in this old fortress of a house. Out there, in the real world, the poor prey upon the wealthy, loath them. I dare say we have witnessed this very injustice upon our own family. Your own son, my beloved nephew, struck down by none other than some worthless peasant, a no gooder. And for what, I ask you? In the hope of a few spare shillings, some food? No!" My heel stomped hard to the floor, causing the din to echo through the upper levels of the house. "If you had seen what I had seen on that day," I went on, prodding at my chest with great purpose, "saw what I had witnessed when venturing back to farmlands, the sight that awaited me, well, I dare say even you would find my reasoning far less cruel."

My sister's mouth hung ajar, half unsure if what she was about to ask was wise or better left unspoken.

"Bodies." I shuddered. "Bodies everywhere. Though I must tell you, it was not the idea of death that disturbed me so. Lord knows I have seen my fair share of the occasional lifeless corpse. It is more the revolting state of which I found them to be. The day was cold and damp when Coull, myself, and several other of my men crossed the Ledmore River, trudging our way towards the settlement. I recall it had rained rather heavily the night before, making the long, tough grass all the more challenging to wade through. We followed the trail leading us to a small dirt path that weaved its way through the hillsides. The morning was peculiarly quiet and still. The steady winds that had stirred the land over the past day had suddenly come to pass, its calming moan that gently shook the tree gone.

"As we made our final bend on the path, the first few dwellings came into view. I should have known right there and then that something was amiss, for what displayed before me was not that of the same bustling community I remembered but more of an unnerving silence, a picture as peaceful as a graveyard. We walked onwards, passing the boundary cottages, the first of which presented absent a door and a roof so miserably sunken that, by all accounts, it could not be worthy for purpose. The inside lay bare and soulless, minus a single possession within its darkened space.

"As we continued stomping through the mud, more stone huts soon emerged, with not so much as a soul to occupy them. It seemed as though the entire community had deserted, the people gone without so much as a trace. However, as I stood by, observing the men as they ventured from hut to hut, Coull insisted with the brief motion of his head that we widen our search to the east side of the farmlands, stating that if anyone was still to remain here, the east side was the most likely place for them to be.

"It took us only a short walk before we arrived at the edge of the settlement, met by a cluster of cottages nestled along a narrow stream that trickled its way through the valley. Unlike the other dwellings we had encountered that morning, the doors of each small cottage appeared to be firmly closed, the windows still intact, and although their structures were in no way pleasing to behold, it begged the question if anyone resided within.

"Without so much as an order from me, Coull made his way towards the nearest cottage, his steps slow and sluggish as he knocked his knuckles upon the door.

"There was no answer. Need I say it, not so much as a peep stirred from inside. He tried again, his knock more forceful. Only this time, the door appeared to open on its own. The hinges groaned, cutting through the bitter air. Inside, the small house appeared dark and dank, giving one the impression that it had stood without an owner for years.

"Coull moved forward, edging through the threshold as his body dispelled into shadows. He remained inside for no longer than a moment. And as the men and myself continued to watch, Coull soon reappeared into the daylight, rushing from the house, soon to find himself fallen to a patch of nearby grass, retching violently as he gasped. His skin was pale, as pale as chalk, as though whatever he had encountered inside had caused his colour to drain from him.

"I encouraged the other men to proceed, myself but a short step behind. But when I entered the cottage, a sour smell struck me. On the ground, the sound of a rodent darted somewhere across the room's corner, its scurrying feet tapping away, desperate for a place to hide. It was then that the men ahead stumbled back with what seemed to have been the greatest shock. One dug into his pocket with urgency, retrieving a handkerchief and smothering it against his nose. At first, I must confess I didn't know what to expect. And in that brief panic, I genuinely feared for my safety.

"It was when the man shifted back towards the light, his body no longer blocking the view ahead, that I saw them—a glimpse into the far side room—that revealed the sight of several bodies lying still upon a bed. They made not a sound as I drew closer. Nor due to their weakened appearance would I have expected as much. A terrible sight, so it was, a scene which no tongue or pen could convey in the same truth. Three famished children, to all appearances dead, lay huddled together under a ragged horse cloth. Their parents, too, likely dead, buried by their own offspring and, in turn, leaving them to fend for themselves. One of the children's ghastly legs, naked from the knees down, hung from the bedside, his features sharpened with hunger and his limbs wasted, displayed little left but bone. A despicable sight. Even now it does not come easy to speak of.

"But these encounters were not short lived. We happened to come by more bodies in the remaining houses that sat along the stream, each interior teeming in the same repulsive state. One hovel housed a family found laying on a blanket of hay, covered in filth—two children, a boy and a girl, a woman, and what I can only guess was once a man, half eaten by rats. How we found them still causes my stomach to knot. They lay together in the most contorted manner, their limbs strained with clenched fists, their faces filled with suffering as though the excruciating want of food still remained in death.

"Another cottage, though much smaller than the previous huts we had searched, presented only a single room, occupied by a skeletal woman. She sat slumped against the stone wall, her shoulders hunched, hair clung to her skin, and eyes so wide and absent that they appeared to gaze right through me. God only knows how long she had been sitting there or how long it had been since she died. But as one of my men stepped closer, the woman's eyes suddenly began to jitter as she let out a low moan. Reaching out, the woman tried to grasp him but failed, begging him for food as she lay upon the floor in a lifeless heap, her body too heavy for her to rise. Her final moments did not last long. Within only seconds, her sobbing began to calm, her gasping ceased, as she lay stone dead across the floor.

"By the time we reached the final house, the sun had peaked its highest, and much to mine and the men's relief, no tenants were found inside. But despite its obnoxious stench, its filth, it housed no more than a single chair. I found myself baffled to find that the stone chimney wall stood warm. But as for the residents, there was not a soul in sight.

"We buried thirty-two people that day, each one removed from their dwelling and lined along the grassy bank—five men, sixteen women, and eleven children, all destined for the same grave. It took us several hours to dig deep enough. And by the time the bodies had been thrown into the earth, the daylight had started to fade as the sun haloed behind the northern mountainside.

"As for the rest of the settlement, we left the village that day very much as it was found, untouched, and returned to the path towards the river. In a silence unbroken, not one man spoke as we walked, our minds clouded by what we had seen, wondering if what we had witnessed that day could ever come to be forgotten."

Chapter 39

The room fell into an uneasy silence, so hushed that only Meredith's sobs seemed to fill the void. It didn't take long for her to gather her composure. Standing up, she made her way towards the window. There she stayed, observing the jackdaw still perched beyond the glass.

"That," she began, her emotions getting the better of her, "is the most heartbreaking tale I've ever heard." Her brow furrowed some as her gaze remained fixed, her imagination holding her trapped. Of course, it was nothing new to me. Even as a small girl, Meredith found ways to immerse herself in a story, allowing her mind to wander into the darkest corners as if the misfortunes of others were hers alone to bear. She would conjure every vivid detail she could envision, hear every voice that played in her head, and often found herself becoming unwell with worry because of it.

"I am sorry to have shared it," I said, watching as she tilted her head and allowed it to solemnly rest against the pane. "But you did insist, did you not?"

"I did," she replied, her voice less fragile than before. "And I must confess that I am in no way sorry for asking, nor do I regret having heard it. However," she looked back, "there is no doubt in my mind that what you and your men endured that day could in some way have been avoided, given the privileged position you held. And yet, for some reason or another, you decided not to. You were cruel, Peter. Bitter and heartless. Stuck in your old stubborn ways. You must see that now? In fact, I know you do. Why else would you have left your beloved home, travelled halfway across Scotland only to be standing here with me, telling me what you have. If you ask me, I believe that you feel the guilt. Guilt from your lack of humanity, the burden of what you witnessed, knowing all too well that you could have done something more to stop it. It has consumed you, Peter, eaten away at you piece by piece. I understand now. I see it. It is as clear as the moon that scrapes through the clouds. You plead for mercy, yearn for it, fearing that no one could possibly understand. It's what keeps you awake at night." Her eyes narrowed. "Why you can't sleep, cannot eat, why these dreams of yours continue to show no end, forcing you to relive it all over again, night after night. Yes, it was a dreadful thing, there is no denying it. Nor would I try to. Yet should you desire forgiveness for the path you have led, know that I, your sister, will in time find my own way to forgive you. Surely that, if anything, is a start?"

I knelt down to the fire and added another log to the grate. A cold breeze funnelled down the chimney, accompanied by the faintest howl.

"You do seek my forgiveness?" Meredith asked. Much to my lack of attention, I had come to realise that she no longer stood by the window, but rather a few steps away from where I knelt, her hands cupped at the waist, anxiously twiddling her thumbs.

"Of course," I answered her, my concentration staying true, unbroken from the flickering flames that forced my eyes to water. "I wish it more than anything. Not only for myself, but for you to see me for the man you always believed me to be."

"Then you shall have it, Peter," replied Meredith, edging towards me with much compassion in her tone.

"But I cannot," I said, clenching my eyes from the heat.

Meredith paused hesitantly in her stead, both feet simultaneously coming to a sudden halt. "You cannot?" she repeated, her partially lit face painted by what one could only perceive as confusion, and rightly so.

"No," I answered. "Not until I have shared with you what was to come. Not until I have told you everything. You see, then and only then could I truly accept your kindness."

She did not move from where she stood, but instead released her hands and, by doing so, allowed them to drop to her sides. There she waited, her chest rising and falling, her troubled breath heard over the spit of the fire.

"There was a woman," I began.

"What do you mean, a woman?" Meredith wrinkled her nose. "You mean at the farmlands?"

I rose slowly from the fireplace.

"Yes," I groaned. "A woman. A woman and two young girls, her daughters, only young little things, so they were. If I were to guess, somewhere between the ages of six and ten."

Meredith gazed on with the blankest expression.

"Please, allow me to explain," I offered, gesturing for her to return to her chair.

She would not budge.

"You see, once we returned to the settlement a day or two later, making sure that all bodies had been found and promptly placed into the ground, I decided to burn what remained of the dwellings, have them destroyed."

"Destroyed?" recounted Meredith.

I shrugged as though in surrender. "I thought it best, my dear. With much death comes many things—vermin mostly, then disease. And by then the farmlands were already seething with them. Rodents everywhere. You would not believe how many if I told you. I, for one, certainly would not have if it weren't for my own two eyes. Rats scurried about the dwellings inside and out, many found feasting upon the dead. Why, I would go as far as to say that if we had not stumbled upon the corpses when we did, there would not have been a single scrap of flesh left on them. Rats—they are filthy creatures, in many ways like the poor they gnawed upon, shrieking the same hideous cry for want. Not forgetting what they carry: plague and lice. So you see, burning what was left of the settlement was purely for the greater good, to cleanse the land of any sickness, as it were."

"And did you?" prompted Meredith. Her eyes were sharp and hard, a mother's stare. She moved closer, stealing the light of the candle behind her.

"I would have, yes. In fact, I distinctly recall shouting the order. But as my men approached the nearest house, they stopped dead in their place, like living statues they were, their torches lowered. At first, I admit I wasn't sure what to think, nor did I give it much thought. That is until I saw her for myself."

"Who?"

"The woman standing at the bank of the stream, a small bucket grasped in hand and two small children sitting at her feet. At first glance, she appeared old. Her sunken cheeks and bony frame gave the impression of a woman far beyond her years. It was not until I stepped closer that I saw much life shone in her eyes; perhaps it was even beauty I glimpsed. For what I saw was no elderly creature, but a young lady who was perhaps not a day past thirty, masked by a raging hunger that riddled deep within. Her children, too, in many ways mirrored their mother's state. Their bulging eyes appeared to pop from their skulls, partially hidden by thick, matted hair, and their bodies, covered by nothing more than tattered cloth, revealed legs and arms so painfully thin it begged the question of how they still were alive at all."

Meredith knelt before me, and with one hand placed upon my shoulder, she gently squeezed. "The poor dears," she remarked. "Please, Peter. Please tell me that you did something to help them in their struggle? That you at least offered this woman, her children, some form of charity."

Meredith gazed at me with large, glassy eyes—eyes so big and round that the reflection of the fireplace seemed to blaze within them.

"I did," I replied, clearing my throat mid-sentence. "I employed the woman."

Meredith looked at me blankly, her grip slightly loosened. "You mean to say you made this poor woman, a mother, no less, near the edge of death, seek your employment?"

My brow deepened some. "My dear, you make it sound as though I had committed some unjust act. Besides, what I offered her was so much more. More than any other respectable man would have."

My sister stayed rooted to her spot on the floor, her expression altering swiftly from relief to sincere worry in the blink of an eye.

"Yes, I took her on as a member of my staff," I continued, "proposing she take on tasks such as tending to the gardens and handling lighter chores around the house—nothing too demanding. In return, I ensured that she and her children were provided for. No longer would they have to endure living within that hovel of theirs, spending their nights huddled together on the ground amidst the squalor. No, I proposed a new lodging for them—a small dwelling located just across the land from Elphin house. A place where they would be close, for me to keep my eye on them. And in the meantime, I would make arrangements for the old settlement to be destroyed."

Meredith's distant expression lasted but a fleeting moment, her face marked by a cloud of concentration. "But, this woman. She had no other family, no husband to care for her?"

"Dead, all of them," I answered plainly. "That is what the young lady told me, at least. As for her husband …" I scratched my head in thought. "If I recall, he was one of the many that made the repeated walk to the nearest workhouse. A gruelling journey, especially when one is without shoes. I was told that one day he simply never returned.

Not that this would have been anything out of the ordinary. Bodies of the poor, they are often found sprawled across the roadside. They seem to have this tendency to drop like flies. A death fitting for such a wasteful life, wouldn't you agree? I expect the same to have occurred to the young woman's husband."

"Enough, Peter!" spouted Meredith, launching up from the floor and clasping both hands to her ears. She began to pace. "Have you no shame in what you say? No pity? Why, you speak of a person's life as though it is nothing more than a mere object at the mercy of your disposal, an inconvenience at most, that one's pain means, well, simply nothing."

Her heavy footsteps echoed about the room, matching the annoyance that brewed within her and the strain that ran along her jaw.

"Meredith," I addressed her delicately. "I have spoken only of what you have asked of me. Furthermore, only what you have yearned to hear, regardless of the detail."

"Detail, indeed," she huffed. "Well, I need not hear it. Nor do I approve of the views." She continued back and forth, her stride never slowing until she came to a weary stop. Flustered and somewhat breathless, Meredith found herself leant upon a bedside cabinet before slowly slumping down and perching at the edge of the bed. "I'm sorry," she uttered, her fists balled down into the linen. "These last few days have seen the better of me. Sleeping, it has been difficult."

So much was true. The woman before me had undergone an overwhelming change. She was no longer the same person who, just a few days earlier, had welcomed me back to the island. The familiar air of the sister I knew had vanished, replaced by her own deep despair. Her heart had been shattered, forcibly ripped from her chest, expelling the very glow that had always shone brightly. All that remained was an emptiness, a darkness that enclosed her soul—a mere shadow of her former self.

"Perhaps you should try," I advised her softly.

Meredith spun around, her neck twisting, determined to catch my gaze. "Nonsense. What of your story?"

"Such things can wait," I claimed. "For now, I suggest you rest."

"Oh, I am tired of resting," she panted. "If I am not to sleep, I am to rest, and right now, I wish for neither." With a sudden movement, Meredith surrendered her weight and flopped back to the bed, her head cushioned by the drop. "There!" she stated. "I am rested."

Her eyes darted at me through the dark, a silent plea for me to proceed.

I continued on, my voice steady. "Within a matter of days, I ensured that Clais Cottage was a suitable home for the woman and her two young children to reside in. Furthermore, I made sure they had the means to sustain themselves. Every day, like clockwork, I provided them with a little food, something to drink. And in due course, this once destitute woman would become part of the housekeeping staff. But, like many things, it was not to last. No good thing ever does."

"Oh …" responded Meredith, her interest once more piquing. "You mean to say the woman crossed you in some way? What was it?"

"Theft," I remarked.

"Oh my," answered Meredith in shock, one hand posed dramatically to her chest. "Then one would suggest you had every right to be angry. It is a sad thing, really, to think that one's money is not secure under their own roof, especially without the worry of suspecting your own staff to be the culprit. Such an act, well, it should not be tolerated."

"Money?" I enquired. "I'm afraid you are mistaken. There was no money stolen. None that I was aware of, at least. And if you were to ask me, nor do I believe this woman had the courage within her to do so. Her crimes, they were much more feeble. Might I say petty."

"Petty?" repeated Meredith, the shock drained from her face. "Well, what do you know her to have stolen, then?"

"Food."

"Food?" she blurted out.

"Very much so," I concurred. The distant memory still caused the blood within me to boil. "And from my own table, no less. Scraps, meagre leftovers from dinners. Bread, meat, a little fruit, whatever morsels she could lay her hands on, she took, and took with the greatest discretion. Heaven knows how long it had been going on, thinking me a fool as she did."

"But why?" remarked Meredith, who by then had retired her resting pose and found herself bolt upright on the bed. "Why steal what you were already willing to offer?"

I shrugged dismissively, watching as the candle on the nightstand again jittered, fighting against the hidden draft.

"She told me …" I answered impatiently. "She claimed that whatever food I offered as payment was simply not enough, that her daughters lay weak and hungry at the cottage. That they had done so for many weeks. Of course, she displayed regret from such a foolish act, in many ways attempting to assure me that no such offence would ever happen again. She grew upset, hysterical, and when I tried to respond, she simply fell to her knees, weeping at my very feet. It was a pitiful display, the state of how she acted, leaving me little choice."

Within but a few seconds, Meredith approached from the bedside, a sorrowful look smeared across her face as she drifted from one side of the room to the other, her dress sweeping up the dust as she walked. She stared into my eyes, refusing to let go, as if the lack of empathy and cruelty was visible on my face. "You offered the woman further charity, I presume?" Her questions went on. "Something to relieve her misery? Further food to aid her young ones?"

"Charity?" I could not help but heckle. "I dare say I did no such thing. Charity … It is all very well and good if given in small doses. But when one becomes too dependent upon it, well, it is hardly charity at all."

"You mean to say you did nothing for her? Nothing at all?" asked Meredith, who by now began to finger the pearls of her necklace anxiously.

A sudden awkwardness lingered between us. The only sounds were that of rats' feet inside the chimney breast wall, darting between the brickwork, and the sound of trapped air entering the house from the attic.

"If I were to reward the woman for her disobedience, to forget the flagrant betrayal of my trust, what lesson would have been learned? What possible good could come from such an act?"

Meredith stood quietly, swaying slightly, her dress softly touching the warm glow of the fire.

"This woman," I continued. "would be led to believe that dishonesty above all things is rewarded and, worse yet, that I, a gentleman, would condone it. I simply could not allow that. I would not. And so to demonstrate my seriousness, I did what I believed was necessary, what any respectable man would have done."

Meredith finally spoke, her hands ceasing their fidgeting with the pearls. "What did you do?"

Beyond the window, a sudden gust stirred, causing the distant trees to quiver as if they were nothing more than tufts of grass in an open field. I glanced at the fire, its flames still burning brightly, offering what little comfort it could.

"Well?" urged Meredith, still standing before me, her voice barely but a whisper. "What did you do?"

"I saw her thrown out," I replied, my voice whispering. "I, I saw her succumb to the cold."

Chapter 40

I picked up the teapot and poured, clumsily missing the cup in the process and allowing the liquid to splash upon the saucer, some to the table. The tea was cold on my lips, the taste bitter.

By the dying fireplace, Meredith remained as stern as ever, watching me, waiting for me to explain, to relieve her of the anxiousness brewing within.

"You…" Meredith paused, swallowing back whatever words she attempted to say. "You banished the poor woman?"

I remained silent, conveying my thoughts through a musing gaze alone. I took another sip from the cup, the familiar bitterness lingering on my tongue. I had no desire to drink more, yet an inner compulsion urged me to do so, a feeble attempt at distraction, perhaps to evade the piercing eyes that awaited me.

"And so," continued Meredith, longing to force the words out of me. "What was to become of her?"

I placed the cup down, observing the teacup tremble as it clunked against the wood.

"It saw the woman to her end," I answered.

She took half a step backwards, looking me up and down, her hands raised to her mouth in utter disbelief. "You mean to say she died, by your own doing no less?"

A howl flowed over the house.

"She did," I eventually answered, worried that the house might not withstand the weather outside and come toppling down upon us. "But it was not an instant end. Neither was it for her daughters."

My sister's expression shifted. Her glazed eyes widening at the sound of a single word. "Surely you don't mean to say …"

"I do." I released a heavy breath. "Moreover, I find myself with no pleasure having to say it. In truth, I'm not quite sure what to feel. After all, they were but minors—unsightly creatures, but children nonetheless. I suppose they did not deserve the ending they received. Her eldest, she passed away not too long after, some illness."

Another tear welled up in the corner of Meredith's eye, its journey down her cheek beginning only to be swiftly brushed away.

"You must understand," I tried to tell her, "it had been a cold winter, a winter with snow so deep it could hide the knee. It is not uncommon for people, especially young children, to fall ill under such circumstances. The cold has a way of seeping into them, bringing forth a chorus of coughs and splutters. I plainly thought nothing more than that. As for the mother, one night, during a storm, she stood outside my home, peering in, yelling. What she called out I could not hear as the storm blew fierce, knocking her slender frame from the window. She clung to something—something in her arms. The form was wrapped to her sickly body, yet I could not discern what. She began to cry, to plead, rapping at the window like an untamed dog. Under no circumstances would I have unbolted my doors, not on that night of all nights. Not when she was acting as she was.

"The noises turned quiet after that, so quiet that not so much as a whimper could be heard. Gone was her shadow at the window. The only trace left behind was the bloodied handprints on the pane. It was not until the very next morning that I would find her. On the ground, squeezed into the corner of the wall space, an odd shape rested. At first, it seemed to be nothing more than a pile of drifted snow windswept by the storm. Yet as the maid continued to loiter by the doorstep, her eyes all puffed up and red as they were, her hands clasped against the seal of her lips if only to cork a scream. It was then I saw it. A face."

"A face?" asked Meredith.

"A face as white as the snow itself. The eyes were closed, frozen stiff like a death mask, the expression as peaceful as sleep itself."

My mind drifted back to that very morning, the memory, the image just as vivid as ever before. I think of her body lying still in the snow, the face all cut and bruised, cheeks sunken, and lips so frostbitten they bore the hue of the coldest blue.

"Peter?"

I think of the people that gathered behind me as the snow was brushed from the corpse, the noises which escape them, the gasps. The horror. Their faces were appalled as they scrambled back into the house like sheep. I think about the bitter breeze as it stabbed at my chest, the sound of untouched snow crunching beneath my feet as I waited, waited as the blanket of ice was removed. Something else lay there. Something small. Something hidden.

"Peter!" Meredith's voice bellowed, her tone rising to the ceiling and snapping me out of my daze.

I looked up, taking note of the blatant expression that plagued her face.

"What of the other child?" she asked me, her voice simmering. "You mentioned there were two?"

A loud crackle spilt out from the hearth, spitting more embers across the floor.

"She was where she had always been." I gulped back, taking in the musty scent of smouldering wood. "The one place she truly belonged—nestled in her mother's arms. Still, if there is any comfort to be found, know that they died together, which is far more than many of their kind are granted."

A shadow fell across my sister's face, her stare striking daggers from above. "Comfort!" Meredith sneered, her voice dripping with contempt. "You speak of comfort, Peter? For whom? For yourself, or the mother and child you saw to their deaths?"

Gone was the confusion she once held, replaced by a look of pure revulsion as she stomped ever closer, towering over me.

"It was dark," I tried to explain. "It was dark and I … I … Well, I did not see the child!"

"And if you had seen the child?" She continued approaching, once again blocking out the little light behind her. "You would have seen them in from the cold, would you? Seen that they were cared for?"

I shifted myself in the chair, reaching out in a vain attempt to soothe her. But my efforts were quickly shot.

She lashed out at every attempt, her arms flailing as she evaded each and every grasp. She stumbled backwards, knocking the table and sending a cup to shatter upon the floor.

"Please, you must listen," I begged.

I listened with a heavy heart as Meredith's words cut through me. "No, I will not," she replied through gritted teeth, her face smeared with tears. "I will not listen. Not anymore. Not tonight. What you have confided. What you have done, Peter. Don't you see? You are not the man I thought you were, nor are you the man I ever thought you could be." Her voice was thick with disgust, stern like a mother. "A woman and her children are dead—dead by your own will, your own ignorance. You tell me to listen to you? Why, I cannot bring myself to look at you. Nor can I bear the thought."

With that, Meredith barged across the room, her dress snagging on the table and tearing at the seam. Her nostrils flared as she passed me, betraying the heavy breath she struggled so hard to hide.

Again, I reached out to stop her, to plead, launching from my seat and grabbing her firmly by the elbow.

She recoiled instantly, causing me to fall. For a moment, I simply lay there, stunned, breathing in the dust and cobwebs, as her footsteps hurried down the hall.

Chapter 41

All was quiet on the staircase as my shadow sulked across the banister. The hall was bleak and still, the open shutters granting the sole means of guidance as the pale moon cast its feeble glow upon the steps.

For a while, I stood and listened, wondering if my mind was playing nothing but cruel tricks or if the doleful sobs of my sister were truly present at all. Releasing the banister, I found myself stumbling across the tiles, driven by an urgent need to find her, the pain in my leg still raw from the fall. One by one, I searched each room, barging through every door. Yet in each chamber, I found only shadows clinging heavily to the corners. I limped down the hall, through the kitchen, and on towards the dining room, where the long table stood neatly set, prepared for the morning's meal.

A clatter of rain drummed on the tall windows, the noise forcing me ahead with an unsettling stride. I ran to the double doors, closing them behind me, pressing my weight as I leant against the wood.

Where is she? I thought. The very question caused me to worry all the more. I tried to yell, to call for her, but I was too weakened, too breathless to even summon a voice. It was then I noticed a faint glimmer, a soft glow, coming from the end of the hall. The light seeped under the crack of a door.

The library.

I edged forward with great discretion, the tired boards beneath my feet bowing under my weight. I listened closely, eager to hear. Without a doubt, it was Meredith's voice that emerged, each sob sharper than the last.

I rapped lightly, softly calling her name and enquiring if I might enter; only the soft weeping of her cries replied. With my hand on the handle, I turned it slowly, the latch resisting with a heavy *click*.

Inside, the room lay dim. The shelves, which held many books, were barely touched by a flickering flame. And there, near the darkened window facing the path to the house, my sister's shape emerged. She sat somewhat bent, one hand shielding her face, fogging the glass with her breath.

I paused in the doorway, my heart heavy, and, in good time, slowly stepped inside.

"Sister?" I spoke the word softly as I drew nearer still. Gently, I placed a hand to her shoulder, the fabric of her dress dampened by her tears. "Please allow me to speak," I urged her, my voice smooth yet shaded with desperation. "Allow me your forgiveness at least?"

It was right then and there that Meredith lifted her head, her eyes puffy from weeping. "Oh, Peter," she huffed, her voice thick and trembling. "Please, do not ask such a thing of me. Even if I did so, I do not believe it would cure the burden you carry, the guilt you bear. Furthermore, I fear that you would not truly want it, that it would just be words. That you, my brother, have not truly seen the error of your ways, the cruelty you have inflicted."

My grip tightened slightly on her shoulder, her accusation hanging even heavier than before.

"You are right," I admitted, my whisper tied with regret. "I have been selfish, cruel in my actions. There is no doubt. I allowed my own pride to cloud my judgment." I paused, swallowing hard past the lump in my throat. "I see it now."

Meredith lifted a shaking hand, sweeping her cold fingers delicately over mine. "Oh, Peter," she sighed. "You truly mean that. Truly?" Her head drooped, her moist cheek coming to rest upon my wrist.

"I do," I answered. A sense of relief suddenly lifted from my chest. "They are not just words. No, they are much, much more. The pain I have caused, the wrongs I have committed. Yes, I dare say I understand now. I understand it all. Everything."

Another gentle squeeze lightly embraced my hand.

"Then don't you see?" she asked me.

"See?"

"That there is still hope, Peter, hope for you yet." She twisted herself around on the seat, and her chin lurched upwards, stretching the course of her neck, her eyes wide and sharp. "If there were some way, some possibility to take back what you have done, would you see it so?"

"But there is not." I stared down blankly.

"No, no, of course, but if there were?"

Releasing my grip on her shoulder, I stepped back, riddled by a whirlwind of thoughts as my hand came to rest against the bookcase.

I took a deep, steadying breath.

"There are many things I would reverse if I could." I paused, allowing the truth of my admission to settle between us.

Meredith remained perched by the window, the slightest tilt of her head a clear question mark through the bleakness.

Pain shimmered across my face. "My travelling to Scotland," I admitted, "purchasing that house. I wish I had left the farmers to their business, allowed them to remain on their land. Maybe even helped them, aided them in some way, done something—anything—to ease their burden." I shook my head, my gaze downcast. "I was blind, Meredith, so stubborn, so determined to my cause that I could not bear to think of anything else, to see what I was doing. The suffering I imposed, the lives I disrupted—it haunts me, Meredith. Every. Single. Day. Every night."

My voice trailed off a little on those last few words, the weight of it all threatening to come crashing down around me. "You must know, I only thought I was doing what was right, what was necessary. But in the end, I was nothing but a callous, selfish fool. So, yes. To answer your question, I would. I would take back everything, every decision that ever saw me led to that terrible place. Foremost, I would see one matter wiped from my mind above all else."

"And what is that?"

"The sight of a mother and child frozen at my door, their deaths dealt by my own will. My own ignorance, no less. I want it gone, Meredith, need it gone! Smeared away from my thoughts as quickly as the tears that shed from your cheek. I wish to never be reminded of that very first day our lives crossed paths—the day I met Martha Ferrell."

A sudden shift in movement caught the corner of my eye, a movement so fleeting that if I had blinked, I would have well nearly missed it entirely. I turned my head, straining to make out the heavy shadows that clung to the room's edge like draping cloth, only to find Meredith standing upright, her form as rigid as stone.

"Martha?" uttered Meredith, her voice barely heard over the din that continued to bounce from the window.

A stroke of lightning struck the sky, immediately followed by an angry clatter, highlighting the blankness of my sister's face. She appeared pale, ghostly, her skin as grey as the frilled collar patterned below her neck.

"But that was *her* name," she managed to voice.

"Whose?" I approached.

"Her name. Patty's name," remarked Meredith. "I always called her Patty for short. My darling girl's."

I stopped in my stead.

"And Ferrell," she went on, the cogs within her head turning. "I had forgotten it. She told me. She said she was to leave with a man of such a name. A farmer called Ferrell. That they planned to travel north, to be married."

That night, I watched as the horror dawned upon my sister's face, her eyes widening with disbelief. She stood there, trembling, as the implications of her words sank in.

"You …" She glared at me, her daydream lost. "You let her struggle when this man she loved died. You allowed her to starve, for her children to starve. It was all you…"

I moved to comfort her, but the words caught in my throat as she quickly began to retreat.

"You … You are the reason she is gone." She wept uncontrollably. "The reason she will never come back here, to me. Because of you, I will never see her again, never see the dimple of her chin, the whites of her eyes, the gleam of her smile."

I searched her face helplessly, hoping against hope to see even the slightest glimmer of understanding.

"Meredith," I beseeched, yearning for her to listen. "If what you say is, in fact, true and the girl you once mothered is the very same woman I wronged, what am I to do, I ask you? How could I have known?"

Within another flash of light, Meredith's form paced forward from her place, teeth clenched tightly, her expression brewing with hatred. Hatred for me.

"There is nothing you can do, don't you see?" she snarled, stopping at my feet as spit formed at the corners of her mouth. "It is too late. Too late for her. Too late for you to repair what has been done, what you have done!" With a violent thud, the hammer of her palms laid down against my chest, one strike swiftly followed by the next, the words gasping from her mouth. "It is all your doing!" She fell to her knees in hysterics, covering her mouth to stop the noise from flooding out. It was a noise so painful I could barely watch. I reached out to help, but she flinched from my slightest touch.

"Please," I asked, my voice unsteady. "Tell me what I must do. How can I make this right?"

She raised a hand, her fingers delicate yet commanding as she pointed towards the door. "Leave," she said crisply, the word escaping through her teeth. "I wish for you to leave."

A heavy sensation befell my lungs just then as her response echoed in my ears. I stood there, still, my heart racing within me, beating for her.

"Very well," I replied. "I shall give you some time, allow you to think, to grieve, to allow the dust to settle. Then perhaps come morning we could talk further?"

The silence that followed lingered, broken only by the faint ticking of a clock hung upon the wall. I searched her face, hoping to find a glimmer of hope, a sign that she might reconsider.

"A night shall not fix such a thing." She crouched down farther, her palms flat against the floorboard, her nails scratching at the wood. "You have broken me," she heaved. "Broken my heart, broken all I hold dear. There is nothing left."

I crouched down to my knees. "What are you saying?"

Her gaze wandered off into the darkness. Her eyes were masked by the many strands of hair that clung across her face. "I need you to go, to leave here, this house. Me. Don't come back."

The storm outside belted at the house with a mighty blow. The lightning that torched the sky struck down from the heavens, igniting a tree in the distance.

I reached out, my fingers wrapping firmly around her wrist.

"No," I insisted, refusing to let go. "No, you don't mean that. You are hurt, your emotions stung."

"And yet, I wish it all the same," she replied, her voice laden with loathing.

"Please," I begged her. "You must hear me. You must understand. The Ferrell woman, Martha, she haunts me, follows me wherever I go. There is no rest from her, no escape, not even here. Everywhere I look I see her face, her eyes. She is within the shadows of every room, the play of every dream. She will not let me rest. She punishes me, Meredith."

With a sudden jerk, my sister ripped her hand away, my nails scraping across her flesh, allowing blood to break the surface. She stood with a breathless stumble, staggering over to a cabinet where a candle still burned brightly.

"You will not speak of her!" she cried aloud, each word hoarse and broken as she continued to dwell with distress. She took a long breath inwards, gazing into the mirror which hung before her, her stare drifting to find me. "I see it now," she said, a sense of realisation dawning on her face. "Yes, I see it all."

"See, Meredith?"

"Why, why you have come here, what is happening to you." She hesitated, her eyes locked with mine through the glass upon the wall. "It is as clear as the reflection I see."

A cloud of confusion washed over me as her words dripped with disdain. I rose to my feet, driven towards the mirror as a sudden wave of discomfort twisted in my gut, the pain swirling within. I drew closer, watching as the shape came into view, my features becoming stronger, clearer, as I stepped into the light.

"You see it?" Meredith asked, sinking back into the shadows. "The truth," she urged. "What you are. What has become of you, your soul."

I leant closer, my nose merely inches from the glass, examining the reflection in front of me. The ridge of my nose, the chalky stubble of my chin, the grey of my eyes—the man I had always known.

"I see only myself," I said without looking back, too focused on the orange glow that danced across my skin.

The faint form of my sister was nothing but an outline loitering somewhere in the blackness.

"Then it is too late for you," she said, her words heavy. "It has you now. It preys upon you. The guilt you carry, it feeds on you all the more. Your curse. Soon, there will be nothing left."

"Curse?"

The sound of her footsteps travelled from somewhere behind me as she slowly emerged back into sight.

"You must leave. Now!" she ordered, her voice filled with a resentful panic. "What has hold of you, whatever it is, I am not the one to resolve it. Do you not understand? It is not me!" She gasped, her hands balled into fists. "Only something pure can stop this, make it go away, something deep that comes from within. Something inside of you."

I didn't understand. How could I? "But, Meredith, I—"

"GET OUT!" she screamed, the sound piercing through the darkness and startling me back to the wall. "LEAVE! NOW!"

I stumbled towards the door, struggling to find the handle hidden from sight. Finally grasping it, I hurried out of the library, squeezing myself through the gap which led back into the hall. Behind me, Meredith's screams grew louder, more painful, her voice wailing, coursing throughout the house, chasing at my heels. Her voice never faded until I found myself gone from the house.

"LEAVE!"

Chapter 42

The wind swept down the ridge of the hill and battered against my back with the force of cannon fire, driving me forward as the garden gate swung open, rattling on its hinges. I followed the path, anticipating the bite of the cold. The way ahead was flooded beneath the depths of murky, unyielding mud. Each hurried step caused my feet to sink and slide.

As I turned to look back, the rain poured down in thick, heavy drops. The downpour was so harsh that I could barely discern the house I fled.

Thunder rumbled overhead, the deep *booming* sound rolling across the land.

Soon, my sodden clothes clung to my skin and the rain ran into my eyes, making it nearly impossible to see the trail ahead. The sounds along the winding path drew to a hushed silence save for the constant pitter-patter of raindrops amidst the sheltering leaves above. Not even the distant hoot of an owl or the familiar rustling of creatures could be heard.

The trees above seemed to close in around me, their branches thickening with each step.

I stopped to try to regain my bearings, noticing that the mud beneath my feet had hardened, replaced by sweeping steps of tall, dark grass.

The trail was gone, lost to the thicket.

With sheer panic, I forced my way through the army of trees, my breath white in the air, the thought of someone watching me from beyond never far away. I fell to the ground more times than I cared to count, tripping on sticks and stones which lay hidden beneath the undergrowth. Each time I clambered up, pushing my way past the branches, my route lay blocked, guarded by a wall of sharp, thorny brambles.

I turned to retrace my steps only to find my recollection compromised, the way gone. Disappeared.

I was lost.

I spun on my heels, terror racing inside of me. Everything appeared the same. Every tree, every bush, every rock was identical to the last. I scanned the forest, searching for a break in the tree line, a clearing that could lead to the coast. But it was no use. The woods stretched on in every direction, the towering oaks hemming me in, refusing my want to pass.

A break in the clouds separated above the treetops as a cold light settled upon the woodland floor, causing the grass to glimmer to a shine and the flicker of moths to dance in the shadowy light.

Far in the distance, a sound reached my ears—the crashing of the sea against the rocks. My heart lifted some, knowing I was close, as I chased the sound of the ocean that spoke through the woods. It called out to me, beckoned me to follow it.

Branches blindfolded the way. The smell of thick, damp earth clotted my nostrils as clouds of breath escaped my lungs. But no matter how quickly I ran, nor how desperately I beseeched the tree line to yield, I could not escape the feeling of something from behind, the sound of pursuing footsteps in my wake. I turned to look back, my feet still pounding the ground as I ran, only to realise I was not running at all, but falling. The ground beneath had given way, turned into a deathly slope. I felt weightless, as though I was floating on the air itself, though it was short-lived. With a hardened thud, I came slamming to the ground, my body rolling, my vision spinning into a haze of nothing but land and sky, a flash of lightning, soon to become nothing at all.

I SIMPLY LAY THERE, THE BEATING RAIN SMACKING THE REAR OF MY head as I drifted between sleep and consciousness.

I awoke with a gasp, my body chilled to the bone. I pushed myself up from the pool I lay in, my muscles protesting the strain. Strange, it was only then that I recalled how I had come to be there, lying in the dirt as I was. I climbed up from my knees, my clothes thick with filth, and peered up at the slope from where I had fallen.

There were no signs of anyone—not a soul, no creature sniffing out my trail, no spirit lurking in the dim. The land appeared just as it always had.

I gathered what little strength I had left, wrapping my arms around myself in a futile attempt to stay warm. My lips quivered from the cold and my eyes squinted against the stinging rain as I urged myself onwards for the coast.

The roar of the waves grew louder. So close were they that I could almost sense the salty spray of the sea. Exhausted, I collapsed against a tired stone wall that blocked the land from the beach. There I rested, powerless, as I stared out at the abyss of darkened water, wondering if I would ever see my sister again.

Of course, I considered returning to the house, to fall on my hands and knees, head hung low, in the hope of her forgiveness, that there was some chance for her to look at me the way she had always done before. I dismissed the thought immediately. The damage had indeed been done, the bond between us torn. Still, I clung to the belief that, in time, there was always a chance to regain her love, to once again hold a dear place within her heart.

As the roar of the waves filled my ears, I clutched the cold, weathered stones, my fingers numb from the chill. I looked out to the shoreline, my focus stopping on a dark, bulky shape that appeared to lay stranded on the bank.

It was a boat—a small wooden boat, its oars wedged, resting in the locks.

Without delay, I followed the course of the wall until a narrow gap in the stonework split the way. I climbed over, cocking my leg, my jacket snagging on the rocks as I stumbled across the sand, cautious of who might have been out there, and on the foulest of nights.

Breathlessly, I reached the boat and searched inside. There were no belongings. Of course not. No bags, no supplies. Even the small compartment located beneath the bench lay bare.

Again, I looked back in every direction, my shoulders hunched against the harsh sea breeze. There was no one. No one at all. Not even a single dwelling sat along the ridge. Whoever the boat belonged to most likely had gone to seek shelter and would return once the storm passed.

I staggered to the edge of the hull, pushing with all my might, trying to get the boat back into the water. My arms trembled, the balls of my feet digging deep into the sand.

A shallow wave soon struck the bow, splitting the water with a calming splash as the bilge slid smoothly out to sea. With no time to waste, I rushed to the side of the boat, breathing deeply as the icy water smacked against my knees. I climbed aboard. The weight of the water weighed me down. The boat rocked hazardously to its side. "Steady now. Steady!" I said, rolling inside and striking my crown on the seat well. So hard was the impact that my vision merged into a blur of blackened blotches.

With stiff, bitten fingers, I grasped the oars, wrapping my hands tightly around the looms. I rowed softly at first but soon increased my strokes as the waves fought to hold me back, pushing the vessel in the direction of the shore. With each pull of the oars, my jaw would chalk from the strain.

I rotated a single oar, navigating the boat back on track as a faint mist seeped over the bow—its form light at first but soon becoming denser, more suffocating, with each passing stroke.

I cast a look back onto Lismore's shore, along the ridge and stone wall, watching the waves that once seemed so large shrink into the distance.

Movement caught my attention from the shoreline.

A person.

At first, I believed it to be none other than my sister. I envisioned her bare feet treading across the sand, her hair flat on her face from the rainfall, hands flailing, pleading for me to come back.

I imagined going back, turning this deadly craft around and rowing like never before, riding the waves to the shallows. I imagined what she might have said to me—that she would hold my hand with kindness, telling me that I was not beyond all hope and that she was willing to see me as her brother once again. My heart lifted, the storm around me dwindling away at the thought as I rose from my seat, the boat rocking beneath me.

I called out her name, my voice cracking, tilting my ear to the sky in hope of hearing her. Yet no voice came. And the longer I waited, the more the mist revealed that it was not my sister at all, but someone else.

A man.

A man cloaked in the darkened haze. He came to an unsure stop, staring out to sea. He carried something with him, the shape swinging at his side. At first glance, I mistook it for a simple walking aid—a stick, no less. But what the man held was nothing of the sort. What the man carried was a gun.

The mists broke.

"Gibbs!" I shouted through the roaring gale. "Over here!" I waved my arms like a madman, watching Gibbs as he stood upon the shore. I tried again, harder that time. My arms thrashed the air, and my yell was stolen by the thunder. But in sheer desperation, I somehow misplaced my footing on the planks, sending myself hurtling down to the seat. I regained myself quickly enough, ignoring the pain, and clambered over the benches to the hull, watching the man from afar.

Gibbs did nothing as he looked into the night. He stood rooted, his attention fixed on the meagre vessel that fought against the sea. For a time, he appeared to look directly at me, or was it through me? I could never quite decide. Not even now. His cloudy features conveyed a stern yet troubled expression, with an intense look cast over his face.

I considered crying out again, to signal the man if I could, somehow. But any opportunity I had was soon to fleet away.

The man on the shore turned his back on me, retracing his route to the ridge that led towards the woodland. His gun rested on his shoulder. He then stopped. With the twist of his neck, Gibbs appeared to turn away, taking one final glance to the ocean, one last look before the fog swallowed me whole.

Chapter 43

The way ahead was lost to me, obscured by thick brumes of fog that sulked over the bow.

It was a wall of endless nothingness.

How long I had been rowing, I was not sure, nor did I care to think, too occupied by the waters that rocked the boat to the point of tipping.

I strained at the oars, my muscles burning with every arduous stroke. The boat shifted violently with every wave as water sloshed over the sides, drenching me to the point of misery. I tried in vain to clear the stinging salt from my eyes, to catch a glimpse of anything beyond the oppressive grey. For the longest time, I yearned for the fog to part, to reveal a course to the harbour, to the safety and warmth I had left behind all those days ago.

Where am I now? I couldn't help but wonder. *How far have I drifted?*

The uncertainty gnawed at me, filling my mind with dark, troubling thoughts.

Have I veered too far off course? Will I ever find my way?

I slouched forward, losing the rhythm of the oars, longing to see the shoreline, the lights of the town. The fog had to break eventually. It had to. I had to believe that or else I risked losing the last traces of hope.

The wind howled a chorus of tormented voices as the boat was tossed by the waves, almost tipping on its side. I screamed in horror. My knuckles were white and shaking as I clasped the oars in an iron grip.

The boat spun round and round in a dizzying spiral, steadying momentarily only to be hit again as the towering body of water thrashed against its side, shortly followed by another, and another, heaving the boat over and sending me tumbling into blackness.

The coldness stabbed at my skin like knives. My lungs burned as I kicked and clawed desperately upwards while my clothes dragged me down.

At last, I broke through the surface, greedily gulping the precious air as I coughed and spluttered.

Clasping the water, I reached out in vain for the boat, capsized and floating adrift. With each crashing surge, the icy water stole another breath, and the relentless swells swept me farther away. A dreaded fear consumed me. I knew I could not tread water for long, yet panic gripped me as I realised how quickly the currents were pulling me farther out to sea.

Without warning, another towering wave crashed over me, submerging me once more into the depths. Darkness pressed onto my eyes. My limbs flailed wildly as I fought to stay afloat. I feared if I did not reach the boat again soon, my strength would fail and I would succumb to the numbing cold. Summoning my last ounce of energy, again I kicked and gasped, desperate to fill my starving lungs.

Finally, I reached the boat, tightly gripping hold of its slippery hull. With what little strength remained, I pulled myself up, collapsing onto the upturned keel as the storm raged on around me.

All I could do was huddle there, shivering and wheezing as I fought to catch my breath, the very thought occurring to me that it would be my end. That my entire life, all my years, had been leading to that very moment.

From out of nowhere, a faint break in the fog began to lift, revealing a glimmer of yellow light in the distance that cut through the endless gloom. It was none other than the glow of Lismore's lighthouse. Like a candle on the water, it threw out its beacon, lighting up the northern cliffside. I could just discern the jagged outline of the cliffs, the waves battering against the rocks.

A sensation of defeat whirled within me, that for all that time I had merely been dragged by the current which coursed the island's channel. That I was still so far from Oban. Helpless and defeated, I simply lay there, my body stiff, stretched out on the slick, wooden planks, bobbing to the rhythm of the sea. I glanced up to the lighthouse. Its circling glow was so comforting, so warm, so near yet so far as it travelled along the cliffside.

What I saw next I cannot begin to explain, to find the right words, yet I know I must try to do so all the same.

I stiffened. A breath caught within my throat.

Way up on the cliff, standing on the edge of its peak, a woman stood deathly still; only her dress wafted in the wind as she looked down to the sheer drop.

"Meredith." I whimpered her name, my hand outstretched, deafened by the roar of the waves. I rubbed the spray from my eyes, hoping against hope that what I saw was merely an illusion, a trick of the failing light. But as the lighthouse's beam swept across the coast, there she was again—my sister, standing at the ledge.

I thought back to that day, the image pinching my emotions, when I believed to have watched as she leapt from that drop, her form vanishing in the blink of an eye. Could this have been the same, nothing but a dream? A cruel repetition? I dared not consider it, for the mere thought filled me with horror. I pushed myself up, gripping the wooden planks of the boat as best I could, not daring to risk another fall.

"Meredith!" I cried out, my voice barely heard above the thunder that angered the sky.

With each sweep of the lighthouse's beam, Meredith's silhouette was lost, swallowed by the haze. I could only pray she would remain there, that she would not make the same fateful leap, just as I had seen before.

Without warning, another wave hit the boat with a violent *smash*, tossing me forward and the vessel back onto its belly. I surfaced promptly, heaving for breath, my extended hand reaching for the bow, pulling myself to safety. With great effort, I tumbled over the side, my breath again lost.

I lifted myself up, waiting with bated breath for the lighthouse beam to reveal her.

It felt like an eternity for the light to return, for my sight to catch even the slightest glimpse of the woman I swore I had seen. But there was no seeing her again. The break in the fog, as quickly as it had opened, had suddenly closed. The cliffs were lost, hidden from the world, the curtain of mist closed.

My eyes strained, desperately searching the darkness, praying that the lighthouse beam would briefly find her one last time. But with each passing sweep, the light fell dimmer. It was no use. She was gone, vanished to the void. As I cried out to her one final time, my voice fighting through the storm, only one thing did I hear through the fog—a sound that caused my hair to prick, my spine to shudder. A faint yet undeniable scream, a scream falling to halt. A scream unfinished. Then there was nothing, nothing but the endless raff of the sea.

Chapter 44

The light bulb overhead gave a momentary spark as Roderick carefully removed the page from the remaining stack and placed it neatly to the side. He glanced up at the shimmering light that stretched across the ceiling. His brow bent as he waited for the flicker to settle.

For some time, Les sat there stunned, slightly bewildered from the tale told to him. To think that man, this Peter Daily, had fled to Lismore in hope of escaping the memory of someone he longed to forget only to discover that very person once held his sister's heart. Martha Ferrell, the woman Les felt in some strange way he knew. The peasant girl who had been taken into riches, raised up only to be cast out and shunned, left to perish by the very same blood that once admired her so.

A hush seemed to settle over the office just then, broken by a stranger's footsteps strolling along the cobbled path that wrapped around the building.

Outside the small window, the world stood pitch black, the office light casting a strong reflection of the inner room.

Les began to stretch, his back stiffened from sitting, as he caught sight of his own true image in the glass. He looked pale and tired. His checked shirt was riddled with creases, and his hair was slightly longer than he was used to, leading down to stubble that cast his face in shadow. Heaven knew what people thought of him, looking the way that he did, the way he carried himself recently. If living in the middle of nowhere did one thing to you, it made you less conscious about the way you looked and perhaps a little forgetful about looking in the mirror every now and then.

"Shoddy electrics," remarked the old man, his stare drifting down from the blinking bulb. "Sodding building needs knocking down and rebuilding brick by brick, that's what I say." He breathed out through his nose. "But what do I know? I've only rented the dump for nigh on twenty years. In all that time, the owner's not done a thing to upkeep it. Not a damn thing!" With a clenched fist, he planted it down upon the table, his frustration brewing all the more as the light continued its endless flickering. "It's not right," he grumbled. "I pay my rent, see to it that the place is cared for, secured, cleaned."

Les's eyes helplessly gazed across the cluttered office floor, unable to pry his sight away from the stacks of papers towering along the walls, the scuffed shoes strewn in the corner, and the rumpled clothes flung atop the cabinets, most likely never to be worn again.

Roderick followed his guest's gaze, the lines on his forehead deepening further if only to mask his embarrassment of the surroundings he called his workspace. "Ah," he mumbled. He wafted his hand. "Pay no attention to all that. I've been meaning to clear it out."

Les shrugged, giving the impression that the mess enclosing him hardly bothered him at all. What did it matter to him if the old bloke chose to live in such a pigsty? Nothing, that's what. Not a thing. In little time at all, Les would be out of there, hurrying down the stairs as fast as his legs could take him, bursting out into the night and drinking back that pure Highland air, air so clean and rich that one could get almost drunk on it.

With nothing more said on the matter, Roderick's attention quickly returned to his desk, his mind focused as he licked the tip of his finger and flicked the edge of several pages ahead.

"So…" Les found his voice, and with some awkwardness tried to revert the conversation back on track. "The woman, she jumped?"

"Hmm?" groaned Roderick, his head still hung low, his mind clearly elsewhere.

Above them, the hanging bulb ceased its flashing, again turning to a solid piss-yellow glow.

"Daily's sister," Les replied. "You mean she fell to her death?"

"Well, she didn't fly," Roderick replied, his voice spilling with sarcasm.

Les discreetly rolled his eyes at the old man's tone.

"You mean to say that's it?" Les asked with a clear sense of disappointment. "The story ends there, with a woman dead and Peter Daily a victim of the sea?"

Roderick let out a long, weary sigh as he leant back in his chair, finally meeting Les's gaze. "Did I say that was it?" he answered sharply. "Did I?" He paused, running a hand through his thinning grey hair, and let out an infectious yawn. "No, that is not *it*. Not for this story, at least. But I'm afraid for the next few days following the events, Daily made no attempt at writing about it. If he did, they have simply become lost. Either one is possible. For the days in between his entries, I had to rely purely on my research alone, solve the puzzle as it were—newspapers, letters, and such. Anything that was obtainable to the public. I tried all the local libraries, of course, though I found them of little use. A name recorded here and there, nothing that gave me sight of the bigger picture, the picture I needed. Be that as it may, I did gain a stroke of luck at the local archives of Inverness. Usually such records are closed to civilians without proper cause, sealed away under lock and key. A fortress."

Les quickly piped up. "Then how did you come to acquire them?"

Roderick smiled at that, a somewhat mysterious smile, to say the least. He tapped a finger to his nose. "My lad, you don't get into this line of business without gaining a connection or two along the way."

The young man sitting across from him leant slightly forward, the side of his face tilted. "Business?"

"Writing."

Les fell back to his chair, his interest deflated as quickly as it began. "Ah."

"Tell me," continued Roderick. "Ever heard of a writer by the name of Lee Kenny?"

Les thought for a moment, knowing all too well he hadn't. He shook his head in turn. "Kenny? No," he exhaled. "Should I have?"

"I suppose not," Roderick replied, twisting his tongue about his cheek. "A nice chap. Decent enough writer too. He had the utmost ability to bring history alive, make it exciting for the reader. You know the sort? A rare skill to come by, especially for our genre."

He picked up his glass, hovering the remaining drag beneath his nose as he came to a sudden halt, his attention stolen by the row of books that stood proudly beside him on the shelf. His books. All written by none other than the great James Roderick, an accomplished historian. Every page bound was his. Every word printed was his own. His research. His accomplishments. A lifetime's worth of dedication, condensed to a single shelf. The old man's stare wandered across the titles, lost in the memory of his work.

"We are a dying breed, Mr Wills," muttered Roderick, his fingertips brushing the row of books until he eventually reached the last. "No longer do we hold the influence we once had. As writers, we spend our days alone, confined and content with our own company, our work. And for what, you might ask yourself."

Les didn't.

"For the simple need to be respected by those you have never met, to be admired, our stories shared, cherished. As for Lee Kenny, the man never stood a chance. Not one."

For the first time since he arrived in the writer's office, Les couldn't help but look upon the old man with a sudden air of suspicion. He seemed to be hiding something. What, at that exact moment, Les couldn't quite put his finger on. But he knew there was something, some secret to the writer's natter, something he longed to get off his chest. He could see it in his face, his eyes. The words wanted to escape. He wanted to clear his conscience. After all, why would he talk to him about such things, to a complete stranger, someone he met little more than a few hours ago?

"What did you do, Roderick?" Les asked. He remained still, his face stern.

Roderick paused, his gaze still fixed on the row of books. "I cheated him," he confessed, and with a throw of his head, swigged back what remained in his glass, exhaling sharply past his teeth. "He was good. Too good, was Kenny," he went on. "Perhaps too good for his own liking. I made up a rumour. What, I would rather not say. But the result saw to it that the man would never be considered by a well-respected house again."

He set his glass on the table, his finger tracing along the rim. "Several months later, once the dust had settled, I managed to get my hands on a project he'd been working on—a fascinating piece of work, to say the least. An historical masterpiece," he mused, a hint of wistfulness in his voice.

Then Roderick's expression hardened. "I stole it. Took the words that he had written, shifted them around a little, and passed the work off as my own."

A sudden wave of what Les could only describe as disgust whirled about his head as the old man's confession sank in. To think that this was a literary idol, a man people had once so admired, and he had stooped to such underhanded tactics. It went without saying that Les knew little about the publishing world, the struggle that so many writers would endure for that single chance to get stories seen, to be loved. Nevertheless, Les knew plagiarism when he heard it.

"Why would you do that?" Les asked. "Ruin someone's career like that, all for the sake of your own vanity?"

The old man's stare lifted, his eyes filled with a haunted sorrow. "I was on top." He simply shrugged. "You wouldn't understand. The literary world is a cutthroat place. It is not as glamorous as some may have you think. Reputation, legacy—it means everything to us. I was competitive, jealous. I suppose in some way I just couldn't bear the thought of being overshadowed by a mere upstart. A young man, no less. He was not the only one. Brown, Jules, Mars—each one suffered the sting of my ever-growing success, each name buried under the pages of my books."

All Les could do was listen, his stomach churning with distrust. He may not have been some fancy writer, nor did he ever consider himself as a man to judge others from their mistakes, but as he sat there quietly, his head swimming from the old man's speech, only one thing seemed to riddle his mind. Only one thought left him stunned.

"Why are you telling me this?"

Roderick squeezed past his own chair, stopping as he leant against the corner of his desk. His gaze fell upon the papers beside him. "Because," a weighted sigh escaped, "I wanted you to know. I needed … I needed to tell someone." Roderick's stare rose, his eyes unblinking. "Further to that, there is something about you, Wills, something that evokes a sense of trust. The kind of trust that assures me that what is spoken of inside this room stays within these walls." He stopped, his expression hardening. "You will not shame me. Neither will you speak of what I have done."

Without noticing, Les's hold on the armrests tightened, his nails digging into the tired leather.

"And you're sure about that?" asked Les, his throat suddenly parched.

"Quite certain." Roderick's torso twisted, his arm stretching down as he reached for the remaining papers. He straightened them out with a small shuffle. "You must believe me when I say I am not proud of what I did. Nor do I find any merit from it." Roderick's expression defaulted to the remaining stack in his hands. "You could say it is why this story means so much to me, why I have spent many years reaching for answers."

He paused briefly, his fingers tracing the edges of the papers almost absently. "Like Peter Daily, I have my own sins to bear, my own guilt to carry, my own curse to hide. I feel his shame now more than ever, the wrongs he made. And very much like the man who wrote these entries," he flipped the pages briskly in front of him, "I, too, yearn for the torment to stop, for the mind to be free from the burden."

With a careful tongue, Les held his voice back, cautious not to provoke the man further. There was something strange about the old writer (if Les could still think of him as such). And as Les observed the old man squeezing past his desk with a grunt, Roderick's face quickly appeared to grow pale, his voice groggy, slurred to some extent, as though he was carrying the weight of his words on his shoulders.

"You alright, Roderick?" Les asked.

The old man paused with a dazed expression, his usually steady voice shaky and strained. "It's all here." He indicated the papers in his hand, and in doing so, he avoided the question entirely. "The last of it. Every bit of it. Everything you wished to know."

He swayed slightly as he walked, passing the papers into Les's hand, and slowly made his way towards the door. He appeared to lose his balance, reaching out to the frame for support, and found himself out in the hall.

Les swivelled his chair and watched as the old man's form drifted into the lightless space, his mind growing concerned for the writer's wellbeing.

"Roderick?" Les called after him.

The man's shadow in the hallway stopped. His raspy voice replied, "I'm fine, son. Just fine. A little flushed, that's all. Nothing that a spell of fresh air won't fix." He coughed, his shadow hunched, as his silhouette descended from the top two steps. "Read on, Mr Wills," he called back, his voice growing distant. "I'll catch up with you in a moment."

Les looked down to what was left of the final documents clutched in his grasp, a measly gathering of pages that would hold all he wished to know. Then he knew he would leave, be gone, out of that office quicker than a fly to shit.

"You're sure?" yelled Les.

The latch clicked from the door below, and a sea breeze tunnelled into the house, feeding into the office upstairs.

Roderick's voice shortly followed as the door fell closed behind him. "Read on, lad. Read on."

Chapter 45

It didn't take long before Les pulled himself up close to the desk, the wheels of the chair grinding under him. He fanned out the pages, making note of the words scrolled with Daily's handwriting and the records Roderick had managed to obtain during his visits at Inverness. He split them into two piles, studying each one carefully, his brow set with concentration. His heart beat wildly in his chest.

He picked up the first pile, a small collection of faded documents, some bound together by a piece of frayed, white string. He glimpsed the front and back, noting the large ink mark stamped on the rear that clearly read *Property of Inverness Archives*. A small brown envelope was nestled amongst them, displaying the same ink mark as the other documents but nothing else. Flipping the envelope over in his hand, Les was surprised to find that the document remained unopened. He could discern the old wax seal once exhibited a single letter and remained unbroken. He considered opening it, snapping the wax and peering inside. He wanted to. His fingers spontaneously felt along the corner of the envelope, his nails searching along the lip.

Les stopped, his head briefly turning towards the open door. It was likely the old man wouldn't be too much longer. Just a few minutes. And when Roderick finally did come back, what would he think to find that Les had taken it upon himself to open such a thing? After all, there was no clear indication that the envelope he held had any relevance to his interest. For all Les knew, the envelope could have simply been placed into the pile by accident—a filing mishap. It was certainly doubtful, but he considered it to be a possibility all the same. There was, after all, no name written, no address nor any other distinguishing markings—nothing other than the faded red stamp, a smudged letter marked on the seal.

With that in mind, Les removed his nail from the corner's groove and, with much reluctance, dropped the envelope to the desk. For that moment, his temptation would have to wait. The old man would be back before he knew it.

Without a second thought, his attention swiftly turned back to the pile of documents. The first one, a small, rectangular paper with well-worn lines that had been folded to a crease, presented some sort of written account. Although the ink had evidently blurred and faded through the years, causing the words to merge together, Les managed, with some effort, to fill in the blanks as he read. It appeared to be an old Port Authority Report.

The report detailed an incident involving one Meredith Durose, who it was suspected had jumped from the island's cliffs and into the ocean depths. According to the aged account, Meredith's brother, one Peter Daily, had said to have heard the scream from his boat, approximately a quarter mile off Oban's shore. Soaked through and having drifted for hours before making it to Oban's port, the shaken and distraught man immediately alerted the authorities.

Les turned the page.

The report went on to state that an extensive search would be conducted of the island, along with the coastline and surrounding waters, once the storm had at last ended, and that the port authority had instructed the unfortunate woman's brother, Mr Peter Daily, to remain at his property or lodgings, informing him not to depart lest further questioning be required.

With little time to digest the information, Les moved on to the second document. It was an old newspaper clipping, or so it appeared, partially torn down the centre. Its date displayed 27th March 1845. Beneath it, the title forced his body to shiver.

He read.

The Ill-Fated Plunge of Widow Durose

Despite the efforts undertaken by the brave men of our port authority, as well as the scores of Oban volunteers summoned from their homes over this past sennight, all hope has now been reluctantly abandoned. The authorities have resigned themselves to the cruel reality that Mrs. Meredith Durose, the fifty-six-year-old widowed gentlewoman of Lismore's Manor, has been claimed forever by the Sea.

Les quickly flipped to yet another clipping that displayed no date. His interest piqued as his hands noticeably began to sweat.

The sombre burial arrangements for the dearly departed Mrs. Meredith Durose shall be held on the morrow at Lismore's own St. Moluag's. Mrs. Durose leaves no surviving kin to mourn her passing. The grand halls of Lismore's Manor now stand empty, a hollow remembrance of a tragic loss.

Confused and somewhat puzzled, Les slung what he read onto the desk, his mind flustered as his hand rubbed firmly against his temple.

A funeral? he thought, rocking back in his seat. *A funeral without so much as a body to bury?*

It seemed sacrilegious, somehow, to Les. He wasn't sure why, but the very idea of such arrangements being made for a body allegedly lost at sea held no logic for him. Nor could he understand any comfort to be found in it.

It went without saying that there was no one left for the poor woman at Lismore—no family, no friends, only the rested souls of forgotten shadows. A husband she had grown to detest. An arrogant son. Even the precious bond of her once adopted daughter Martha Ferrell had long left that life. And in no time at all, she would become just like them—a few words etched upon stone, a name forgotten, hidden in the corner of the churchyard.

Despite Les's attempts not to paint such a morbid picture in his head, he could not help in doing so. Yes, he had never met Meredith

Durose. Nor did he, upon hearing her story, consider himself to know her well. Regardless, there was something about her final days that seemed to have struck a chord with him. He thought it her loss, or maybe it was simply her loneliness that he found he could relate to. He was no stranger to it, after all.

In little time, he found his eyes lowered once more to his lap or, more so, to what remained there—the final document. He picked it up, guiding it closer to the light as he quickly scanned the writing.

Odd, he thought. It was handwriting he somehow knew. Les froze, his body bracing as he read the signature marked at the bottom of the page. "Coull?"

His head jerked back, his eyes refusing to release their hold as he let out a breathless gasp. What he held before him was nothing other than a letter written to Roderick from Michael Coull himself some ten years ago.

The sheet of paper danced wildly in Les's hands as they shook. His heart pounded all the while with the implications of what he held. As he read, Les could almost hear Coull's voice echoing in his mind, the flow of each word transporting him back in time to when his friend was alive. Alive and well. It was as if Coull himself was speaking to him from beyond the grave, ready to reveal what Les so desperately sought to know.

Dear Roderick,

I depart from Oban tomorrow. I will not stay another day. No matter what you ask of me, nothing will change my mind.

I do not belong here, Roderick. Nor do I have reason to stay. Not now. Now that I have done what you have asked of me.

I caught the ferry to Lismore this morning, just as you asked. When I handed over the fare to the ferry-man, he looked at me with the strangest gaze. He told me that no one travels to the island anymore. Not for the longest time. People have no reason to go there, to set foot *on the shore. Not now the island is empty. Not anymore. Not with the locals long gone. Their homes wilted to ruin.*

As the boat sailed through the choking fog, I could not help but envision what you once spoke of on that miserable night - of the woman drowned at sea. Yes, I remember it true enough. And as the dark form of Lismore's cliffs peeked through the clouds, the very thought of such a fall sent a chill down my spine. A ghastly ending.

True to the ferryman's word, I walked the island's trail and saw no one. Not a soul. I followed the directions you spoke of. The north cliff path that wound through the woods, turning right at the old milestone and up towards the manor. I must say, the house is not as I envisioned it. It stands no longer as a landmark: its windows shattered, walls battered, its roof gone. It exists only as an unwelcoming reminder. A memory as crooked as the Daily name itself.

The day had grown late by the time I reached the chapel. It, too, was a shadow of what I imagined. Its arch crumbling to utter despair. Its once-white walls shrouded by veils of hanging vines.

With much effort, I waded through the churchyard, fighting my way through the brambles and waving grass. Grass so dense it concealed whatever headstones lay buried beneath.

It took some time, but I finally found it. Found what you wished me to find. The small headstone, slanted at the corner of the grounds, bearing the name Meredith Durose. Of course, the stone had taken some damage over the years, its letters diminished, its surface cloaked in moss, but I have no doubt it was hers. No doubt at all.

I remained in the forgotten church for the rest of the day. And would you believe it? For the first time since I stepped foot on Lismore, I managed to grow a conscience, my mind questioning the very act of what I was about to do. I admit, writing this now, that the thought had crossed my mind to abandon the charade entirely. To head back to the dock and never look back. To redeem myself for what I was about to do. To make up some story of never finding her. But what good would that have done? You would not have believed me, have listened. You simply would have done only what you do best - come up with some other atrocious plan for me to do your dirty work. I couldn't have that. Not when I had already come so far. Not when our bargain had already been struck, our hands shaken.

Damn you.

By the time I left the church that evening, the world had turned cold. The churchyard deathly quiet. So quiet that not even the birds dared to cause a peep. I looked out onto the night, watching the silver moonlight bathe the tops of each headstone with a glistening of white frost. I knew there and then that it was now or never. That if I was about to do the unspeakable, the time would have to be now.

The coffin was empty. Just as you said. Just as bare, just as dark as a soulless pit. There was never a body buried here, you were right so much about that.

Nothing but an empty space. No clothes, no belongings. Nothing inside but the one thing you desired most. I have it, Roderick, carry it in my possession, snatched from the grave. I hold it now as I write this letter, the thing you yearn for most. The very object you will stop at nothing to gain. I have it. Do not worry, it will be yours soon enough.

And so, my job is done. The matter closed. Finished! No more will I do for you, and no more will you ask of me. I have done quite enough, kept my side of the bargain. My word. Retrieved what you wished of me. It is all here with this letter. Now it is time for you to keep yours. That is, if your word counts for anything. No more threats, Roderick. No more blackmail. See to it that my family's name is stripped clear from the twisted pages of your book. And that the name Coull will never again be referenced within the same sentence as that heartless beast.

You will not hear from me again after this. Nor will you come knocking at my door should you ever need me. If you do, Roderick, I will not be held accountable for what happens. This is my final warning to you.

Let this be the end of it.

M. Coull

For some seconds, Les could do nothing but stare blankly at the message in front of him, his eyes drifting over the read sentences as the same question forced itself to the forefront of his mind. "I have it," he spoke aloud. "What did you have, Coull? What did you find down there?"

His attention shifted to the remaining entries from Daily's journal, piled on the desk—the man's final words. If he had any chance of knowing what happened to Peter Daily or what Coull was talking about, it was then. All or nothing. He picked up the papers, straightening them neatly, his eyes catching sight of the bottle of whiskey accompanied by a single glass. Surely Roderick wouldn't mind if he indulged in just one drink—a small one. Just a tipple. Needless to say, he needed it. He grabbed the bottle, sloshing the beverage into the glass and throwing it back in one gulp. His eyes bulged, a slight tickle prompting him to cough as he breathed back the burning fumes.

He hunched forward, his gaze fixed, an anxiousness building within him as the light cast a menacing shadow across the parchment. Les couldn't shake the feeling that the words he was about to read held some dark meaning—a secret that Coull had uncovered all those years ago.

Chapter 46

5TH April 1847

I sat in the carriage, awaiting to depart, listening to the townspeople scurry about, their useless lives already forgetful of the loss across the shore, of her body, gone, lost to the sea.

Outside, Campbell huffed and puffed about the horses, reining them in. The sound of their tails whipped in the morning breeze.

As I waited, I glanced out the window, catching a glimpse of the ocean fading into fog. The haunting thought all the while occurred to me that my sister may still be out there, her lifeless body riding against the waves, all battered and bruised, torn to pieces by the piercing rocks. And as I stared out into the distance, my gaze caught the peak of the far-off lighthouse, the memory of that night creeping back into my thoughts forevermore. So vivid. So real that I can almost feel the chill of the sea on my back, the rain as it ran down my face, and hear the terrifying scream of her voice as she leapt. I cringe every time at the thought, even now as I write this.

There was no one at the funeral, no one but I. No friends, no loved ones. Not even Gibbs saw fit to attend, his belongings gone from the keeper's lodge. He most likely fled for the mainland in search of work, abandoning my dear sister's memory in his haste.

As they lowered the empty casket into the ground, I watched, numb, unable to shed another tear. The grief had long since given way to a deep, aching hollowness—a void that threatened to destroy me. I had hoped, foolishly, that some semblance of her life would be honoured, that those she once knew would come to show their final respects, to say goodbye. But there was no one. Not a soul to care. Their lives were untouched by the tragedy, the great loss of Lismore's fairest.

As the wheels began to turn, the carriage rocked, jolting in time with the horses. Their breath clouded the air as they trailed the road out of town.

It was a cold, drizzly day, and the road was scattered with pools of water. The buildings along the roadside merged into a distant blur as we passed. The faces of the people standing on their doorsteps were just as indistinct, nothing more than a haze of watchful eyes.

As I write this, I do not recall if I have said what I am about to do, yet I will not go back and reread the pages I have written. I do not believe I can face them—not now. Not ever. I will never again return to Lismore. That much is certain.

The house will be signed over to me in good time, for that I am sure, though I will take no pleasure in receiving it. Nor shall I attempt to see it sold, to see it loved by others. It was her house after all. Hers. And will forever be so. A memory suspended in time's embrace, a place where some part of her may still linger—a place that she called home.

As for me, I shall return to Elphin, at least for a short time. Be that as it may, I have no intention of staying, not in the slightest. I will see my affairs in order there and the house sold before returning to London. Very much like Lismore, I will never go back again. Of that, I am sure. To that end, I pledge my word.

7TH APRIL 1847

It has been two days' journey since we departed Oban, and the rain has not since stopped. The sky remains as miserable as when we first left, a dull and sinister grey that threatens to remain. The roads have turned to mud, making our progress slow and tough as the carriage wades through the earth. As more time passes, I find myself growing increasingly weary, both in body and in mind, as we inch our way farther north. The journey is one I have dreaded undertaking the most, yet I feel compelled by a sense of duty to see it through.

Lismore, with all its sorrows, feels a lifetime away. And yet the memory of that place, that island, clings to me like the damp chill that seeps through the carriage frame, rotting it to its core. I still cannot shake the feeling that I am running, fleeing from ghosts that will never cease haunting me. I cannot help but ask myself if this will ever end.

8TH APRIL 1847

Last night, I insisted we take rest at a small inn just on the outskirts of Beauly. A poor establishment, old and shabby, located near the edge of the village, its wind-swept walls bore the scars of many storms.

The chambers were sparse, to say the least—a narrow, lumpy bed, a small table with a guttering candle, and a rickety chair that stood lonely in the corner. Still, I was content enough to spend the night there, away from the jarring bumps and jolts of the road, the smell of the horses. A good night's sleep was all I needed—one final rest before Elphin.

I FOUND LITTLE SLUMBER THAT NIGHT, MY SLEEP DISTURBED BY THE rowdy laughter drifting up through the floorboards. For hours, I lay awake, eyes straining against the darkness, until I finally abandoned any prospect of sleep at all. Instead, I found myself arched at the small table, quill in hand, feeling an eager need to write.

As I sat there listening to the voices from the tavern below, my thoughts would often drift to Meredith, of the last time we spoke, the last time I really heard her voice. In many ways, I felt regret for those final moments, the heartache I caused, that the last recollection I held of her would forever be a tainted one, a cursed memory never to be healed. What I wouldn't give to take it all back, to see the smile on her face once more, to turn back the clock. To have her alive and well, reunited with her Martha. The girl she raised. The woman I wronged.

But it is all too late. There is no going back from such things. There is only hope. The hope that death may see them together again.

THE NEXT MORNING, I SAT IN SILENT REFLECTION, MY MIND consumed above all else with the words Meredith had spoken to me. I could hear them as clearly as if she was sitting beside me, forever repeating, refusing to stop.

"*It has you now,*" she said to me. "*It preys upon you. The guilt you carry, it feeds on you all the more. Your curse. Soon, there will be nothing left.*"

My gaze drifted beyond the window, watching the world as it rolled by.

Your curse, I thought to myself, wishing I could make sense of what she had meant, what she had seen in me on that night.

Perhaps she was right. Perhaps I truly was cursed—not in body, but in the mind, pestered always and forever by my shackled thoughts, my own wrongdoings, my nightmares. Would I be forever reminded of those I ill-treated, saw to shallow graves? It was a sentence fit only for a monster, a wretched soul, a soul like mine.

Oh, how I have longed to see it end, for the torment to stop, the voices, the visions. Yet I fear it shall remain with me for all time. There is no remedy that will see me well from such a thing, no cure to see me whole again. No hope, no chance. No chance but one.

I buried it. It is with her now, with her spirit, hidden deep below the soil's surface, sealed away in the darkness. Maybe one day someone will find it. "*Something pure,*" she once said, *"something deep from within."*

Maybe she will finally know my desperation. Maybe now she will finally understand.

THE NIGHT HAD GROWN COLD. THE SKY WAS BLACK SAVE FOR THE scattered pinpricks of starlight that weakly shimmered through the clouds.

The road ahead was no longer far. The bends and curves of the route were familiar to me as I was rocked back and forth on the seat.

No, it would not be long. And soon enough, Elphin would emerge from those distant shadows, the house too painted in its veil of night, just as I had left it not so long ago. I thought of the emptiness it would bring, the rooms within so still and quiet.

My pulse quickened, sending tremors through my frame and causing sweat to bead upon my brow. I implored the driver to halt.

No sooner had I asked than a fierce snort broke out from one of the horses. The commanding tone of Campbell's voice soon followed as the carriage came to a weary stop.

With a rising panic, I flung open the carriage door. I hurried outside, left the road, and paced towards the bank, carpeted in tall, mossy grass. There I stopped, my eyes shut, both hands clasped at my knees, listening to the breeze as it flurried about me, catching my hair in its flow. Far too distant was I to notice the tread of approaching footsteps, my mind elsewhere, too distracted to hear the voice.

A hand rested firmly on my shoulder, startling me backwards.

"Everythin' alright, sir?" asked Campell, jumping back, his expression of surprise half visible in the bleak light. "Not too far now," he continued, guiding his arm to a point. "Just beyond the curve of the road there."

He watched me closely, observing the anxiety on his master's face.

"For what it's worth, I'm sorry for your loss, Mr Daily," said Campbell, placing his hands deep in his pockets. "A bleedin' shame, so it was, for a lady to go the way she did. Though let it be said that there wasn't a man's or woman's tongue at Oban who did not praise her name. I heard them talk, their gossip. The kindest of souls, they said."

As if prompted by what he said, a sudden rain began to fall, showering down in heavy clumps.

With a weary sigh, I pulled myself upright, turning my back on his sympathy. "You will not speak of her, Campbell," I told him, my voice masked by the falling rain. "Not a word from you."

For a moment, he said nothing, his presence made known only by the labour of his breath and the slight ruffle of his coat.

"Leave me," I mumbled. "You do not know loss like I have, Campbell, the pain I feel, the love I felt." I scowled hard. "How dare you speak of her to me."

Again, the man said not a word, not right away, at least. He remained quiet, his stance stern. It was so stern that I had almost mistaken him to have left, to have quietly retraced to his post.

"Then you would be wrong, sir."

He seemed closer, his voice clearer, travelling over my shoulder.

Yet I did not turn to face him. Instead, I held my ground, watching a loch in the distance mirror the stars above.

"A sibling, like you. A sister," the man continued. "Separated as children. Torn apart from one another. She was taken into care, looked after and given a loving home, a family. I, on the other hand, was not as fortunate. It was the workhouse for me. A small boy, thrown into the mills. No courtesy of a bed to sleep on, no blanket. Nothing but a cold stone floor to see me through night after night. Many of the younger boys, they perished during the winters. If the cold didn't get to them, the lack of food certainly did. There were many a night we would go without, with not so much as a scrap, a morsel in our bellies, most too weak to fight for it. There were days when I thought my time was up, that I too would be found one morning laying stiff upon the stone, frozen, the breath gone from my chest. A miserable end to a miserable life."

I slowly turned to face him, my feet squelching into the soft, mossy ground.

The barrel of a pistol stared back at me.

"But I did not die, Mr Daily," said Campbell with a glint of wildness in his eyes. "The young boy I speak of, the runt of a child, nothing but skin and bone, was far too stubborn, far too foolish to succumb to that. But you … You, sir, will."

A chill ran down my spine, watching the weight of the pistol shake madly in his hand.

A metallic *click* rang out into the open, piercing through the rain.

"Now," he spoke calmly, "don't that sound just chalk your jaw?"

Without realising, my hands were raised, both palms flat. "I'm afraid I don't understand, Campbell," I said, my voice measured if only to see him calm.

"You wouldn't, would you?" He jabbed the pistol forth, the barrel's end mere inches from my face, so close that I could almost discern the gunpowder that coated the tip, feel the cool steel pressed hard against my skin.

With his one free hand, he raised a finger, pressing the dirt on his nail against his lips.

"Just you hold your tongue now, sir," he sneered. "Keep it muzzled, hush now, or the last thing you'll be seein' is a bullet from this here pistol scrambling a hole in your head."

I swallowed nervously, my shaking hands uplifted as I offered a fearful nod.

Campbell's eyes narrowed, an unsettling glint of triumph within them. "That's a good man," he murmured, a nervous smile tilting a corner of his mouth. Rain smashed down against his brow, funnelling down and dripping at the point of his nose. "No, I did not die," he repeated. "I did not give in. Instead, I chose to survive, to endure that filth-infested place, for each day to go hungry, to not fall like so many others, forever knowing, longing, that one day the cruelness would stop. How foolish I was to think so, that the world outside those walls was different, that kindness marked the face of every man."

He paused briefly, his nostrils flared.

"By the time I was a boy of eleven years, I was thrown out onto the streets. Discarded, left to live like a rat in the sewers, watching as men like you walked on by day in and day out, the look of disgust painted on their faces.

"After some years, I found myself travelling back to the place I was born. I found passage on a boat, stowing away amongst the cargo. When I finally made it home, I was met only by ruin. The village had long since vanished, and the home that once sheltered my family stood empty, crumbling to ruin."

I looked at him, baffled. My arms lowered gently as I opened my mouth to speak.

"Shut your gob!" The gun jabbed forward again, the muzzle pressed firmly against my head. "You'll learn," he snarled. "You'll see. Right after I left that old house, I bumped into a man near the docks—a groundsman, an old fellow. A man by the name of Gibbs."

My eyes went wide.

"Ah, rings a bell, does it?" He leant in closer, his foul breath washing over my face. "It came as no surprise that the man didn't recognise me, not at first. Why would he have? I was no longer the boy he had carted off to the workhouse, hidden away and forgotten. But oh, I remembered him sure enough. Yes, I recalled him very well—the look on his face as he led me through those tall workhouse doors, the sound of his boots as he turned and walked away. And when I inquired about my sister, where she might be found, I was struck to hear that she had long since gone, run away with some farmhand, fallen in love.

"Some years went by after that. I found work on the outskirts of Oban, a cattle farm, a place to lay my head. It wasn't much, but it was far better than the spike. I stayed in the barn most nights, burrowing under the hay, often wondering if I'd ever see her again, what she might look like now or if she even remembered her long-lost brother. So, when Gibbs showed his face one spring morning to inform me he had heard rumours of her residing up north, in a place called Elphin, needless to say, I set off to find her.

"It took me many days by foot, many a night walking alone with only a name written on a scrunched-up piece of parchment—my only source to find her."

Campbell placed a hand into his jacket pocket, digging deeply. With a flick of his wrist, he threw something to the ground. “Pick it up!” he demanded, his eyes blazing.

I looked down, then slowly bent a knee, grabbing the paper as it flittered at my feet.

“Read it,” Campbell commanded.

I cleared my throat nervously “*Elphin*. That is all it says.”

“The other side,” he inclined with the twirl of his finger.

I turned the paper over with quivering hands, shielding the surface from the rain. The writing was smudged, hardly legible. I looked up at the gun, the hand of the man who held it. The paper released from my grasp, taken by the wind.

“Aye,” remarked Campbell, straightening out his arm. “Ferrell.”

My heart sank as it dawned on me. I should have known.

“But your name, there must be some mistake,” I blurted out. “Campbell. It was not her family name. It was …” I paused, racking my brain, trying to think.

“Ó Súilleabháin,” he said, the name rolling off his tongue with ease. “There is no Campbell, Daily. Never was one,” he went on. “You see, by the time I arrived at Elphin and learned of my sister’s passing, I swiftly moved on. After all, there was no reason to stay, no reason to question. Like most of the farmlands, the people had perished—lack of food, the workhouses full to the brim. As far as I was concerned, her death was no different from any other soul that had fallen dead upon the fields.”

He stopped, his gaze narrowing. “Then … Then I heard of you, Daily.”

Behind him, a horse nickered softly, its ears pricking forward as if sensing something in the air.

“Me?” I asked him.

“Aye. None other,” he replied, a touch of anger in his voice. “After I left Elphin, I travelled onwards, following the road. I didn’t care where I was headed or where I’d wind up. Any place was as good as another. You might say I was left to God’s good graces.”

A smile briefly shadowed his face.

“After a few days of walking, I found myself at a place called Strathan, squandering what little coin I had left at the local inn. It was there, by chance, that I heard of you through a drunken exchange between two gentlemen. One of them, a coachman, was said to be heading south, driving some rich toff to the coast, blundering on and on how he had visited Elphin only last winter, and that the man he was to transport was a ‘no-gooder.’ A monster, I believe he called him.”

He shrugged, and his finger on the trigger somewhat eased.

"Well, I must admit, at first I thought little of the man's slurs, his rambling. That was until something particular caught my ear—a name. My sister's name, along with her two daughters. You, Daily, you allowed them to die."

His lips quivered as he spoke, his grief etched into everything he said.

My lips parted.

"Shut it!" His grip tightened more around the gun, his finger poised "Do you have any clue, Daily?" he asked me, his eyes burning. "Any idea of how it felt to learn that the man who ended her life shared the same name, the same blood, as the very woman who sundered us forever? I could not abide that. I would not. And so, as the hour turned late, I waited for the coachman to leave, watched him stagger through the streets, falling at the wheel of his coach. I stole it. That and the horses. I made my way to Elphin. I made my way to you."

The air grew thick as the man steadied the gun at my face, its cold steel glinting in the light.

"Why now?" I asked of him, still in shock. "Why not have shot me when you first had the chance?"

The man's brow lifted slightly, his expression one of secrecy. "It was never I who intended to pull the trigger, Daily, but Gibbs. That was the plan. That was the deal for sending me off to that dreadful place. If only you hadn't fled the island. Damn you!"

Thick droplets pelted the man's face, flattening his hair against his forehead as he tilted his head to the sky.

"Aye. A sister for a sister," he remarked, his words carried by the wind. "I hear you're a cursed man, Mr Daily." His eyes narrowed dangerously. "Though I have no doubt of the truth in that. Now, your curse ends here."

His finger strained as I lunged forward, my hand grasping his arm in a desperate attempt to stop him. Straining, I pushed against him, my fingers clawing at his arm. A struggle of breaths clouded my hearing, the grunts and groans of his voice fighting, seething against me as several blows of his fist landed deep in my side. I bellowed aloud in pain.

"Damn you!" yelled the man, his teeth as knitted as the hatred that blared in his eyes.

A thunderous *crack* echoed through the gale, the deafening sound of a bullet tearing from the barrel as we stood knotted in our stance, our grip as rigid as fate.

Chapter 47

I fled. Ran as swiftly as my legs could carry me, leaving the body slumped upon the ground, the eyes visible as I glanced back through the rain—eyes as wide as shillings.

It had all transpired so rapidly, the discharge of the pistol, as my mind grappled to comprehend it all, what had occurred as the man began to choke for air, straining with every ounce of his being to gurgle those final words. So much blood spilt from his shirt as he held me, refusing to let go.

The road turned to muck as I ran, my feet plummeting into puddles that lay hidden along the trail, causing me to trip and stumble. I followed the way as best I could. The moonlight had long vanished from the sky, cloaking the path ahead with nothing more than shadows, forcing me to stop and look back.

There was no one.

Nothing.

Yet no matter how long I stood alone, my steps having carried me far from the scene, my conscience began to dawn.

It was not my fault, I tried to convince myself. *If only he had listened. If only he had heard me.*

A shift in the grass caught my ear, the sound so clearly of footsteps wading through the marsh.

I BARGED UP AGAINST THE DOOR OF ELPHIN HOUSE, THE STONE building looming over me with the deepest gloom. So bleak was its shade that I almost missed it from the road.

Desperately, I twisted the handle, the doorknob slipping uselessly in my trembling hands. With panic rising, I pounded on the door, praying that someone— anyone—might be within.

Yet even as I beat my fists against the panel, I knew no one would answer. The house was empty, just as I had left it.

In my chaotic state, I had quite forgotten about the key tucked safely in my pocket.

From behind, shadows seemed to press in around me, the muffled sounds of my pursuers drawing ever closer. I quickly glanced over my shoulder, half-expecting to see a figure emerging from the gates, their dead eyes fixed upon me.

I fumbled in my pocket, feeling the key slide against my palm. I grasped it tightly and rushed it to the door, twisting it in the lock with a violent thrust.

The latch *clicked* as the door swung wide. I stumbled forth, the key clattering to the floor as I slammed the door shut behind me, sealing myself inside.

From deep within the house, an unwelcoming silence followed, broken only by the hollow chime of a familiar clock.

DARKNESS LIFTED FROM THE ROOM AS I LIT THE OIL LAMP. I hurried from one room to the next, drawing the heavy curtains closed over every window, ensuring not even the slightest crack could be seen.

With the last room sealed, I cowered in a corner, catching my breath, my heart racing. I had to be certain no one would find me, to see the light seeping from the house. The outcome of being found was too grave to risk.

Cautiously, I crept to my writing desk. Retrieving some tattered papers from the drawer, I began to scribble under the meagre lamplight, documenting the last few days, recording every detail, every movement that saw me back to this loathsome place—a diary of memories before they gradually slipped away, turned to nothing.

It remained silent for a long time after that, but it felt like there was more to it—a quiet that held a deeper purpose. For many hours, I sat motionless, too consumed by fear to stir from the spot, terrified that any movement might bring about some horrifying event, something dreadful.

I recall the clock chiming beside me, its final toll fading to a faint ring. Closing my eyes, I drifted in and out of a restless sleep, each time jolted upright by the *tap-tap-tapping* at the window—a sound that existed in my mind alone.

It was not until the clock struck ten that I finally mustered the courage to rise from my desk. By then, the weather had subsided, the rain upon the rooftop having given way to a calming peace that settled over the house.

I crept into my quarters, my gaze immediately drawn to the unmade bed, the sheets lying precisely as I had left them. I bolted the door behind me and inspected the room, searching for any sign of intrusion. I checked the wardrobes, rifled through the drawers of my bureau, ensured that all was in its place. Only then did I allow myself to let out a guarded breath.

I sank to the edge of the bed and ran my hands over the rumpled sheets. Yet from the corner of my eye, I could not help but notice a twinkling light outside, its glow casting a weak, wavering shimmer across the room.

Standing promptly, I hurried to the window and peered out, making sure the latch remained firmly locked as my eyes widened from what I saw. Out across the darkened moors, the Ferrell cottage stood upon the hill. Hanging by the entrance, a lantern swung lazily, its glow growing stronger by the moment as if trying to draw me in.

I scampered backwards, knocking into the bedframe's post.

A sound reached my ears, a sound I well knew. It was a sound that forced the blood within to run cold.

Tap, tap, tap.

It was not merely in my dreams that time. The noise coming from below was real. The lantern burning across the moors, too, was real.

Tap, tap, tap, tap.

It grew louder, so loud that I was sure the glass below might shatter at any moment, breaking into hundreds of shards upon the floor.

Tap, tap, whack, whack, whack!

My chest tightened as I pressed my back against the wall, scanning the room in hope of finding a weapon, something to defend myself. Something blunt. Anything. I lurched forward, racing across the space, my steps faltering, catching sight of my image in the mirror.

I stood motionless, gazing through the dusky light. Retrieving the lamp and lifting it to the glass, I finally saw my reflection. In the waning glow, I could see myself, my own eyes, etched with fear. Yet the face that gazed back was not my own.

"Who are you?" I heard myself say.

I set the shaking lantern on the nightstand, its flame casting an orange shimmer across my skin.

What looked back at me from the mirror was not the man I had known, nor was it a face I recognised, at least not at first. It was gaunt and saddened. The eyes, so perfectly round and sunken, dove into the depths of my soul. The skin was taut and sallow, stretched painfully tight over the nose and chin. The cheeks appeared hollowed out, the bones jutting sharply, as if the face I studied had slowly been wasting away.

I lifted a hand, certain what I was witnessing could be explained by nothing short of my own imagination, my own fear. Yet as I watched the reflection mirror my movement, my hand gently swept across my face, feeling the deep grooves and dents of weather-worn skin, the wrinkles that carved along my sun-baked bones. The figure I looked upon was none other than me.

The noise coming from below had ceased. The tapping was gone, faded, bringing with it only a chilling quietness that lingered throughout the house.

I swallowed hard, my mouth as dry as soot, attention never drifting, never swaying from the mirror fixed upon the wall, from the face of this wretched soul. But what was it that loitered just beyond? A drifting shadow passed my shoulder, a presence of motion sulking from the far reaches of the corner's depths. Its form drew nearer, slowly gliding ever closer, drifting at my heels—the hazy shape of a woman.

Chapter 48

The room fell dark as the bulb above Les's head burst into blackness, showering him with bits of glass that finely cut his ear.

Startled, Les pushed his chair back, looking wildly around the room, his focus swinging back to the window. He was sure he had seen someone leering in, an old, haggard frame watching him. But as soon as it appeared, it had vanished, gone, leaving only the yellow light burning from the street below.

"Roderick!" Les yelled towards the doorway, sucking in a breath as he did so. He cradled his ear. "Roderick!"

There was no reply, though Les had never truly expected one. He didn't know where the old man had wandered off to or when he planned to return. But the one thing Les did know was that he wouldn't still be there when Roderick did return.

Holding out a hand to dull the blindness, Les carefully stepped towards the door, barely making out the dark passage which loomed beyond. With outstretched hands, he felt his way along the wall, his knees knocking into piles of papers, scattering them across the floor.

By the time he reached the archway, Les grabbed at the frame and pulled himself through, stopping as a sudden feeling overtook him. He couldn't explain what it was as he twisted his neck to look back to where the dim light of the outside world shone on the surface of the desk.

The letter.

The envelope, still sealed, lay amongst the papers. It seemed to be calling to him, yearning for him to reach out and grab it, to take it with him.

Les wet his lips.

Every part of his being told him to leave it, to get the hell out of there, to flee down the steps as fast as he could and never look back. To run. But what message lay beneath that sealed wax that the writer had not shared, that was not yet told to him?

Les knew he wanted to take it. After all, he had come that far, hadn't he? And if he didn't take the opportunity at that moment, it was certain he would never have the chance again. Not in his lifetime. He would always look back on that very moment and wonder how he could have been so stupid, how he could have let such a thing slip right through his fingers.

Les was no fool. He knew that much. He may not have been the brightest spark, but he knew what he wanted. And if he wanted to know everything, everything he could, his chance was right then. Not later. There was no second chance.

Turning around, he found himself back at the old man's desk, using what little light there was to guide him. With a swift motion of his wrist, he snatched the letter, carelessly crumpling it into the depth of his pocket before staggering back towards the hall, stomping down the stairs.

It was cold out. By the time Les reached his car, an old, rundown Citroën ZX, the chill had already taken hold of him. He unlocked the door and fell into the driver's seat, shivering from head to toe as he jiggled the key in the ignition. The old engine turned over with a rumbling roar as Les flicked on the headlights. He released the handbrake and pressed his foot down on the accelerator, speeding through the winding streets, past the dark, masked building he had come from, and out onto the Highland road, hardly glancing at the give way.

It was a short drive back to Coull's place. He had made the drive often enough. Les knew he could get there even faster if he kept his speed above fifty. But the roads leading to Elphin were nothing short of risky, especially come nightfall—single lanes with passing places, twisting around hidden bends. No, he needed to stay calm. He needed to keep his wits about him.

As Les eased off the pedal, he couldn't help but notice the twinkling lights of Ullapool grow distant in his rearview mirror, leaving him with nothing in sight but the road ahead and the trees that tunnelled the way.

As the road channelled through the rocky terrain, the tyres of the car crunched over the wet and slippery gravel, the sound echoing in Les's ears. His grip remained stern on the wheel, his knuckles tightening as he peered forward, focusing for the turn ahead.

All the while, thoughts of Daily's final account plagued Les's mind, never letting go. He thought about the woman that Daily had stated he saw in the mirror, the reflection that mirrored his own true self, his cruelty—the very thing he despised most.

Was it all in the old man's head? Les thought. The guilt he carried, the delusion that the face he saw staring back at him was not the man he knew, that he had become something else entirely, something unspeakable, had Daily imagined it?

A cold shiver found its way running up Les's spine. It was a quiver so deep he felt the steering wheel shake under his fingers.

Les was never one to believe in curses. To him, such things were a matter of pure superstition, irrational beliefs. Then again, he had never taken to believing in ghosts before, either. Not in all his years. Not until Elphin. Could what Daily have seen really been possible? That what pestered his every waking moment were not the ghosts of his past that haunted him, but something more? Something else entirely?

Les's thoughts drifted to Roderick, the writer who had dashed off so abruptly, leaving Les alone in his office. It went without saying that the old timer had not looked at all well before he left, not that Les felt as though he knew the historian well, of course. After all, they had been acquainted for only a few hours. Despite that, Les knew something weighed heavily on the man. It was as clear as the look on his face, the way he spoke. Les just wasn't sure what it was. Still, he couldn't help but wonder if Roderick's hasty departure had been driven by some strange sense of premonition, with his skin pasty and brow sweating. Or was the writer simply overwhelmed by the weight of revelations he had uncovered, the dark secrets that were soon to come to light?

Wherever Roderick was, Les hoped the old writer was alright, hoped that he had not gotten himself into some kind of trouble.

Les's imagination thought of the worst, conjuring visions of Roderick lying face first on the pavement or huddled up against some dark alley, not to be found until the next morning, his hand still clutched to his chest, his face marked with distress. Dead.

"Oh, knock it off!" he grumbled to himself, shaking off the morbid thought. "The old sod likely just went out for a walk to catch some air."

The idea settled his mind some as he made a sharp left-hand turn, the brakes squealing as the tyres slowed. As soon as he returned home, he would call Roderick's office. He didn't have the number, but Les was sure he had seen an old telephone book stashed away in the cupboard somewhere. And if he couldn't find the number, well, he was confident there would be someone he could contact—Roderick's agent, a publisher perhaps? Anyone who would be able to get in touch with the man directly.

The sky opened as he continued to drive, the trees that concealed the vehicle becoming sparse silhouettes until there were none at all. He turned off the heater and cracked open the window, allowing the bitter breeze to funnel inside, forcing his eyelids to narrow against the chill.

In the distance, the dark cast of familiar mountains lay ahead as the road weaved down into the open valley where the Ledmore River meandered, its churning waters glinting from the headlights on passing.

THE CAR GROUND TO A GRADUAL STOP ALONG THE PEBBLED driveway. The main beams shone upon the house, stirring the dogs inside as their curious, wide-eyed faces approached the windows, tails wagging with excitement.

Les took a deep breath, gathering himself, before stepping out of the car. As he opened the door, the sound of barking and the patter of paws against the tiles reached his ears. A small smile crossed his lips; the familiar sight and sound of his friends never failed to ease him.

With the turn of the doorknob, both dogs bounded through the gap, their long legs galloping them around the front of the house before returning to their master. Both jumped up to Les's chest, paws swiping for leverage as their tongues slapped at his face, covering his chin with drool.

Les chuckled, wrapping his arms around the two lively canines, giving them a playful scratch behind the ears. "Down, you bloody idiots! You're going to knock me flat before I even step foot through the door."

With the first command, both dogs heeled, their eyes remaining focused on Les as they followed him back to the house.

Les was glad to have such loyal company out there. Sure enough, the dogs didn't bring much to the table in terms of conversation, but Les had no doubt in his mind that the slobbering mutts knew him better than any person did. And despite the loneliness since taking on Coull's old place, the silent nights, the countless days where he barely breathed a word, their two scruffy faces were all he needed to come home to. They were all he wanted.

When Coull died, they didn't even have names. Les changed that, training them to respond to his call. He called the smaller one, a rugged mix of Doberman and Greyhound, or at least that's what he thought, Max. The larger dog, Angus, was a burly Scottish deerhound with a shaggy grey coat, though his gentle manner belied his sturdy size. The two dogs' certainly formed an unlikely pair. Les always thought so, at least.

He pushed the door open, kicking off his shoes immediately as the dogs sprinted past him like a whirlwind, neck and neck, racing for the armchair. He took off his coat, hung it next to Coull's (it still remained hooked on the rack), and flicked on the light. Quickly, he made his way down the hallway.

LES SPENT WHAT FELT LIKE THE BETTER PART OF AN HOUR emptying the cluttered space beneath the stairs. He moved out old boxes that nearly fell apart in his hands. Most contained items Coull had hoarded over the years—old clothes, photographs of people Les could only assume were his relatives, documents, books, tools. The list went on.

Les didn't have the heart to throw any of it away. They were Coull's belongings, his things. In many ways, Les never felt like the house he had inherited, a generous gift from his old friend, was ever truly his. He was there purely to look after it—to keep the place spick and span, to care for the dogs, until Coull returned. Although, of course, he never would.

It was funny. On some nights, as he sat in his chair reading, he would often drift from the words on the page, imagining Coull sitting across from him, content by the fire as he talked of the land, a drink in one hand and a cigarette in the other. He remembered Coull's laugh the most, big belly-deep laughs that were as contagious as they were loud. God, he missed him, missed him more than he ever thought he could miss another person, and he wasn't ashamed to admit it. Not out loud, not in front of the dogs, at least, though Les was sure those two scruffy canines missed Coull most of all.

He rummaged in the back of the cupboard, grunting as he reached for the stack of catalogues that stood piled and submerged in the corner. Carefully, Les pulled out the phone book, trying his best to stop the remaining stack from toppling. He stood, feeling the aches and pains in his back from kneeling too long, and made his way back down the hall, flicking through the pages as he went.

In the living room, both Max and Angus lay asleep on the sofa, their bodies curved around each other for warmth. Snores from both beasts filled the quiet room—snores and groans so loud that Les's focus momentarily broke from his search.

He sat in Coull's old chair by the unlit hearth, a small table next to him that held only a landline phone and empty ashtray. Page by page, Les searched through the list of Ullapool numbers, his finger guiding the way, until he found the address he was looking for. Granted, the phone book he held was a decade or more old, but he could only try. What other choice did he have?

Folding over the book, Les placed the open page on his lap. He picked up the receiver, wedging it between his ear and shoulder, the cord dangling at his chin. After studying the number with much attention, he dialed.

Nothing.

He tried again.

No answer.

And again.

Nothing but a solid tone in his ear. There wasn't so much as an answering machine.

By the fifth attempt, Les placed the receiver back in its cradle, his knee beginning to nervously twitch, heel tapping as his worry for Roderick returned. He grabbed his laptop, which sat nestled between the cushions, and opened it in hope of finding help. The internet was poor, as was usually typical for the location of the house. Still, with some patience, he managed to find some contacts for local authors.

Les typed up an email to Roderick's agent, then another to his publisher, who had released several of Roderick's books, both relaying the same message and his greatest concern for the writer. It wasn't much, but it was certainly better than nothing.

He thought of calling the local authorities, too, though he persuaded himself to hold off. He needed to calm himself, to think. Despite his best judgment, he didn't know if the old man was in trouble or not. For all Les knew, Roderick could have been home, safe and sound, tucked up in bed.

Les's head fell back against the chair, his eyes creeping to a close. The worst case would be that the emails he sent would not be read until the following morning. If that were the case, Roderick would be contacted around noon, perhaps a little later. But by then, it could have been too late.

He continued to think, his mind unable to let go of the scenario as his foot continued to tap, his hands clenching firmly against the fabric of the armrests.

Maybe ... Les thought. *Maybe I could drive back into town in the morning. Get up early, meet the old man at his office door. He would apologise, of course, when he saw me, come up with some excuse for wandering off, leaving me alone as he did. I'd give him a shrug, explain to him that I left after the bulbs blew out, and that would be the end of it. I'd get my peace of mind, and he'd feel better about disappearing the way he did.*

Yes, that would be his plan. It wasn't the most cunning of ideas, but it was a plan at least. As the idea settled into his mind, a sudden calmness came. He began to feel relaxed, content, almost free from the worries he carried. There were still questions, of course there were, one above all others. But as the twitching of his foot subsided, his eyes rolled back in his head, sending Les into the deepest, most calming of sleeps.

HE AWOKE TO THE SOUND OF NOTHING. NOT EVEN A WHISPER OF A breeze outside disturbed the stillness that had settled over the cottage.

He stretched his back, feeling the stiffness in his legs from sitting all night. With half-open eyes, he looked over at the two dogs, who remained unmoved on the sofa, still lost in their peaceful sleep.

Rubbing the tiredness from his eyes, Les glanced around the dimly lit room. He blinked groggily. The unlit hearth stood cold and empty at his feet, and the old clock on the mantelpiece ticked away with a muted rhythm. He didn't catch the time, nor did he truly care.

Letting out a quiet sigh, Les eased himself up from the chair, his joints protesting the movement. He contemplated stroking the dogs as he passed but decided against it, not wanting to disturb the peaceful scene. Instead, he carefully made his way to the window, peering out into the night sky that was as inky as it was black, before stepping out to the hall.

Bed was calling him.

With tired, shuffling steps, Les headed for the front door, ensuring the lock was tightly bolted. A large yawn escaped him as he turned for the stairs, his mouth so wide it caused his jaw to crack.

On the doormat, his shoes lay strewn from where he left them earlier. Rather than bending down, Les gave them a small kick, watching as they slid across the floor, landing on something that leant against the skirting.

Les looked down, stopping in his tracks.

"The letter," he murmured, crouching down and sweeping up the envelope.

In truth, he had forgotten all about it. The sheer rush of getting out of that place when the lights blew out, and the drive home, had caused him to forget that he had even borrowed it. Stolen would have been a more accurate.

Turning the envelope over, Les felt a growing sense of unease as the light revealed what once was the letter *D* imprinted on the seal. It wasn't just any ordinary letter—it was the one thing that might tie Daily's final accounts together, the one thing that could help conclude what Coull demanded he'd have no part in. Why was he so against finding out the truth? Les didn't know. And in that moment, he was too preoccupied by the snap of the wax between his fingers to dwell on it, too anxious as he unfolded the paper from its sleeve to care. Far too immersed in reading was he as he walked by the entrance of the living room that he never even noticed the swaying flames from the fire.

Carefully ironing out the old creases, Les continued down the hall, entering the kitchen, which looped back to the room where he had started. He found himself sitting back down in the same familiar chair, the seat still warm. All the while, his eyes never left the paper.

The twisted letters were written in none other than Daily's shaking hand. He read the words again, slowly, taking it all in, word by word. His mind was puzzled by their riddled meaning, their intent. What it all truly meant, Les wasn't sure, couldn't understand.

His hands began to quake as he looked down at the writings he held, knowing where they had come from, visualising Coull digging through the mud, his old friend stealing from the grave.

What was not clear, however, was why Roderick wanted to find what had been concealed in the dark so badly, and after so many years. It was but paper, a simple poem, a scribbled note at best. Why was it so important to him? What would drive Roderick to such lengths?

Les slouched back into the chair, bewildered, a pounding beginning to drum inside his head. Rubbing his temples, he closed his eyes briefly, searching his memory for any clues that could explain Roderick's only focus. There had to be something more, some deeper meaning.

Relentless to give in, Les raised the note to his line of sight, the writing caught perfectly as the old brown paper turned golden in lamplight, the words taunting him as he found himself reading again, reading the words aloud.

He paused as he finished the last sentence. The final words lingered on his tongue, leaving a bad taste and a chill to stay with him. It was only then that his attention shifted from the pages in front of him to the sound of crackling near his feet.

The fire. He noticed. It burned with a steady blaze, the flames licking at the logs and sending sudden bursts of sparks about his feet.

Les jolted upright, his stance as stiff as a board, sweat appearing on his brow. How had he not noticed the fire before, the orange glow spilling from the grate, the heat warming his feet?

Something was wrong, he knew that much—very wrong. It was so wrong that all Les could do was stand there, mulling it over, his feet nailed to the floor. At his side, the lamp began to dim, the glow that filled the room dying as though life itself was draining away until only the flare of the grate was left.

Without warning, a sharp bark pierced into Les's ear, sending another flinch through him as the shape of Max stood upright on the sofa. The black dog stood to attention, his ears pinned back, the snarl of his fangs just about visible in the wavering light, his eyes reflecting the fire.

"It's just the power, Max," said Les, unable to fight the cowardness in his voice. "Hush now. It'll be back up in a moment. You'll see. Any second."

The anxious dog let out another burst of roaring barks, leading to a threatening growl.

It was just then that Les caught sight of the unusual way the dog moved his head, like he was following something, watching as whatever it was moved directly in front of him.

Les's attention shifted, following the trusty dog's gaze, his stare remaining fixed on the long bay window.

Something did move.

Something outside.

He caught a glimpse of it just then, just for a second, maybe not even that. A shadow moved past the edge of the pane, drifting out of sight. It wasn't until he edged closer, his feet scraping along the rug, that he saw it, what was displayed on the glass—a sight so familiar, smeared with red clots—the visible print of a hand.

THE DRILL OF THE TELEPHONE BLASTED THROUGH THE QUIETNESS, the ringing sound cutting through the air and echoing throughout the room, causing Max to cease his insistent yelps and lower himself to the cushions, his muzzle sinking between his paws.

With a sharp twist of his neck, Les looked back at the small table, following its spindly legs upwards from the floor, almost afraid to meet the ringing phone. In some way, he wished it would stop, wished for the jarring sound to end, for the quiet to return.

It did not.

Plucking up the courage from within, Les drank back a long breath, holding it as he marched across the floor space, towering over what called to him. He picked it up, pressing the groove of the receiver hard against his ear, and released the tension of his lungs.

"Hello?" he answered.

The line gently crackled in response, the connection somewhat disrupted by a sharp yet scrambled *hiss*.

"Anyone there?" asked Les, his tone much louder.

There was no answer back, nothing but the persistent hum of static that tunnelled down his ear. He was about to give in. A few more seconds and he would have, if it weren't for the sound he swore he heard—coughing, faint at first, fed through the line. Les pressed the phone harder to his ear, so hard, yet he barely noticed the pain.

"Hello?" Les tried again, listening to the noise of coughs and splutters that fought their way through the static.

"Mr Wills?" a voice replied, the words all cracked and jittered as another wave of coughs broke the line.

"Roderick?" asked Les, recognising the voice in an instant. "Roderick, is that you?"

The line fell quiet. The static seemed to settle as the wheeze of the old writer's breath fell clearly down the line.

"Roderick, something's happened," remarked Les sternly, his head spinning about the room. "Something is here. I know it. I need you to tell me. Tell me why? Tell me why she is here. You know. I know you know."

With another sharp glance around the room, Les stepped back into the alcove, his bare feet treading on papers that rustled about his feet. He looked down—the final pages of Peter Daily, no longer golden in the stark amber light, were littered about his feet.

Roderick's breathing halted in Les's ear. The static, too, mellowed instantly into dreadful nothingness.

Les's eyes couldn't tear away from the writings on the floor. The final sentence reached out to him, clutching him from the darkness, never letting go, until the old writer's voice returned, his words hushed to a whisper and his raspy tone just as cold as the grave.

"Did you read it?"

In shadows deep, my soul doth dwell,
A darkness veiled, a woeful knell.
Within this frame, my essence fades,
My mortal coil, in silent shades.

Visions grim assail my sight,
Phantoms lurk in haunted night.
Whispers cold, a chilling breath,
Foretell this creeping grasp of death.

My form doth waste, my spirit wanes,
As time's cruel hand leaves its stains.
In corners dark, where demons play,
I linger on in disarray.

To you who reads this, I now confess
This burden mine, this deep distress.
As shadows lengthen, and night falls anew,
This curse I pass, I pass to you.

Acknowledgments

This project has been challenging, and I couldn't have completed it without the support of my wife, Emma. Thank you for pushing me to keep on writing even on days when I could think of nothing better to do than sit on the sofa watching Netflix.

To my two children, Brandon and Meredith: I can be a pretty uncool dad, but writing stories makes me feel connected with the kids.

To Sue Scott: Your constant support of my writing knows no bounds. Thank you for your time and commitment to editing my work and making me look like I know what I'm doing.

A big thank you to my family who support my work endlessly. My father, Tim, my mother, Annette, and my two sisters, Jodie and Olivia.

To Heather Ann Larson: Thank you for doing what you do best. Your support is amazing.

I'm not the most social person, but there are a few authors within the community whom I'd like to thank for their friendship, support, and interest while writing this book: Leigh Kenny, Liz Brown, Nick Roberts, Steven Pajak, Ben Young, Lauren Young, Sammy Scott, Jonathan Edward Durham, and Felix Blackwell. Additionally, another shout out to Nick Roberts for such a great author blurb.

To my top Patreon members: You guys are awesome! Thank you for spreading the word about my work and becoming such good friends along the way.

Andrea Johnson
Kristal Shanahan
Sara Smith
Kelly-Louise Whelan
Sherri Childs
Alysha Yuhas
Jen Ramsden
Katie Forsman
Mark Shayler
Paige French
Charlotte Peel
Rhiannon Williams
Lori Hamilton
Davy Arnold
Jonathan Edward Durham
Talees McDonald
Rhonda Potter
Nicky Ryan
Hollie Brimble

Join my Patreon to gain access to all works in progress, exclusive updates, and freebies!

About the Author

Born and bred in the county of Staffordshire. Matt is a keen reader of classical, horror and fantasy literature and enjoys writing in the style of traditional ghost stories. During his working life, Matt joined the ambulance service in 2009, transporting critically ill patients all over the UK. After writing his first novel, Matt now dedicates his time on future releases. His hobbies include genealogy and hiking, and he enjoys spending time with his wife, Emma, his children, and his family.

Connect with M. L. Rayner

Connect with M. L. Rayner
Website: M. L. Rayner Signed Books
Email: Crane.Publishing@hotmail.com

facebook.com/MLRayner
instagram.com/m.l.rayner.author
patreon.com/MLRaynerAuthor
goodreads.com/M_L_Rayner

Also by M. L. Rayner

Amongst the Mists

Bloodline: Every Root Holds a Secret

Lost Souls Series

Echoes of Home: A Ghost Story (Book 1)

Wretched: An Echoes of Home Story (Book 2)

Printed in Great Britain
by Amazon

35eb1580-c4bc-4c36-b2ae-5c97a68041dcR01